L. Bannerji
July 98

16/2

ANNALS OF THE PARISH

and

THE AYRSHIRE LEGATEES

ANNALS OF THE PARISH

and

THE AYRSHIRE LEGATEES

JOHN GALT

Introduction by
IAN CAMPBELL

THE MERCAT PRESS
EDINBURGH

The text of *Annals of the Parish* and *The Ayrshire Legatees*
is a facsimile of the editions published by
Macmillan and Co. in 1895
This combined edition with new Introduction
published 1994 by Mercat Press
James Thin, 53 South Bridge, Edinburgh

Introduction © Ian Campbell, 1994

ISBN 1873644310

The publisher acknowledges subsidy from
the Scottish Arts Council towards
the publication of this volume

Printed in Great Britain by The Cromwell Press
Broughton Gifford, Wiltshire

CONTENTS

New Introduction by Ian Campbell   vii

Annals of the Parish

Contents   xix
List of Illustrations   xxvii
Text   1-188

The Ayrshire Legatees
(Independent pagination)

Contents   vii
List of Illustrations   viii
Text   1-142

NEW INTRODUCTION
to
Annals of the Parish
and
The Ayrshire Legatees

It has taken a long time for John Galt to emerge from the shadow he created for himself with his most successful work, *Annals of the Parish* (1821), the supposed autobiography of a country minister whose fifty years in Dalmailing cover the momentous decades of war and revolution from 1760 to 1810. But the Reverend Micah Balwhidder is a deceptive figure, and the white-haired stereotype, sitting in his study in retirement to tell the story of his life, is very far from being the whole of John Galt's intention in writing the *Annals*, and still less a reflection of Galt himself. His success has been hard to live down. Galt the local historian, Galt the Scottish painter of a rural idyll, Galt the genial satirist, Galt the regretful describer of a vanishing Scotland—all true, all most successfully achieved, all partial. The real John Galt, at last, is a little more visible.

But to go back to the other Galt, the stereotype, to the picture of Mr Balwhidder in the Autumn of his days in the study, looking back over a vanished Scotland—it would be very misleading to brush that Galt aside simply because the reality was more complicated. It may overlay that Galt, but that too was part of his experience: the *Annals*, he was to confirm, did not arise exactly from experience but they incorporated memory and historical event and personage, they incorporated the memory of real places and real changes in a real Scotland. The choice of 1760-1810 could hardly have been better. At the outset of the *Annals*, Scotland seems timeless. Dalmailing is a rural centre, poor, hard-working, intensely centred on its Church. How else could we explain a riot over the choice of Balwhidder as minister, 'imposed' by the local landowner rather than chosen by democratic ballot? It is noteworthy that Balwhidder does not need, in his early diaries, to discuss the attendance figures in a Church doubtless always full, where his public utterances would probably hit the whole community, where

vii

his political and social attitudes, no matter how naive or under-informed, would be accepted as gospel.

Dalmailing is to be transformed in Galt's hands, rather than in Balwhidder's. For Galt begins to emerge himself, however much we focus on the kindly minister: the minister is a front, a spokesman, a voice, but never the totality of the book. The reader always retains an ironic distance from the minister, noting his kindliness, his generosity, his Christian mission and his many likeable human qualities: noting also his naive attempts to disguise his passion for Mrs Malcolm, his snobbery, his timidity, his rustic self-satisfaction, his readiness to enjoy the world's good things, his entire unfitness to keep up with a world changing too fast for him to understand—and one which in any case he hardly tries to keep up with.

The entire narrative method of Galt's *Annals*—and his *Ayrshire Legatees* (1820)—is to create this double reading from the outset, keep it up, and maintain in the narrative what Coleridge called 'the perfect irony of self-delusion' which allows the character in the book to believe the implied reader will accept the narrative at face value—while the reader sees something bigger, something different, something perhaps the character in the book would much rather keep quiet. Like Provost Pawkie in *The Provost*, like the central character of *The Member*, Mr Balwhidder of *Annals of the Parish* thinks he is in control. It is, after all, his book, his annals of his Parish. Because he has chosen to spend all his adult life there, with infrequent and uncomfortable excursions to Glasgow and Edinburgh, Balwhidder thinks himself on safe territory in Dalmailing. Looked up to at the outset as an imposed minister who convinces and wins over his flock by the devotion of his ministry, he metamorphoses during fifty years' work at the centre of the parish into the white-haired patriarch who is offered an assistant in 1809 (though he pawkily sees no need for it, when he can hold forth half an hour longer on any topic than he could in his younger days) and accepts, reluctantly, the inevitable in 1810 and retires, his memory failing, his physical infirmity consoled by the third Mrs Balwhidder whom he prudently chooses to care for him in his declining years. This has been his world, and he has built up a central consciousness of it despite the rapidly accelerating change he chronicles towards the end of the eighteenth century, and the bewildering years of the Napoleonic Wars which opened the nineteenth. Whatever happens in the outside world—dangerous and murderous when it comes close to home and kills Charlie Malcolm—Dalmailing is safe, secure, unchangingly Scottish.

Is it? To Balwhidder, perhaps. He lets slips little hints of change: the local landowner Lord Eaglesham, who had the power to impose a minister in 1760 and was the unquestioned authority and source of local power and change in 1760, has long since disappeared. Mr Cayenne the mill owner had become a much more important figure, though even he has risen and had his day during Mr Balwhidder's long ministry.

Significantly, there is no Mr Cayenne, no single figure with whom Balwhidder can identify, or argue with, towards the end of his description of Dalmailing. Lord Eaglesham was distant but approachable: Cayenne irritable but human: but the enemies the Church faces in 1810 are impersonal, and do not yield to the simple approaches and remedies of 1760 and the Divinity Hall of Glasgow College. In a telling passage, Balwhidder notices a falling-off in the attendances at Church of the young weavers, and summons them to the Manse. The ironies are rich: while the weavers are summoned (and come, out of deference to a minister plainly out of touch with their world which he never once describes nor apparently visits for first-hand experience of a growing part of his parish) the interview is a disaster, for the weavers run circles round Balwhidder, and use his arguments as 'the light sayings of a vain man'. His arguments, he proudly tells us, are those he was taught in the 1750s in Glasgow, a different world from that of the new industrial poor of the 1780s, who (as it turns out in the diary for 1790) not only know more than the minister, but even subscribe from their miserable wages to take a daily London newspaper to keep up with events in France. The ironic contrast could hardly be more skilfully pointed up by Galt. The parish minister, revered in earlier years as source of all information, sacred and secular, has been completely sidelined in a new world where harder, fresher news is available—at a price—quite outside the Church and its institutions. Balwhidder himself, though he gives us the information on which we can build this picture—his breathless description of a bookshop stuffed with nicknacks, though he hardly mentions the books and the newspaper—cannot see how far he is out of step with his times. It apparently does not cross his mind to buy a newspaper himself, to catch up with events, to try to appeal to the new underclass of his parish, to read some new Divinity to freshen his discourses. Not he. He tells us about the bookshop, and we ironically deduce the rest.

NEW INTRODUCTION

The real Galt is coming closer. Galt is the product of that little secure world of Dalmailing in mid-century, albeit from the slightly more cosmopolitan Port Glasgow and Greenock area, in touch with a mighty trading route from the Clyde to the industrial heartlands of England and beyond, a young man fired by ambition which took him through education to enterprise, to a business career as writer and as entrepreneur and manager in England and Scotland, and very widely in Canada, to success and to financial ruin, to literary fame and to literary disillusion. While he had an insider's knowledge of rural Dalmailing, he had by 1821 an outsider's awareness that there was a larger world beyond, and an ironist's ability to play off the limitations of the people in his novels against the wider knowledge his readers brought. *Annals of the Parish* was published in 1821, by which time the revolution in Dalmailing was finished, indeed was old hat. The new industrial proletariat were an established fact, the wars had given travel and wider knowledge to a whole generation, and the kirks were fast emptying from that secure position they had enjoyed when Balwhidder was placed in 1760. The Cayennes and the Eagleshams had had their day, and Britain increasingly was run by the impersonal, the centralised forces which subtly displace in Galt's narrative the face-to-face contact with aristocrat and local millowner which had sufficed for Dalmailing in the previous century. No longer can the Kirk Session and its modest coffers handle small problems of local poverty and distress: no longer can a single Mrs Malcolm, fallen on hard times but scratching a modest living, stand out by her exceptional nature. Dalmailing is part of the larger world, for better or worse, and perhaps the greatest part of Galt's description of that process is Balwhidder's failure to recognise it.

The Galt of the wider world is very much present in the plot of his first success, *The Ayrshire Legatees*, which is reprinted along with the *Annals* in this volume. Here, with a vengeance, is a book about the wider world, dawning slowly on people who come from a secure smaller one, on people who simultaneously want it and fear it, their fortunes reflected in a wonderful series of letters which not only go back to their sleepy parish of Garnock (not a thousand miles from Dalmailing) but are read aloud there by session clerk and schoolmaster, seamstress and gossip, young and old, sophisticated and apparently clodhopper. From the moment Dr Pringle and his country family learn of their inheritance and resolve to leave their country Manse a while and venture to London, Galt has the scene set for a masterly investigation of what he had himself lived, and what the Scotland of his time was learning to live with—the fact of a larger world outside, the dubious pleasure of learning about that world, the fate of the old when the new intrudes and presents a more attractive face. Balwhidder took refuge, all too often, from that world by pretending it could not exist, and considering the plot of *Annals* (in which he visits the cities hardly at all, and cannot get home fast enough) that was easy for him. In *The Ayrshire Legatees* this will not be so simple. The epistolary novel begins with the Doctor's fearful leaving of his parish, and ends with his triumphant return, enriched, emboldened, his innocence a little lost, the tell-tale signs of the new coach and the newly-Englished manner and dress betraying the sophisticate. Pringle has seen the outside world that Balwhidder feared to encounter: he has gained something compared with Balwhidder (something more, that is, than the cool quarter-million pounds of his inheritance). But he has lost something too.

Balwhidder remains, pretty well to the end of his novel, a loveable and delightful man, quaint, 'pawky', picturesque in his appearance, shameless in his sexist assumptions and his businesslike approach to choosing a wife. He could only survive in this character, through the turbulent second half of the eighteenth century, by being cut off from the mainstream of change, and we accept this without demur from the ironic position we enjoy as modern readers. But Pringle thinks himself better informed than someone like Balwhidder, and he has higher ambitions for himself and his family. Balwhidder certainly wants the best for his family—placing his son in business even drags him to Glasgow—but no inheritance makes him move in the circles of the aristocracy and the royal family in London. He does not mix, as Pringle does, with rich lawyers like Argent, nor with the upwardly mobile Captain Sabre with his eyes fixed on Pringle's daughter, as much no doubt for her looks as for the enormous dowry she would bring. Balwhidder's three wives apparently show little ambition to move beyond Dalmailing, even though his second one transforms the quiet Manse to a hive of industry. In *The Ayrshire Legatees* people move on: even Mrs Pringle, though she is very much against London and its ways, learns from London and even reluctantly admits that some of its ways are better than Garnock's. Though her frugal habits persist even after her elevation to financial riches—she tosses bawbees to the children from the returning coach, less extravagant than her husband's pennies—she consents to the buying of richer clothes and London goods for their return to Garnock.

Two very strong points are made by Galt in the concluding part of *The Ayrshire Legatees* which would not have been in place in the *Annals*. One concerns the younger generation, people like himself who grow up in Scotland and move on, driven partly by ambition and partly by the need to leave a much-loved Scotland in search of work or career prospects. In *The Ayrshire Legatees* the younger generation cannot wait to get rid of their Scottish background. While Balwhidder's children naturally get on in the world, they seem happy with their parents' solid Christian values, and respect the provincial setting they came from. Not so the repellent Andrew and Rachel Pringle. As soon as they can, they cut the tie and use their new-found riches to start a new life, as far from their Garnock roots as they can. Andrew enters the world of parliamentary politics (and we know from *The Member* how little respect Galt felt for that line of work) and Rachel marries into fashionable English society, her affected and sentimental letters to Garnock not hiding for a moment her satisfaction at moving onward and upward. Nor does Garnock, for a moment, fail to see through the affectation and politeness of the younger Pringles' letters; after all, they have known Andrew and Rachel all their lives.

The other point concerns their parents. That the minister and his wife feel their roots are in Garnock, and that (give or take a new coach and a new coat) their obvious path is the path back home, is in many ways admirable, but Galt shrewdly points our attention at the assistant minister, Mr Snodgrass, left in charge during Pringle's absence, a well-travelled and able young man who has not only seen more of the world than Garnock, but is more up to date than even his senior colleague—he surreptitiously is reading Scott, for instance, in a village where the activity would be anathema to many of the older and more strait-laced. Andrew Pringle recognises Snodgrass's qualities, but only to say he is sorry that they are wasted in a place like Garnock. All the more credit to Andrew Pringle's father, then, that the old Doctor is able to see Garnock with new eyes, and himself with new eyes, after London. Unlike his fashionable children, he does not slip on a ready-made identity from English society; he wants to retain his Scottishness, but not blindly. Almost his first act on reaching home is to check that the parish is in good order: but after that he loses no time in preparing to step aside, and hand the parish over to the younger and more flexible

NEW INTRODUCTION

hands of Mr Snodgrass while he and Mrs Pringle retire to a new life as
laird and lady in a nearby country house, fallen vacant by good timing.
Galt's affectionate satire is spot-on in describing the first Sunday
service after their return.

> And some little change had taken place during his absence in his visible
> equipage. His stockings, which were wont to be of worsted, had undergone
> a translation into silk; his waistcoat, instead of the venerable Presbyterian
> flap-covers to the pockets, which were of Johnsonian magnitude, was
> become plain—his coat, in all times single-breasted, with no collar, still,
> however, maintained its ancient characteristics; instead, however, of the
> former bright black cast-horn, the buttons were covered with cloth. But the
> chief alteration was discernible in the furniture of the head. He had
> exchanged the simplicity of his own respectable grey hairs for the
> cauliflower hoariness of a PARRISH wig, on which he wore a broad-
> brimmed hat, turned up a little at each side behind, in a portentous manner,
> indicatory of Episcopalian predilections. This, however, was not justified
> by any alteration in his principles, being merely an innocent variation of
> fashion, the natural result of a Doctor of Divinity buying a hat and wig in
> London.
> The moment that the Doctor made his appearance, his greeting and
> salutation was quite delightful; it was that of a father returned to his
> children, and a king to his people.

Of course Galt is hinting at all kinds of things here, the genuine slip
towards the Episcopalian, the manner of the king to his people, the not
very unconscious imitation of Dr Johnson. But the parish receives him
with affectionate respect, as they receive his wife rustling in her
London clothes with a new veneration 'neither unobserved nor
unappreciated by that acute and perspicacious lady'. Nothing has
changed, everything has changed. The Moneypennies estate is bought
by Dr Pringle 'as a great bargain', but 'It was not . . . on account of the
advantageous nature of the purchase that our friend valued this
acquisition, but entirely because it was situated in his own parish, and
part of the lands marching with the Glebe'. No doubt. Pringle has the
sense to move out of Manse and pulpit, for a few months in London has
changed him beyond moving back to his much-loved earlier self. The
inside of the man is as changed as the outside coat and wig.
The outside of Garnock has changed, too, as little details in Galt's
description confirm. When the Pringles' coach comes into the village
from London, Galt pointedly contrasts the welcome of the older poor

people—who reverently doff their bonnets to the minister—with that of the younger workers,with their 'green aprons and thin yellow faces', products of a new weaving factory generation who look on with 'a melancholy smile', pleased enough to see their minister back, but quite without the older generation's instinctive reverence. The position is exactly the same as in Balwhidder's Dalmailing, where the older minister has lost that enormous part of his congregation who either have given up church-going, or prefer the livelier service in Cayenneville. But while Balwhidder cannot comprehend the notion, Pringle does something about it: he stands aside for a younger man who has a chance to be minister to a mixed parish like the one Garnock has become.

More than any other of his books, *The Ayrshire Legatees* catches the paradoxical nature of Galt's Scottishness, since it never ceases to juxtapose the world of the traveller, the man of business, the Scot of the world, with the never-to-be-forgotten roots of the Scottish character and the Scottish imagination. Galt was a product of both, and while his bodily existence was to be one of strenuous travel and effort—and bitter disappointment when his Canadian business went sour and he was recalled in disgrace by his employers—his mental existence was very much one of exercise of the memory, recreating a vanishing Scotland, one remembered far away, one reconstructed from gossip and local history, one imagined by comparing the here and now of the 1820s—the aftermath of an enormous war, the still ongoing industrial revolution, the country revolutionised by transport and trade—with sleepy Garnock and Dalmailing.

'A certain distance', he wrote in his Autobiography, 'in all limning is necessary to enable an artist to contemplate, in the most picturesque point of view, the objects he would represent'. Galt argues for the advantage of having been away, of not having been too close to the Scotland he depicts in these books. 'The vraisemblance of my pictures ought to have been . . . regarded as a proof that I could not have been very intimately near those things which I have chosen to depict; although in all of them there may be a bringing together of homogenous circumstances, so obvious, that the mere mirroring of the mind is not their sole merit . . .' In a much-quoted passage Galt rebukes people for taking his *Annals* as literal autobiography: 'to myself it has ever been a kind of treatise on the history of society in the west of Scotland during the reign of King George the Third; and when it was written, I had no idea it would ever have been received as a novel, Fables are often a better way of illustrating philosophical truths than abstract reasoning; and in this class of composition I would place the *Annals of the Parish*; but the public consider it as a novel, and it is of no use to think of altering the impression with which it has been received'. Galt acknowledged some of the characters were recognisably linked to 'real' people, but denied his readers the pleasure of source hunting, holding that his creations were 'things of which the originals are, or were, actually in nature,but brought together into composition by art'. And there it has to remain.

One thing this volume should do, forcibly, is undermine the impression sometimes given that Galt is a novelist of the kailyard, clinging profitably but exploitatively to a vanished Scotland and representing that Scotland as the one, true picture to an audience eager to be deceived into believing in a Dalmailing or a Garnock, still there, still waiting to be discovered. Galt's fiction, as shown in this volume, combines highly profitable writing with a sharp-eyed recognition of the inevitability of change in Scotland. Balwhidder's clinging to the past and all its values is, ultimately, futile: Cayenneville grows without him, the church empties, the world of the 1760s is far away indeed when white-haired old Balwhidder sits down in 1810 to write his memoirs. And everything about Pringle's visit to London shows the futility of coming back to Garnock, and pretending that nothing has changed. That the Pringles came back, loyal to their roots, yet made a new life for themselves in which the real change they had experienced—and recognised in their homely village—could be assimilated, is Galt's message to his Scottish readers. The annals of his parish are annals of change: the legacy of a trip to London is not retreat to comforting familiarity, but the bitter-sweet recognition that there is no going back. Rather, like Galt himself, his characters learn to adapt and live with the new world. He gives his readers the pleasure of the old world and all its distinctive Scottish character: but the future lies not in burying one's head in the past, but in learning to live with the present. Galt's message to his readers, Scots and non-Scots, is as relevant today as it was in the 1820s when his novels raised him to the rank of best-seller. *Annals of the Parish* and *The Ayrshire Legatees*, as they are read, will only enhance his reputation in the 1990s.

IAN CAMPBELL

ANNALS OF THE PARISH:

OR THE

CHRONICLE OF DALMAILING

DURING THE MINISTRY OF

THE REV. MICAH BALWHIDDER

WRITTEN BY HIMSELF

ARRANGED AND EDITED

BY THE AUTHOR OF 'THE AYRSHIRE LEGATEES,' ETC.

CONTENTS

ANNALS OF THE PARISH

INTRODUCTION . . . . . . Page 1

CHAPTER I—YEAR 1760

The placing of Mr. Balwhidder—The resistance of the parishioners—Mrs. Malcolm, the widow—Mr. Balwhidder's marriage . 5

CHAPTER II—YEAR 1761

The great increase of smuggling—Mr. Balwhidder disperses a tea-drinking par.y of gossips—He records the virtues of Nanse Banks, the schoolmistress—The servant of a military man, who had been prisoner in France, comes into the parish, and opens a dancing-school 11

CHAPTER III—YEAR 1762

Havoc produced by the small-pox—Charles Malcolm is sent off a cabin-boy on a voyage to Virginia—Mizy Spaewell dies on Hallowe'en—Tea begins to be admitted at the manse, but the minister continues to exert his authority against smuggling . 16

CHAPTER IV—YEAR 1763

Charles Malcolm's return from sea—Kate Malcolm is taken to live with Lady Macadam—Death of the first Mrs. Balwhidder . 20

xix

CHAPTER V—Year 1764

He gets a headstone for Mrs. Balwhidder, and writes an epitaph for it—He is afflicted with melancholy, and thinks of writing a book—Nichol Snipe the gamekeeper's device when reproved in church . . . . . . Page 24

CHAPTER VI—Year 1765

Establishment of a whisky distillery—He is again married to Miss Lizy Kibbock—Her industry in the dairy—Her example diffuses a spirit of industry through the parish . . . 29

CHAPTER VII—Year 1766

The burning of the Breadland—A new bell, and also a steeple—Nanse Birrel found drowned in a well—The parish troubled with wild Irishmen 33

CHAPTER VIII—Year 1767

Lord Eglesham meets with an accident, which is the means of getting the parish a new road—I preach for the benefit of Nanse Banks, the schoolmistress, reduced to poverty . . . 39

CHAPTER IX—Year 1768

Lord Eglesham uses his interest in favour of Charles Malcolm—The finding of a new schoolmistress—Miss Sabrina Hookie gets the place—Change of fashions in the parish . . . 44

CHAPTER X—Year 1769

A toad found in the heart of a stone—Robert Malcolm, who had been at sea, returns from a northern voyage—Kate Malcolm's clandestine correspondence with Lady Macadam's son . . 48

CONTENTS

CHAPTER XI—YEAR 1770

This year a happy and tranquil one—Lord Eglesham establishes a fair in the village—The show of Punch appears for the first time in the parish . . . . . Page 53

CHAPTER XII—YEAR 1771·

The nature of Lady Macadam's amusements—She intercepts letters from her son to Kate Malcolm 54

CHAPTER XIII—YEAR 1772

The detection of Mr. Heckletext's guilt—He threatens to prosecute the elders for defamation—The Muscovy duck gets an operation performed on it 59

CHAPTER XIV—YEAR 1773

The new schoolhouse—Lord Eglesham comes down to the castle—I refuse to go and dine there on Sunday, but go on Monday, and meet with an English dean 63

CHAPTER XV—YEAR 1774

The murder of Jean Glaikit—The young Laird Macadam comes down and marries Kate Malcolm—The ceremony performed by me, and I am commissioned to break the matter to Lady Macadam—Her behaviour 67

CHAPTER XVI—YEAR 1775

Captain Macadam provides a house and an annuity for old Mrs. Malcolm—Miss Betty Wudrife brings from Edinburgh a new-fashioned silk mantle, but refuses to give the pattern to old Lady Macadam—Her revenge 71

CHAPTER XVII—Year 1776

A recruiting party comes to Irville—Thomas Wilson and some others enlist—Charles Malcolm's return . . . Page 75

CHAPTER XVIII—Year 1777

Old Widow Mirkland—Bloody accounts of the war—He gets a newspaper—Great flood 80

CHAPTER XIX—Year 1778

Revival of the smuggling trade—Betty and Janet Pawkie, and Robin Bicker, an exciseman, come to the parish—Their doings—Robin is succeeded by Mungo Argyle—Lord Eglesham assists William Malcolm 84

CHAPTER XX—Year 1779

He goes to Edinburgh to attend the General Assembly—Preaches before the Commissioner 89

CHAPTER XXI—Year 1780

Lord George Gordon—Report of an illumination . . 94

CHAPTER XXII—Year 1781

Argyle, the exciseman, grows a gentleman—Lord Eglesham's concubine—His death—The parish children afflicted with the measles 96

CHAPTER XXIII—Year 1782

News of the victory over the French fleet—He has to inform Mrs. Malcolm of the death of her son Charles in the engagement 100

CONTENTS

CHAPTER XXIV—YEAR 1783

Janet Gaffaw's death and burial   .   .   .   Page 102

CHAPTER XXV—YEAR 1784

A year of sunshine and pleasantness   105

CHAPTER XXVI—YEAR 1785

Mr. Cayenne comes to the parish—A passionate character—His outrageous behaviour at the Session-house   .   .   .   107

CHAPTER XXVII—YEAR 1786

Repairs required for the manse—By the sagacious management of Mr.
Kibbock, the heritors are made to give a new manse altogether—
They begin, however, to look upon me with a grudge, which pro-
vokes me to claim an augmentation, which I obtain   .   111

CHAPTER XXVIII—YEAR 1787

Lady Macadam's house is changed into an inn—The making of jelly
becomes common in the parish—Meg Gaffaw is present at a payment of victual—Her behaviour   114

CHAPTER XXIX—YEAR 1788

A cotton-mill is built—The new spirit which it introduces among the
people   117

CHAPTER XXX—YEAR 1789

William Malcolm comes to the parish and preaches—The opinions
upon his sermon   121

CHAPTER XXXI—YEAR 1790

A bookseller's shop is set up among the houses of the weavers at Cayenneville . . . . . Page 122

CHAPTER XXXII—YEAR 1791

I place my son Gilbert in a counting-house at Glasgow—My observations on Glasgow—On my return I preach against the vanity of riches, and begin to be taken for a black-neb . . 125

CHAPTER XXXIII—YEAR 1792

Troubled with low spirits—Accidental meeting with Mr. Cayenne, who endeavours to remove the prejudices entertained against me 127

CHAPTER XXXIV—YEAR 1793

I dream a remarkable dream, and preach a sermon in consequence, applying to the events of the times—Two democratical weaver lads brought before Mr. Cayenne, as justice of peace . 130

CHAPTER XXXV—YEAR 1794

The condition of the parish, as divided into government men and Jacobins—I endeavour to prevent Christian charity from being forgotten in the phraseology of utility and philanthropy . 133

CHAPTER XXXVI—YEAR 1795

A recruiting party visits the town—After them, players—then preaching Quakers—The progress of philosophy among the weavers 135

CHAPTER XXXVII—YEAR 1796

Death of second Mrs. Balwhidder—I look out for a third, and fix upon Mrs. Nugent, a widow—Particulars of the courtship . 139

CONTENTS

CHAPTER XXXVIII—YEAR 1797

Mr. Henry Melcomb comes to the parish to see his uncle, Mr. Cayenne—From some jocular behaviour on his part, Meg Gaffaw falls in love with him—The sad result of the adventure when he is married .   .   .   .   .   Page 143

CHAPTER XXXIX—YEAR 1798

A dearth—Mr. Cayenne takes measures to mitigate the evil—He receives kindly some Irish refugees—His daughter's marriage   147

CHAPTER XL—YEAR 1799

My daughter's marriage — Her large portion — Mrs. Malcolm's death   151

CHAPTER XLI—YEAR 1800

Return of an inclination towards political tranquillity—Death of the schoolmistress   154

CHAPTER XLII—YEAR 1801

An account of Colin Mavis, who becomes a poet   .   .   157

CHAPTER XLIII—YEAR 1802

The political condition of the world felt in the private concerns of individuals— Mr. Cayenne comes to ask my advice, and acts according to it   159

CHAPTER XLIV—YEAR 1803

Fear of an invasion—Raising of volunteers in the parish—The young ladies embroider a stand of colours for the regiment   .   162

CHAPTER XLV—YEAR 1804

The Session agrees that church censures shall be commuted with fines—
Our parish has an opportunity of seeing a turtle, which is sent to
Mr. Cayenne—Some fears of popery—Also about a preacher of
universal redemption—Report of a French ship appearing in the
west, which sets the volunteers astir   .   .   Page 167

CHAPTER XLVI—YEAR 1805

Retrenchment of the extravagant expenses usual at burials—I use an
expedient for putting even the second service out of fashion .   171

CHAPTER XLVII—YEAR 1806

The deathbed behaviour of Mr. Cayenne—A schism in the parish,
and a subscription to build a meeting-house   .   .   173

CHAPTER XLVIII—YEAR 1807

Numerous marriages—Account of a pay-wedding made to set up a
shop   177

CHAPTER XLIX—YEAR 1808

Failure of Mr. Speckle, the proprietor of the cotton-mill—The melancholy end of one of the overseers and his wife   .   .   179

CHAPTER L—YEAR 1809

Opening of a meeting-house—The elders come to the manse, and offer
me a helper   183

CHAPTER LI—YEAR 1810

Conclusion—I repair to the church for the last time—Afterwards
receive a silver server from the parishioners—And still continue
to marry and baptize   184

LIST OF ILLUSTRATIONS

ANNALS OF THE PARISH

	PAGE
'We were obligated to go in by a window' . .	6
'Mr. Macskipnish'	15
'The very parrot was a participator'	22
'A figure was seen in the upper flat'	35
'One of the older men set and tempered to me two razors' .	38
'It was a droll curiosity to see his lordship clad in my garments'	41
'He came to show himself in his regimentals to his mother' .	52
'Covered her face with her hands, and wept bitterly' . .	57
'Extraordinary condescending towards me' . . .	65
'The murderer was brought back to the parish' . .	68
'Miss Sabrina showed him the way'	78
'She ripped up the tikeing, and sent all the tea floating away' .	88
'Words passed, and the exciseman shot my lord' . .	98
'With all the due formality common on such occasions' .	104
'He attempted to fling it at Sambo'	109
'Debating about the affairs of the French' . . .	119
'She entertained me sometimes with a tune' . . .	129
'The actor who did the part of King Macbeth made a most polite bow of thankfulness'	138
'A kindly nip on her sonsy arm'	142

ANNALS OF THE PARISH

	PAGE
'Handed her over the kirk stile'	145
'A pair of old marrowless stockings'	156
'So he lay down, and I tumbled over him' . . .	166
'Mr. Cayenne got a turtle-fish sent to him' . . .	169
'I knelt down and prayed for him with great sincerity' .	175
'The elders, in a body, came to me in the manse' . .	185

TO

JOHN WILSON, Esquire,

PROFESSOR OF MORAL PHILOSOPHY IN THE

UNIVERSITY OF EDINBURGH;

AS A SMALL EXPRESSION OF THE AUTHOR'S REGARD

FOR HIS WORTH AND TALENTS

INTRODUCTION

IN the same year, and on the same day of the same month, that his Sacred Majesty King George, the third of the name, came to his crown and kingdom, I was placed and settled as the minister of Dalmailing. When about a week thereafter this was known in the parish, it was thought a wonderful thing, and everybody spoke of me and the new king as united in our trusts and temporalities, marvelling how the same should come to pass, and thinking the hand of Providence was in it, and that surely we were preordained to fade and flourish in fellowship together; which has really been the case, for, in the same season that his Most Excellent Majesty, as he was very properly styled in the proclamations for the general fasts and thanksgivings, was set by as a precious vessel which had received a crack or a flaw, and could only be serviceable in the way of an ornament, I was obliged, by reason of age and the growing infirmities of my recollection, to consent to the earnest entreaties of the Session, and to accept of Mr. Amos to be my helper. I was long reluctant to do so, but the great respect that my people had for me, and the love that I bore towards them, over and above the sign that was given to me in the removal of the royal candlestick from its place, worked upon my heart and understanding, and I could not stand out. So, on the last Sabbath of the year 1810, I preached my last sermon, and it was a moving discourse. There were few dry eyes in the kirk that day, for I had been with the aged from the beginning —the young considered me as their natural pastor—and my bidding them all farewell was, as when of old among the heathen, an idol was taken away by the hands of the enemy.

At the close of the worship, and before the blessing, I

addressed them in a fatherly manner, and although the kirk was fuller than ever I saw it before, the fall of a pin might have been heard—at the conclusion there was a sobbing and much sorrow. I said :

'My dear friends, I have now finished my work among you for ever. I have often spoken to you from this place the words of truth and holiness, and, had it been in poor frail human nature to practise the advice and counselling that I have given in this pulpit to you, there would not need to be any cause for sorrow on this occasion—the close and latter end of my ministry. But, nevertheless, I have no reason to complain, and it will be my duty to testify, in that place where I hope we are all one day to meet again, that I found you a docile and a tractable flock, far more than at first I could have expected. There are among you still a few, but with grey heads and feeble hands now, that can remember the great opposition that was made to my placing, and the stout part they themselves took in the burly, because I was appointed by the patron ; but they have lived to see the error of their way, and to know that preaching is the smallest portion of the duties of a faithful minister. I may not, my dear friends, have applied my talent in the pulpit so effectually as perhaps I might have done, considering the gifts that it pleased God to give me in that way, and the education that I had in the Orthodox University of Glasgow, as it was in the time of my youth, nor can I say that, in the works of peacemaking and charity, I have done all that I should have done. But I have done my best, studying no interest but the good that was to rise according to the faith in Christ Jesus.

'To my young friends I would, as a parting word, say, Look to the lives and conversation of your parents—they were plain, honest, and devout Christians, fearing God and honouring the king. They believed the Bible was the word of God, and when they practised its precepts, they found, by the good that came from them, that it was truly so. They bore in mind the tribulation and persecution of their fore-fathers for righteousness' sake, and were thankful for the quiet and protection of the government in their day and generation. Their land was tilled with industry, and they ate the bread of carefulness with a contented spirit, and, verily, they had

2

the reward of well-doing even in this world, for they beheld on all sides the blessing of God upon the nation, and the tree growing, and the plough going, where the banner of the oppressor was planted of old, and the war-horse trampled in the blood of martyrs. Reflect on this, my young friends, and know, that the best part of a Christian's duty in this world of much evil, is to thole and suffer with resignation, as lang as it is possible for human nature to do. I do not counsel passive obedience; that is a doctrine that the Church of Scotland can never abide; but the divine right of resistance, which, in the days of her trouble, she so bravely asserted against popish and prelatic usurpations, was never resorted to till the attempt was made to remove the ark of the tabernacle from her. I therefore counsel you, my young friends, no to lend your ears to those that trumpet forth their hypothetical politics, but to believe that the laws of the land are administered with a good intent, till in your own homes and dwellings ye feel the presence of the oppressor—then, and not till then, are ye free to gird your loins for battle—and woe to him, and woe to the land where that is come to, if the sword be sheathed till the wrong be redressed.

'As for you, my old companions, many changes have we seen in our day, but the change that we ourselves are soon to undergo will be the greatest of all. We have seen our bairns grow to manhood—we have seen the beauty of youth pass away—we have felt our backs become unable for the burthen, and our right hand forget its cunning. Our eyes have become dim, and our heads grey—we are now tottering with short and feckless steps towards the grave; and some, that should have been here this day, are bed-rid, lying, as it were, at the gates of death, like Lazarus at the threshold of the rich man's door, full of ails and sores, and having no enjoyment but in the hope that is in hereafter. What can I say to you but farewell! Our work is done—we are weary and worn out, and in need of rest — may the rest of the blessed be our portion!—and, in the sleep that all must sleep, beneath the cold blanket of the kirkyard grass, and on that clay pillow where we must shortly lay our heads, may we have pleasant dreams, till we are awakened to partake of the everlasting banquet of the saints in glory.'

When I had finished, there was for some time a great

3

solemnity throughout the kirk, and, before giving the blessing, I sat down to compose myself, for my heart was big, and my spirit oppressed with sadness.

As I left the pulpit, all the elders stood on the steps to hand me down, and the tear was in every eye, and they helped me into the session house; but I could not speak to them, nor them to me. Then Mr. Dalziel, who was always a composed and sedate man, said a few words of prayer, and I was comforted therewith, and rose to go home to the manse; but in the churchyard all the congregation was assembled, young and old, and they made a lane for me to the back-yett that opened into the manse-garden. Some of them put out their hands and touched me as I passed, followed by the elders, and some of them wept. It was as if I was passing away, and to be no more—verily, it was the reward of my ministry—a faithful account of which, year by year, I now sit down, in the evening of my days, to make up, to the end that I may bear witness to the work of a beneficent Providence, even in the narrow sphere of my parish, and the concerns of that flock of which it was His most gracious pleasure to make me the unworthy shepherd.

CHAPTER I

The placing of Mr. Balwhidder—The resistance of the parishioners—
Mrs. Malcolm, the widow—Mr. Balwhidder's marriage.

THE Ann. Dom. one thousand seven hundred and sixty was
remarkable for three things in the parish of Dalmailing.
First and foremost, there was my placing; then the coming
of Mrs. Malcolm with her five children to settle among us;
and next, my marriage upon my own cousin, Miss Betty
Lanshaw, by which the account of this year naturally divides
itself into three heads or portions.

First, of the placing. It was a great affair; for I was put
in by the patron, and the people knew nothing whatsoever of
me, and their hearts were stirred into strife on the occasion,
and they did all that lay within the compass of their power
to keep me out, insomuch, that there was obliged to be a
guard of soldiers to protect the presbytery; and it was a thing
that made my heart grieve when I heard the drum beating and
the fife playing as we were going to the kirk. The people
were really mad and vicious, and flung dirt upon us as we
passed, and reviled us all, and held out the finger of scorn
at me; but I endured it with a resigned spirit, compassion-
ating their wilfulness and blindness. Poor old Mr. Kilfuddy
of the Braehill got such a clash of glar on the side of his face,
that his eye was almost extinguished.

When we got to the kirk door, it was found to be nailed
up, so as by no possibility to be opened. The sergeant of the
soldiers wanted to break it, but I was afraid that the heritors
would grudge and complain of the expense of a new door, and
I supplicated him to let it be as it was; we were, therefore,

5

'We were obligated to go in by a window.'

obligated to go in by a window, and the crowd followed us, in the most unreverent manner, making the Lord's house like an inn on a fair day, with their grievous yellyhooing. During the time of the psalm and the sermon, they behaved themselves better, but when the induction came on, their clamour was dreadful; and Thomas Thorl, the weaver, a pious zealot in that time, he got up and protested, and said, 'Verily, verily, I say unto you, he that entereth not by the door into the sheepfold, but climbeth up some other way, the same is a thief and a robber.' And I thought I would have a hard and sore time of it with such an outstrapolous people. Mr. Given, that was then the minister of Lugton, was a jocose man, and would have his joke even at a solemnity. When the laying of the hands upon me was a-doing, he could not get near enough to put on his, but he stretched out his staff and touched my head, and said, to the great diversion of the rest, 'This will do well enough, timber to timber,' but it was an unfriendly saying of Mr. Given, considering the time and the place, and the temper of my people.

After the ceremony, we then got out at the window, and it was a heavy day to me, but we went to the manse, and there we had an excellent dinner, which Mrs. Watts of the new inns of Irville prepared at my request, and sent her chaise-driver to serve, for he was likewise her waiter, she having then but one chaise, and that no often called for.

But, although my people received me in this unruly manner, I was resolved to cultivate civility among them; and therefore, the very next morning I began a round of visitations; but oh, it was a steep brae that I had to climb, and it needed a stout heart. For I found the doors in some places barred against me; in others, the bairns, when they saw me coming, ran crying to their mothers, 'Here's the feckless Mess-John'; and then when I went in into the houses, their parents would no ask me to sit down, but with a scornful way, said, 'Honest man, what's your pleasure here?' Nevertheless, I walked about from door to door, like a dejected beggar, till I got the almous deed of a civil reception, and who would have thought it, from no less a person than the same Thomas Thorl that was so bitter against me in the kirk on the foregoing day. Thomas was standing at the door with his green duffle apron and his red Kilmarnock nightcap—I mind him as well

7

as if it was but yesterday—and he had seen me going from house to house, and in what manner I was rejected, and his bowels were moved, and he said to me in a kind manner, 'Come in, sir, and ease yoursel'; this will never do, the clergy are God's gorbies, and for their Master's sake it behoves us to respect them. There was no ane in the whole parish mair against you than mysel', but this early visitation is a sympton of grace that I couldna have expectit from a bird out the nest of patronage.' I thanked Thomas, and went in with him, and we had some solid conversation together, and I told him that it was not so much the pastor's duty to feed the flock, as to herd them well; and that although there might be some abler with the head than me, there wasna a he within the bounds of Scotland more willing to watch the fold by night and by day. And Thomas said he had not heard a mair sound observe for some time, and that if I held to that doctrine in the poopit, it wouldna be lang till I would work a change. 'I was mindit,' quoth he, 'never to set my foot within the kirk door while you were there; but to testify, and no to condemn without a trial, I'll be there next Lord's day, and egg my neighbours to be likewise, so ye'll no have to preach just to the bare walls and the laird's family.'

I have now to speak of the coming of Mrs. Malcolm. She was the widow of a Clyde shipmaster, that was lost at sea with his vessel. She was a genty body, calm and methodical. From morning to night she sat at her wheel, spinning the finest lint, which suited well with her pale hands. She never changed her widow's weeds, and she was aye as if she had just been ta'en out of a bandbox. The tear was aften in her e'e when the bairns were at the school; but when they came home, her spirit was lighted up with gladness, although, poor woman, she had many a time very little to give them. They were, however, wonderful well-bred things, and took with thankfulness whatever she set before them, for they knew that their father, the bread-winner, was away, and that she had to work sore for their bit and drap. I daresay, the only vexation that ever she had from any of them, on their own account, was when Charlie, the eldest laddie, had won fourpence at pitch and toss at the school, which he brought home with a proud heart to his mother. I happened to be daunrin' by at the time, and just looked in at the door to say gude-night:

8

It was a sad sight. There was she sitting with the silent tear on her cheek, and Charlie greeting as if he had done a great fault, and the other four looking on with sorrowful faces. Never, I am sure, did Charlie Malcolm gamble after that night.

I often wondered what brought Mrs. Malcolm to our clachan, instead of going to a populous town, where she might have taken up a huxtry-shop, as she was but of a silly constitution, the which would have been better for her than spinning from morning to far in the night, as if she was in verity drawing the thread of life. But it was, no doubt, from an honest pride to hide her poverty; for when her daughter Effie was ill with the measles—the poor lassie was very ill—nobody thought she could come through, and when she did get the turn, she was for many a day a heavy handful;—our Session being rich, and nobody on it but cripple Tammy Daidles, that was at that time known through all the country-side for begging on a horse, I thought it my duty to call upon Mrs. Malcolm in a sympathising way, and offer her some assistance, but she refused it.

'No, sir,' said she, 'I canna take help from the poor's-box, although it's very true that I am in great need; for it might hereafter be cast up to my bairns, whom it may please God to restore to better circumstances when I am no to see't; but I would fain borrow five pounds, and if, sir, you will write to Mr. Maitland, that is now the Lord Provost of Glasgow, and tell him that Marion Shaw would be obliged to him for the lend of that soom, I think he will not fail to send it.'

I wrote the letter that night to Provost Maitland, and, by the retour of the post, I got an answer, with twenty pounds for Mrs. Malcolm, saying, 'that it was with sorrow he heard so small a trifle could be serviceable.' When I took the letter and the money, which was in a bank-bill, she said, 'This is just like himsel'.' She then told me, that Mr. Maitland had been a gentleman's son of the east country, but driven out of his father's house, when a laddie, by his step-mother; and that he had served as a servant lad with her father, who was the Laird of Yillcogie, but ran through his estate, and left her, his only daughter, in little better than beggary with her auntie, the mother of Captain Malcolm, her husband that was. Provost Maitland in his servitude had ta'en a notion of her,

9

and when he recovered his patrimony, and had become a great Glasgow merchant, on hearing how she was left by her father, he offered to marry her, but she had promised herself to her cousin the captain, whose widow she was. He then married a rich lady, and in time grew, as he was, Lord Provost of the City; but his letter with the twenty pounds to me, showed that he had not forgotten his first love. It was a short, but a well-written letter, in a fair hand of write, containing much of the true gentleman; and Mrs. Malcolm said, 'Who knows but out of the regard he once had for their mother, he may do something for my five helpless orphans.'

Thirdly, upon the subject of taking my cousin, Miss Betty Lanshaw, for my first wife, I have little to say. It was more out of a compassionate habitual affection, than the passion of love. We were brought up by our grandmother in the same house, and it was a thing spoken of from the beginning, that Betty and me were to be married. So when she heard that the Laird of Breadland had given me the presentation of Dalmailing, she began to prepare for the wedding. And as soon as the placing was well over, and the manse in order, I gaed to Ayr, where she was, and we were quietly married, and came home in a chaise, bringing with us her little brother Andrew, that died in the East Indies, and he lived and was brought up by us.

Now, this is all, I think, that happened in that year worthy of being mentioned, except that at the Sacrament, when old Mr. Kilfuddy was preaching in the tent, it came on such a thunder-plump, that there was not a single soul staid in the kirkyard to hear him; for the which he was greatly mortified, and never after came to our preachings.

CHAPTER II

YEAR 1761

The great increase of smuggling—Mr. Balwhidder disperses a tea-drinking
party of gossips—He records the virtues of Nanse Banks, the schoolmistress—The servant of a military man, who had been prisoner in
France, comes into the parish, and opens a dancing-school.

IT was in this year that the great smuggling trade corrupted
all the west coast, especially the Laigh Lands about the Troon
and the Loans. The tea was going like the chaff, the brandy
like well-water, and the wastrie of all things was terrible.
There was nothing minded but the riding of cadgers by day,
and excisemen by night—and battles between the smugglers
and the king's men, both by sea and land. There was a
continual drunkenness and debauchery; and our Session, that
was but on the lip of this whirlpool of iniquity, had an awful
time o't. I did all that was in the power of nature to keep my
people from the contagion; I preached sixteen times from the
text, Render to Cæsar the things that are Cæsar's. I visited,
and I exhorted; I warned, and I prophesied; I told them
that, although the money came in like sclate stones, it would
go like the snow off the dyke. But for all I could do, the evil
got in among us, and we had no less than three contested
bastard bairns upon our hands at one time, which was a thing
never heard of in a parish of the shire of Ayr, since the Reformation. Two of the bairns, after no small sifting and
searching, we got fathered at last; but the third, that was by
Meg Glaiks, and given to one Rab Rickerton, was utterly
refused, though the fact was not denied; but he was a terma-
gant fellow, and snappit his fingers at the elders. The next
day he listed in the Scotch Greys, who were then quartered at
Ayr, and we never heard more of him, but thought he had
been slain in battle, till one of the parish, about three years
since, went up to London to lift a legacy from a cousin, that
died among the Hindoos; when he was walking about, seeing
the curiosities, and among others Chelsea Hospital, he
happened to speak to some of the invalids, who found out from
his tongue that he was a Scotchman; and speaking to the

invalids, one of them, a very old man, with a grey head, and a leg of timber, inquired what part of Scotland he was come from; and when he mentioned my parish, the invalid gave a great shout, and said he was from the same place himself; and who should this old man be, but the very identical Rab Rickerton, that was art and part in Meg Glaiks' disowned bairn. Then they had a long converse together, and he had come through many hardships, but had turned out a good soldier; and so, in his old days, was an indoor pensioner, and very comfortable; and he said that he had, to be sure, spent his youth in the devil's service, and his manhood in the king's, but his old age was given to that of his Maker, which I was blithe and thankful to hear; and he inquired about many a one in the parish, the blooming and the green of his time, but they were all dead and buried; and he had a contrite and penitent spirit, and read his Bible every day, delighting most in the Book of Joshua, the Chronicles and the Kings.

Before this year, the drinking of tea was little known in the parish, saving among a few of the heritors' houses on a Sabbath evening, but now it became very rife, yet the commoner sort did not like to let it be known that they were taking to the new luxury, especially the elderly women, who, for that reason, had their ploys in outhouses and byplaces, just as the witches lang syne had their sinful possets and galravitchings; and they made their tea for common in the pint-stoup, and drank it out of caps and luggies, for there were but few among them that had cups and saucers. Well do I remember one night in harvest, in this very year, as I was taking my twilight dauner aneath the hedge along the back side of Thomas Thorl's yard, meditating on the goodness of Providence, and looking at the sheafs of victual on the field, that I heard his wife, and two three other carlins, with their bohea in the inside of the hedge, and no doubt but it had a lacing of the conek,[1] for they were all cracking like pen-guns. But I gave them a sign by a loud host, that Providence sees all, and it skailed the bike; for I heard them, like guilty creatures, whispering and gathering up their truck-pots and trenchers, and cowering away home.

It was in this year that Patrick Dilworth (he had been schoolmaster of the parish from the time, as his wife said, of

[1] Cogniac.

Anna Regina, and before the Rexes came to the crown) was disabled by a paralytic, and the heritors, grudging the cost of another schoolmaster as long as he lived, would not allow the Session to get his place supplied, which was a wrong thing, I must say of them; for the children of the parishioners were obliged, therefore, to go to the neighbouring towns for their schooling, and the custom was to take a piece of bread and cheese in their pockets for dinner, and to return in the evening always voracious for more, the long walk helping the natural crave of their young appetites. In this way Mrs. Malcolm's two eldest laddies, Charlie and Robert, were wont to go to Irville, and it was soon seen that they kept themselves aloof from the other callans in the clachan, and had a genteeler turn than the grulshy bairns of the cotters. Her bit lassies, Kate and Effie, were better off; for some years before, Nanse Banks had taken up a teaching in a garret-room of a house, at the corner where John Bayne has biggit the sclate-house for his grocery-shop. Nanse learnt them reading and working stockings, and how to sew the semplar, for twal-pennies a week. She was a patient creature, well cut out for her calling, with bleer eyn, a pale face, and a long neck, but meek and contented withal, tholing the dule of this world with a Christian submission of the spirit; and her garret-room was a cordial of cleanliness, for she made the scholars set the house in order, time and time about, every morning; and it was a common remark for many a day, that the lassies who had been at Nanse Banks's school were always well spoken of, both for their civility, and the trigness of their houses, when they were afterwards married. In short, I do not know, that in all the long epoch of my ministry, any individual body did more to improve the ways of the parishioners, in their domestic concerns, than did that worthy and innocent creature, Nanse Banks, the schoolmistress; and she was a great loss when she was removed, as it is to be hoped, to a better world; but anent this I shall have to speak more at large hereafter.

It was in this year that my patron, the Laird of Breadland, departed this life, and I preached his funeral-sermon; but he was none beloved in the parish, for my people never forgave him for putting me upon them, although they began to be more on a familiar footing with myself. This was partly owing to my first wife, Betty Lanshaw, who was an active through-going woman, and wonderfu' useful to many of the cotters' wives at their lying-in ; and when a death happened among them, her helping hand, and anything we had at the manse, was never wanting ; and I went about myself to the bed-sides of the frail, leaving no stone unturned to win the affections of my people, which, by the blessing of the Lord, in process of time, was brought to a bearing.

But a thing happened in this year, which deserves to be recorded, as manifesting what effect the smuggling was beginning to take in the morals of the country-side. One Mr. Macskipnish, of Highland parentage, who had been a *valet-de-chambre* with a major in the campaigns, and taken a prisoner with him by the French, he having come home in a cartel, took up a dancing-school at Irville, the which art he had learnt in the genteelest fashion, in the mode of Paris, at the French Court. Such a thing as a dancing-school had never, in the memory of man, been known in our country-side ; and there was such a sound about the steps and cotillions of Mr. Macskipnish, that every lad and lass, that could spare time and siller, went to him, to the great neglect of their work. The very bairns on the loan, instead of their wonted play, gaed linking and louping in the steps of Mr. Macskipnish, who was, to be sure, a great curiosity, with long spindle legs, his breast shot out like a duck's, and his head powdered and frizzled up like a tappit-hen. He was, indeed, the proudest peacock that could be seen, and he had a ring on his finger, and when he came to drink his tea at the Breadland, he brought no hat on his head, but a droll cockit thing under his arm, which, he said, was after the manner of the courtiers at the petty suppers of one Madam Pompadour, who was at that time the concubine of the French king.

I do not recollect any other remarkable thing that happened in this year. The harvest was very abundant, and the meal so cheap, that it caused a great defect in my stipend, so that I was obligated to postpone the purchase of a mahogany scrutoire for my study, as I had intended. But I had not the heart to complain of this ; on the contrary, I rejoiced thereat, for what made me want my scrutoire till another year, had carried blitheness into the hearth of the cotter, and made the widow's heart sing with joy ; and I would have been an unnatural creature, had I not joined in the universal gladness, because plenty did abound.

'Mr. Macskipnish.'

Copyright 1895 by Macmillan & Co.

CHAPTER III

YEAR 1762

Havoc produced by the small-pox—Charles Malcolm is sent off a cabin-boy, on a voyage to Virginia—Mizy Spaewell dies on Hallowe'en—Tea begins to be admitted at the manse, but the minister continues to exert his authority against smuggling.

THE third year of my ministry was long held in remembrance for several very memorable things. William Byres of the Loanhead had a cow that calved two calves at one calving; Mrs. Byres, the same year, had twins, male and female; and there was such a crop on his fields, testifying that the Lord never sends a mouth into the world without providing meat for it. But what was thought a very daunting sign of something, happened on the Sacrament Sabbath at the conclusion of the action sermon, when I had made a very suitable discourse. The day was tempestuous, and the wind blew with such a pith and birr, that I thought it would have twirled the trees in the kirkyard out by the roots, and, blowing in this manner, it tirled the thack from the rigging of the manse stable; and the same blast that did that, took down the lead that was on the kirk-roof, which hurled off, as I was saying, at the conclusion of the action sermon, with such a dreadful sound, as the like was never heard, and all the congregation thought that it betokened a mutation to me. However, nothing particular happened to me; but the small-pox came in among the weans of the parish, and the smashing that it made of the poor bits o' bairns was indeed woeful.

One Sabbath, when the pestilence was raging, I preached a sermon about Rachel weeping for her children, which Thomas Thorl, who was surely a great judge of good preaching, said, 'was a monument of divinity whilk searched the heart of many a parent that day'; a thing I was well pleased to hear, for Thomas, as I have related at length, was the most zealous champion against my getting the parish; but, from this time, I set him down in my mind for the next vacancy among the elders. Worthy man! it was not permitted him to arrive at that honour.   In the fall of that year he took an income in his legs, and could no go about, and was laid up for the remainder of his days, a perfect Lazarus, by the fireside.   But he was well supported in his affliction.   In due season, when it pleased HIM that alone can give and take, to pluck him from this life, as the fruit ripened and ready for the gathering, his death, to all that knew him, was a gentle dispensation, for truly he had been in sore trouble.

It was in this year that Charlie Malcolm, Mrs. Malcolm's eldest son, was sent to be a cabin-boy in the *Tobacco* trader, a three-masted ship, that sailed between Port-Glasgow and Virginia in America.   She was commanded by Captain Dickie, an Irville man ; for at that time the Clyde was supplied with the best sailors from our coast, the coal trade with Ireland being a better trade for bringing up good mariners than the long voyages in the open sea ; which was the reason, as I often heard said, why the Clyde shipping got so many of their men from our country-side.   The going to sea of Charlie Malcolm was, on divers accounts, a very remarkable thing to us all, for he was the first that ever went from our parish, in the memory of man, to be a sailor, and everybody was concerned at it, and some thought it was a great venture of his mother to let him, his father having been lost at sea.   But what could the forlorn widow do ?   She had five weans, and little to give them ; and, as she herself said, he was aye in the hand of his Maker, go where he might, and the will of God would be done, in spite of all earthly wiles and devices to the contrary.

On the Monday morning, when Charlie was to go away to meet the Irville carrier on the road, we were all up, and I walked by myself from the manse into the clachan to bid him farewell, and I met him just coming from his mother's door, as blithe as a bee, in his sailor's dress, with a stick, and a bundle tied in a Barcelona silk handkerchief hanging o'er his shoulder, and his two little brothers were with him, and his sisters, Kate and Effie, looking out from the door all begreeten ; but his mother was in the house, praying to the Lord to protect her orphan, as she afterwards told me.   All the weans of the clachan were gathered at the kirkyard yett to see him pass, and they gave him three great shouts as he was going by ; and everybody was at their doors, and said something

C   17

encouraging to him; but there was a great laugh when auld Mizy Spaewell came hirpling with her bachle in her hand, and flung it after him for gude luck. Mizy had a wonderful faith in freats, and was just an oracle of sagacity at expounding dreams, and bodes of every sort and description—besides, she was reckoned one of the best howdies in her day; but by this time she was grown frail and feckless, and she died the same year on Hallowe'en, which made everybody wonder, that it should have so fallen out for her to die on Hallowe'en.

Shortly after the departure of Charlie Malcolm, the Lady of Breadland, with her three daughters, removed to Edinburgh, where the young laird, that had been my pupil, was learning to be an advocate, and the Breadland House was set to Major Gilchrist, a nabob from India; but he was a narrow ailing man, and his maiden-sister, Miss Girzie, was the scrimpetest creature that could be; so that, in their hands, all the pretty policy of the Breadlands, that had cost a power of money to the old laird, that was my patron, fell into decay and disorder; and the bonny yew trees, that were cut into the shape of peacocks, soon grew out of all shape, and are now doleful monuments of the major's tack, and that of Lady Skim-milk, as Miss Girzie Gilchrist, his sister, was nicknamed by every ane that kent her.

But it was not so much on account of the neglect of the Breadland, that the incoming of Major Gilchrist was to be deplored. The old men, that had a light labour in keeping the policy in order, were thrown out of bread, and could do little; and the poor women, that whiles got a bit and a drap from the kitchen of the family, soon felt the change, so that by little and little, we were obligated to give help from the Session; insomuch, that before the end of the year, I was necessitated to preach a discourse on almsgiving, specially for the benefit of our own poor, a thing never before known in the parish.

But one good thing came from the Gilchrists to Mrs. Malcolm. Miss Girzie, whom they called Lady Skim-milk, had been in a very penurious way as a seamstress, in the Gorbals of Glasgow, while her brother was making the fortune in India, and she was a clever needlewoman—none better, as it was said; and she having some things to make, took Kate Malcolm to help her in the coarse work; and Kate, being a nimble and birky thing, was so useful to the lady, and the complaining man the major, that they invited her to stay with them at the Breadland for the winter, where, although she was holden to her seam from morning to night, her food lightened the hand of her mother, who, for the first time since her coming into the parish, found the penny for the day's dark more than was needed for the meal-basin; and the tea-drinking was beginning to spread more openly, insomuch, that, by the advice of the first Mrs. Balwhidder, Mrs. Malcolm took in tea to sell, and in this way was enabled to eke something to the small profits of her wheel. Thus the tide, that had been so long ebbing to her, began to turn; and here I am bound in truth to say, that although I never could abide the smuggling, both on its own account, and the evils that grew therefrom to the country-side, I lost some of my dislike to the tea, after Mrs. Malcolm began to traffic in it, and we then had it for our breakfast in the morning at the manse, as well as in the afternoon. But what I thought most of it for, was, that it did no harm to the head of the drinkers, which was not always the case with the possets that were in fashion before. There is no meeting now in the summer evenings, as I remember often happened in my younger days, with decent ladies coming home with red faces, tozy and cosh from a posset masking; so, both for its temperance, and on account of Mrs. Malcolm's sale, I refrained from the November in this year to preach against tea; but I never lifted the weight of my displeasure from off the smuggling trade, until it was utterly put down by the strong hand of government.

There was no other thing of note in this year, saving only that I planted in the garden the big pear tree, which had the two great branches that we call the Adam and Eve. I got the plant, then a sapling, from Mr. Graft, that was Lord Eglesham's head-gardener; and he said it was, as indeed all the parish now knows well, a most juicy sweet pear, such as was not known in Scotland, till my lord brought down the father plant from the king's garden in London, in the forty-five, when he went up to testify his loyalty to the House of Hanover.

CHAPTER IV

YEAR 1763

Charles Malcolm's return from sea—Kate Malcolm is taken to live with
Lady Macadam—Death of the first Mrs. Balwhidder.

THE Ann. Dom. 1763, was, in many a respect, a memorable
year, both in public and in private. The king granted peace
to the French, and Charlie Malcolm, that went to sea in the
Tobacco trader, came home to see his mother. The ship,
after being at America, had gone down to Jamaica, an island
in the West Indies, with a cargo of live lumber, as Charlie
told me himself, and had come home with more than a
hundred and fifty hoggits of sugar, and sixty-three puncheons
full of rum ; for she was, by all accounts, a stately galley, and
almost two hundred tons in the burden, being the largest
vessel then sailing from the creditable town of Port-Glasgow.
Charlie was not expected ; and his coming was a great thing
to us all, so I will mention the whole particulars.

One evening, towards the gloaming, as I was taking my
walk of meditation, I saw a brisk sailor laddie coming towards
me. He had a pretty green parrot, sitting on a bundle, tied
in a Barcelona silk handkerchief, which he carried with a
stick over his shoulder, and in this bundle was a wonderful big
nut, such as no one in our parish had ever seen. It was called
a cocker-nut. This blithe callant was Charlie Malcolm, who
had come all the way that day his leaful lane, on his own legs
from Greenock, where the *Tobacco* trader was then 'livering
her cargo. I told him how his mother, and his brothers, and
his sisters were all in good health, and went to convoy him
home ; and as we were going along, he told me many curious
things, and he gave me six beautiful yellow limes, that he had
brought in his pouch all the way across the seas, for me to make
a bowl of punch with, and I thought more of them than if they
had been golden guineas, it was so mindful of the laddie.

When we got to the door of his mother's house, she was
sitting at the fireside, with her three other bairns at their
bread and milk, Kate being then with Lady Skim-milk, at the

Breadland, sewing. It was between the day and dark, when the shuttle stands still till the lamp is lighted. But such a shout of joy and thankfulness as rose from that hearth when Charlie went in ! The very parrot, ye would have thought, was a participator, for the beast gied a skraik that made my whole head dirl ; and the neighbours came flying and flocking to see what was the matter, for it was the first parrot ever seen within the bounds of the parish, and some thought it was but a foreign hawk, with a yellow head and green feathers.

In the midst of all this, Effie Malcolm had run off to the Breadland for her sister Kate, and the two lassies came flying breathless, with Miss Girzie Gilchrist, the Lady Skim-milk, pursuing them like desperation, or a griffon, down the avenue ; for Kate, in her hurry, had flung down her seam, a new printed gown, that she was helping to make, and it had fallen into a boyne of milk that was ready for the creaming, by which ensued a double misfortune to Miss Girzie, the gown being not only ruined, but licking up the cream. For this, poor Kate was not allowed ever to set her face in the Breadland again.

When Charlie Malcolm had staid about a week with his mother, he returned to his birth in the *Tobacco* trader, and shortly after his brother Robert was likewise sent to serve his time to the sea, with an owner that was master of his own bark, in the coal trade at Irville. Kate, who was really a surprising lassie for her years, was taken off her mother's hands by the old Lady Macadam, that lived in her jointure house, which is now the Cross Keys Inns. Her Ladyship was a woman of high-breeding, her husband having been a great general, and knighted by the king for his exploits ; but she was lame, and could not move about in her dining-room without help, so hearing from the first Mrs. Balwhidder how Kate had done such an unatonable deed to Miss Girzie Gilchrist, she sent for Kate, and finding her sharp and apt, she took her to live with her as a companion. This was a vast advantage, for the lady was versed in all manner of accomplishments, and could read and speak French, with more ease than any professor at that time in the College of Glasgow ; and she had learnt to sew flowers on satin, either in a nunnery abroad, or in a boarding-school in England, and took pleasure in teaching Kate all she knew, and how to behave herself like a lady.

In the summer of this year, old Mr. Patrick Dilworth, that

'*The very parrot was a participator.*'

had so long been doited with the paralytics, died, and it was a great relief to my people, for the heritors could no longer refuse to get a proper schoolmaster; so we took on trial Mr. Lorimore, who has ever since the year after, with so much credit to himself, and usefulness to the parish, been school-master, session-clerk, and precentor—a man of great mildness and extraordinary particularity. He was then a very young man, and some objection was made on account of his youth, to his being session-clerk, especially as the smuggling im-morality still gave us much trouble in the making up of irregular marriages; but his discretion was greater than could have been hoped for from his years; and after a twelve-month's probation in the capacity of schoolmaster, he was in-stalled in all the offices that had belonged to his predecessor, old Mr. Patrick Dilworth that was.

But the most memorable thing that befell among my people this year, was the burning of the lint-mill on the Lugton Water, which happened, of all the days of the year, on the very self-same day that Miss Girzie Gilchrist, better known as Lady Skim-milk, hired the chaise from Mrs. Watts of the New Inns of Irville, to go with her brother the major to consult the faculty in Edinburgh concerning his complaints. For, as the chaise was coming by the mill, William Huckle, the miller that was, came flying out of the mill like a demented man, crying fire!—and it was the driver that brought the melan-choly tidings to the clachan—and melancholy they were; for the mill was utterly destroyed, and in it not a little of all that year's crop of lint in our parish. The first Mrs. Balwhidder lost upwards of twelve stone, which we had raised on the glebe with no small pains, watering it in the drouth, as it was intended for sarking to ourselves, and sheets and napery. A great loss indeed it was, and the vexation thereof had a visible effect on Mrs. Balwhidder's health, which from the spring had been in a dwining way. But for it, I think she might have wrestled through the winter; however, it was ordered other-wise, and she was removed from mine to Abraham's bosom on Christmas day, and buried on Hogmanae, for it was thought uncanny to have a dead corpse in the house on the New Year's day. She was a worthy woman, studying with all her capa-city to win the hearts of my people towards me—in the which good work she prospered greatly; so that when she died,

23

there was not a single soul in the parish that was not contented with both my walk and conversation. Nothing could
be more peaceable than the way we lived together. Her
brother Andrew, a fine lad, I had sent to the College at Glasgow, at my own cost, and when he came out to the burial, he
staid with me a month, for the manse after her decease was
very dull, and it was during this visit that he gave me an inkling of his wish to go out to India as a cadet, but the transactions anent that fall within the scope of another year—as
well as what relates to her headstone, and the epitaph in
metre, which I indited myself thereon ; John Truel, the mason,
carving the same, as may be seen in the kirkyard, where it
wants a little reparation and setting upright, having settled the
wrong way when the second Mrs. Balwhidder was laid by her
side. But I must not here enter upon an anticipation.

CHAPTER V

YEAR 1764

He gets a headstone for Mrs. Balwhidder, and writes an epitaph for it—
    He is afflicted with melancholy, and thinks of writing a book—
    Nichol Snipe the gamekeeper's device when reproved in church.

THIS year well deserved the name of the monumental year in
our parish ; for the young Laird of the Breadland, that had
been my pupil, being learning to be an advocate among. the
faculty in Edinburgh, with his lady mother, who had removed
thither with the young ladies her daughters, for the benefit of
education, sent out to be put up in the kirk, under the loft
over the family vault, an elegant marble headstone, with an
epitaph engraven thereon, in fair Latin, setting forth many
excellent qualities which the old laird, my patron that was, the
inditer thereof, said he possessed. I say the inditer, because
it could no have been the young laird himself, although he got
the credit o't on the stone, for he was nae daub in my aught
at the Latin or any other language. However, he might
improve himself at Edinburgh, where a' manner of genteel
things were then to be got at an easy rate, and doubtless, the

young laird got a probationer at the College to write the epitaph ; but I have often wondered sin' syne, how he came to make it in Latin, for assuredly his dead parent, if he could have seen it, could not have read a single word o't, notwithstanding it was so vaunty about his virtues, and other civil and hospitable qualifications.

The coming of the laird's monumental stone had a great effect on me, then in a state of deep despondency for the loss of the first Mrs. Balwhidder ; and I thought I could not do a better thing, just by way of diversion in my heavy sorrow, than to get a well-shapen headstone made for her—which, as I have hinted at in the record of the last year, was done and set up. But a headstone without an epitaph is no better than a body without the breath of life in't ; and so it behoved me to make a posey for the monument, the which I conned and pondered upon for many days. I thought as Mrs. Balwhidder, worthy woman as she was, did not understand the Latin tongue, it would not do to put on what I had to say in that language, as the laird had done—nor indeed would it have been easy, as I found upon the experimenting, to tell what I had to tell in Latin, which is naturally a crabbed language, and very difficult to write properly. I therefore, after mentioning her age and the dates of her birth and departure, composed in sedate poetry, the following epitaph, which may yet be seen on the tombstone.

EPITAPH

' A lovely Christian, spouse, and friend,
Pleasant in life, and at her end.
A pale consumption dealt the blow
That laid her here, with dust below.
Sore was the cough that shook her frame ;
That cough her patience did proclaim—
And as she drew her latest breath,
She said, "The Lord is sweet in death."
O pious reader, standing by,
Learn like this gentle one to die.
The grass doth grow and fade away,
And time runs out by night and day ;
The King of Terrors has command
To strike us with his dart in hand.
Go where we will by flood or field,

He will pursue and make us yield.
But though to him we must resign
The vesture of our part divine,
There is a jewel in our trust,
That will not perish in the dust,
A pearl of price, a precious gem,
Ordain'd for Jesus' diadem :
Therefore be holy while you can,
And think upon the doom of man.
Repent in time and sin no more,
That when the strife of life is o'er,
On wings of love your soul may rise,
To dwell with angels in the skies,
Where psalms are sung eternally,
And martyrs ne'er again shall die ;
But with the saints still bask in bliss,
And drink the cup of blessedness.'

This was greatly thought of at the time, and Mr. Lorimore, who had a nerve for poesy himself in his younger years, was of opinion that it was so much to the purpose and suitable withal, that he made his scholars write it out for their examination copies, at the reading whereof before the heritors, when the examination of the school came round, the tear came into my eye, and every one present sympathised with me in my great affliction for the loss of the first Mrs. Balwhidder.

Andrew Lanshaw, as I have recorded, having come from the Glasgow College to the burial of his sister, my wife that was, staid with me a month to keep me company ; and staying with me, he was a great cordial, for the weather was wet and sleety, and the nights were stormy, so that I could go little out, and few of the elders came in, they being at that time old men in a feckless condition, not at all qualified to warsle with the blasts of winter. But when Andrew left me to go back to his classes, I was eirie and lonesome, and but for the getting of the monument ready, which was a blessed entertainment to me in those dreary nights, with consulting anent the shape of it with John Truel, and meditating on the verse for the epitaph, I might have gone altogether demented. However, it pleased HIM, who is the surety of the sinner, to help me through the Slough of Despond, and to set my feet on firm land, establishing my way thereon.

But the work of the monument, and the epitaph, could not

endure for a constancy, and after it was done, I was again in great danger of sinking into the hypochonderies a second time. However, I was enabled to fight with my affliction, and by and by, as the spring began to open her green lattice, and to set out her flower-pots to the sunshine, and the time of the singing of birds was come, I became more composed, and like myself, so I often walked in the fields, and held communion with nature, and wondered at the mysteries thereof.

On one of these occasions, as I was sauntering along the edge of Eglesham Wood, looking at the industrious bee going from flower to flower, and the idle butterfly, that layeth up no store, but perisheth ere it is winter, I felt as it were a spirit from on high descending upon me, a throb at my heart, and a thrill in my brain, and I was transported out of myself, and seized with the notion of writing a book—but what it should be about, I could not settle to my satisfaction : sometimes I thought of an orthodox poem, like *Paradise Lost*, by John Milton, wherein I proposed to treat more at large of Original Sin, and the great mystery of Redemption ; at others, I fancied that a connect treatise on the efficacy of Free Grace would be more taking ; but although I made divers beginnings in both subjects, some new thought ever came into my head, and the whole summer passed away and nothing was done. I therefore postponed my design of writing a book till the winter, when I would have the benefit of the long nights. Before that, however, I had other things of more importance to think about : my servant lasses, having no eye of a mistress over them, wastered everything at such a rate, and made such a galravitching in the house, that, long before the end of the year, the year's stipend was all spent, and I did not know what to do. At lang and length I mustered courage to send for Mr. Auld, who was then living, and an elder. He was a douce and discreet man, fair and well-doing in the world, and had a better handful of strong common sense than many even of the heritors. So I told him how I was situated, and conferred with him, and he advised me, for my own sake, to look out for another wife as soon as decency would allow, which he thought might very properly be after the turn of the year, by which time the first Mrs. Balwhidder would be dead more than twelve months ; and when I mentioned my design to write a book, he said (and he was a man of good discretion) that the doing of the book was a thing that would keep, but wasterful servants were a growing evil; so, upon his counselling, I resolved not to meddle with the book till I was married again, but employ the interim, between then and the turn of the year, in looking out for a prudent woman to be my second wife, strictly intending, as I did perform, not to mint a word about my choice, if I made one, till the whole twelve months and a day, from the date of the first Mrs. Balwhidder's interment, had run out.

In this the hand of Providence was very visible, and lucky for me it was that I had sent for Mr. Auld when I did send, as the very week following, a sound began to spread in the parish, that one of my lassies had got herself with bairn, which was an awful thing to think had happened in the house of her master, and that master a minister of the Gospel. Some there were, for backbiting appertaineth to all conditions, that jaloused and wondered if I had not a finger in the pye; which, when Mr. Auld heard, he bestirred himself in such a manful and godly way in my defence, as silenced the clash, telling that I was utterly incapable of any such thing, being a man of a guileless heart, and a spiritual simplicity, that would be ornamental in a child. We then had the latheron summoned before the Session, and was not long of making her confess that the father was Nichol Snipe, Lord Glencairn's gamekeeper; and both her and Nichol were obligated to stand in the kirk, but Nichol was a graceless reprobate, for he came with two coats, one buttoned behind him, and another buttoned before him, and two wigs of my lord's, lent him by the valet-de-chamer; the one over his face, and the other in the right way; and he stood with his face to the church wall. When I saw him from the pu'pit, I said to him, 'Nichol, you must turn your face towards me!' At the which, he turned round to be sure, but there he presented the same show as his back. I was confounded, and did not know what to say, but cried out, with a voice of anger, 'Nichol, Nichol! if ye had been a' back, ye would nae hae been there this day'; which had such an effect on the whole congregation, that the poor fellow suffered afterwards more derision, than if I had rebuked him in the manner prescribed by the Session.

This affair, with the previous advice of Mr. Auld, was,

however, a warning to me, that no pastor of his parish should be long without a helpmate. Accordingly, as soon as the year was out, I set myself earnestly about the search for one, but as the particulars fall properly within the scope and chronicle of the next year, I must reserve them for it ; and I do not recollect that anything more particular befell in this, excepting that William Mutchkins, the father of Mr. Mutchkins, the great spirit-dealer in Glasgow, set up a change-house in the clachan, which was the first in the parish, and which, if I could have helped, it would have been the last ; for it was opening a howf to all manner of wickedness, and was an immediate get and offspring of the smuggling trade, against which I had so set my countenance. But William Mutchkins himself was a respectable man, and no house could be better ordered than his change. At a stated hour he made family worship, for he brought up his children in the fear of God and the Christian religion ; and although the house was full, he would go into the customers, and ask them if they would want anything for half an hour, for that he was going to make exercise with his family ; and many a wayfaring traveller has joined in the prayer. There is no such thing, I fear, nowadays, of publicans entertaining travellers in this manner.

CHAPTER VI

YEAR 1765

Establishment of a whisky distillery—He is again married to Miss Lizy Kibbock—Her industry in the dairy—Her example diffuses a spirit of industry through the parish.

As there was little in the last year that concerned the parish, but only myself, so in this the like fortune continued ; and saving a rise in the price of barley, occasioned, as was thought, by the establishment of a house for brewing whisky in a neighbouring parish, it could not be said that my people were exposed to the mutations and influences of the stars which ruled in the seasons of Ann. Dom. 1765. In the winter there was a dearth of fuel, such as has not been since ; for when the spring loosened the bonds of the ice, three new coal-heughs were shanked in the Douray Moor, and ever since there has been a great plenty of that necessary article. Truly, it is very wonderful to see how things come round ; when the talk was about the shanking of their heughs, and a paper to get folk to take shares in them, was carried through the circumjacent parishes, it was thought a gowk's errand ; but no sooner was the coal reached, but up sprung such a traffic, that it was a God-send to the parish, and the opening of a trade and commerce that has, to use an old bye-word, brought gold in gowpins amang us. From that time my stipend has been on the regular increase, and therefore I think that the incoming of the heritors must have been in like manner augmented.

Soon after this, the time was drawing near for my second marriage. I had placed my affections, with due consideration, on Miss Lizy Kibbock, the well-brought-up daughter of Mr. Joseph Kibbock of the Gorbyholm, who was the first that made a speculation in the farming way in Ayrshire, and whose cheese were of such an excellent quality, that they have, under the name of Delap cheese, spread far and wide over the civilised world. Miss Lizy and me were married on the 29th day of April, with some inconvenience to both sides, on account of the dread that we had of being married in May, for it is said,

> ' Of the marriages in May,
> The bairns die of a decay.'

However, married we were, and we hired the Irville chaise, and with Miss Jenny her sister, and Becky Cairns her niece, who sat on a portmanty at our feet, we went on a pleasure jaunt to Glasgow, where we bought a miracle of useful things for the manse, that neither the first Mrs. Balwhidder nor me ever thought of ; but the second Mrs. Balwhidder that was, had a geni for management, and it was extraordinary what she could go through. Well may I speak of her with commendations, for she was the bee that made my honey, although at first things did not go so clear with us. For she found the manse rookit and herrit, and there was such a supply of plenishing of all sort wanted, that I thought myself ruined and undone by her care and industry. There was such a buying of wool to make blankets, with a booming of the meikle wheel to spin the same, and such birring of the little wheel for sheets and napery, that the manse was for many a day like an organ kist. Then we had milk cows, and the calves to bring up, and a kirning of butter, and a making of cheese; in short, I was almost by myself with the jangle and din, which prevented me from writing a book as I had proposed, and I for a time thought of the peaceful and kindly nature of the first Mrs. Balwhidder with a sigh; but the outcoming was soon manifest. The second Mrs. Balwhidder sent her butter on the market-days to Irville, and her cheese from time to time to Glasgow, to Mrs. Firlot, that kept the huxtry in the Saltmarket, and they were both so well made, that our dairy was just a coining of money, insomuch, that after the first year, we had the whole tot of my stipend to put untouched into the bank.

But I must say, that although we were thus making siller like sclate stones, I was not satisfied in my own mind that I had got the manse merely to be a factory of butter and cheese, and to breed up veal calves for the slaughter; so I spoke to the second Mrs. Balwhidder, and pointed out to her what I thought the error of our way; but she had been so ingrained with the profitable management of cows and grumphies in her father's house, that she could not desist, at the which I was greatly grieved. By and by, however, I began to discern that there was something as good in her example as the giving of alms to the poor folk. For all the wives of the parish were stirred up by it into a wonderful thrift, and nothing was heard of in every house, but of quiltings and wabs to weave; insomuch, that before many years came round, there was not a better-stocked parish, with blankets and napery, than mine was, within the bounds of Scotland.

It was about the Michaelmas of this year that Mrs. Malcolm opened her shop, which she did chiefly on the advice of Mrs. Balwhidder, who said it was far better to allow a little profit on the different haberdasheries that might be wanted, than to send to the neighbouring towns an end's errand on purpose for them, none of the lasses that were so sent ever thinking of making less than a day's play on every such occasion. In a word, it is not to be told how the second Mrs. Balwhidder, my wife, showed the value of flying time, even to the concerns of this world, and was the mean of giving a life and energy to the housewifery of the parish,

that has made many a one beek his shins in comfort, that
would otherwise have had but a cold coal to blow at. Indeed,
Mr. Kibbock, her father, was a man beyond the common,
and had an insight of things, by which he was enabled to
draw profit and advantage, where others could only see risk
and detriment. He planted mounts of fir-trees on the bleak
and barren tops of the hills of his farm, the which everybody,
and I among the rest, considered as a thrashing of the water,
and raising of bells. But as his tack ran his trees grew,
and the plantations supplied him with stabs to make *stake
and rice* between his fields, which soon gave them a trig
and orderly appearance, such as had never before been seen
in the west country ; and his example has, in this matter,
been so followed, that I have heard travellers say, who have
been in foreign countries, that the shire of Ayr, for its bonny
round green plantings on the tops of the hills, is above comparison either with Italy or Switzerland, where the hills are,
as it were, in a state of nature.

Upon the whole, this was a busy year in the parish, and
the seeds of many great improvements were laid. The king's
road, which then ran through the Vennel, was mended ; but
it was not till some years after, as I shall record by and by,
that the trust road, as it was called, was made, the which
had the effect of turning the town inside out.

Before I conclude, it is proper to mention that the kirk-
bell, which had to this time, from time immemorial, hung on
an ash-tree, was one stormy night cast down by the breaking
of the branch, which was the cause of the heritors agreeing
to build the steeple. The clock was a mortification to the
parish from the Lady Breadland, when she died some years
after.

CHAPTER VII

YEAR 1766

The burning of the Breadland—A new bell, and also a steeple—Nanse Birrel found drowned in a well—The parish troubled with wild Irishmen.

IT was in this Ann. Dom. that the great calamity happened, the which took place on a Sabbath evening in the month of February. Mrs. Balwhidder had just infused or masket the tea, and we were set round the fireside to spend the night in an orderly and religious manner, along with Mr. and Mrs. Petticrew, who were on a friendly visitation to the manse, the mistress being full cousin to Mrs. Balwhidder. Sitting, as I was saying, at our tea, one of the servant lasses came into the room with a sort of a panic laugh, and said, 'What are ye all doing there when the Breadland's in a low?' 'The Breadland in a low!' cried I. 'Oh, ay,' cried she; 'bleezing at the windows and the rigging, and out at the lum, like a killogie.' Upon the which, we all went to the door, and there, to be sure, we did see that the Breadland was burning, the flames crackling high out o'er the trees, and the sparks flying like a comet's tail in the firmament.

Seeing this sight, I said to Mr. Petticrew that, in the strength of the Lord, I would go and see what could be done, for it was as plain as the sun in the heavens, that the ancient place of the Breadlands would be destroyed; whereupon he accorded to go with me, and we walked at a lively course to the spot, and the people from all quarters were pouring in, and it was an awsome scene. But the burning of the house, and the droves of the multitude, were nothing to what we saw when we got forenent the place. There was the rafters crackling, the flames raging, the servants running, some with bedding, some with looking-glasses, and others with chamber utensils, as little likely to be fuel to the fire, but all testifications to the confusion and alarm. Then there was a shout, 'Whar's Miss Girzie? whar's the major?' The major, poor man, soon cast up, lying upon a feather-bed, ill with his complaints, in the garden; but Lady Skim-milk was nowhere to be found. At last, a figure was seen in the upper flat, pursued by the flames, and that was Miss Girzie. Oh! it was a terrible sight to look at her in that jeopardy at the window, with her gold watch in the one hand and the silver teapot in the other, skreighing like desperation for a ladder and help. But before a ladder or help could be found, the floor sunk down, and the roof fell in, and poor Miss Girzie, with her idols, perished in the burning. It was a dreadful business; I think to this hour, how I saw her at the window, how the fire came in behind her, and claught her like a fiery Belzebub, and bore her into perdition before our eyes. The next morning the atomy of the body was found among the rubbish, with a piece of metal in what had been each of its hands, no doubt the gold watch and the silver teapot. Such was the end of Miss Girzie, and the Breadland, which the young laird, my pupil that was, by growing a resident at Edinburgh, never rebuilt. It was burnt to the very ground, nothing was spared but what the servants in the first flaught gathered up in a hurry and ran with, but no one could tell how the major, who was then, as it was thought by the faculty, past the power of nature to recover, got out of the house, and was laid on the feather-bed in the garden. However, he never got the better of that night, and before Whitsunday he was dead too, and buried beside his sister's bones at the south side of the kirkyard dyke, where his cousin's son, that was his heir, erected the handsome monument, with the three urns and weeping cherubims, bearing witness to the great valour of the major among the Hindoos, as well as other commendable virtues, for which, as the epitaph says, he was universally esteemed and beloved by all who knew him, in his public and private capacity.

But although the burning of the Breadland House was justly called the great calamity, on account of what happened to Miss Girzie, with her gold watch and silver teapot, yet, as Providence never fails to bring good out of evil, it turned out a catastrophe that proved advantageous to the parish; for the laird, instead of thinking to build it up, was advised to let the policy out as a farm, and the tack was taken by Mr. Coulter, than whom there had been no such man in the agriculturing line among us before, not even excepting Mr. Kibbock of the Gorbyholm, my father-in-law that was. Of the stabling, Mr.

'A figure was seen in the upper flat.'

Coulter made a comfortable dwelling-house, and having rugget out the evergreens and other unprofitable plants, saving the twa ancient yew-trees which the near-begun major and his sister had left to go to ruin about the mansion-house, he turned all to production, and it was wonderful what an increase he made the land bring forth. He was from far beyond Edinburgh, and had got his insight among the Lothian farmers, so that he knew what crop should follow another, and nothing could surpass the regularity of his rigs and furrows. Well do I remember the admiration that I had, when, in a fine sunny morning of the first spring after he took the Breadland, I saw his braird on what had been the cows' grass, as even and pretty as if it had been worked and stripped in the loom with a shuttle. Truly, when I look back at the example he set, and when I think on the method and dexterity of his management, I must say, that his coming to the parish was a great God-send, and tended to do far more for the benefit of my people, than if the young laird had rebuilded the Breadland House in a fashionable style, as was at one time spoken of.

But the year of the great calamity was memorable for another thing. In the December foregoing, the wind blew, as I have recorded in the chronicle of the last year, and broke down the bough of the tree, whereon the kirk-bell had hung from the time, as was supposed, of the Persecution, before the bringing over of King William. Mr. Kibbock, my father-in-law then that was, being a man of a discerning spirit, when he heard of the unfortunate fall of the bell, advised me to get the heritors to big a steeple, but which, when I thought of the expense, I was afraid to do. He, however, having a great skill in the heart of man, gave me no rest on the subject, but told me, that if I allowed the time to go by, till the heritors were used to come to the kirk without a bell, I would get no steeple at all. I often wondered what made Mr. Kibbock so fond of a steeple, which is a thing that I never could see a good reason for, saving that it is an ecclesiastical adjunct, like the gown and bands. However, he set me on to get a steeple proposed, and after no little argol-bargling with the heritors, it was agreed to. This was chiefly owing to the instrumentality of Lady Moneyplack, who in that winter was much subjected to the rheumatics, she having one cold and raw Sunday morning, there being no bell to announce the time, come half an hour too soon to the kirk, made her bestir herself to get an interest awakened among the heritors in behalf of a steeple.

But when the steeple was built, a new contention arose. It was thought that the bell, which had been used in the ash-tree, would not do in a stone and lime fabric, so, after great agitation among the heritors, it was resolved to sell the old bell to a foundry in Glasgow, and buy a new bell suitable to the steeple, which was a very comely fabric. The buying of the new bell led to other considerations, and the old Lady Breadland, being at the time in a decaying condition, and making her will, she left a mortification to the parish, as I have intimated, to get a clock, so that, by the time the steeple was finished, and the bell put up, the Lady Breadland's legacy came to be implemented, according to the ordination of the testatrix.

Of the casualties that happened in this year, I should not forget to put down, as a thing for remembrance, that an aged woman, one Nanse Birrel, a distillator of herbs, and well skilled in the healing of sores, who had a great repute among the quarriers and colliers,—she having gone to the physic well in the sandy hills to draw water, was found with her feet uppermost in the well by some of the bairns of Mr. Lorimore's school; and there was a great debate whether Nanse had fallen in by accident head-foremost, or, in a temptation, thrown herself in that position, with her feet sticking up to the evil one; for Nanse was a curious discontented blear-eyed woman, and it was only with great ado that I could get the people keepit from calling her a witchwife.

I should likewise place on record, that the first ass that had ever been seen in this part of the country came in the course of this year with a gang of tinklers, that made horn-spoons and mended bellows. Where they came from never was well made out, but being a blackaviced crew, they were generally thought to be Egyptians. They tarried about a week among us, living in tents, with their little ones squattling among the litter; and one of the older men of them set and tempered to me two razors, that were as good as nothing, but which he made better than when they were new.

Shortly after, but I am not quite sure whether it was in

37

'One of the older men set and tempered to me two razors.'

the end of this year or the beginning of the next, although I have a notion that it was in this, there came over from Ireland a troop of wild Irish, seeking for work, as they said, but they made free quarters, for they herrit the roosts of the clachan, and cutted the throat of a sow of ours, the carcase of which they no doubt intended to steal, but something came over them, and it was found lying at the back-side of the manse, to the great vexation of Mrs. Balwhidder, for she had set her mind on a clecking of pigs, and only waited for the China boar, that had been brought down from London by Lord Eglesham, to mend the breed of pork—a profitable commodity that her father, Mr. Kibbock, cultivated for the Glasgow market. The destruction of our sow, under such circumstances, was therefore held to be a great crime and cruelty, and it had the effect to raise up such a spirit in the clachan that the Irish were obligated to decamp; and they set out for Glasgow, where one of them was afterwards hanged for a fact, but the truth concerning how he did it, I either never heard, or it has passed from my mind, like many other things I should have carefully treasured.

CHAPTER VIII

YEAR 1767

Lord Eglesham meets with an accident, which is the means of getting the parish a new road—I preach for the benefit of Nanse Banks, the schoolmistress, reduced to poverty.

ALL things in our parish were now beginning to shoot up into a great prosperity. The spirit of farming began to get the upper hand of the spirit of smuggling, and the coal-heughs that had been opened in the Douray now brought a pour of money among us. In the manse, the thrift and frugality of the second Mrs. Balwhidder throve exceedingly, so that we could save the whole stipend for the bank.

The king's highway, as I have related in the foregoing, ran through the Vennel, which was a narrow and a crooked street, with many big stones here and there, and every now and then, both in the spring and the fall, a gathering of middens for the fields, insomuch that the coal carts from the Dowray Moor were often reested in the middle of the causeway, and on more than one occasion some of them laired altogether in the middens, and others of them broke down. Great complaint was made by the carters anent these difficulties, and there was for many a day a talk and sound of an alteration and amendment, but nothing was fulfilled in the matter till the month of March in this year, when the Lord Eglesham was coming from London to see the new lands that he had bought in our parish. His lordship was a man of a genteel spirit, and very fond of his horses, which were the most beautiful creatures of their kind that had been seen in all the country-side. Coming, as I was noting, to see his new lands, he was obliged to pass through the clachan one day, when all the middens were gathered out reeking and sappy in the middle of the causeway. Just as his lordship was driving in with his prancing steeds like a Jehu at the one end of the Vennel, a long string of loaded coal carts came in at the other, and there was hardly room for my lord to pass them. What was to be done? his lordship could not turn back, and the coal carts were in no less perplexity. Everybody was out of doors to see and to help, when, in trying to get his lordship's carriage over the top of a midden, the horses gave a sudden loup, and couped the coach, and threw my lord, head-foremost, into the very scent-bottle of the whole commodity, which made him go perfect mad, and he swore like a trooper, that he would get an Act of Parliament to put down the nuisance—the which now ripened in the course of this year into the undertaking of the trust road.

His lordship being in a woeful plight, left the carriage and came to the manse, till his servant went to the castle for a change for him; but he could not wait nor abide himself, so he got the lend of my best suit of clothes, and was wonderful jocose both with Mrs. Balwhidder and me, for he was a portly man, and I but a thin body, and it was really a droll curiosity to see his lordship clad in my garments.

Out of this accident grew a sort of a neighbourliness between that Lord Eglesham and me, so that when Andrew Lanshaw, the brother that was of the first Mrs. Balwhidder, came to think of going to India, I wrote to my lord for his

40

'It was a droll curiosity to see his lordship clad in my garments.'

behoof, and his lordship got him sent out as a cadet, and was extraordinary discreet to Andrew when he went up to London to take his passage, speaking to him of me as if I had been a very saint, which the Searcher of Hearts knows I am far from thinking myself.

But to return to the making of the trust road, which, as I have said, turned the town inside out. It was agreed among the heritors that it should run along the back-side of the south houses ; and that there should be steadings fewed off on each side, according to a plan that was laid down, and this being gone into, the town gradually, in the course of years, grew up into that orderliness which makes it now a pattern to the country-side—all which was mainly owing to the accident that befell the Lord Eglesham, which is a clear proof how improvements come about, as it were, by the immediate instigation of Providence, which should make the heart of man humble, and change his eyes of pride and haughtiness into a lowly demeanour.

But although this making of the trust road was surely a great thing for the parish, and of an advantage to my people, we met, in this year, with a loss not to be compensated,—that was the death of Nanse Banks, the schoolmistress. She had been long in a weak and frail state, but, being a methodical creature, still kept on the school, laying the foundation for many a worthy wife and mother. However, about the decline of the year her complaints increased, and she sent for me to consult about her giving up the school ; and I went to see her on a Saturday afternoon, when the bit lassies, her scholars, had put the house in order, and gone home till the Monday.

She was sitting in the window-nook reading THE WORD to herself, when I entered, but she closed the book, and put her spectacles in for a mark when she saw me ; and, as it was expected I would come, her easy-chair, with a clean cover, had been set out for me by the scholars, by which I discerned that there was something more than common to happen, and so it appeared when I had taken my seat.

' Sir,' said she, ' I hae sent for you on a thing troubles me sairly. I have warsled with poortith in this shed, which it has pleased the Lord to allow me to possess, but my strength is worn out, and I fear I maun yield in the strife' ; and she wiped her eye with her apron. I told her, however, to be of good cheer; and then she said, 'that she could no longer thole the din of the school, and that she was weary, and ready to lay herself down to die whenever the Lord was pleased to permit. But,' continued she, 'what can I do without the school; and alas! I can neither work nor want; and I am wae to go on the Session, for I am come of a decent family.' I comforted her, and told her that I thought she had done so much good in the parish that the Session was deep in her debt, and that what they might give her was but a just payment for her service. 'I would rather, however, sir,' said she, 'try first what some of my auld scholars will do, and it was for that I wanted to speak with you. If some of them would but just, from time to time, look in upon me, that I may not die alane; and the little pick and drap that I require would not be hard upon them—I am more sure that in this way their gratitude would be no discredit, than I am of having any claim on the Session.'

As I had always a great respect for an honest pride, I assured her that I would do what she wanted, and accordingly, the very morning after, being Sabbath, I preached a sermon on the helplessness of them that have no help of man, meaning aged single women, living in garret-rooms, whose forlorn state, in the gloaming of life, I made manifest to the hearts and understandings of the congregation, in such a manner that many shed tears, and went away sorrowful.

Having thus roused the feelings of my people, I went round the houses on the Monday morning, and mentioned what I had to say more particularly about poor old Nanse Banks the schoolmistress, and truly I was rejoiced at the condition of the hearts of my people. There was a universal sympathy among them; and it was soon ordered that, what with one and another, her decay should be provided for. But it was not ordained that she should be long heavy on their goodwill. On the Monday the school was given up, and there was nothing but wailing among the bit lassies, the scholars, for getting the vacance, as the poor things said, because the mistress was going to lie down to dee. And, indeed, so it came to pass, for she took to her bed the same afternoon, and, in the course of the week, dwindled away, and slippet out of this howling wilderness into the kingdom of heaven, on the Sabbath following, as quietly as a blessed saint could do.

And here I should mention, that the Lady Macadam, when I told her of Nanse Banks's case, inquired if she was a snuffer, and being answered by me that she was, her ladyship sent her a pretty French enamel box full of Macabaw, a fine snuff that she had in a bottle; and among the Macabaw was found a guinea, at the bottom of the box, after Nanse Banks had departed this life, which was a kind thing of Lady Macadam to do.

About the close of this year there was a great sough of old prophecies, foretelling mutations and adversities, chiefly on account of the canal that was spoken of to join the rivers of the Clyde and the Forth, it being thought an impossible thing to be done; and the Adam and Eve pear-tree in our garden budded out in an awful manner, and had divers flourishes on it at Yule, which was thought an ominous thing, especially as the second Mrs. Balwhidder was at the down-lying with my eldest son Gilbert, that is the merchant in Glasgow, but nothing came o't, and the howdie said she had an easy time when the child came into the world, which was on the very last day of the year, to the great satisfaction of me, and of my people, who were wonderful lifted up because their minister had a man-child born unto him.

CHAPTER IX

YEAR 1768

Lord Eglesham uses his interest in favour of Charles Malcolm—The finding of a new schoolmistress—Miss Sabrina Hookie gets the place— Change of fashions in the parish.

IT's a surprising thing how time flieth away, carrying off our youth and strength, and leaving us nothing but wrinkles and the ails of old age. Gilbert, my son, that is now a corpulent man, and a Glasgow merchant, when I take up my pen to record the memorables of this Ann. Dom., seems to me yet but a suckling in swaddling clothes, mewing and peevish in the arms of his mother, that has been long laid in the cold kirkyard, beside her predecessor, in Abraham's bosom. It is not, however, my design to speak much anent my own affairs, which would be a very improper and uncomely thing, but only of what happened in the parish, this book being for a witness and testimony of my ministry. Therefore, setting out of view both me and mine, I will now resuscitate the concerns of Mrs. Malcolm and her children ; for, as I think, never was there such a visible preordination seen in the lives of any persons, as was seen in that of this worthy decent woman and her well-doing offspring. Her morning was raw, and a sore blight fell upon her fortunes, but the sun looked out on her mid-day, and her evening closed loun and warm, and the stars of the firmament, that are the eyes of Heaven, beamed, as it were, with gladness when she lay down to sleep the sleep of rest.

Her son Charles was by this time grown up into a stout buirdly lad, and it was expected that before the return of the *Tobacco* trader, he would have been out of his time, and a man afore the mast, which was a great step of preferment, as I heard say by persons skilled in sea-faring concerns; But this was not ordered to happen ; for, when the *Tobacco* trader was lying in the harbour of Virginia in the North America, a pressgang, that was in need of men for a man-of-war, came on board, and pressed poor Charles, and sailed away with him on a cruise, nobody, for many a day, could tell where, till I thought of the Lord Eglesham's kindness. His lordship having something to say with the king's government, I wrote to him, telling him who I was, and how jocose he had been when buttoned in my clothes, that he might recollect me, thanking him at the same time for his condescension and patronage to Andrew Lanshaw, in his way to the East Indies. I then slipped in, at the end of the letter, a bit *nota bene* concerning the case of Charles Malcolm, begging his lordship, on account of the poor lad's widow mother, to inquire at the government if they could tell us anything about Charles. In the due course of time, I got a most civil reply from his lordship, stating all about the name of the man-of-war, and where she was ; and at the conclusion his lordship said, that I was lucky in having the brother of a Lord of the Admiralty on this occasion for my agent, as otherwise, from the vagueness of my statement, the information might not have been procured ; which remark of his lordship was long a great riddle to me, for I could not think what he meant about an agent, till, in the course of the year, we heard that his own brother was concerned in the Admiralty; so that all his lordship meant was only to crack a joke with me, and that he was ever ready and free to do, as shall be related in the sequel, for he was an excellent man.

There being a vacancy for a schoolmistress, it was proposed to Mrs. Malcolm, that, under her superintendence, her daughter Kate, that had been learning great artifices in needle-work so long with Lady Macadam, should take up the school, and the Session undertook to make good to Kate the sum of five pounds sterling per annum, over and above what the scholars were to pay. But Mrs. Malcolm said she had not strength herself to warsle with so many unruly brats, and that Kate, though a fine lassie, was a tempestuous spirit, and might lame some of the bairns in her passion; and that self-same night, Lady Macadam wrote me a very complaining letter, for trying to wile away her companion; but her ladyship was a canary-headed woman, and given to flights and tantrums, having in her youth been a great toast among the quality. It would, however, have saved her from a sore heart had she never thought of keeping Kate Malcolm. For this year her only son, who was learning the art of war at an academy in France, came to pay her, his lady mother, a visit. He was a brisk and light-hearted stripling, and Kate Malcolm was budding into a very rose of beauty; so between them a hankering began, which, for a season, was productive of great heaviness of heart to the poor old cripple lady; indeed, she assured me herself, that all her rheumatics were nothing to the heartache which she suffered in the progress of this business. But that will be more treated of hereafter; suffice it to say for the present, that we have thus recorded how the plan for making Kate Malcolm our schoolmistress came to nought. It pleased however Him, from whom cometh every good and perfect gift, to send at this time among us a Miss Sabrina Hookie, the daughter of old Mr. Hookie, who had been schoolmaster in a neighbouring parish. She had gone after his death to live with an auntie in Glasgow, that kept a shop in the Gallowgate. It was thought that the old woman would have left her heir to all her gatherings, and so she said she would, but alas! our life is but within our lip. Before her testament was made, she was carried suddenly off by an apoplectick, an awful monument of the uncertainty of time, and the nearness of eternity, in her own shop, as she was in the very act of weighing out an ounce of snuff to a Professor of the College, as Miss Sabrina herself told me. Being thus destitute, it happened that Miss Sabrina heard of the vacancy in our parish, as it were, just by the cry of a passing bird, for she could not tell how; although I judge myself that William Keckle the elder had a hand in it, as he was at the time in Glasgow; and she wrote me a wonderful well-penned letter, bespeaking the situation, which letter came to hand on the morn following Lady Macadam's stramash to me about Kate Malcolm, and I laid it before the Session the same day; so that by the time her auntie's concern was taken off her hands, she had a home and a howff among us to come to, in the which she lived upwards of thirty years in credit and respect, although some thought she had not the art of her predecessor, and was more uppish in her carriage than befitted the decorum of her vocation. Hers, however, was but a harmless vanity; and, poor woman, she needed all manner of graces to set her out, for she was made up of odds and ends, and had but one good eye, the other being blind, and just like a blue bead; at first she plainly set her cap for Mr. Lorimore, but after ogling and gogling at him every Sunday in the kirk for a whole half year and more, Miss Sabrina desisted in despair.

But the most remarkable thing about her coming into the parish was the change that took place in Christian names among us. Old Mr. Hookie, her father, had, from the time he read his Virgil, maintained a sort of intromission with the Nine Muses, by which he was led to baptize her Sabrina, after a name mentioned by John Milton in one of his works. Miss Sabrina began by calling our Jennies, Jessies, and our Nannies, Nancies; alas! I have lived to see even these likewise grow old-fashioned. She had also a taste in the mantua-making line, which she had learnt in Glasgow, and I could date from the very Sabbath of her first appearance in the kirk, a change growing in the garb of the younger lassies, who from that day began to lay aside the silken plaidie over the head, the which had been the pride and bravery of their grandmothers, and instead of the snood, that was so snod and simple, they hided their heads in round-eared bees-cap mutches, made of gauze and catgut, and other curious contrivances of French millendery; all which brought a deal of custom to Miss Sabrina, over and above the incomings and Candlemas offerings of the school; insomuch, that she saved money, and in the course of three years had ten pounds to put in the bank.

At the time, these alterations and revolutions in the parish were thought a great advantage; but now when I look back upon them, as a traveller on the hill over the road he has passed, I have my doubts. For with wealth come wants, like a troop of clamorous beggars at the heels of a generous man, and it's hard to tell wherein the benefit of improvement in a country parish consists, especially to those who live by the sweat of their brow. But it is not for me to make reflections, my task and duty is to note the changes of time and habitudes.

CHAPTER X

YEAR 1769

A toad found in the heart of a stone—Robert Malcolm, who had been at sea, returns from a northern voyage—Kate Malcolm's clandestine correspondence with Lady Macadam's son.

I HAVE my doubts whether it was in the beginning of this year, or in the end of the last, that a very extraordinary thing came to light in the parish; but howsoever that may be, there is nothing more certain than the fact, which it is my duty to record. I have mentioned already how it was that the toll, or trust road, was set agoing, on account of the Lord Eglesham's tumbling on the midden in the Vennel. Well, it happened to one of the labouring men, in breaking the stones to make metal for the new road, that he broke a stone that was both large and remarkable, and in the heart of it, which was boss, there was found a living creature, that jumped out the moment it saw the light of heaven, to the great terrification of the man, who could think it was nothing but an evil spirit that had been imprisoned therein for a time. The man came to me like a demented creature, and the whole clachan gathered out, young and old, and I went at their head, to see what the miracle could be, for the man said it was a fiery dragon, spuing smoke and flames. But when we came to the spot, it was just a yird toad, and the laddie weans nevelled it to death with stones, before I could persuade them to give over. Since then I have read of such things coming to light in the *Scots Magazine*, a very valuable book.

Soon after the affair of 'the wee deil in the stane,' as it was called, a sough reached us that the Americas were seized with the rebellious spirit of the ten tribes, and were snapping their fingers in the face of the king's government. The news came on a Saturday night, for we had no newspapers in those days, and was brought by Robin Modiwort, that fetched the letters from the Irville post. Thomas Fullarton (he has been dead many a day) kept the grocery-shop in Irville, and he had been in at Glasgow, as was his yearly custom, to settle his accounts, and to buy a hogshead of tobacco, with sugar and other spiceries; and being in Glasgow, Thomas was told by the merchant of a great rise in tobacco, that had happened by reason of the contumacity of the plantations, and it was thought that blood would be spilt before things were ended, for that the king and Parliament were in a great passion with them. But as Charles Malcolm, in the king's ship, was the only one belonging to the parish that was likely to be art and part in the business, we were in a manner little troubled at the time with this first gasp of the monster of war, who, for our sins, was ordained to swallow up and devour so many of our fellow-subjects, before he was bound again in the chains of mercy and peace.

I had, in the meantime, written a letter to the Lord Eglesham to get Charles Malcolm out of the clutches of the press-gang in the man-of-war; and about a month after, his lordship sent me an answer, wherein was inclosed a letter from the captain of the ship, saying, that Charles Malcolm was so good a man, that he was reluctant to part with him, and that Charles himself was well contented to remain aboard. Anent which, his lordship said to me, that he had written back to the captain to make a midshipman of Charles, and that he would take him under his own protection, which was great joy on two accounts to us all, especially to his mother; first, to hear that Charles was a good man, although in years still but a youth; and secondly, that my lord had of his own free will taken him under the wing of his patronage.

E   49

But the sweet of this world is never to be enjoyed without some of the sour. The coal bark between Irville and Belfast, in which Robert Malcolm, the second son of his mother, was serving his time to be a sailor, got a charter, as it was called, to go with to Norway for deals, which grieved Mrs. Malcolm to the very heart, for there was then no short cut by the canal, as now is, between the rivers of the Forth and Clyde, but every ship was obligated to go far away round by the Orkneys, which, although a voyage in the summer not overly dangerous, there being long days and short nights then, yet in the winter it was far otherwise, many vessels being frozen up in the Baltic till the spring; and there was a story told at the time, of an Irville bark coming home in the dead of the year, that lost her way altogether, and was supposed to have sailed north into utter darkness, for she was never more heard of; and many an awful thing was said of what the auld mariners about the shore thought concerning the crew of that misfortunate vessel. However, Mrs. Malcolm was a woman of great faith, and having placed her reliance on Him who is the orphant's stay and widow's trust, she resigned her bairn into his hands, with a religious submission to His pleasure, though the mother's tear of weak human nature was on her cheek and in her e'e. And her faith was well rewarded, for the vessel brought him safe home, and he had seen such a world of things, that it was just to read a story-book to hear him tell of Elsineur and Gottenburgh, and other fine and great places that we had never heard of till that time; and he brought me a bottle of Riga balsam, which for healing cuts was just miraculous, besides a clear bottle of Rososolus for his mother, a spirit which for cordiality could not be told; for though since that time we have had many a sort of Dantzick cordial, I have never tasted any to compare with Robin Malcolm's Rososolus. The Lady Macadam, who had a knowledge of such things, declared it was the best of the best sort; for Mrs. Malcolm sent her ladyship some of it in a doctor's bottle, as well as to Mrs. Balwhidder, who was then at the down-lying with our daughter Janet—a woman now in the married state, that makes a most excellent wife, having been brought up with great pains, and well educated, as I shall have to record by and by.

About the Christmas of this year, Lady Macadam's son

having been perfected in the art of war at a school in France, had, with the help of his mother's friends, and his father's fame, got a stand of colours in the Royal Scots regiment; he came to show himself in his regimentals to his lady mother, like a dutiful son, as he certainly was. It happened that he was in the kirk in his scarlets and gold, on the same Sunday that Robert Malcolm came home from the long voyage to Norway for deals; and I thought when I saw the soldier and the sailor from the pulpit, that it was an omen of war among our harmless country folks, like swords and cannon amidst ploughs and sickles, coming upon us, and I became laden in spirit, and had a most weighty prayer upon the occasion, which was long after remembered, many thinking, when the American war broke out, that I had been gifted with a glimmering of prophecy on that day.

It was during this visit to his lady mother, that young Laird Macadam settled the correspondence with Kate Malcolm, which, in the process of time, caused us all so much trouble; for it was a clandestine concern, but the time is not yet ripe for me to speak of it more at large. I should however mention, before concluding this annal, that Mrs. Malcolm herself was this winter brought to death's door by a terrible host that came on her in the kirk, by taking a kittling in her throat. It was a terrification to hear her sometimes; but she got the better of it in the spring, and was more herself thereafter than she had been for years before; and her daughter Effie, or Euphemia, as she was called by Miss Sabrina, the schoolmistress, was growing up to be a gleg and clever quean; she was, indeed, such a spirit in her way, that the folks called her Spunkie; while her son William, that was the youngest of the five, was making a wonderful proficiency with Mr. Lorimore. He was indeed a douce, well-doing laddie, of a composed nature; insomuch that the master said he was surely chosen for the ministry. In short, the more I think on what befell this family, and of the great meekness and Christian worth of the parent, I verily believe there never could have been in any parish such a manifestation of the truth, that they who put their trust in the Lord are sure of having a friend that will never forsake them.

'_He came to show himself in his regimentals to his mother._'

Copyright 1895 by Macmillan & Co.

CHAPTER XI

YEAR 1770

This year a happy and tranquil one—Lord Eglesham establishes a fair in the village—The show of Punch appears for the first time in the parish.

THIS blessed Ann. Dom. was one of the Sabbaths of my ministry; when I look back upon it, all is quiet and good order; the darkest cloud of the smuggling had passed over, at least from my people, and the rumours of rebellion in America were but like the distant sound of the bars of Ayr. We sat, as it were, in a lown and pleasant place, beholding our prosperity, like the apple-tree adorned with her garlands of flourishes, in the first fair mornings of the spring, when the birds were returning thanks to their Maker for the coming again of the seed-time, and the busy bee goeth forth from her cell, to gather honey from the flowers of the field, and the broom of the hill, and the blue-bells and gowans, which Nature, with a gracious and a gentle hand, scatters in the valley, as she walketh forth in her beauty, to testify to the goodness of the Father of all mercies.

Both at the spring and the harvest sacraments, the weather was as that which is in Paradise; there was a glad composure in all hearts, and the minds of men were softened towards each other. The number of communicants was greater than had been known for many years, and the tables were filled by the pious from many a neighbouring parish; those of my hearers who had opposed my placing declared openly for a testimony of satisfaction and holy thankfulness, that the tent, so surrounded as it was on both occasions, was a sight they never had expected to see. I was, to be sure, assisted by some of the best divines then in the land, but I had not been a sluggard myself in the vineyard.

Often, when I think on this year, so fruitful in pleasant intimacies, has the thought come into my mind, that as the Lord blesses the earth from time to time with a harvest of more than the usual increase, so, in like manner, he is some-times for a season pleased to pour into the breasts of mankind a larger portion of goodwill and charity, disposing them to love one another, to be kindly to all creatures, and filled with the delight of thankfulness to himself, which is the greatest of blessings.

It was in this year that the Earl of Eglesham ordered the fair to be established in the village; and it was a day of wonderful festivity to all the bairns, and lads and lassies, for miles round. I think, indeed, that there has never been such a fair as the first since; for although we have more mountebanks and Merry-andrews now, and richer cargoes of groceries and packman's stands, yet there has been a falling off in the light-hearted daffing, while the hobble-shows in the change-houses have been awfully augmented. It was on this occasion that Punch's opera was first seen in our country-side, and surely never was there such a funny curiosity; for although Mr. Punch himself was but a timber idol, he was as droll as a true living thing, and napped with his head so comical; but oh he was a sorrowful contumacious captain, and it was just a sport to see how he rampaged, and triumphed, and sang. For months after, the laddie weans did nothing but squeak and sing like Punch. In short, a blithe spirit was among us throughout this year, and the briefness of the chronicle bears witness to the innocency of the time.

CHAPTER XII

YEAR 1771

The nature of Lady Macadam's amusements—She intercepts letters from her son to Kate Malcolm.

IT was in this year that my troubles with Lady Macadam's affair began. She was a woman, as I have by hint here and there intimated, of a prelatic disposition, seeking all things her own way, and not overly scrupulous about the means, which I take to be the true humour of prelacy. She was come of a high episcopal race in the east country, where sound doctrine had been long but little heard, and she considered the comely humility of a presbyter as the wickedness of hypocrisy; so that, saving in the way of neighbourly visitation, there was no sincere communion between us. Nevertheless, with all her vagaries, she had the element of a kindly spirit, that would sometimes kythe in actions of charity, that showed symptoms of a true Christian grace, had it been properly cultivated; but her morals had been greatly neglected in her youth, and she would waste her precious time in the long winter nights, playing at the cards with her visitors; in the which thriftless and sinful pastime, she was at great pains to instruct Kate Malcolm, which I was grieved to understand. What, however, I most misliked in her ladyship was a lightness and juvenility of behaviour altogether unbecoming her years, for she was far past threescore, having been long married without children. Her son, the soldier officer, came so late, that it was thought she would have been taken up as an evidence in the Douglas cause. She was, to be sure, crippled with the rheumatics, and no doubt the time hung heavy on her hands; but the best friends of recreation and sport must allow, that an old woman, sitting whole hours jingling with that paralytic chattel a spinet, was not a natural object! What then could be said for her singing Italian songs, and getting all the newest from Vauxhall in London, a boxful at a time, with new novel-books, and trinkum-trankum flowers and feathers, and sweetmeats, sent to her by a lady of the blood royal of Paris? As for the music, she was at great pains to instruct Kate, which, with the other things she taught, were sufficient, as my lady said herself, to qualify poor Kate for a duchess or a governess, in either of which capacities, her ladyship assured Mrs. Malcolm, she would do honour to her instructor, meaning her own self; but I must come to the point anent the affair.

One evening, early in the month of January, as I was sitting by myself in my closet studying the *Scots Magazine*, which I well remember the new number had come but that very night, Mrs. Balwhidder being at the time busy with the lasses in the kitchen, and superintending, as her custom was, for she was a clever woman, a great wool-spinning we then had, both little wheel and meikle wheel, for stockings and blankets—sitting, as I was saying, in the study, with the fire well gathered up, for a night's reflection, a prodigious knocking came to the door, by which the book was almost startled out of my hand, and all the wheels in the house were silenced at once. This was her ladyship's flunkey, to beg me to go to her, whom he described as in a state of desperation. Christianity required that I should obey the summons; so, with what haste I could, thinking that perhaps, as she had been low-spirited for some time about the young laird's going to the Indies, she might have got a cast of grace, and been wakened in despair to the state of darkness in which she had so long lived, I made as few steps of the road between the manse and her house as it was in my ability to do.

On reaching the door, I found a great light in the house— candles burning upstairs and downstairs, and a sough of some-thing extraordinar going on. I went into the dining-room, where her ladyship was wont to sit; but she was not there— only Kate Malcolm all alone, busily picking bits of paper from the carpet. When she looked up, I saw that her eyes were red with weeping, and I was alarmed, and said, ' Katy, my dear, I hope there is no danger?' Upon which the poor lassie rose, and flinging herself in a chair, covered her face with her hands, and wept bitterly.

'What is the old fool doing with the wench?' cried a sharp angry voice from the drawing-room—'why does not he come to me?' It was the voice of Lady Macadam herself, and she meant me. So I went to her; but, oh, she was in a far different state from what I had hoped. The pride of this world had got the upper hand of her, and was playing dreadful antics with her understanding. There was she, painted like a Jezebel, with gum-flowers on her head, as was her custom every afternoon, sitting on a settee, for she was lame, and in her hand she held a letter. ' Sir,' said she, as I came into the room, ' I want you to go instantly to that young fellow, your clerk (meaning Mr. Lorimore, the schoolmaster, who was likewise session-clerk and precentor), and tell him I will give him a couple of hundred pounds to marry Miss Malcolm without delay, and undertake to procure him a living from some of my friends.'

'Softly, my lady, you must first tell me the meaning of all this haste of kindness,' said I, in my calm methodical manner. At the which she began to cry and sob like a petted bairn, and to bewail her ruin, and the dishonour of her family. I

'Covered her face with her hands, and wept bitterly.'

was surprised, and beginning to be confounded, at length out it came. The flunkie had that night brought two London letters from the Irville post, and Kate Malcolm being out of the way when he came home, he took them both in to her ladyship on the silver server, as was his custom; and her ladyship, not jealousing that Kate could have a correspondence with London, thought both the letters were for herself, for they were franked, so, as it happened, she opened the one that was for Kate, and this, too, from the young laird, her own son. She could not believe her eyes when she saw the first words in his hand of write, and she read, and she better read, till she read all the letter, by which she came to know that Kate and her darling were trysted, and that this was not the first love-letter which had passed between them. She therefore tore it in pieces, and sent for me, and screamed for Kate; in short, went, as it were, off at the head, and was neither to bind nor to hold on account of this intrigue, as she in her wrath stigmatised the innocent gallanting of poor Kate and the young laird.

I listened in patience to all she had to say anent the discovery, and offered her the very best advice; but she derided my judgment, and because I would not speak outright to Mr. Lorimore, and get him to marry Kate off-hand, she bade me good-night with an air, and sent for him herself. He, however, was on the brink of marriage with his present worthy helpmate, and declined her ladyship's proposals, which angered her still more. But although there was surely a great lack of discretion in all this, and her ladyship was entirely overcome with her passion, she would not part with Kate, nor allow her to quit the house with me, but made her sup with her as usual that night, calling her sometimes a perfidious baggage, and at other times, forgetting her delirium, speaking to her as kindly as ever. At night Kate as usual helped her ladyship into her bed (this she told me with tears in her eyes next morning), and when Lady Macadam, as was her wont, bent to kiss her for good-night, she suddenly recollected 'the intrigue,' and gave Kate such a slap on the side of the head, as quite dislocated for a time the intellects of the poor young lassie. Next morning Kate was solemnly advised never to write again to the laird, while the lady wrote him a letter, which, she said, would be as good as a birch to the breech of

58

the boy. Nothing therefore, for some time, indeed throughout the year, came of this matter, but her ladyship, when Mrs. Balwhidder soon after called on her, said that I was a nose of wax, and that she never would speak to me again, which surely was not a polite thing to say to Mrs. Balwhidder, my second wife.

This stramash was the first time that I had interposed in the family concerns of my people, for it was against my nature to make or meddle with private actions, saving only such as in course of nature came before the Session; but I was not satisfied with the principles of Lady Macadam, and I began to be weary about Kate Malcolm's situation with her ladyship, whose ways of thinking I saw were not to be depended on, especially in those things wherein her pride and vanity were concerned. But the time ran on—the butterflies and the blossoms were succeeded by the leaves and the fruit, and nothing of a particular nature further molested the general tranquillity of this year; about the end of which there came on a sudden frost after a tack of wet weather. The roads were just a sheet of ice, like a frozen river; insomuch, that the coal-carts could not work; and one of our cows (Mrs. Balwhidder said, after the accident, it was our best, but it was not so much thought of before) fell in coming from the glebe to the byre, and broke its two hinder legs, which obligated us to kill it, in order to put the beast out of pain. As this happened after we had salted our mart, it occasioned us to have a double crop of puddings, and such a show of hams in the kitchen as was a marvel to our visitors to see.

CHAPTER XIII

YEAR 1772

The detection of Mr. Heckletext's guilt—He threatens to prosecute the elders for defamation—The Muscovy duck gets an operation performed on it.

ON New Year's night, this year, a thing happened, which, in its own nature, was a trifle, but it turned out as a mustard-seed that grows into a great tree. One of the elders, who has long been dead and gone, came to the manse about a fact that was found out in the clachan, and after we had discoursed on it some time, he rose to take his departure. I went with him to the door with the candle in my hand—it was a clear frosty night, with a sharp wind, and the moment I opened the door, the blast blew out the candle, so that I heedlessly, with the candlestick in my hand, walked with him to the yett without my hat, by which I took a sore cold in my head, that brought on a dreadful toothache; insomuch, that I was obligated to go into Irville to get the tooth drawn, and this caused my face to swell to such a fright, that on the Sabbath day I could not preach to my people. There was, however, at that time, a young man, one Mr. Heckletext, tutor in Sir Hugh Montgomerie's family, and who had shortly before been licenced. Finding that I would not be able to preach myself, I sent to him, and begged he would officiate for me, which he very pleasantly consented to do, being, like all the young clergy, thirsting to show his light to the world. 'Twixt the fore and afternoon's worship, he took his check of dinner at the manse, and I could not but say that he seemed both discreet and sincere. Judge, however, what was brewing, when the same night Mr. Lorimore came and told me, that Mr. Heckletext was the suspected person anent the fact, that had been instrumental in the hand of a chastising Providence, to afflict me with the toothache, in order, as it afterwards came to pass, to bring the hidden hypocrisy of the ungodly preacher to light. It seems that the donsie lassie who was in fault had gone to the kirk in the afternoon, and seeing who was in the pulpit, where she expected to see me, was seized with the hystericks, and taken with her crying on the spot, the which being untimely, proved the death of both mother and bairn before the thing was properly laid to the father's charge.

This caused a great uproar in the parish. I was sorely blamed to let such a man as Mr. Heckletext go up into my pulpit, although I was as ignorant of his offences as the innocent child that perished; and, in an unguarded hour, to pacify some of the elders, who were just distracted about the disgrace, I consented to have him called before the Session. He obeyed the call, and in a manner that I will never forget, for he was a sorrow of sin and audacity, and demanded to

know why and for what reason he was summoned. I told him
the whole affair in my calm and moderate way, but it was oil
cast upon a burning coal. He flamed up in a terrible passion,
threepit at the elders that they had no proof whatever of his
having had any trafficking in the business, which was the case,
for it was only a notion, the poor deceased lassie never having
made a disclosure ; called them libellous conspirators against
his character, which was his only fortune, and concluded by
threatening to punish them, though he exempted me from the
injury which their slanderous insinuations had done to his
prospects in life. We were all terrified, and allowed him to
go away without uttering a word ; and sure enough he did
bring a plea in the courts of Edinburgh against Mr. Lorimore
and the elders for damages, laid at a great sum.

What might have been the consequence, no one can tell ;
but soon after he married Sir Hugh's housekeeper, and went
with her into Edinburgh, where he took up a school, and
before the trial came on—that is to say, within three months of
the day that I myself married them—Mrs. Heckletext was
delivered of a thriving lad bairn, which would have been a
witness for the elders, had the worst come to the worst. This
was, indeed, we all thought, a joyous deliverance to the parish,
and it was a lesson to me never to allow any preacher to
mount my pulpit unless I knew something of his moral
character.

In other respects, this year passed very peaceably in the
parish ; there was a visible increase of worldly circumstances,
and the hedges which had been planted along the toll-road
began to put forth their branches, and to give new notions of
orderliness and beauty to the farmers. Mrs. Malcolm heard
from time to time from her son Charles, on board the man-of-
war the *Avenger*, where he was midshipman, and he had found
a friend in the captain, that was just a father to him. Her
second son Robert, being out of his time at Irville, went to
the Clyde to look for a berth, and was hired to go to Jamaica,
in a ship called the *Trooper*. He was a lad of greater sobriety
of nature than Charles ; douce, honest, and faithful ; and when
he came home, though he brought no limes to me to make
punch, like his brother, he brought a Muscovy duck to Lady
Macadam, who had, as I have related, in a manner educated
his sister Kate. That duck was the first of the kind we had

ever seen, and many thought it was of the goose species, only with short bowly legs.   It was however, a tractable and homely beast, and after some confabulation, as my lady herself told Mrs. Balwhidder, it was received into fellowship by her other ducks and poultry.   It is not, however, so much on account of the rarity of the creature, that I have introduced it here, as for the purpose of relating a wonderful operation that was performed on it by Miss Sabrina, the schoolmistress.

There happened to be a sack of beans in our stable, and Lady Macadam's hens and fowls, which were not overly fed at home, through the inattention of her servants, being great stravaggers for their meat, in passing the door, went in to pick, and the Muscovy seeing a hole in the bean-sack, dabbled out a crap-full before she was disturbed.   The beans swelled on the poor bird's stomach, and her crap bellied out like the kyte of a Glasgow magistrate, until it was just a sight to be seen with its head back on its shoulders.   The bairns of the clachan followed it up and down, crying, the lady's muckle jock's aye growing bigger, till every heart was wae for the creature.   Some thought it was afflicted with a tympathy, and others, that it was the natural way for such like ducks to cleck their young.   In short, we were all concerned, and my lady having a great opinion of Miss Sabrina's skill, had a consultation with her on the case, at which Miss Sabrina advised, that what she called the Cæsarian operation should be tried, which she herself performed accordingly, by opening the creature's crap, and taking out as many beans as filled a mutchkin stoup, after which she sewed it up, and the Muscovy went its way to the water-side, and began to swim, and was as jocund as ever ; insomuch, that in three days after it was quite cured of all the consequences of its surfeit.

I had at one time a notion to send an account of this to the *Scots Magazine*, but something always came in the way to prevent me ; so that it has been reserved for a place in this chronicle, being, after Mr. Heckletext's affair, the most memorable thing in our history of this year.

CHAPTER XIV

YEAR 1773

The new schoolhouse—Lord Eglesham comes down to the castle—I refuse to go and dine there on Sunday, but go on Monday, and meet with an English dean.

IN this Ann. Dom. there was something like a plea getting to a head, between the Session and some of the heritors, about a new schoolhouse; the thatch having been torn from the rigging of the old one by a blast of wind, on the first Monday of February, by which a great snow-storm got admission, and the school was rendered utterly uninhabitable. The smaller sort of lairds were very willing to come into the plan with an extra contribution, because they respected the master, and their bairns were at the school; but the gentlemen who had tutors in their own houses were not so manageable, and some of them even went so far as to say, that the kirk being only wanted on Sunday, would do very well for a school all the rest of the week, which was a very profane way of speaking, and I was resolved to set myself against any such thing, and to labour according to the power and efficacy of my station to get a new school built.

Many a meeting the Session had on the subject, and the heritors debated and discussed, and revised their proceedings, and still no money for the needful work was forthcoming. Whereupon it happened one morning, as I was rummaging in my scrutoire, that I laid my hand on the Lord Eglesham's letter anent Charles Malcolm, and it was put into my head at that moment, that if I was to write his lordship, who was the greatest heritor, and owned now the major part of the parish, that by his help and influence, I might be an instrument to the building of a comfortable new school; accordingly I sat down and wrote my lord all about the accident, and the state of the schoolhouse, and the divisions and seditions among the heritors, and sent the letter to him at London by the post the same day, without saying a word to any living soul on the subject.

This in me was an advised thought, for, by the return of post, his lordship, with his own hand, in a most kind manner, authorised me to say that he would build a new school at his own cost, and bade me go over and consult about it with his steward, at the castle, to whom he had written by the same post the necessary instructions. Nothing could exceed the gladness which the news gave to the whole parish, and none said more in behalf of his lordship's bounty and liberality than the heritors; especially those gentry who grudged the undertaking, when it was thought that it would have to come out of their own pock-nook.

In the course of the summer, just as the roof was closing in of the schoolhouse, my lord came to the castle with a great company, and was not there a day till he sent for me to come over on the next Sunday to dine with him; but I sent him word that I could not do so, for it would be a transgression of the Sabbath, which made him send his own gentleman to make his apology for having taken so great a liberty with me, and to beg me to come on the Monday, which I accordingly did, and nothing could be better than the discretion with which I was used. There was a vast company of English ladies and gentlemen, and his lordship, in a most jocose manner, told them all how he had fallen on the midden, and how I had clad him in my clothes, and there was a wonder of laughing and diversion; but the most particular thing in the company was a large round-faced man, with a wig, that was a dignitary in some great Episcopalian church in London, who was extraordinary condescending towards me, drinking wine with me at the table, and saying weighty sentences in a fine style of language, about the becoming grace of simplicity and innocence of heart, in the clergy of all denominations of Christians, which I was pleased to hear; for really he had a proud red countenance, and I could not have thought he was so mortified to humility within, had I not heard with what sincerity he delivered himself, and seen how much reverence and attention was paid to him by all present, particularly by my lord's chaplain, who was a pious and pleasant young divine, though educated at Oxford for the Episcopalian persuasion.

One day soon after, as I was sitting in my closet conning a sermon for the next Sunday, I was surprised by a visit from the dean, as the dignitary was called. He had come, he said, to wait on me as rector of the parish, for so it seems they call a pastor in England, and to say, that, if it was agreeable, he

' Extraordinary condescending towards me.'

would take a family dinner with us before he left the castle. I could make no objection to this kindness, but said I hoped my lord would come with him, and that we would do our best to entertain them with all suitable hospitality. About an hour or so after he had returned to the castle, one of the flunkies brought a letter from his lordship to say, that not only he would come with the dean, but that they would bring his other guests with them, and that, as they could only drink London wine, the butler would send me a hamper in the morning, assured, as he was pleased to say, that Mrs. Balwhidder would otherwise provide good cheer.

This notification, however, was a great trouble to my wife, who was only used to manufacture the produce of our glebe and yard to a profitable purpose, and not used to the treatment of deans and lords, and other persons of quality. However, she was determined to stretch a point on this occasion, and we had, as all present declared, a charming dinner; for fortunately one of the sows had a litter of pigs a few days before, and, in addition to a goose, that is but a boss bird, we had a roasted pig, with an apple in its mouth, which was just a curiosity to see; and my lord called it a tythe pig, but I told him it was one of Mrs. Balwhidder's own clecking, which saying of mine made no little sport when expounded to the dean.

But, och how! this was the last happy summer that we had for many a year in the parish; and an omen of the dule that ensued, was in a sacrilegious theft that a daft woman, Jenny Gaffaw, and her idiot daughter, did in the kirk, by tearing off and stealing the green serge lining of my lord's pew, to make, as they said, a hap for their shoulders in the cold weather—saving, however, the sin, we paid no attention at the time to the mischief and tribulation that so unheard-of a trespass boded to us all. It took place about Yule, when the weather was cold and frosty, and poor Jenny was not very able to go about seeking her meat as usual. The deed, however, was mainly done by her daughter, who, when brought before me, said, 'her poor mother's back had mair need of claes than the kirk-boards,' which was so true a thing, that I could not punish her, but wrote anent it to my lord, who not only overlooked the offence, but sent orders to the servants at the castle to be kind to the poor woman, and the natural, her daughter.

CHAPTER XV

YEAR 1774

The murder of Jean Glaikit—The young Laird Macadam comes down and marries Kate Malcolm—The ceremony performed by me, and I am commissioned to break the matter to Lady Macadam—Her behaviour.

WHEN I look back on this year, and compare what happened therein with the things that had gone before, I am grieved to the heart, and pressed down with an afflicted spirit. We had, as may be read, trials and tribulations in the days that were past, and in the rank and boisterous times of the smuggling there was much sin and blemish among us, but nothing so dark and awful as what fell out in the course of this unhappy year. The evil omen of daft Jenny Gaffaw, and her daughter's sacrilege, had soon a bloody verification.

About the beginning of the month of March in this year, the war in America was kindling so fast that the government was obligated to sent soldiers over the sea, in the hope to quell the rebellious temper of the plantations, and a party of a regiment that was quartered at Ayr was ordered to march to Greenock, to be there shipped off. The men were wild and wicked profligates, without the fear of the Lord before their eyes, and some of them had drawn up with light women in Ayr, who followed them on their march. This the soldiers did not like, not wishing to be troubled with such gear in America; so the women, when they got the length of Kilmarnock, were ordered to retreat, and go home, which they all did, but one Jean Glaikit, who persisted in her intent to follow her jo, Patrick O'Neil, a Catholic Irish corporal. The man did, as he said, all in his capacity to persuade her to return, but she was a contumacious limmer, and would not listen to reason, so that, in passing along our toll-road, from less to more, the miserable wretches fell out, and fought, and the soldier put an end to her, with a hasty knock on the head with his firelock, and marched on after his comrades.

The body of the woman was, about half an hour after,

found by the scholars of Mr. Lorimore's school, who had got the play to see the marching, and to hear the drums of the

'*The murderer was brought back to the parish.*'
Copyright 1895 by Macmillan & Co.

soldiers. Dreadful was the shout and the cry throughout the parish at this foul work. Some of the farmer lads followed the soldiers on horseback, and others ran to Sir Hugh, who was a justice of the peace, for his advice. Such a day as that was !

However, the murderer was taken, and, with his arms tied behind him with a cord, he was brought back to the parish, where he confessed before Sir Hugh the deed, and how it happened. He was then put in a cart, and being well guarded by six of the lads, was taken to Ayr jail.

It was not long after this that the murderer was brought to trial, and, being found guilty on his own confession, he was sentenced to be executed, and his body to be hung in chains near the spot where the deed was done. I thought that all in the parish would have run to desperation with horror when the news of this came, and I wrote immediately to the Lord Eglesham to get this done away by the merciful power of the government, which he did to our great solace and relief.

In the autumn, the young Laird Macadam, being ordered with his regiment for the Americas, got leave from the king to come and see his lady-mother, before his departure. But it was not to see her only, as will presently appear.

Knowing how much her ladyship was averse to the notion he had of Kate Malcolm, he did not write of his coming, lest she would send Kate out of the way, but came in upon them at a late hour, as they were wasting their precious time, as was the nightly wont of my lady, with a pack of cards ; and so far was she from being pleased to see him, that no sooner did she behold his face, but like a tap of tow, she kindled upon both him and Kate, and ordered them out of her sight and house. The young folk had discretion : Kate went home to her mother, and the laird came to the manse, and begged us to take him in. He then told me what had happened, and that having bought a captain's commission, he was resolved to marry Kate, and hoped I would perform the ceremony, if her mother would consent. ' As for mine,' said he, ' she will never agree ; but, when the thing is done, her pardon will not be difficult to get, for, with all her whims and caprice, she is generous and affectionate.' In short, he so wiled and beguiled me, that I consented to marry them, if Mrs. Malcolm was agreeable. ' I will not disobey my mother,' said he, ' by asking her consent, which I know she will refuse ; and, therefore, the sooner it is done the better.' So we then stepped over to

Mrs. Malcolm's house, where we found that saintly woman, with Kate and Effie, and Willie, sitting peacefully at their fireside, preparing to read their Bibles for the night. When we went in and when I saw Kate, that was so ladylike there with the decent humility of her parent's dwelling, I could not but think she was destined for a better station ; and when I looked at the captain, a handsome youth, I thought surely their marriage is made in Heaven ; and so I said to Mrs. Malcolm, who after a time consented, and likewise agreed that her daughter should go with the captain to America, for her faith and trust in the goodness of Providence was great and boundless, striving, as it were, to be even with its tender mercies. Accordingly, the captain's man was sent to bid the chaise wait that had taken him to the lady's, and the marriage was sanctified by me before we left Mrs. Malcolm's. No doubt, they ought to have been proclaimed three several Sabbaths, but I satisfied the Session, at our first meeting, on account of the necessity of the case. The young couple went in the chaise travelling to Glasgow, authorising me to break the matter to Lady Macadam, which was a sore task, but I was spared from the performance. For her ladyship had come to herself, and thinking on her own rashness in sending away Kate and the captain in the way she had done, she was like one by herself; all the servants were scattered out and abroad in quest of the lovers, and some of them, seeing the chaise drive from Mrs. Malcolm's door, with them in it, and me coming out, jealoused what had been done, and told their mistress outright of the marriage, which was to her like a clap of thunder ; insomuch that she flung herself back in her settee, and was beating and drumming with her heels on the floor, like a madwoman in Bedlam, when I entered the room. For some time she took no notice of me, but continued her din ; but, by and by, she began to turn her eyes in fiery glances upon me, till I was terrified lest she would fly at me with her claws in her fury. At last she stopped all at once, and, in a calm voice, said, ' But it cannot now be helped, where are the vagabonds ? ' ' They are gone,' replied I. ' Gone ? ' cried she, ' gone where ? ' ' To America, I suppose,' was my answer ; upon which she again threw herself back in the settee, and began again to drum and beat with her feet as before. But not to dwell on small particularities, let it suffice to say, that she sent her coachman on one of her coach horses, which being old and stiff, did not overtake the fugitives till they were in their bed at Kilmarnock, where they stopped that night ; but when they came back to the lady's in the morning, she was as cagey and meikle taken up with them, as if they had gotten her full consent and privilege to marry from the first. Thus was the first of Mrs. Malcolm's children well and creditably settled. I have only now to conclude with observing that my son Gilbert was seized with the small-pox about the beginning of December, and was blinded by them for seventeen days ; for the inoculation was not in practice yet among us, saving only in the genteel families, that went into Edinburgh for the education of their children, where it was performed by the faculty there.

CHAPTER XVI

YEAR 1775

Captain Macadam provides a house and an annuity for old Mrs. Malcolm —Miss Betty Wudrife brings from Edinburgh a new-fashioned silk mantle, but refuses to give the pattern to old Lady Macadam—Her revenge.

THE regular course of nature is calm and orderly, and tempests and troubles are but lapses from the accustomed sobriety with which Providence works out the destined end of all things. From Yule till Pace-Monday there had been a gradual subsidence of our personal and parochial tribulations, and the spring, though late, set in bright and beautiful, and was accompanied with the spirit of contentment, so that, excepting the great concern that we all began to take in the American rebellion, especially on account of Charles Malcolm that was in the man-of-war, and of Captain Macadam that had married Kate, we had throughout the better half of the year but little molestation of any sort. I should, however, note the upshot of the marriage.

By some cause that I do not recollect, if I ever had it properly told, the regiment wherein the captain had bought his commission was not sent to the plantations, but only over to Ireland, by which the captain and his lady were allowed to prolong their stay in the parish with his mother, and he, coming of age, while he was among us, in making a settlement on his wife, bought the house at the braehead, which was then just built by Thomas Shivers the mason, and he gave that house, with a judicious income, to Mrs. Malcolm, telling her that it was not becoming, he having it in his power to do the contrary, that she should any longer be dependent on her own industry. For this the young man got a name like a sweet odour in all the country-side ; but that whimsical and prelatic lady his mother just went out of all bounds, and played such pranks, for an old woman, as cannot be told. To her daughter-in-law, however, she was wonderful kind ; and in fitting her out for going with the captain to Dublin, it was extraordinary to hear what a paraphernalia she provided her with. But who could have thought that in this kindness a sore trial was brewing for me !

It happened that Miss Betty Wudrife, the daughter of an heritor, had been on a visit to some of her friends in Edinburgh ; and, being in at Edinburgh, she came out with a fine mantle, decked and adorned with many a ribbon-knot, such as had never been seen in the parish. The Lady Macadam, hearing of this grand mantle, sent to beg Miss Betty to lend it to her, to make a copy for young Mrs. Macadam. But Miss Betty was so vogie with her gay mantle, that she sent back word, it would be making it o'er common ; which so nettled the old courtly lady, that she vowed revenge, and said the mantle would not be long seen on Miss Betty. Nobody knew the meaning of her words ; but she sent privately for Miss Sabrina, the schoolmistress, who was aye proud of being invited to my lady's, where she went on the Sabbath night to drink tea, and read Thomson's *Seasons* and Hervey's *Meditations* for her ladyship's recreation. Between the two, a secret plot was laid against Miss Betty and her Edinburgh mantle ; and Miss Sabrina, in a very treacherous manner, for the which I afterwards chided her severely, went to Miss Betty, and got a sight of the mantle, and how it was made, and all about it, until she was in a capacity to make another like it ; by which my lady and her, from old silk and satin *negligées* which her ladyship had worn at the French court, made up two mantles of the self-same fashion as Miss Betty's, and, if possible, more sumptuously garnished, but in a flagrant fool way. On the

72

Sunday morning after, her ladyship sent for Jenny Gaffaw, and her daft daughter Meg, and showed them the mantles, and said she would give them half-a-crown if they would go with them to the kirk, and take their place on the bench beside the elders, and after worship, walk home before Miss Betty Wudrife. The two poor natural things were just transported with the sight of such bravery, and needed no other bribe; so, over their bits of ragged duds, they put on the pageantry, and walked away to the kirk like peacocks, and took their place on the bench, to the great diversion of the whole congregation.

I had no suspicion of this, and had prepared an affecting discourse about the horrors of war, in which I touched, with a tender hand, on the troubles that threatened families and kindred in America; but all the time I was preaching, doing my best, and expatiating till the tears came into my eyes, I could not divine what was the cause of the inattention of my people. But the two vain haverels were on the bench under me, and I could not see them; where they sat, spreading their feathers and picking their wings, stroking down and setting right their finery, with such an air as no living soul could see and withstand; while every eye in the kirk was now on them, and now at Miss Betty Wudrife, who was in a worse situation than if she had been on the stool of repentance.

Greatly grieved with the little heed that was paid to my discourse, I left the pulpit with a heavy heart; but when I came out into the kirkyard, and saw the two antics linking like ladies, and aye keeping in the way before Miss Betty, and looking back and around in their pride and admiration, with high heads and a wonderful pomp, I was really overcome, and could not keep my gravity, but laughed loud out among the graves, and in the face of all my people, who, seeing how I was vanquished in that unguarded moment by my enemy, made a universal and most unreverent breach of all decorum, at which Miss Betty, who had been the cause of all, ran into the first open door, and almost fainted away with mortification.

This affair was regarded by the elders as a sinful trespass on the orderliness that was needful in the Lord's house, and they called on me at the manse that night, and said it would be a guilty connivance, if I did not rebuke and admonish Lady Macadam of the evil of her way ; for they had questioned daft Jenny, and had got at the bottom of the whole plot and mischief. But I, who knew her ladyship's light way, would fain have had the elders to overlook it, rather than expose myself to her tantrums ; but they considered the thing as a great scandal, so I was obligated to conform to their wishes. I might, however, have as well stayed at home, for her ladyship was in one of her jocose humours when I went to speak to her on the subject ; and it was so far from my power to make a proper impression on her of the enormity that had been committed, that she made me laugh, in spite of my reason, at the fantastical drollery of her malicious prank on Miss Betty Wudrife.

It, however, did not end here ; for the Session knowing that it was profitless to speak to the daft mother and daughter, who had been the instruments, gave orders to Willy Howking, the betheral, not to let them again so far into the kirk, and Willy, having scarcely more sense than them both, thought proper to keep them out next Sunday altogether. They twa said nothing at the time, but the adversary was busy with them ; for, on the Wednesday following, there being a meeting of the Synod at Ayr, to my utter amazement, the mother and daughter made their appearance there in all their finery, and raised a complaint against me and the Session, for debarring them from church privileges. No stage play could have produced such an effect ; I was perfectly dumbfoundered, and every member of the Synod might have been tied with a straw, they were so overcome with this new device of that endless woman, when bent on provocation—the Lady Macadam ; in whom the saying was verified, that old folk are twice bairns, for in such plays, pranks, and projects, she was as play-rife as a very lassie at her sampler, and this is but a swatch to what lengths she would go. The complaint was dismissed, by which the Session and me were assoilzied ; but I'll never forget till the day of my death what I suffered on that occasion, to be so put to the wall by two born idiots.

CHAPTER XVII

YEAR 1776

A recruiting party comes to Irville—Thomas Wilson and some others
enlist—Charles Malcolm's return.

IT belongs to the chroniclers of the realm, to describe the
damage and detriment which fell on the power and prosperity
of the kingdom, by reason of the rebellion that was fired into
open war against the name and authority of the king in the
plantations of America; for my task is to describe what
happened within the narrow bound of the pasturage of the
Lord's flock, of which, in His bounty and mercy, He made
me the humble, willing, but alas! the weak and ineffectual
shepherd.

About the month of February, a recruiting party came to
our neighbour town of Irville, to beat up for men to be soldiers
against the rebels; and thus the battle was brought, as it were,
to our gates, for the very first man that took on with them was
one Thomas Wilson, a cotter in our clachan, who, up to that
time, had been a decent and creditable character. He was at
first a farmer lad, but had forgathered with a doited tawpy,
whom he married, and had offspring three or four. For some
time it was noticed that he had a down and thoughtful look,
that his cleeding was growing bare, and that his wife kept an
untrig house, which, it was feared by many, was the cause of
Thomas going o'er often to the change-house; he was, in
short, during the greater part of the winter, evidently a man
foregone in the pleasures of this world, which made all that
knew him compassionate his situation.

No doubt, it was his household ills that burdened him past
bearing, and made him go into Irville, when he heard of the
recruiting, and take on to be a soldier. Such a wally-wallying
as the news of this caused at every door; for the redcoats,—
from the persecuting days, when the black-cuffs rampaged
through the country,—soldiers that fought for hire, were held
in dread and as a horror among us, and terrible were the
stories that were told of their cruelty and sinfulness; indeed,

there had not been wanting in our own time a sample of what they were, as witness the murder of Jean Glaikit by Patrick O'Neil, the Irish corporal, anent which I have treated at large in the memorables of the year 1774.

A meeting of the Session was forthwith held; for here was Thomas Wilson's wife and all his weans, an awful cess, thrown upon the parish; and it was settled outright among us that Mr. Docken, who was then an elder, but is since dead, a worthy man, with a soft tongue and a pleasing manner, should go to Irville, and get Thomas, if possible, released from the recruiters. But it was all in vain, the serjeant would not listen to him, for Thomas was a strapping lad; nor would the poor infatuated man himself agree to go back, but cursed like a cadger, and swore that if he staid any longer among his plagues, he would commit some rash act; so we were saddled with his family, which was the first taste and preeing of what war is when it comes into our hearths, and among the breadwinners.

The evil, however, did not stop here. Thomas, when he was dressed out in the king's clothes, came over to see his bairns, and take a farewell of his friends, and he looked so gallant, that the very next market-day another lad of the parish listed with him; but he was a ramplor, roving sort of a creature, and, upon the whole, it was thought he did well for the parish when he went to serve the king.

The listing was a catching distemper. Before the summer was over, other three of the farming lads went off with the drum, and there was a wailing in the parish, which made me preach a touching discourse. I likened the parish to a widow woman with a small family, sitting in their cottage by the fireside, herself spinning with an eydent wheel, ettling her best to get them a bit and a brat, and the poor weans all canty about the hearthstane — the little ones at their playocks, and the elder at their tasks—the callans working with hooks and lines to catch them a meal of fish in the morning—and the lassies working stockings to sell at the next Marymas fair. And then I likened war to a calamity coming among them—the callans drowned at their fishing— the lassies led to a misdoing—and the feckless wee bairns laid on the bed of sickness, and their poor forlorn mother sitting by herself at the embers of a cauldrife fire; her tow

76

done, and no a bodle to buy more; dropping a silent and salt tear for her babies, and thinking of days that war gone, and, like Rachel weeping for her children, she would not be comforted. With this I concluded, for my own heart filled full with the thought, and there was a deep sob in the church, verily, it was Rachel weeping for her children.

In the latter end of the year, the man-of-war, with Charles Malcolm in her, came to the Tail of the Bank at Greenock, to press men as it was thought, and Charles got leave from his captain to come and see his mother; and he brought with him Mr. Howard, another midshipman, the son of a great Parliament man in London, which, as we had tasted the sorrow, gave us some insight into the pomp of war. Charles was now grown up into a fine young man, rattling, light-hearted, and just a cordial of gladness, and his companion was every bit like him. They were dressed in their fine gold-laced garbs, and nobody knew Charles when he came to the clachan, but all wondered, for they were on horseback, and rode to the house where his mother lived when he went away, but which was then occupied by Miss Sabrina and her school. Miss Sabrina had never seen Charles, but she had heard of him, and when he inquired for his mother, she guessed who he was, and showed him the way to the new house that the captain had bought for her.

Miss Sabrina, who was a little overly perjink at times, behaved herself on this occasion with a true spirit, and gave her lassies the play immediately, so that the news of Charles's return was spread by them like wild-fire, and there was a wonderful joy in the whole town. When Charles had seen his mother, and his sister Effie, with that douce and well-mannered lad William, his brother, for of their meeting I cannot speak, not being present, he then came with his friend to see me at the manse, and was most jocose with me, and in a way of great pleasance, got Mrs. Balwhidder to ask his friend to sleep at the manse. In short, we had just a ploy the whole two days they staid with us, and I got leave from Lord Eglesham's steward to let them shoot on my lord's land, and I believe every laddie wean in the parish attended them to the field. As for old Lady Macadam, Charles being, as she said, a near relation, and she having likewise some knowledge of his comrade's family, she was

'Miss Sabrina showed him the way.'

Copyright 1895 by Macmillan & Co.

just in her element with them, though they were but youths, for she was a woman naturally of a fantastical, and, as I have narrated, given to comical devices and pranks to a degree. She made for them a ball, to which she invited all the bonniest lassies, far and near, in the parish, and was out of the body with mirth, and had a fiddler from Irville ; and it was thought by those that were there, that had she not been crippled with the rheumatics, she would have danced herself. But I was concerned to hear both Charles and his friend, like hungry hawks, rejoicing at the prospect of the war, hoping thereby, as soon as their midship term was out, to be made lieutenants ; saving this, there was no allay in the happiness they brought with them to the parish, and it was a delight to see how auld and young of all degrees made of Charles, for we were proud of him, and none more than myself, though he began to take liberties with me, calling me old governor ; it was, however, in a warm-hearted manner, only I did not like it when any of the elders heard. As for his mother, she deported herself like a saint on the occasion. There was a temperance in the pleasure of her heart, and in her thankfulness, that is past the compass of words to describe. Even Lady Macadam, who never could think a serious thought all her days, said, in her wild way, that the gods had bestowed more care in the making of Mrs. Malcolm's temper, than on the bodies and souls of all the saints in the calendar. On the Sunday the strangers attended divine worship, and I preached a sermon purposely for them, and enlarged at great length and fulness on how David overcame Goliah ; and they both told me that they had never heard such a good discourse, but I do not think they were great judges of preachings. How, indeed, could Mr. Howard know anything of sound doctrine, being educated, as he told me, at Eton school, a prelatic establishment. Nevertheless, he was a fine lad, and though a little given to frolic and diversion, he had a principle of integrity, that afterwards kithed into much virtue ; for, during this visit, he took a notion of Effie Malcolm, and the lassie of him, then a sprightly and blooming creature, fair to look upon, and blithe to see ; and he kept up a correspondence with her till the war was over, when, being a captain of a frigate, he came down among us, and they were married by me, as shall be related in its proper place.

CHAPTER XVIII

YEAR 1777

Old Widow Mirkland—Bloody accounts of the war—He gets
a newspaper—Great flood.

THIS may well be called the year of the heavy heart, for we
had sad tidings of the lads that went away as soldiers to
America. First, there was a boding in the minds of all their
friends that they were never to see them more, and their
sadness, like a mist spreading from the waters and covering
the fields, darkened the spirit of the neighbours. Secondly, a
sound was bruited about, that the king's forces would have a
hot and a sore struggle before the rebels were put down, if
they were ever put down. Then came the cruel truth of all
that the poor lads' friends had feared; but it is fit and proper
that I should relate at length, under their several heads, the
sorrows and afflictions as they came to pass.

One evening, as I was taking my walk alone, meditating
my discourse for the next Sabbath—it was shortly after
Candlemas—it was a fine clear frosty evening, just as the sun
was setting. Taking my walk alone, and thinking of the
dreadfulness of Almighty Power, and how that if it was not
tempered and restrained by infinite goodness, and wisdom,
and mercy, the miserable sinner man, and all things that live,
would be in a woeful state, I drew near the beild where old
Widow Mirkland lived by herself, who was grandmother to
Jock Hempy, the ramplor lad that was the second who took
on for a soldier. I did not mind of this at the time, but
passing the house, I heard the croon, as it were, of a laden
soul, busy with the Lord, and, not to disturb the holy workings
of grace, I paused, and listened. It was old Mizy Mirkland
herself, sitting at the gable of the house, looking at the sun
setting in all his glory behind the Arran hills; but she was
not praying—only moaning to herself,—an oozing out, as it
might be called, of the spirit from her heart, then grievously
oppressed with sorrow, and heavy bodements of grey hairs
and poverty. 'Yonder it slips awa',' she was saying, 'and my

poor bairn, that's o'er the seas in America, is maybe looking on its bright face, thinking of his hame, and aiblins of me, that did my best to breed him up in the fear of the Lord ; but I couldna warsle wi' what was ordained. Ay, Jock ! as ye look at the sun gaun down, as many a time, when ye were a wee innocent laddie at my knee here, I hae bade ye look at him as a type of your Maker, you will hae a sore heart ; for ye hae left me in my need, when ye should hae been near at hand to help me, for the hard labour and industry with which I brought you up. But it's the Lord's will,—blessed be the name of the Lord, that makes us to thole the tribulations of this world, and will reward us, through the mediation of Jesus, hereafter.' She wept bitterly as she said this, for her heart was tried, but the blessing of a religious contentment was shed upon her ; and I stepped up to her, and asked about her concerns, for, saving as a parishioner, and a decent old woman, I knew little of her. Brief was her story, but it was one of misfortune. ' But I will not complain,' she said, ' of the measure that has been meted unto me. I was left myself an orphan ; when I grew up, and was married to my gudeman, I had known but scant and want. Our days of felicity were few, and he was ta'en awa' from me shortly after my Mary was born—a wailing baby, and a widow's heart, was a' he left me. I nursed her with my salt tears, and bred her in straits, but the favour of God was with us, and she grew up to womanhood, as lovely as the rose, and as blameless as the lily. In her time she was married to a farming lad ; there never was a brawer pair in the kirk, than on that day when they gaed there first as man and wife. My heart was proud, and it pleased the Lord to chastise my pride—to nip my happiness even in the bud. The very next day he got his arm crushed. It never got well again, and he fell into a decay, and died in the winter, leaving my Mary far on in the road to be a mother.

'When her time drew near, we both happened to be working in the yard. She was delving to plant potatoes, and I told her it would do her hurt, but she was eager to provide something, as she said, for what might happen. Oh, it was an ill-omened word. The same night her trouble came on, and before the morning she was a cauld corpse, and another wee wee fatherless baby was greeting at my bosom. It was him that's noo awa' in America. He grew up to be a fine bairn, with a warm heart, but a light head, and, wanting the rein of a father's power upon him, was no sae douce as I could have wished; but he was no man's foe save his own. I thought, and hoped, as he grew to years of discretion, he would have sobered, and been a consolation to my old age; but he's gone, and he'll never come back—disappointment is my portion in this world, and I have no hope; while I can do, I will seek no help, but threescore and fifteen can do little, and a small ail is a great evil to an aged woman who has but the distaff for her breadwinner.'

I did all that I could to bid her be of good cheer, but the comfort of a hopeful spirit was dead within her; and she told me, that by many tokens she was assured her bairn was already slain. 'Thrice,' said she, 'I have seen his wraith. The first time he was in the pride of his young manhood, the next he was pale and wan, with a bloody and a gashy wound in his side, and the third time there was a smoke, and when it cleared away, I saw him in a grave, with neither winding-sheet nor coffin.'

The tale of this pious and resigned spirit dwelt in mine ear, and when I went home, Mrs. Balwhidder thought that I had met with an o'ercome, and was very uneasy; so she got the tea soon ready to make me better, but scarcely had we tasted the first cup when a loud lamentation was heard in the kitchen. This was from that tawpy the wife of Thomas Wilson, with her three weans. They had been seeking their meat among the farmer houses, and, in coming home, forgathered on the road with the Glasgow carrier, who told them that news had come in the *London Gazette*, of a battle, in which the regiment that Thomas had listed in was engaged, and had suffered loss both in rank and file; none doubting that their head was in the number of the slain, the whole family grat aloud, and came to the manse, bewailing him as no more; and it afterwards turned out to be the case, making it plain to me that there is a far-seeing discernment in the spirit, that reaches beyond the scope of our incarnate senses.

But the weight of the war did not end with these afflictions; for, instead of the sorrow that the listing caused, and the anxiety after, and the grief of the bloody tidings, operating as wholesome admonition to our young men, the natural perversity of the human heart was more and more manifested. A wonderful interest was raised among us all to hear of what was going on in the world, insomuch, that I myself was no longer contented with the relation of the news of the month in the *Scots Magazine*, but joined with my father-in-law, Mr. Kibbock, to get a newspaper twice a week from Edinburgh. As for Lady Macadam, who being naturally an impatient woman, she had one sent to her three times a week from London, so that we had something fresh five times every week ; and the old papers were lent out to the families who had friends in the wars. This was done on my suggestion, hoping it would make all content with their peaceable lot, but dominion for a time had been given to the power of contrariness, and it had quite an opposite effect. It begot a curiosity, egging on to enterprise, and, greatly to my sorrow, three of the brawest lads in the parish, or in any parish, all in one day took on with a party of the Scots Greys that were then lying in Ayr ; and nothing would satisfy the callans at Mr. Lorimore's school, but, instead of their innocent plays with girs and shintys, and sicklike, they must go ranking like soldiers, and fight sham-fights in bodies. In short, things grew to a perfect hostility, for a swarm of weans came out from the schools of Irville on a Saturday afternoon, and, forgathering with ours, they had a battle with stones on the toll-road, such as was dreadful to hear of, for many a one got a mark that day he will take to the grave with him.

It was not, however, by accidents of the field only, that we were afflicted ; those of the flood, too, were sent likewise against us. In the month of October, when the corn was yet in the holms, and on the cold land by the river-side, the water of Irville swelled to a great speat, from bank to brae, sweeping all before it, and roaring, in its might, like an agent of divine displeasure sent forth to punish the inhabitants of the earth. The loss of the victual was a thing reparable, and those that suffered did not greatly complain ; for, in other respects, their harvest had been plenteous ; but the river, in its fury, not content with overflowing the lands, burst through the sandy hills with a raging force, and a riving asunder of the solid ground, as when the fountains of the great deep were broken up. All in the parish was afoot, and on the hills, some weeping and wringing their hands not knowing what would happen, when they beheld the landmarks of the waters deserted, and the river breaking away through the country, like the war-horse set loose in his pasture, and glorying in his might. By this change in the way and channel of the river, all the mills in our parish were left more than half a mile from dam or lade ; and the farmers through the whole winter, till the new mills were built, had to travel through a heavy road with their victual, which was a great grievance, and added not a little to the afflictions of this unhappy year, which to me were not without a particularity, by the death of a full cousin of Mrs. Balwhidder, my first wife ; she was grievously burnt by looting over a candle. Her mutch, which was of the high structure then in vogue, took fire, and being fastened with corking pins to a great toupee, it could not be got off until she had sustained a deadly injury, of which, after lingering long, she was kindly eased by her removal from trouble. This sore accident was to me a matter of deep concern and cogitation ; but as it happened in Tarbolton, and no in our parish, I have only alluded to it to show, that when my people were chastised by the hand of Providence, their pastor was not spared, but had a drop from the same vial.

CHAPTER XIX

Year 1778

Revival of the smuggling trade — Betty and Janet Pawkie, and Robin Bicker, an exciseman, come to the parish — Their doings — Robin is succeeded by Mungo Argyle — Lord Eglesham assists William Malcolm.

THIS year was as the shadow of the bygane ; there was less actual suffering, but what we came through cast a gloom among us, and we did not get up our spirits till the spring was far advanced ; the corn was in the ear, and the sun far towards midsummer height, before there was any regular show of gladness in the parish.

It was clear to me that the wars were not to be soon over, for I noticed, in the course of this year, that there was a greater christening of lad bairns than had ever been in any year during my incumbency; and grave and wise persons, observant of the signs of the times, said, that it had been long held as a sure prognostication of war, when the births of male children outnumbered that of females.

Our chief misfortune in this year was a revival of that wicked mother of many mischiefs, the smuggling trade, which concerned me greatly; but it was not allowed to it to make anything like a permanent stay among us, though in some of the neighbouring parishes its ravages, both in morals and property, were very distressing, and many a mailing was sold to pay for the triumphs of the cutters and gaugers; for the Government was by this time grown more eager, and the war caused the king's ships to be out and about, which increased the trouble of the smugglers, whose wits in their turn were thereby much sharpened.

After Mrs. Malcolm, by the settlement of Captain Macadam, had given up her dealing, two maiden-women, that were sisters, Betty and Janet Pawkie, came in among us from Ayr, where they had friends in league with some of the laigh land folk, that carried on the contraband with the Isle of Man, which was the very eye of the smuggling. They took up the tea-selling, which Mrs. Malcolm had dropped, and did business on a larger scale, having a general huxtry, with parliament-cakes, and candles, and pin-cushions, as well as other groceries, in their window. Whether they had any contraband dealings, or were only back-bitten, I cannot take it upon me to say, but it was jealoused in the parish, that the meal in the sacks, that came to their door at night, and was sent to the Glasgow market in the morning, was not made of corn. They were, however, decent women, both sedate and orderly; the eldest, Betty Pawkie, was of a manly stature, and had a long beard, which made her have a coarse look, but she was, nevertheless, a worthy, well-doing creature, and at her death she left ten pounds to the poor of the parish, as may be seen in the morti-fication board that the Session put up in the kirk as a testifica-tion and an example.

Shortly after the revival of the smuggling, an exciseman was put among us, and the first was Robin Bicker, a very civil lad, that had been a flunkie with Sir Hugh Montgomerie, when he was a residenter in Edinburgh, before the old Sir

Hugh's death. He was a queer fellow, and had a coothy way of getting in about folk, the which was very serviceable to him in his vocation; nor was he overly gleg, but when a job was ill done, and he was obliged to notice it, he would often break out on the smugglers for being so stupid, so that for an exciseman he was wonderful well liked, and did not object to a waught of brandy at a time, when the auld wives ca'd it well-water. It happened, however, that some unneighbourly person sent him notice of a clecking of tea chests, or brandy kegs, at which both Jenny and Betty Pawkie were the howdies. Robin could not but therefore enter their house; however, before going in, he just cried at the door to somebody on the road, so as to let the twa industrious lassies hear he was at hand. They were not slack in closing the trance-door, and putting stoups and stools behind it, so as to cause trouble, and give time before anybody could get in. They then emptied their chaff-bed, and filled the tikeing with tea, and Betty went in on the top, covering herself with the blanket, and graining like a woman in labour. It was thought that Robin Bicker himself would not have been overly particular in searching the house, considering there was a woman seemingly in the dead thraws; but a sorner, an incomer from the east country, and that hung about the change-house as a divor hostler, that would rather gang a day's journey in the dark than turn a spade in daylight, came to him as he stood at the door, and went in with him to see the sport. Robin, for some reason, could not bid him go away, and both Betty and Janet were sure he was in the plot against them; indeed, it was always thought he was an informer, and no doubt he was something not canny, for he had a down look.

It was some time before the doorway was cleared of the stoups and stools, and Jenny was in great concern, and flustered, as she said, for her poor sister, who was taken with a heart-cholic. 'I'm sorry for her,' said Robin, 'but I'll be as quiet as possible'; and so he searched all the house, but found nothing, at the which his companion, the divor east-country hostler, swore an oath that could not be misunderstood, so, without more ado, but as all thought against the grain, Robin went up to sympathise with Betty in the bed, whose groans were loud and vehement. 'Let me feel your pulse,' said Robin, and he looted down as she put forth her

86

arm from aneath the clothes, and laying his hand on the bed, cried, 'Hey! what's this? this is a costly filling.' Upon which Betty jumpet up quite recovered, and Jenny fell to the wailing and railing, while the hostler from the east country took the bed of tea on his back, to carry it to the change-house, till a cart was gotten to take it into the custom-house at Irville.

Betty Pawkie being thus suddenly cured, and grudging the lose of property, took a knife in her hand, and as the divor was crossing the burn at the stepping-stones that lead to the back of the change-house, she ran after him, and ripped up the tikeing, and sent all the tea floating away on the burn, which was thought a brave action of Betty, and the story not a little helped to lighten our melancholy meditations.

Robin Bicker was soon after this affair removed to another district, and we got in his place one Mungo Argyle, who was as proud as a provost, being come of Highland parentage. Black was the hour he came among my people, for he was needy and greedy, and rode on the top of his commission. Of all the manifold ills in the train of smuggling, surely the excisemen are the worst, and the setting of this rabiator over us was a severe judgment for our sins. But he suffered for't, and peace be with him in the grave, where the wicked cease from troubling.

Willie Malcolm, the youngest son of his mother, had by this time learnt all that Mr. Lorimore, the schoolmaster, could teach, and as it was evidenced to everybody, by his mild manners and saintliness of demeanour, that he was a chosen vessel, his mother longed to fulfil his own wish, which was doubtless the natural working of the act of grace that had been shed upon him; but she had not the wherewithal to send him to the College of Glasgow, where he was desirous to study, and her just pride would not allow her to cess his brother-in-law, the Captain Macadam, whom, I should now mention, was raised, in the end of this year, as we read in the newspapers, to be a major. I thought her in this some-what unreasonable, for she would not be persuaded to let me write to the captain; but when I reflected on the good that Willie Malcolm might in time do as a preacher, I said nothing more to her, but indited a letter to the Lord Eglesham, setting forth the lad's parts, telling who he was and all about

'She ripped up the tikeing, and sent all the tea floating away.'

Copyright 1895 by Macmillan & Co.

his mother's scruples; and, by the retour of the post from London, his lordship sent me an order on his steward, to pay me twenty pounds towards equipping my *protégé*, as he called Willie, with a promise to pay for his education, which was such a great thing for his lordship to do off-hand on my recommendation, that it won him much affection throughout the country-side; and folk began to wonder, rehearsing the great things, as was said, that I had gotten my lord at different times, and on divers occasions, to do, which had a vast of influence among my brethren of the presbytery, and they grew into a state of greater cordiality with me, looking on me as a man having authority; but I was none thereat lifted up, for not being gifted with the power of a kirk-filling eloquence, I was but little sought for at sacraments and fasts, and solemn days, which was doubtless well ordained, for I had no motive to seek fame in foreign pulpits, but was left to walk in the paths of simplicity within my own parish. To eschew evil myself, and to teach others to do the same, I thought the main duties of the pastoral office, and with a sincere heart endeavoured what in me lay to perform them with meekness, sobriety, and a spirit wakeful to the inroads of sin and Satan. But oh the sordidness of human nature!— The kindness of the Lord Eglesham's own disposition was ascribed to my influence, and many a dry answer I was obliged to give to applicants that would have me trouble his lordship, as if I had a claim upon him. In the ensuing year, the notion of my cordiality with him came to a great head, and brought about an event that could not have been forethought by me as a thing within the compass of possibility to bring to pass.

CHAPTER XX

YEAR 1779

He goes to Edinburgh to attend the General Assembly—Preaches before the Commissioner.

I WAS named in this year for the General Assembly, and Mrs. Balwhidder, by her continual thrift, having made our purse able to stand a shake against the wind, we resolved to go into Edinburgh in a creditable manner. Accordingly, in conjunct with Mrs. Dalrymple, the lady of a major of that name, we hired the Irville chaise, and we put up in Glasgow at the Black Boy, where we staid all night. Next morning by seven o'clock we got into the fly coach for the capital of Scotland, which we reached after a heavy journey, about the same hour in the evening, and put up at the public where it stopped, till the next day; for really both me and Mrs. Balwhidder were worn out with the undertaking, and found a cup of tea a vast refreshment.

Betimes, in the morning, having taken our breakfast, we got a caddy to guide us and our wallise to Widow M'Vicar's, at the head of the Covenanters' Close. She was a relation to my first wife, Betty Lanshaw, my own full cousin that was, and we had advised her, by course of post, of our coming, and intendment to lodge with her, as uncos and strangers. But Mrs. M'Vicar kept a cloth shop, and sold plaidings and flannels, besides Yorkshire superfines, and was used to the sudden incoming of strangers, especially visitants, both from the West and the North Highlands, and was withal a gawsy furthy woman, taking great pleasure in hospitality and every sort of kindliness and discretion. She would not allow of such a thing as our being lodgers in her house, but was so cagey to see us, and to have it in her power to be civil to a minister, as she was pleased to say, of such repute, that nothing less would content her, but that we must live upon her, and partake of all the best that could be gotten for us within the walls of 'the gude town.'

When we found ourselves so comfortable, Mrs. Balwhidder and me waited on my patron's family, that was, the young ladies, and the laird, who had been my pupil, but was now an advocate high in the law. They likewise were kind also. In short, everybody in Edinburgh were in a manner wearisome kind, and we could scarcely find time to see the Castle and the palace of Holyrood House, and that more sanctified place, where the Maccabeus of the Kirk of Scotland, John Knox, was wont to live.

Upon my introduction to his Grace the Commissioner, I was delighted and surprised to find the Lord Eglesham at the levee, and his lordship was so glad on seeing me, that he made me more kenspeckle than I could have wished to have been in his Grace's presence; for, owing to the same, I was required to preach before his Grace, upon a jocose recommendation of his lordship; the which gave me great concern, and daunted me, so that in the interim I was almost bereft of all peace and studious composure of mind. Fain would I have eschewed the honour that was thus thrust upon me, but both my wife and Mrs. M'Vicar were just lifted out of themselves with the thought.

When the day came, I thought all things in this world were loosened from their hold, and that the sure and steadfast earth itself was grown coggly beneath my feet, as I mounted the pulpit. With what sincerity I prayed for help that day, and never stood man more in need of it, for through all my prayer the congregation was so watchful and still, doubtless to note if my doctrine was orthodox, that the beating of my heart might have been heard to the uttermost corners of the kirk.

I had chosen as my text, from Second Samuel, xixth chapter, and 35th verse, these words—'Can I hear any more the voice of singing men and singing women? wherefore then should thy servant be yet a burden to the king?' And hardly had I with a trembling voice read the words, when I perceived an awful stir in the congregation, for all applied the words to the state of the Church, and the appointment of his Grace the Commissioner. Having paused after giving out the text, the same fearful and critical silence again ensued, and every eye was so fixed upon me, that I was for a time deprived of courage to look about; but Heaven was pleased to compassionate my infirmity, and as I proceeded, I began to warm as in my own pulpit. I described the gorgeous Babylonian harlot riding forth in her chariots of gold and silver, with trampling steeds, and a hurricane of followers, drunk with the cup of abominations, all shouting with revelry, and glorying in her triumph, treading down in their career those precious pearls, the saints and martyrs, into the mire beneath their swinish feet. 'Before her you may behold Wantonness playing the tinkling cymbal, Insolence beating the drum, and Pride blowing the trumpet. Every vice is there with his emblems, and the seller of pardons, with his crucifix and triple crown, is distributing his largess of perdition. The voices of men shout to set wide the gates, to give entrance to the Queen of nations, and the gates are set wide, and they all enter. The avenging gates close on them—they are all shut up in hell.'

There was a sough in the kirk as I said these words, for the vision I described seemed to be passing before me as I spoke, and I felt as if I had witnessed the everlasting destruction of Antichrist, and the worshippers of the beast. But soon recovering myself, I said, in a soft and gentle manner, 'Look at yon lovely creature in virgin-raiment, with the Bible in her hand. See how mildly she walks along, giving alms to the poor as she passes on towards the door of that lowly dwelling. Let us follow her in. She takes her seat in the chair at the bedside of the poor old dying sinner, and as he tosses in the height of penitence and despair, she reads to him the promise of the Saviour, "This night thou shalt be with me in Paradise"; and he embraces her with transports, and falling back on his pillow, calmly closes his eyes in peace. She is the true religion; and when I see what she can do even in the last moments of the guilty, well may we exclaim, when we think of the symbols and pageantry of the departed superstition, Can I hear any more the voice of singing men and singing women? No; let us cling to the simplicity of the Truth that is now established in our native land.'

At the conclusion of this clause of my discourse, the congregation, which had been all so still and so solemn, never coughing, as was often the case among my people, gave a great rustle, changing their positions, by which I was almost overcome; however, I took heart, and ventured on, and pointed out, that with our Bible and an orthodox priesthood, we stood in no need of the king's authority, however bound we were in temporal things to respect it, and I showed this at some length, crying out, in the words of my text, 'Wherefore then should thy servant be yet a burden to the king?' in the saying of which I happened to turn my eyes towards his Grace the Commissioner, as he sat on the throne, and I thought his countenance was troubled, which made me add, that he might not think I meant him any offence, That the King of the Church was one before whom the great, and the wise, and the good,—all doomed and sentenced convicts—implore his mercy. 'It is true,' said I, 'that in the days of his tribulation he was wounded for our iniquities, and died to save us; but, at his death, his greatness was proclaimed by the quick and

ANNALS OF THE PARISH

the dead. There was sorrow, and there was wonder, and there was rage, and there was remorse ; but there was no shame there—none blushed on that day at that sight but yon glorious luminary.' The congregation rose and looked round, as the sun that I pointed at shone in at the window. I was disconcerted by their movement, and my spirit was spent, so that I could say no more.

When I came down from the pulpit, there was a great pressing in of acquaintance and ministers, who lauded me exceedingly ; but I thought it could be only in derision, therefore I slipped home to Mrs. M'Vicar's as fast as I could.

Mrs. M'Vicar, who was a clever, hearing-all sort of a neighbour, said my sermon was greatly thought of, and that I had surprised everybody ; but I was fearful there was something of jocularity at the bottom of this, for she was a flaunty woman, and liked well to give a good-humoured jibe or jeer. However, his Grace the Commissioner was very thankful for the discourse, and complimented me on what he called my apostolical earnestness ; but he was a courteous man, and I could not trust to him, especially as my Lord Eglesham had told me in secrecy before—it's true, it was in his gallanting way,—that, in speaking of the king's servant as I had done, I had rather gone beyond the bounds of modern moderation. Altogether, I found neither pleasure nor profit in what was thought so great an honour, but longed for the privacy of my own narrow pasture and little flock.

It was in this visit to Edinburgh that Mrs. Balwhidder bought her silver teapot, and other ornamental articles ; but this was not done, as she assured me, in a vain spirit of bravery, which I could not have abided, but because it was well known, that tea draws better in a silver pot, and drinks pleasanter in a china cup, than out of any other kind of cup or teapot.

By the time I got home to the manse, I had been three whole weeks and five days absent, which was more than all my absences together, from the time of my placing, and my people were glowing with satisfaction when they saw us driving in a Glasgow chaise through the clachan to the manse.

The rest of the year was merely a quiet succession of small incidents, none of which are worthy of notation, though they were all severally, no doubt, of aught somewhere, as they took up both time and place in the coming to pass, and nothing comes to pass without helping onwards to some great end; each particular little thing that happens in the world, being a seed sown by the hand of Providence to yield an increase, which increase is destined, in its turn, to minister to some higher purpose, until at last the issue affects the whole earth. There is nothing in all the world that doth not advance the cause of goodness; no, not even the sins of the wicked, though, through the dim casement of her mortal tabernacle, the soul of man cannot discern the method thereof.

CHAPTER XXI

YEAR 1780

Lord George Gordon—Report of an illumination.

THIS was, among ourselves, another year of few events. A sound, it is true, came among us of a design on the part of the government in London to bring back the old harlotry of papistry; but we spent our time in the lea of the hedge, and the lown of the hill. Some there were that a panic seized upon, when they heard of Lord George Gordon, that zealous Protestant, being committed to the Tower; but for my part, I had no terror upon me, for I saw all things around me going forward improving, and I said to myself, it is not so when Providence permits scathe and sorrow to fall upon a nation. Civil troubles, and the casting down of thrones, is always fore-warned by want and poverty striking the people. What I have, therefore, chiefly to record as the memorables of this year are things of small import,—the main of which are, that some of the neighbouring lairds, taking example by Mr. Kibbock, my father-in-law that was, began in this fall to plant the tops of their hills with mounts of fir-trees; and Mungo Argyle, the exciseman, just herried the poor smugglers to death, and made a power of prize-money, which, however, had not the wonted effect of riches; for it brought him no honour, and he lived in the parish like a leper, or any other kind of excommunicated person.

But I should not forget a most droll thing that took place with Jenny Gaffaw and her daughter. They had been missed from the parish for some days, and folk began to be uneasy about what could have become of the two silly creatures; till one night, at the dead hour, a strange light was seen beaming and burning at the window of the bit hole where they lived. It was first observed by Lady Macadam, who never went to bed at any Christian hour, but sat up reading her new French novels and play-books with Miss Sabrina, the schoolmistress. She gave the alarm, thinking that such a great and continuous light from a lone house, where never candle had been seen before, could be nothing less than the flame of a burning. And sending Miss Sabrina and the servants to see what was the matter, they beheld daft Jenny, and her as daft daughter, with a score of candle doups (Heaven only knows where they got them!) placed in the window, and the twa fools dancing, and linking, and admiring before the door. 'What's all this about, Jenny?' said Miss Sabrina. 'Awa' wi' you, awa' wi' you —ye wicked pope, ye whore of Babylon. Isna it for the glory of God and the Protestant religion? d'ye think I will be a pope as long as light can put out darkness?' And with that the mother and daughter began again to leap and dance as madly as before.

It seems that poor Jenny having heard of the luminations that were lighted up through the country, on the ending of the Popish Bill, had, with Meg, travelled by themselves into Glasgow, where they had gathered or begged a stock of candles, and coming back under the cloud of night, had surprised and alarmed the whole clachan by lighting up their window in the manner that I have described. Poor Miss Sabrina, at Jenny's uncivil salutation, went back to my lady with her heart full, and would fain have had the idiots brought to task before the Session for what they had said to her. But I would not hear tell of such a thing, for which Miss Sabrina owed me a grudge, that was not soon given up. At the same time, I was grieved to see the testimonies of joyfulness for a holy victory brought into such disrepute by the ill-timed demonstrations of the two irreclaimable naturals, that had not a true conception of the cause for which they were triumphing.

CHAPTER XXII

YEAR 1781

Argyle, the exciseman, grows a gentleman—Lord Eglesham's concubine—
His death—The parish children afflicted with the measles.

IF the two last years passed o'er the heads of me and my people
without any manifest dolour, which is a great thing to say
for so long a period in this world, we had our own trials and
tribulations, in the one of which I have now to make mention.
Mungo Argyle, the exciseman, waxing rich, grew proud and
petulant, and would have ruled the country-side with a rod of iron.
Nothing less would serve him than a fine horse to ride on, and
a world of other conveniences and luxuries, as if he had been
on an equality with gentlemen. And he bought a grand gun,
which was called a fowling-piece ; and he had two pointer
dogs, the like of which had not been seen in the parish since
the planting of the Eglesham Wood on the moorland, which
was four years before I got the call. Everybody said the man
was fey, and truly, when I remarked him so gallant and gay
on the Sabbath at the kirk, and noted his glowing face and
gleg e'en, I thought at times there was something no canny
about him. It was indeed clear to be seen, that the man was
hurried out of himself, but nobody could have thought that the
death he was to dree would have been what it was.

About the end of summer my Lord Eglesham came to the
castle, bringing with him an English madam, that was his
Miss. Some days after he came down from London, as he
was riding past the manse, his lordship stopped to inquire for
my health, and I went to the door to speak to him. I thought
that he did not meet me with that blithe countenance he was
wont, and in going away, he said with a blush, ' I fear I dare
not ask you to come to the castle.' I had heard of his concubine, and I said, ' In saying so, my lord, you show a spark
of grace, for it would not become me to see what I have
heard ; and I am surprised, my lord, you will not rather take
a lady of your own.' He looked kindly, but confused, saying,
he did not know where to get one ; so seeing his shame, and
not wishing to put him out of conceit entirely with himself, I

96

replied, 'Na, na, my lord, there's nobody will believe that, for there never was a silly Jock, but there was as silly a Jenny,' at which he laughed heartily, and rode away. But I know not what was in't, I was troubled in mind about him, and thought, as he was riding away, that I would never see him again ; and sure enough it so happened, for the next day, being airing in his coach with Miss Spangle, the lady he had brought, he happened to see Mungo Argyle with his dogs and his gun, and my lord being as particular about his game as the other was about boxes of tea and kegs of brandy, he jumped out of the carriage, and ran to take the gun. Words passed, and the exciseman shot my lord. Never shall I forget that day ; such riding, such running, the whole country-side afoot ; but the same night my lord breathed his last, and the mad and wild reprobate that did the deed was taken up and sent off to Edinburgh. This was a woeful riddance of that oppressor, for my lord was a good landlord and a kind-hearted man ; and albeit, though a little thoughtless, was aye ready to make his power, when the way was pointed out, minister to good works. The whole parish mourned for him, and there was not a sorer heart in all its bounds than my own. Never was such a sight seen as his burial : The whole country-side was there, and all as solemn as if they had been assembled in the valley of Jehoshaphat in the latter day. The hedges where the funeral was to pass were clad with weans, like bunches of hips and haws, and the kirkyard was as if all its own dead were risen. Never, do I think, was such a multitude gathered together. Some thought there could not be less than three thousand grown men, besides women and children.

Scarcely was this great public calamity past, for it could be reckoned no less, when one Saturday afternoon, as Miss Sabrina, the schoolmistress, was dining with Lady Macadam, her ladyship was stricken with the paralytics, and her face so thrown in the course of a few minutes, that Miss Sabrina came flying to the manse for the help and advice of Mrs. Balwhidder. A doctor was gotten with all speed by express, but her lady-ship was smitten beyond the reach of medicine. She lived, however, some time after ; but oh, she was such an object, that it was a grief to see her. She could only mutter when she tried to speak, and was as helpless as a baby. Though she never liked me, nor could I say there was many things in her

'Words passed, and the exciseman shot my lord.'

Copyright 1895 by Macmillan & Co.

demeanour that pleased me, yet she was a free-handed woman to the needful, and when she died she was more missed than it was thought she could have been.

Shortly after her funeral, which was managed by a gentleman sent from her friends in Edinburgh, that I wrote to about her condition, the major, her son, with his lady, Kate Malcolm, and two pretty bairns, came and stayed in her house for a time, and they were a great happiness to us all, both in the way of drinking tea, and sometimes taking a bit dinner, their only mother now, the worthy and pious Mrs. Malcolm, being regularly of the company.

Before the end of the year, I should mention that the fortune of Mrs. Malcolm's family got another shove upwards, by the promotion of her second son, Robert Malcolm, who, being grown an expert and careful mariner, was made captain of a grand ship, whereof Provost Maitland of Glasgow, that was kind to his mother in her distresses, was the owner. But that douce lad Willie, her youngest son, who was at the University of Glasgow, under the Lord Eglesham's patronage, was like to have suffered a blight ; however, Major Macadam, when I spoke to him anent the young man's loss of his patron, said, with a pleasant generosity, he should not be stickit ; and, accordingly, he made up, as far as money could, for the loss of his lordship, but there was none that made up for the great power and influence, which, I have no doubt, the earl would have exerted in his behalf, when he was ripened for the church. So that, although in time William came out a sound and heart-searching preacher, he was long obliged, like many another unfriended saint, to cultivate sand, and wash Ethiopians in the shape of an east-country gentleman's camstrairy weans ; than which, as he wrote me himself, there cannot be on earth a greater trial of temper. However, in the end he was rewarded, and is not only now a placed minister, but a doctor of divinity.

The death of Lady Macadam was followed by another parochial misfortune, for, considering the time when it happened, we could count it as nothing less : Auld Thomas Howkings, the betherel, fell sick, and died in the course of a week's illness, about the end of November, and the measles coming at that time upon the parish, there was such a smashery of the poor weans, as had not been known for an age ; insomuch, that James Banes, the lad who was Thomas Howkings's helper, rose in open rebellion against the Session, during his superior's illness, and we were constrained to augment his pay, and to promise him the place, if Thomas did not recover, which it was then thought he could not do. On the day this happened, there were three dead children in the clachan, and a panic and consternation spread about the burial of them, when James Banes's insurrection was known, which made both me and the Session glad to hush up the affair, that the heart of the public might have no more than the sufferings of individuals to hurt it. Thus ended a year, on many accounts, heavy to be remembered.

CHAPTER XXIII

YEAR 1782

News of the victory over the French fleet—He has to inform Mrs. Malcolm of the death of her son Charles in the engagement.

ALTHOUGH I have not been particular in noticing it, from time to time there had been an occasional going off, at fairs and on market-days, of the lads of the parish as soldiers, and when Captain Malcolm got the command of his ship, no less than four young men sailed with him from the clachan ; so that we were deeper and deeper interested in the proceedings of the doleful war that was raging in the plantations. By one post we heard of no less than three brave fellows belonging to us being slain in one battle, for which there was a loud and general lamentation.

Shortly after this, I got a letter from Charles Malcolm, a very pretty letter it indeed was ; he had heard of my Lord Eglesham's murder, and grieved for the loss, both because his lordship was a good man, and because he had been such a friend to him and his family. ' But,' said Charles, ' the best way that I can show my gratitude for his patronage is to prove myself a good officer to my king and country.' Which I thought a brave sentiment, and was pleased thereat ; for somehow Charles, from the time he brought me the limes to make a bowl of punch, in his pocket from Jamaica, had built a nest of affection in my heart. But, oh! the wicked wastry of life in war. In less than a month after, the news came of a victory over the French fleet, and by the same post I got a letter from Mr. Howard, that was the midshipman who came to see us with Charles, telling me that poor Charles had been mortally wounded in the action, and had afterwards died of his wounds. ' He was a hero in the engagement, said Mr. Howard, ' and he died as a good and a brave man should.' These tidings gave me one of the sorest hearts I ever suffered, and it was long before I could gather fortitude to disclose the tidings to poor Charles's mother. But the callants of the school had heard of the victory, and were going shouting about, and had set the steeple bell a-ringing, by which Mrs. Malcolm heard the news; and knowing that Charles's ship was with the fleet, she came over to the manse in great anxiety, to hear the particulars, somebody telling her that there had been a foreign letter to me by the postman.

When I saw her I could not speak, but looked at her in pity, and the tear fleeing up into my eyes, she guessed what had happened. After giving a deep and sore sigh, she inquired, ' How did he behave? I hope well, for he was aye a gallant laddie!'—and then she wept very bitterly. However, growing calmer, I read to her the letter, and when I had done, she begged me to give it to her to keep, saying, ' It's all that I have now left of my pretty boy; but it's mair precious to me than the wealth of the Indies'; and she begged me to return thanks to the Lord, for all the comforts and manifold mercies with which her lot had been blessed, since the hour she put her trust in Him alone, and that was when she was left a penniless widow, with her five fatherless bairns.

It was just an edification of the spirit, to see the Christian resignation of this worthy woman. Mrs. Balwhidder was confounded, and said, there was more sorrow in seeing the deep grief of her fortitude than tongue could tell.

Having taken a glass of wine with her, I walked out to conduct her to her own house, but in the way we met with a severe trial. All the weans were out parading with napkins and kail-blades on sticks, rejoicing and triumphing in the glad tidings of victory. But when they saw me and Mrs. Malcolm coming slowly along, they guessed what had happened, and threw away their banners of joy; and, standing all up in a row, with silence and sadness, along the kirkyard wall as we passed, showed an instinct of compassion that penetrated to my very soul. The poor mother burst into fresh affliction, and some of the bairns into an audible weeping; and, taking one another by the hand, they followed us to her door, like mourners at a funeral. Never was such a sight seen in any town before. The neighbours came to look at it, as we walked along, and the men turned aside to hide their faces, while the mothers pressed their babies fondlier to their bosoms, and watered their innocent faces with their tears.

I prepared a suitable sermon, taking as the words of my text, 'Howl, ye ships of Tarshish, for your strength is laid waste.' But when I saw around me so many of my people, clad in complimentary mourning for the gallant Charles Malcolm, and that even poor daft Jenny Gaffaw, and her daughter, had on an old black ribbon; and when I thought of him, the spirited laddie, coming home from Jamaica, with his parrot on his shoulder, and his limes for me, my heart filled full, and I was obliged to sit down in the pulpit, and drop a tear.

After a pause, and the Lord having vouchsafed to compose me, I rose up, and gave out that anthem of triumph, the 124th Psalm; the singing of which brought the congregation round to themselves; but still I felt that I could not preach as I had meant to do, therefore I only said a few words of prayer, and singing another psalm, dismissed the congregation.

CHAPTER XXIV

YEAR 1783

Janet Gaffaw's death and burial.

THIS was another Sabbath year of my ministry. It has left me nothing to record, but a silent increase of prosperity in the parish. I myself had now in the bank more than a thousand pounds, and everything was thriving around. My two bairns, Gilbert, that is now the merchant in Glasgow, was grown into a sturdy ramplor laddie, and Janet, that is married upon Dr.

Kittleword, the minister of Swappington, was as fine a lassie for her years as the eye of a parent could desire to see.

Shortly after the news of the peace, an event at which all gave themselves up to joy, a thing happened among us that at the time caused much talk; but although very dreadful, was yet not so serious, somehow or other, as such an awsome doing should have been. Poor Jenny Gaffaw happened to take a heavy cold, and soon thereafter died. Meg went about from house to house, begging dead-clothes, and got the body straighted in a wonderful decent manner, with a plate of earth and salt placed upon it—an admonitory type of mortality and eternal life that has ill-advisedly gone out of fashion. When I heard of this, I could not but go to see how a creature that was not thought possessed of a grain of understanding could have done so much herself. On entering the door, I beheld Meg sitting with two or three of the neighbouring kimmers, and the corpse laid out on a bed. 'Come awa', sir,' said Meg, 'this is an altered house; they're gane that keepit it bein; but, sir, we maun a' come to this—we maun pay the debt o' nature—death is a grim creditor, and a doctor but brittle bail when the hour of reckoning's at han'! What a pity it is, mother, that you're now dead, for here's the minister come to see you. Oh, sir, but she would have had a proud heart to see you in her dwelling, for she had a genteel turn, and would not let me, her only daughter, mess or mell wi' the lathron lasses of the clachan. Ay, ay, she brought me up with care, and edicated me for a lady; nae coarse wark darkened my lily-white hands. But I maun work now, I maun dree the penalty of man.'

Having stopped some time, listening to the curious maunnering of Meg, I rose to come away, but she laid her hand on my arm, saying, ' No, sir, ye maun taste before ye gang! My mother had aye plenty in her life, nor shall her latter day be needy.'

Accordingly, Meg, with all the due formality common on such occasions, produced a bottle of water, and a dram glass, which she filled and tasted, then presented to me, at the same time offering me a bit of bread on a slate. It was a consternation to everybody how the daft creature had learnt all the ceremonies, which she performed in a manner past the power of pen to describe, making the solemnity of death, by her

'*With all the due formality common on such occasions.*'

strange mockery, a kind of merriment, that was more painful than sorrow; but some spirits are gifted with a faculty of observation, that, by the strength of a little fancy, enables them to make a wonderful and truth-like semblance of things and events which they never saw, and poor Meg seemed to have this gift.

The same night the Session having provided a coffin, the body was put in, and removed to Mr. Mutchkin's brew-house, where the lads and lassies kept the late-wake.

Saving this, the year flowed in a calm, and we floated on in the stream of time towards the great ocean of eternity, like ducks and geese in the river's tide, that are carried down without being sensible of the speed of the current. Alas! we have not wings like them, to fly back to the place we set out from.

CHAPTER XXV

YEAR 1784

A year of sunshine and pleasantness.

I HAVE ever thought that this was a bright year, truly an Ann. Dom., for in it many of the lads came home that had listed to be soldiers; and Mr. Howard, that was the midshipman, being now a captain of a man-of-war, came down from England and married Effie Malcolm, and took her up with him to London, where she wrote to her mother, that she found his family people of great note, and more kind to her than she could write. By this time, also, Major Macadam was made a colonel, and lived with his lady in Edinburgh, where they were much respected by the genteeler classes, Mrs. Macadam being considered a great unco among them for all manner of ladylike ornaments, she having been taught every sort of perfection in that way by the old lady, who was educated at the court of France, and was, from her birth, a person of quality. In this year, also, Captain Malcolm, her brother, married a daughter of a Glasgow merchant, so that Mrs. Malcolm, in her declining years, had the prospect of a bright setting; but nothing could change the

sober Christianity of her settled mind; and although she was
strongly invited, both by the Macadams and the Howards, to
see their felicity, she ever declined the same, saying—'No! I
have been long out of the world, or rather, I have never been
in it; my ways are not as theirs; and although I ken their
hearts would be glad to be kind to me, I might fash their
servants, or their friends might think me unlike other folk, by
which, instead of causing pleasure, mortification might ensue;
so I will remain in my own house, trusting that when they can
spare the time, they will come and see me.'

There was a spirit of true wisdom in this resolution, for it
required a forbearance that in weaker minds would have
relaxed; but though a person of a most slender and delicate
frame of body, she was a Judith in fortitude, and in all the
fortune that seemed now smiling upon her, she never was
lifted up, but bore always that pale and meek look, which
gave a saintliness to her endeavours in the days of her suffering
and poverty.

But when we enjoy most, we have least to tell. I look
back on this year as on a sunny spot in the valley, amidst the
shadows of the clouds of time; and I have nothing to record,
save the remembrance of welcomings and weddings, and a
meeting of bairns and parents, that the wars and the waters
had long raged between. Contentment within the bosom lent
a livelier grace to the countenance of Nature, and everybody
said, that in this year the hedges were greener than common,
the gowans brighter on the brae, and the heads of the statelier
trees adorned with a richer coronal of leaves and blossoms.
All things were animated with the gladness of thankfulness,
and testified to the goodness of their Maker.

CHAPTER XXVI

YEAR 1785

Mr. Cayenne comes to the parish—A passionate character—His outrageous
behaviour at the Session-house.

WELL may we say, in the pious words of my old friend and
neighbour, the Reverend Mr. Keekie of Loupinton, that the
world is such a wheel-carriage, that it might very properly be
called the WHIRL'D. This reflection was brought home to me
in a very striking manner, while I was preparing a discourse
for my people, to be preached on the anniversary day of my
placing, in which I took a view of what had passed in the
parish during the five-and-twenty years that I had been, by
the grace of God, the pastor thereof. The bairns, that were
bairns when I came among my people, were ripened unto
parents, and a new generation was swelling in the bud around
me. But it is what happened that I have to give an account of.

This year the Lady Macadam's jointure-house that was,
having been long without a tenant, a Mr. Cayenne and his
family, American loyalists, came and took it, and settled
among us for a time. His wife was a clever woman, and they
had two daughters, Miss Virginia and Miss Carolina; but he
was himself an etter-cap, a perfect spunkie of passion, as ever
was known in town or country. His wife had a terrible time
o't with him, and yet the unhappy man had a great share of
common sense, and, saving the exploits of his unmanageable
temper, was an honest and creditable gentleman. Of his
humour we soon had a sample, as I shall relate at length all
about it.

Shortly after he came to the parish, Mrs. Balwhidder and
me waited upon the family, to pay our respects, and Mr.
Cayenne, in a free and hearty manner, insisted on us staying
to dinner. His wife, I could see, was not satisfied with this,
not being, as I discerned afterwards, prepared to give an
entertainment to strangers; however, we fell into the misfortune of staying, and nothing could exceed the happiness of

Mr. Cayenne. I thought him one of the blithest bodies I had ever seen, and had no notion that he was such a tap of tow as in the sequel he proved himself.

As there was something extra to prepare, the dinner was a little longer of being on the table than usual, at which, he began to fash, and every now and then took a turn up and down the room, with his hands behind his back, giving a short melancholious whistle. At length the dinner was served, but it was more scanty than he had expected, and this upset his good-humour altogether. Scarcely had I asked the blessing when he began to storm at his blackamoor servant, who was, however, used to his way, and did his work without minding him; but by some neglect there was no mustard down, which Mr. Cayenne called for in the voice of a tempest, and one of the servant lassies came in with the pot, trembling. It happened that, as it had not been used for a day or two before, the lid was clagged, and, as it were, glewed in, so that Mr. Cayenne could not get it out, which put him quite wud, and he attempted to fling it at Sambo, the black lad's head, but it stottit against the wall, and the lid flying open, the whole mustard flew in his own face, which made him a sight not to be spoken of. However it calmed him; but really, as I had never seen such a man before, I could not but consider the accident as a providential reproof, and trembled to think what greater evil might fall out in the hands of a man so left to himself in the intemperance of passion.

But the worst thing about Mr. Cayenne was his meddling with matters in which he had no concern, for he had a most irksome nature, and could not be at rest, so that he was truly a thorn in our side. Among other of his strange doings, was the part he took in the proceedings of the Session, with which he had as little to do, in a manner, as the man in the moon; but having no business on his hands, he attended every sederunt, and from less to more, having no self-government, he began to give his opinion in our deliberations; and often bred us trouble, by causing strife to arise.

It happened, as the time of the summer occasion was drawing near, that it behoved us to make arrangements about the assistance; and upon the suggestion of the elders, to which I paid always the greatest deference, I invited Mr. Keekie of Loupinton, who was a sound preacher, and a great expounder of the kittle parts of the Old Testament, being a man well versed in the Hebrew and etymologies, for which he

' He attempted to fling it at Sambo.'

was much reverenced by the old people that delighted to search the Scriptures. I had also written to Mr. Sprose of Annock, a preacher of another sort, being a vehement and powerful thresher of the word, making the chaff and vain babbling of corrupt commentators to fly from his hand. He was not, however, so well liked, as he wanted that connect method which is needful to the enforcing of doctrine. But he had never been among us, and it was thought it would be a godly treat to the parish to let the people hear him. Besides Mr. Sprose, Mr. Waikle of Gowanry, a quiet hewer-out ot the image of holiness in the heart, was likewise invited, all in addition to our old stoops from the adjacent parishes.

None of these three preachers were in any estimation with Mr. Cayenne, who had only heard each of them once ; and he happening to be present in the Session-house at the time, inquired how we had settled. I thought this not a very orderly question, but I gave him a civil answer, saying, that Mr. Keekie of Loupinton would preach on the morning of the fast-day, Mr. Sprose of Annock in the afternoon, and Mr. Waikle of Gowanry on the Saturday. Never shall I or the elders, while the breath of life is in our bodies, forget the reply. Mr. Cayenne struck the table like a clap of thunder, and cried, ' Mr. Keekie ˙ of Loupinton, and Mr. Sprose of Annock, and Mr. Waikle of Gowanry, and all such trash, may go to — and be —— ! ' and out of the house he bounced, like a hand-ball stotting on a stone.

The elders and me were confounded, and for some time we could not speak, but looked at each other, doubtful if our ears heard aright. At long and length I came to myself, and, in the strength of God, took my place at the table, and said, this was an outrageous impiety not to be borne, which all the elders agreed to ; and we thereupon came to a resolve, which I dictated myself, wherein we debarred Mr. Cayenne from ever after entering, unless summoned, the Session-house, the which resolve we directed the Session-clerk to send to him direct, and thus we vindicated the insulted privileges of the church.

Mr. Cayenne had cooled before he got home, and our paper coming to him in his appeased blood, he immediately came to the manse, and made a contrite apology for his hasty temper, which I reported, in due time and form, to the Session, and there the matter ended. But here was an example plain to be seen of the truth of the old proverb, that as one door shuts another opens; for scarcely were we in quietness by the decease of that old light-headed woman, the Lady Macadam, till a full equivalent for her was given in this hot and fiery Mr. Cayenne.

CHAPTER XXVII

YEAR 1786

Repairs required for the manse—By the sagacious management of Mr. Kibbock, the heritors are made to give a new manse altogether—They begin, however, to look upon me with a grudge, which provokes me to claim an augmentation, which I obtain.

FROM the day of my settlement, I had resolved, in order to win the affections of my people, and to promote unison among the heritors, to be of as little expense to the parish as possible; but by this time the manse had fallen into a sore state of decay—the doors were wormed on the hinges—the casements of the windows chattered all the winter, like the teeth of a person perishing with cold, so that we had no comfort in the house; by which, at the urgent instigations of Mrs. Balwhidder, I was obligated to represent our situation to the Session. I would rather, having so much saved money in the bank, paid the needful repairs myself than have done this, but she said it would be a rank injustice to our own family; and her father, Mr. Kibbock, who was very long-headed, with more than a common man's portion of understanding, pointed out to me, that as my life was but in my lip, it would be a wrong thing towards whomsoever was ordained to be my successor, to use the heritors to the custom of the minister paying for the reparations of the manse, as it might happen he might not be so well able to afford it as me. So in a manner, by their persuasion, and the constraint of the justice of the case, I made a report of the infirmities both of doors and windows, as well as of the rotten state of the floors, which were constantly in want of cobbling. Over and above all, I told them of the sarking of the roof, which was as frush as a puddock stool; insomuch, that in every blast, some of the pins lost their grip, and the slates came hurling off.

The heritors were accordingly convened, and, after some deliberation, they proposed that the house should be seen to, and white-washed and painted; and I thought this might do, for I saw they were terrified at the expense of a thorough repair; but when I went home and repeated to Mrs. Balwhidder what had been said at the meeting, and my thankfulness at getting the heritors' consent to do so much, she was excessively angry, and told me that all the painting and white-washing in the world would avail nothing, for that the house was as a sepulchre full of rottenness; and she sent for Mr. Kibbock, her father, to confer with him on the way of getting the matter put to rights.

Mr. Kibbock came, and hearing of what had passed, pondered for some time, and then said, 'All was very right! The minister (meaning me) has just to get tradesmen to look at the house, and write out their opinion of what it needs. There will be plaster to mend; so, before painting, he will get a plasterer. There will be a slater wanted; he has just to get a slater's estimate, and a wright's, and so forth, and when all is done, he will lay them before the Session and the heritors, who, no doubt, will direct the reparations to go forward.'

This was very pawkie counselling of Mr. Kibbock, and I did not see through it at the time, but did as he recommended, and took all the different estimates, when they came in, to the Session. The elders commended my prudence exceedingly for so doing, before going to work; and one of them asked me what the amount of the whole would be, but I had not cast it up. Some of the heritors thought that a hundred pounds would be sufficient for the outlay, but judge of our consternation, when, in counting up all the sums of the different estimates together, we found them well on towards a thousand pounds. 'Better big a new house at once than do this!' cried all the elders, by which I then perceived the draughtiness of Mr. Kibbock's advice. Accordingly, another meeting of the heritors was summoned, and after a great deal of controversy, it was agreed that a new manse should be erected; and, shortly after, we contracted with Thomas Trowel, the mason, to build one for six hundred pounds, with all the requisite appurtenances, by which a clear gain was saved to the parish, by the foresight of Mr. Kibbock, to the amount of nearly four hundred pounds. But the heritors did not mean to have allowed the sort of repair that his plan comprehended. He was, however, a far forecasting man, the like of him for natural parts not being in our country-side, and nobody could get the whip-hand of him, either in a bargain or an improvement, when he once was sensible of the advantage. He was, indeed, a blessing to the shire, both by his example as a farmer, and by his sound and discreet advice in the contentions of his neighbours, being a man, as was a saying among the commonality, 'wiser than the law and the fifteen lords of Edinburgh.'

The building of the new manse occasioned a heavy cess on the heritors, which made them overly ready to pick holes in the coats of me and the elders; so that, out of my forbearance and delicacy in time past, grew a lordliness on their part, that was an ill return for the years that I had endured no little inconveniency for their sake. It was not in my heart or principles to harm the hair of a dog; but when I discerned the austerity with which they were disposed to treat their minister, I bethought me, that, for the preservation of what was due to the establishment and the upholding of the decent administration of religion, I ought to set my face against the sordid intolerance by which they were actuated. This notion I weighed well before divulging it to any person, but when I had assured myself as to the rectitude thereof, I rode over one day to Mr. Kibbock's, and broke my mind to him about claiming out of the teinds an augmentation of my stipend, not because I needed it, but in case, after me, some bare and hungry gorbie of the Lord should be sent upon the parish, in no such condition to plea with the heritors as I was. Mr. Kibbock highly approved of my intent, and by his help, after much tribulation, I got an augmentation, both in glebe and income; and to mark my reason for what I did, I took upon me to keep and clothe the wives and orphans of the parish who lost their breadwinners in the American war. But for all that, the heritors spoke of me as an avaricious Jew, and made the hard-won fruits of Mrs. Balwhidder's great thrift and good management a matter of reproach against me. Few of them would come to the church, but stayed away, to the detriment of their own souls hereafter, in order, as they thought, to punish me; so that, in the course of this year there was a visible decay of the sense of religion among the better orders of the parish, and, as will be seen in the sequel, their evil example infected the minds of many of the rising generation.

It was in this year that Mr. Cayenne bought the mailing of the Wheatrigs, but did not begin to build his house till the following spring ; for being ill to please with a plan, he fell out with the builders, and on one occasion got into such a passion with Mr. Trowel, the mason, that he struck him a blow in the face, for which he was obligated to make atonement. It was thought the matter would have been carried before the Lords ; but, by the mediation of Mr. Kibbock, with my helping hand, a reconciliation was brought about, Mr. Cayenne indemnifying the mason with a sum of money to say no more anent it ; after which, he employed him to build his house, a thing that no man could have thought possible, who reflected on the enmity between them.

CHAPTER XXVIII

YEAR 1787

Lady Macadam's house is changed into an inn—The making of jelly becomes common in the parish—Meg Gaffaw is present at a payment of victual—Her behaviour.

THERE had been, as I have frequently observed, a visible improvement going on in the parish. From the time of the making of the toll-road, every new house that was built in the clachan was built along that road. Among other changes thereby caused, the Lady Macadam's jointure-house that was, which stood in a pleasant parterre, inclosed within a stone wall and an iron gate, having a pillar with a pine-apple head on each side, came to be in the middle of the town. While Mr. Cayenne inhabited the same, it was maintained in good order, but on his flitting to his own new house on the Wheatrigs, the parterre was soon overrun with weeds, and it began to wear the look of a waste place. Robert Toddy, who then kept the change-house, and who had from the lady's death rented the coach-house for stabling, in this juncture thought of it for an inn; so he set his own house to Thomas Treddles, the weaver, whose son, William, is now the great Glasgow manufacturer, that has cotton mills and steam-engines; and took 'the Place,' as it was called, and had a fine sign, THE CROSS KEYS, painted and put up in golden characters, by which it became one of the most noted inns anywhere to be seen; and the civility of Mrs. Toddy was commended by all strangers. But although this transmutation from a change-house to an inn was a vast amendment, in a manner, to the parish, there was little amendment of manners thereby, for the farmer lads began to hold dancings and other riotous proceedings there, and to bring, as it were, the evil practices of towns into the heart of the country. All sort of licence was allowed as to drink and hours, and the edifying example of Mr. Mutchkins, and his pious family, was no longer held up to the imitation of the wayfaring man.

Saving the mutation of 'the Place' into an inn, nothing very remarkable happened in this year. We got into our new manse about the middle of March, but it was rather damp, being new plastered, and it caused me to have a severe attack of the rheumatics in the fall of the year.

I should not, in my notations, forget to mark a new luxury that got in among the commonality at this time. By the opening of new roads, and the traffic thereon with carts and carriers, and by our young men that were sailors going to the Clyde, and sailing to Jamaica and the West Indies, heaps of sugar and coffee-beans were brought home, while many, among the kail-stocks and cabbages in their yards, had planted grozet and berry bushes; which two things happening together, the fashion to make jam and jelly, which hitherto had been only known in the kitchens and confectionaries of the gentry, came to be introduced into the clachan. All this, however, was not without a plausible pretext, for it was found that jelly was an excellent medicine for a sore throat, and jam a remedy as good as London candy for a cough, or a cold, or a shortness of breath. I could not, however, say, that this gave me so much concern as the smuggling trade, only it occasioned a great fasherie to Mrs. Balwhidder; for, in the berry time, there was no end to the borrowing of her brass pan, to make jelly and jam, till Mrs. Toddy, of the Cross Keys, bought one, which, in its turn, came into request, and saved ours.

It was in the Martinmas quarter of this year that I got the first payment of my augmentation. Having no desire to rip up old sores, I shall say no more anent it, the worst being anticipated in my chronicle of the last year; but there was a thing happened in the payment that occasioned a vexation at the time of a very disagreeable nature. Daft Meg Gaffaw, who, from the tragical death of her mother, was a privileged subject, used to come to the manse on the Saturdays for a meal of meat; and it so fell out, that as, by some neglect of mine, no steps had been taken to regulate the disposal of the victual that constituted the means of the augmentation, some of the heritors, in an ungracious temper, sent what they called the tythe-boll (the Lord knows it was not the fiftieth) to the manse, where I had no place to put it. This fell out on a Saturday night, when I was busy with my sermon, thinking not of silver or gold, but of much better; so that I was greatly molested and disturbed thereby. Daft Meg, who sat by the kitchen chimlay-lug hearing a', said nothing for a time, but when she saw how Mrs. Balwhidder and me were put to, she cried out with a loud voice, like a soul under the inspiration of prophecy—'When the widow's creuse had filled all the vessels in the house, the Lord stopped the increase; verily, verily, I say unto you, if your barns be filled, and your girnel-kists can hold no more, seek till ye shall find the tume basins of the poor, and therein pour the corn, and the oil, and the wine of your abundance; so shall ye be blessed of the Lord.' The which words I took for an admonition, and directing the sacks to be brought into the dining-room, and other chambers of the manse, I sent off the heritors' servants, that had done me this prejudice, with an unexpected thankfulness. But this, as I afterwards was informed, both them and their masters attributed to the greedy grasp of avarice, with which they considered me as misled; and having said so, nothing could exceed their mortification on Monday, when they heard (for they were of those who had deserted the kirk) that I had given by the precentor notice to every widow in the parish that was in need, to come to the manse, and she would receive her portion of the partitioning of the augmentation. Thus, without any offence on my part, saving the strictness of justice, was a division made between me and the heritors; but the people were with me; and my own conscience was with me,

and though the fronts of the lofts and the pews of the heritors
were but thinly filled, I trusted that a good time was coming,
when the gentry would see the error of their way.   So I bent
the head of resignation to the Lord, and, assisted by the
wisdom of Mr. Kibbock, adhered to the course I had adopted ;
but at the close of the year, my heart was sorrowful for the
schism, and my prayer on Hogmanay was one of great
bitterness of soul, that such an evil had come to pass.

CHAPTER XXIX

YEAR 1788

A cotton-mill is built—The new spirit which it introduces among
the people.

IT had been often remarked by ingenious men, that the Brawl
burn, which ran through the parish, though a small, was yet
a rapid stream, and had a wonderful capability for damming,
and to turn mills.   From the time that the Irville water
deserted its channel this brook grew into repute, and several
mills and dams had been erected on its course.   In this year
a proposal came from Glasgow to build a cotton-mill on its
banks, beneath the Witch-linn, which being on a corner of the
Wheatrig, the property of Mr. Cayenne, he not only consented
thereto, but took a part in the profit or loss therein ; and,
being a man of great activity, though we thought him, for
many a day, a serpent plague sent upon the parish, he proved
thereby one of our greatest benefactors.   The cotton-mill was
built, and a spacious fabric it was—nothing like it had been
seen before in our day and generation—and, for the people
that were brought to work in it, a new town was built in the
vicinity, which Mr. Cayenne, the same being founded on his
land, called Cayenneville, the name of the plantation in
Virginia that had been taken from him by the rebellious
Americans.   From that day Fortune was lavish of her favours
upon him ; his property swelled, and grew in the most
extraordinary manner, and the whole country-side was stirring
with a new life.   For, when the mill was set agoing, he got

weavers of muslin established in Cayenneville; and shortly after, but that did not take place till the year following, he brought women all the way from the neighbourhood of Manchester in England, to teach the lassie bairns in our old clachan tambouring.

Some of the ancient families, in their turreted houses, were not pleased with this innovation, especially when they saw the handsome dwellings that were built for the weavers of the mills, and the unstinted hand that supplied the wealth required for the carrying on of the business. It sank their pride into insignificance, and many of them would almost rather have wanted the rise that took place in the value of their lands, than have seen this incoming of what they called o'er-sea speculation. But, saving the building of the cotton-mill, and the beginning of Cayenneville, nothing more memorable happened in this year, still it was nevertheless a year of a great activity. The minds of men were excited to new enterprises; a new genius, as it were, had descended upon the earth, and there was an erect and outlooking spirit abroad that was not to be satisfied with the taciturn regularity of ancient affairs. Even Miss Sabrina Hookie, the schoolmistress, though now waned from her meridian, was touched with the enlivening rod, and set herself to learn and to teach tambouring, in such a manner as to supersede by precept and example that old time-honoured functionary, as she herself called it, the spinning-wheel, proving, as she did one night, to Mr. Kibbock and me, that, if more money could be made by a woman tambouring than by spinning, it was better for her to tambour than to spin.

But, in the midst of all this commercing and manufacturing, I began to discover signs of decay in the wonted simplicity of our country ways. Among the cotton-spinners and muslin-weavers of Cayenneville, were several unsatisfied and ambitious spirits, who clubbed together, and got a London news-paper to the Cross Keys, where they were nightly in the habit of meeting and debating about the affairs of the French, which were then gathering towards a head. They were represented to me as lads by common in capacity, but with unsettled notions of religion. They were, however, quiet and orderly, and some of them since, at Glasgow, Paisley, and Manchester, even, I am told, in London, have grown into a topping way.

'*Debating about the affairs of the French.*'

Copyright 1895 by Macmillan & Co.

It seems they did not like my manner of preaching, and on that account absented themselves from public worship ; which, when I heard, I sent for some of them, to convince them of their error with regard to the truth of divers points of doctrine ; but they confounded me with their objections, and used my arguments, which were the old and orthodox proven opinions of the Divinity Hall, as if they had been the light sayings of a vain man.   So that I was troubled, fearing that some change would ensue to my people, who had hitherto lived amidst the boughs and branches of the gospel unmolested by the fowler's snare, and I set myself to watch narrowly, and with a vigilant eye, what would come to pass.

There was a visible increase among us of worldly prosperity in the course of this year ; insomuch, that some of the farmers, who were in the custom of taking their vendibles to the neighbouring towns on the Tuesdays, the Wednesdays, and Fridays, were led to open a market on the Saturdays in our own clachan, the which proved a great convenience.   But I cannot take it upon me to say whether this can be said to have well begun in the present Ann. Dom., although I know that in the summer of the ensuing year it was grown into a settled custom ; which I well recollect by the Macadams coming with their bairns to see Mrs. Malcolm their mother suddenly on a Saturday afternoon ; on which occasion me and Mrs. Balwhidder were invited to dine with them, and Mrs. Malcolm bought in the market for the dinner that day both mutton and fowls, such as twenty years before could not have been got for love or money on such a pinch.   Besides, she had two bottles of red and white wine from the Cross Keys, luxuries which, saving in the Breadland House in its best days, could not have been had in the whole parish, but must have been brought from a borough town ; for Eglesham Castle is not within the bounds of Dalmailing, and my observe does not apply to the stock and stores of that honourable mansion, but only to the dwellings of our own heritors, who were in general straitened in their circumstances, partly with upsetting, and partly by the eating rust of family pride, which hurt the edge of many a clever fellow among them, that would have done well in the way of trade, but sunk into divors for the sake of their genteelity.

CHAPTER XXX

YEAR 1789

William Malcolm comes to the parish and preaches—The opinions
upon his sermon.

THIS I have always reflected upon as one of our blessed years.
It was not remarkable for any extraordinary occurrence, but
there was a hopefulness in the minds of men, and a planning
of new undertakings, of which, whatever may be the upshot,
the devising is ever rich in the cheerful anticipations of good.

Another new line of road was planned, for a shorter cut to
the cotton-mill, from the main road to Glasgow, and a public-
house was opened in Cayenneville; the latter, however, was
not an event that gave me much satisfaction, but it was a
convenience to the inhabitants, and the carriers that brought
the cotton-bags and took away the yarn twice a week, needed
a place of refreshment. And there was a stage-coach set up
thrice every week from Ayr, that passed through the town, by
which it was possible to travel to Glasgow between breakfast
and dinner time, a thing that could not, when I came to the
parish, have been thought within the compass of man.

This stage-coach I thought one of the greatest conveniences
that had been established among us; and it enabled Mrs.
Balwhidder to send a basket of her fresh butter into the
Glasgow market, by which, in the spring and the fall of the
year, she got a great price, for the Glasgow merchants are fond
of excellent eatables, and the payment was aye ready money—
Tam Whirlit the driver paying for the one basket when he
took up the other.

In this year William Malcolm, the youngest son of the
widow, having been some time a tutor in a family in the east
country, came to see his mother, as indeed he had done every
year from the time he went to the College, but this occasion
was made remarkable by his preaching in my pulpit. His old
acquaintance were curious to hear him, and I myself had a
sort of a wish likewise, being desirous to know how far he was
orthodox; so I thought fit, on the suggestion of one of the

elders, to ask him to preach one day for me, which, after some fleeching, he consented to do. I think, however, there was a true modesty in his diffidence, although his reason was a weak one, being lest he might not satisfy his mother, who had as yet never heard him. Accordingly, on the Sabbath after, he did preach, and the kirk was well packed, and I was not one of the least attentive of the congregation. His sermon assuredly was well put together, and there was nothing to object to in his doctrine ; but the elderly people thought his language rather too Englified, which I thought likewise, for I never could abide that the plain auld Kirk of Scotland, with her sober presbyterian simplicity, should borrow, either in word or in deed, from the language of the prelatic hierarchy of England. Nevertheless, the younger part of the congregation were loud in his praise, saying, there had not been heard before such a style of language in our side of the country. As for Mrs. Malcolm, his mother, when I spoke to her anent the same, she said but little, expressing only her hope that his example would be worthy of his precepts ; so that, upon the whole, it was a satisfaction to us all that he was likely to prove a stoop and upholding pillar to the Kirk of Scotland. And his mother had the satisfaction, before she died, to see him a placed minister, and his name among the authors of his country ; for he published at Edinburgh a volume of *Moral Essays*, of which he sent me a pretty bound copy, and they were greatly creditable to his pen, though lacking somewhat of that birr and smeddum that is the juice and flavour of books of that sort.

CHAPTER XXXI

YEAR 1790

A bookseller's shop is set up among the houses of the weavers at Cayenneville.

THE features of this Ann. Dom. partook of the character of its predecessor. Several new houses were added to the clachan ; Cayenneville was spreading out with weavers' shops, and growing up fast into a town. In some respects it got the start of ours, for one day, when I was going to dine with Mr. Cayenne, at Wheatrig House, not a little to my amazement, did I behold a bookseller's shop opened there, with sticks of red and black wax, pouncet-boxes, pens, pocket-books, and new publications, in the window, such as the like of was only to be seen in cities and borough towns. And it was lighted at night by a patent lamp, which shed a wonderful beam, burning oil, and having no smoke. The man sold likewise perfumery, powder-puffs, trinkets, and Dublin dolls, besides penknives, Castile soap, and walking-sticks, together with a prodigy of other luxuries too tedious to mention.

Upon conversing with the man, for I was enchanted to go into this phenomenon, for as no less could I regard it, he told me that he had a correspondence with London, and could get me down any book published there within the same month in which it came out, and he showed me divers of the newest come out, of which I did not read even in the *Scots Magazine*, till more than three months after, although I had till then always considered that work as most interesting for its early intelligence. But what I was most surprised to hear, was that he took in a daily London newspaper for the spinners and weavers, who paid him a penny a week apiece for the same ; they being all greatly taken up with what, at the time, was going on in France.

This bookseller in the end, however, proved a whawp in our nest, for he was in league with some of the English reformers, and when the story took wind three years after, concerning the plots and treasons of the Corresponding Societies and democrats, he was fain to make a moonlight flitting, leaving his wife for a time to manage his affairs. I could not, however, think any ill of the man notwithstanding ; for he had very correct notions of right and justice, in a political sense, and when he came into the parish he was as orderly and well-behaved as any other body ; and conduct is a test that I have always found as good for a man's principles as professions. Nor, at the time of which I am speaking, was there any of that dread or fear of reforming the government that has since been occasioned by the wild and wasteful hand which the French employed in their Revolution.

But, among other improvements, I should mention that a Dr. Marigold came and settled in Cayenneville, a small, round, happy-tempered man, whose funny stories were far better liked than his drugs. There was a doubt among some of the weavers if he was a skilful Esculapian, and this doubt led to their holding out an inducement to another medical man, Dr. Tanzey, to settle there likewise, by which it grew into a saying, that at Cayenneville there was a doctor for health as well as sickness. For Dr. Marigold was one of the best hands in the country at a pleasant punch-bowl, while Dr. Tanzey had all the requisite knowledge of the faculty for the bedside.

It was in this year, that the hour-plate and hand on the kirk-steeple were renewed, as indeed may yet be seen by the date, though it be again greatly in want of fresh gilding ; for it was by my advice that the figures of the Ann. Dom. were placed one in each corner. In this year, likewise, the bridge over the Brawl burn was built, a great convenience, in the winter time, to the parishioners that lived on the north side ; for when there happened to be a speat on the Sunday, it kept them from the kirk, but I did not find that the bridge mended the matter, till after the conclusion of the war against the democrats, and the beginning of that which we are now waging with Boney, their child and champion. It is, indeed, wonderful to think of the occultation of grace that was taking place about this time, throughout the whole bound of Christendom ; for I could mark a visible darkness of infidelity spreading in the corner of the vineyard committed to my keeping, and a falling away of the vines from their wonted props and confidence in the truths of Revelation. But I said nothing. I knew that the faith could not be lost, and that it would be found purer and purer the more it was tried ; and this I have lived to see, many now being zealous members of the church, that were abundantly lukewarm at the period of which I am now speaking.

CHAPTER XXXII

YEAR 1791

I place my son Gilbert in a counting-house at Glasgow—My observations on Glasgow—On my return I preach against the vanity of riches, and begin to be taken for a black-neb.

IN the spring of this year, I took my son Gilbert into Glasgow, to place him in a counting-house. As he had no inclination for any of the learned professions, and not having been there from the time when I was sent to the General Assembly, I cannot express my astonishment at the great improvements, surpassing far all that was done in our part of the country, which I thought was not to be paralleled. When I came afterwards to reflect on my simplicity in this, it was clear to me that we should not judge of the rest of the world by what we see going on around ourselves, but walk abroad into other parts, and thereby enlarge our sphere of observation, as well as ripen our judgment of things.

But although there was no doubt a great and visible increase of the city, loftier buildings on all sides, and streets that spread their arms far into the embraces of the country, I thought the looks of the population were impaired, and that there was a greater proportion of long white faces in the Trongate, than when I attended the Divinity class. These, I was told, were the weavers and others concerned in the cotton trade, which I could well believe, for they were very like in their looks to the men of Cayenneville; but from living in a crowded town, and not breathing a wholesome country air between their tasks, they had a stronger cast of unhealthy melancholy. I was, therefore, very glad that Providence had placed in my hand the pastoral staff of a country parish, for it cut me to the heart to see so many young men, in the rising prime of life, already in the arms of a pale consumption. 'If, therefore,' said I to Mrs. Balwhidder, when I returned home to the manse, 'we live, as it were, within the narrow circle of ignorance, we are spared from the pain of knowing many an evil; and, surely, in much knowledge, there is sadness of heart.'

But the main effect of this was to make me do all in my power to keep my people contented with their lowly estate ; for in that same spirit of improvement, which was so busy everywhere, I could discern something like a shadow, that showed it was not altogether of that pure advantage, which avarice led all so eagerly to believe. Accordingly, I began a series of sermons on the evil and vanity of riches, and, for the most part of the year, pointed out in what manner they led the possessor to indulge in sinful luxuries, and how indulgence begat desire, and desire betrayed integrity and corrupted the heart, making it evident, that the rich man was liable to forget his unmerited obligations to God, and to oppress the laborious and the needful when he required their services.

Little did I imagine, in thus striving to keep aloof the ravenous wolf Ambition from my guileless flock, that I was giving cause for many to think me an enemy to the king and government, and a perverter of Christianity, to suit levelling doctrines. But so it was. Many of the heritors considered me a black-neb, though I knew it not, but went on in the course of my duty, thinking only how best to preserve peace on earth, and goodwill towards men. I saw, however, an altered manner in the deportment of several, with whom I had long lived in friendly terms. It was not marked enough to make me inquire the cause, but sufficiently plain to affect my ease of mind. Accordingly, about the end of this year, I fell into a dull way : my spirit was subdued, and at times I was aweary of the day, and longed for the night, when I might close my eyes in peaceful slumbers. I missed my son Gilbert, who had been a companion to me in the long nights, while his mother was busy with the lasses, and their ceaseless wheels and cardings, in the kitchen. Often could I have found it in my heart to have banned that never-ceasing industry, and to tell Mrs. Balwhidder, that the married state was made for something else than to make napery, and beetle blankets ; but it was her happiness to keep all at work, and she had no pleasure in any other way of life, so I sat many a night by the fireside with resignation ; sometimes in the study, and sometimes in the parlour, and, as I was doing nothing, Mrs. Balwhidder said it was needless to light the candle. Our daughter Janet was in this time at a boarding-school in Ayr, so that I was really a most solitary married man.

CHAPTER XXXIII

YEAR 1792

Troubled with low spirits—Accidental meeting with Mr. Cayenne, who
endeavours to remove the prejudices entertained against me.

WHEN the spring in this year began to brighten on the brae,
the cloud of dulness, that had darkened and oppressed me all
the winter, somewhat melted away, and I could now and then
joke again at the never-ending toil and trouble of that busiest
of all bees, the second Mrs. Balwhidder. But still I was far
from being right, a small matter affected me, and I was overly
given to walking by myself, and musing on things that I could
tell nothing about—my thoughts were just the rack of a dream
without form, and driving witlessly as the smoke that mounteth
up, and is lost in the airy heights of the sky.

Heeding little of what was going on in the clachan, and
taking no interest in the concerns of anybody, I would have
been contented to die, but I had no ail about me. An
accident, however, fell out, that, by calling on me for an effort,
had the blessed influence of clearing my vapours almost
entirely away.

One morning, as I was walking on the sunny side of the
road, where the footpath was in the next year made to the
cotton-mill, I fell in with Mr. Cayenne, who was seemingly
much fashed—a small matter could do that at any time ; and he
came up to me with a red face and an angry eye. It was not
my intent to speak to him, for I was grown loth to enter into
conversation with anybody, so I bowed and passed on.
'What,' cried Mr. Cayenne, 'and will you not speak to me?'
I turned round, and said meekly, 'Mr. Cayenne, I have no
objections to speak to you ; but having nothing particular to
say, it did not seem necessary just now.'

He looked at me like a gled, and in a minute exclaimed,
'Mad, by Jupiter! as mad as a March hare!' He then
entered into conversation with me, and said, that he had
noticed me an altered man, and was just so far on his way to
the manse, to inquire what had befallen me. So, from less to

127

more, we entered into the marrow of my case; and I told him how I had observed the estranged countenances of some of the heritors; at which he swore an oath, that they were a parcel of the damn'dest boobies in the country, and told me how they had taken it into their heads that I was a leveller. 'But I know you better,' said Mr. Cayenne, 'and have stood up for you as an honest conscientious man, though I don't much like your humdrum preaching. However, let that pass; I insist upon your dining with me to-day, when some of these arrant fools are to be with us, and the devil's in't, if I don't make you friends with them.' I did not think Mr. Cayenne, however, very well qualified for a peacemaker, but, nevertheless, I consented to go; and having thus got an inkling of the cause of that cold back-turning which had distressed me so much, I made such an effort to remove the error that was entertained against me, that some of the heritors, before we separated, shook me by the hands with the cordiality of renewed friendship; and, as if to make amends for past neglect, there was no end to their invitations to dinner, which had the effect of putting me again on my mettle, and removing the thick and muddy melancholious humour out of my blood.

But what confirmed my cure, was the coming home of my daughter Janet from the Ayr boarding-school, where she had learnt to play on the spinet, and was become a conversible lassie, with a competent knowledge, for a woman, of geography and history; so that when her mother was busy with the wearyful booming wheel, she entertained me sometimes with a tune, and sometimes with her tongue, which made the winter nights fly cantily by.

Whether it was owing to the malady of my imagination, throughout the greatest part of this year, or that really nothing particular did happen to interest me, I cannot say, but it is very remarkable that I have nothing remarkable to record—farther, than that I was at the expense myself of getting the manse rough cast, and the window cheeks painted, with roans put up, rather than apply to the heritors; for they were always sorely fashed when called upon for outlay.

'*She entertained me sometimes with a tune.*'

Copyright 1895 by Macmillan & Co.

CHAPTER XXXIV

Year 1793

I dream a remarkable dream, and preach a sermon in consequence,
applying to the events of the times—Two democratical weaver lads
brought before Mr. Cayenne, as justice of peace.

On the first night of this year I dreamt a very remarkable
dream, which, when I now recall to mind, at this distance of
time, I cannot but think that there was a cast of prophecy in
it. I thought that I stood on the tower of an old popish kirk,
looking out at the window upon the kirkyard, where I beheld
ancient tombs, with effigies and coats of arms on the wall
thereof, and a great gate at the one side, and a door that led
into a dark and dismal vault at the other. I thought all the
dead, that were lying in the common graves, rose out of their
coffins ; at the same time, from the old and grand monuments,
with the effigies and coats of arms, came the great men, and
the kings of the earth with crowns on their heads, and globes
and sceptres in their hands.

I stood wondering what was to ensue, when presently I
heard the noise of drums and trumpets, and anon I beheld
an army with banners entering in at the gate ; upon which
the kings and the great men came also forth in their power
and array, and a dreadful battle was foughten ; but the multitude, that had risen from the common graves, stood afar off,
and were but lookers-on.

The kings and their host were utterly discomfited. They
were driven within the doors of their monuments, their coats
of arms were broken off, and their effigies cast down, and the
victors triumphed over them with the flourishes of trumpets
and the waving of banners. But while I looked, the vision
was changed, and I then beheld a wide and a dreary waste, and
afar off the steeples of a great city, and a tower in the midst,
like the tower of Babel, and on it I could discern written in
characters of fire, 'Public Opinion.' While I was pondering
at the same, I heard a great shout, and presently the con-
querors made their appearance, coming over the desolate moor.
They were going in great pride and might towards the city,

but an awful burning rose, afar as it were in the darkness, and the flames stood like a tower of fire that reached unto the heavens. And I saw a dreadful hand and an arm stretched from out of the cloud, and in its hold was a besom made of the hail and the storm, and it swept the fugitives like dust; and in their place I saw the churchyard, as it were, cleared and spread around, the graves closed, and the ancient tombs, with their coats of arms and their effigies of stone, all as they were in the beginning. I then awoke, and behold it was a dream.

This vision perplexed me for many days, and when the news came that the King of France was beheaded by the hands of his people, I received, as it were, a token in confirmation of the vision that had been disclosed to me in my sleep, and I preached a discourse on the same, and against the French Revolution, that was thought one of the greatest and soundest sermons that I had ever delivered in my pulpit.

On the Monday following, Mr. Cayenne, who had been some time before appointed a justice of the peace, came over from Wheatrig House to the Cross Keys, where he sent for me and divers other respectable inhabitants of the clachan, and told us that he was to have a sad business, for a warrant was out to bring before him two democratic weaver lads, on a suspicion of high treason. Scarcely were the words uttered, when they were brought in, and he began to ask them how they dared to think of dividing, with their liberty and equality of principles, his and every other man's property in the country. The men answered him in a calm manner, and told him they sought no man's property, but only their own natural rights; upon which he called them traitors and reformers. They denied they were traitors, but confessed they were reformers, and said they knew not how that should be imputed to them as a fault, for that the greatest men of all times had been reformers,—'Was not,' they said, 'our Lord Jesus Christ a reformer?' 'And what the devil did He make of it?' cried Mr. Cayenne, bursting with passion; 'was He not crucified?'

I thought, when I heard these words, that the pillars of the earth sunk beneath me, and that the roof of the house was carried away in a whirlwind. The drums of my ears crackit, blue starns danced before my sight, and I was fain to leave the house and hie me home to the manse, where I sat down in my study, like a stupified creature awaiting what would betide. Nothing, however, was found against the weaver lads ; but I never from that day could look on Mr. Cayenne as a Christian, though surely he was a true government man.

Soon after this affair there was a pleasant re-edification of a gospel-spirit among the heritors, especially when they heard how I had handled the regicides of France ; and on the following Sunday, I had the comfortable satisfaction to see many a gentleman in their pews, that had not been for years within a kirk door. The democrats, who took a world of trouble to misrepresent the actions of the gentry, insinuated that all this was not from any new sense of grace, but in fear of their being reported as suspected persons to the king's government. But I could not think so, and considered their renewal of communion with the church as a swearing of allegiance to the King of kings, against that host of French atheists, who had torn the mort-cloth from the coffin, and made it a banner, with which they were gone forth to war against the Lamb. The whole year was, however, spent in great uneasiness, and the proclamation of the war was followed by an appalling stop in trade. We heard of nothing but failures on all hands, and among others that grieved me, was that of Mr. Maitland of Glasgow, who had befriended Mrs. Malcolm in the days of her affliction, and gave her son Robert his fine ship. It was a sore thing to hear of so many breakings, especially of old respected merchants like him, who had been a Lord Provost, and was far declined into the afternoon of life. He did not, however, long survive the mutation of his fortune, but bending his aged head in sorrow, sunk down beneath the stroke to rise no more.

CHAPTER XXXV

YEAR 1794

The condition of the parish, as divided into government men and Jacobins—I endeavour to prevent Christian charity from being forgotten in the phraseology of utility and philanthropy.

THIS year had opened into all the leafiness of midsummer before anything memorable happened in the parish, further than that the sad division of my people into government men and Jacobins was perfected. This calamity, for I never could consider such heart-burning among neighbours as anything less than a very heavy calamity, was assuredly occasioned by faults on both sides, but it must be confessed that the gentry did nothing to win the commonality from the errors of their way. A little more condescension on their part would not have made things worse, and might have made them better; but pride interposed, and caused them to think that any show of affability from them would be construed by the democrats into a terror of their power. While the democrats were no less to blame; for hearing how their compeers were thriving in France, and demolishing every obstacle to their ascendency, they were crouse and really insolent, evidencing none of that temperance in prosperity that proves the possessors worthy of their good fortune.

As for me, my duty in these circumstances was plain and simple. The Christian religion was attempted to be brought into disrepute; the rising generation were taught to jibe at its holiest ordinances; and the kirk was more frequented as a place to while away the time on a rainy Sunday, than for any insight of the admonitions and revelations in the sacred book. Knowing this, I perceived that it would be of no effect to handle much the mysteries of the faith; but as there was at the time a bruit and a sound about universal benevolence, philanthropy, utility, and all the other disguises with which an infidel philosophy appropriated to itself the charity, brotherly love, and well-doing inculcated by our holy religion, I set myself to task upon these heads, and thought it no robbery to use a little of the stratagem employed against Christ's Kingdom, to promote the interests thereof in the hearts and understandings of those whose ears would have been sealed against me had I attempted to expound higher things. Accordingly on one day it was my practice to show what the nature of Christian charity was, comparing it to the light and warmth of the sun that shines impartially on the just and the unjust—showing that man, without the sense of it as a duty, was as the beasts that perish, and that every feeling of his nature was intimately selfish, but that when actuated by this divine impulse, he rose out of himself and became as a god, zealous to abate the sufferings of all things that live. And on the next day, I demonstrated that the new benevolence which had come so much into vogue was but another version of this Christian virtue. In like manner I dealt with brotherly love, bringing it home to the business and bosoms of my hearers, that the Christianity of it was neither enlarged nor bettered by being baptized with the Greek name of philanthropy. With well-doing, however, I went more roundly to work. I told my people that I thought they had more sense than to secede from Christianity to become Utilitarians, for that it would be a confession of ignorance of the faith they deserted, seeing that it was the main duty inculcated by our religion to do all in morals and manners to which the new-fangled doctrine of utility pretended.

These discourses, which I continued for some time, had no great effect on the men; but, being prepared in a familiar household manner, they took the fancies of the young women, which was to me an assurance that the seed I had planted would in time shoot forth; for I reasoned with myself, that if the gudemen of the immediate generation should continue free-thinkers, their wives will take care that those of the next shall not lack that spunk of grace; so I was cheered under that obscurity which fell upon Christianity at this time, with a vista beyond, in which I saw, as it were, the children unborn, walking on the bright green, and in the unclouded splendour of the faith.

But, what with the decay of trade, and the temptation of the king's bounty, and over all, the witlessness that was in the spirit of man at this time, the number that enlisted in the course of the year from the parish was prodigious. In one week no less than three weavers and two cotton-spinners went over to Ayr, and took the bounty for the Royal Artillery.   But I could not help remarking to myself, that the people were grown so used to changes and extraordinary adventures, that the single enlistment of Thomas Wilson, at the beginning of the American war, occasioned a far greater grief and work among us, than all the swarms that went off week after week in the months of November and December of this year.

CHAPTER XXXVI

YEAR 1795

A recruiting party visits the town—After them, players—then preaching quakers—The progress of philosophy among the weavers.

THE present Ann. Dom. was ushered in with an event that I had never dreaded to see in my day, in our once sober and religious country parish.   The number of lads that had gone over to Ayr to be soldiers from among the spinners and weavers of Cayenneville had been so great, that the government got note of it, and sent a recruiting party to be quartered in the town ; for the term clachan was beginning by this time to wear out of fashion ; indeed the place itself was outgrowing the fitness of that title.   Never shall I forget the dunt that the first tap of the drum gied to my heart as I was sitting on Hansel Monday by myself at the parlour fireside, Mrs. Balwhidder being throng with the lasses looking out a washing, and my daughter at Ayr, spending a few days with her old comrades of the boarding-school.   I thought it was the enemy, and then anon the sound of the fife came shrill to the ear ; for the night was lown and peaceful.   My wife and all the lasses came flying in upon me, crying all, in the name of Heaven, what could it be ? by which I was obligated to put on my big coat, and, with my hat and staff, go out to inquire. The whole town was aloof, the aged at the doors in clusters, and the bairns following the tattoo, as it was called, and at every doubling beat of the drum, shouting as if they had been in the face of their foemen.

Mr. Archibald Dozendale, one of my elders, was saying to several persons around him, just as I came up, ' Hech, sirs ! but the battle draws near our gates,' upon which there was a heavy sigh from all that heard him ; and then they told me of the serjeant's business, and we had a serious communing together anent the same. But while we were thus standing discoursing on the causeway, Mrs. Balwhidder and the servant lasses could thole no longer, but in a troop came in quest of me to hear what was doing. In short, it was a night both of sorrow and anxiety. Mr. Dozendale walked back to the manse with us, and we had a sober tumbler of toddy together, marvelling exceedingly where these fearful portents and changes would stop, both of us being of opinion that the end of the world was drawing nearer and nearer.

Whether it was, however, that the lads belonging to the place did not like to show themselves with the enlistment cockades among their acquaintance, or that there was any other reason, I cannot take it upon me to say, but certain it is, the recruiting party came no speed, and in consequence were removed about the end of March.

Another thing happened in this year, too remarkable for me to neglect to put on record, as it strangely and strikingly marked the rapid revolutions that were going on. In the month of August, at the time of the fair, a gang of play-actors came, and hired Thomas Thacklan's barn for their enactments. They were the first of that clanjamfrey who had ever been in the parish, and there was a wonderful excitement caused by the rumours concerning them. Their first performance was *Douglas Tragedy*, and the *Gentle Shepherd;* and the general opinion was, that the lad who played Norval in the play, and Patie in the farce, was an English lord's son, who had run away from his parents, rather than marry an old cracket lady, with a great portion. But, whatever truth there might be in this notion, certain it is the whole pack was in a state of perfect beggary ; and yet, for all that, they not only in their parts, as I was told, laughed most heartily, but made others do the same ; for I was constrained to let my daughter go to see them, with some of her acquaintance, and she gave me such an account of what they did, that I thought I would have liked to have gotten a keek at them myself. At the same time, I must own this was a sinful curiosity, and I stifled it to

the best of my ability.   Among other plays that they did was
one called *Macbeth and the Witches*, which the Miss Cayennes
had seen performed in London, when they were there in the
winter time, with their father, for three months, seeing the
world, after coming from the boarding-school.   But it was no
more like the true play of Shakespeare the poet, according to
their account, than a duddy betherel set up to fright the
sparrows from the pease is like a living gentleman.   The
hungry players, instead of behaving like guests at the royal
banquet, were voracious on the needful feast of bread, and the
strong ale, that served for wine in decanters ; but the greatest
sport of all was about a kail-pot that acted the part of a
cauldron, and which should have sunk with thunder and
lightning into the earth ; however, it did quite as well, for it
made its exit, as Miss Virginia said, by walking quietly off,
being pulled by a string fastened to one of its feet.   No scene
of the play was so much applauded as this one ; and the actor
who did the part of King Macbeth made a most polite bow of
thankfulness to the audience, for the approbation with which
they had received the performance of the pot.

We had likewise, shortly after the *omnes exeunt* of the
players, an exhibition of a different sort in the same barn.   This
was by two English quakers, and a quaker lady, tanners from
Kendal, who had been at Ayr on some leather business, where
they preached, but made no proselytes.   The travellers were
all three in a whisky, drawn by one of the best-ordered horses,
as the hostler at the Cross Keys told me, ever seen.   They
came to the inn to their dinner, and, meaning to stay all night,
sent round to let it be known that they would hold a meeting
in friend Thacklan's barn ; but Thomas denied they were
either kith or kin to him ; this, however, was their way of
speaking.

In the evening, owing to the notice, a great congregation
was assembled in the barn, and I myself, along with Mr.
Archibald Dozendale, went there likewise, to keep the people
in awe ; for we feared the strangers might be jeered and
insulted.   The three were seated aloft on a high stage
prepared on purpose, with two mares and scaffold-deals,
borrowed from Mr. Trowel the mason.   They sat long, and
silent ; but at last the spirit moved the woman, and she rose
and delivered a very sensible exposition of Christianity.   I

'*The actor who did the part of King Macbeth made a most polite bow of thankfulness.*

was really surprised to hear such sound doctrine; and Mr. Dozendale said, justly, that it was more to the purpose than some that my younger brethren from Edinburgh endeavoured to teach. So, that those who went to laugh at the sincere simplicity of the pious quakers were rebuked by a very edifying discourse on the moral duties of a Christian's life.

Upon the whole, however, this, to the best of my recollection, was another unsatisfactory year. In this we were doubtless brought more into the world, but we had a greater variety of temptation set before us, and there was still jealousy and estrangement in the dispositions of the gentry and the lower orders, particularly the manufacturers. I cannot say, indeed, that there was any increase of corruption among the rural portion of my people; for their vocation calling them to work apart, in the purity of the free air of heaven, they were kept uncontaminated by that seditious infection which fevered the minds of the sedentary weavers, and working like flatulence in the stomachs of the cotton-spinners, sent up into their heads a vain and diseased fume of infidel philosophy.

CHAPTER XXXVII

YEAR 1796

Death of second Mrs. Balwhidder—I look out for a third, and fix upon Mrs. Nugent, a widow—Particulars of the courtship.

THE prosperity of fortune is like the blossoms of spring, or the golden hue of the evening cloud. It delighteth the spirit, and passeth away.

In the month of February my second wife was gathered to the Lord. She had been very ill for some time with an income in her side, which no medicine could remove. I had the best doctors in the country-side to her, but their skill was of no avail, their opinions being that her ail was caused by an internal abscess, for which physic has provided no cure. Her death was to me a great sorrow, for she was a most excellent wife, industrious to a degree, and managed everything with so brisk a hand, that nothing went wrong that she put it to.

With her I had grown richer than any other minister in the presbytery; but above all, she was the mother of my bairns, which gave her a double claim upon me.

I laid her by the side of my first love, Betty Lanshaw, my own cousin that was, and I inscribed her name upon the same headstone; but time had drained my poetical vein, and I have not yet been able to indite an epitaph on her merits and virtues, for she had an eminent share of both. Her greatest fault—the best have their faults—was an over-earnestness to gather gear; in the doing of which I thought she sometimes sacrificed the comforts of a pleasant fireside, for she was never in her element but when she was keeping the servants eydent at their work. But, if by this she subtracted something from the quietude that was most consonant to my nature, she has left cause, both in bank and bond, for me and her bairns to bless her great household activity.

She was not long deposited in her place of rest till I had occasion to find her loss. All my things were kept by her in a most perjink and excellent order, but they soon fell into an amazing confusion, for, as she often said to me, I had a turn for heedlessness; insomuch that although my daughter Janet was grown up, and able to keep the house, I saw that it would be necessary, as soon as decency would allow, for me to take another wife. I was moved to this chiefly by foreseeing that my daughter would in time be married, and taken away from me, but more on account of the servant lasses, who grew out of all bounds, verifying the proverb, 'Well kens the mouse when the cat's out of the house.' Besides this, I was now far down in the vale of years, and could not expect to be long without feeling some of the penalties of old age, although I was still a hail and sound man. It therefore behoved me to look in time for a helpmate to tend me in my approaching infirmities.

Upon this important concern I reflected, as I may say, in the watches of the night, and, considering the circumstances of my situation, I saw it would not do for me to look out for an overly young woman, nor yet would it do for one of my ways to take an elderly maiden, ladies of that sort being liable to possess strong-set particularities. I therefore resolved that my choice should lie among widows of a discreet age; and I had a glimmer in my mind of speaking to Mrs. Malcolm, but when I reflected on the saintly steadiness of her character, I was satisfied it would be of no use to think of her. Accordingly I bent my brows, and looked towards Irville, which is an abundant trone for widows and other single women; and I fixed my purpose on Mrs. Nugent, the relic of a Professor in the University of Glasgow, both because she was a well-bred woman, without any children to plea about the interest of my own two, and likewise because she was held in great estimation by all who knew her, as a lady of a Christian principle.

It was some time in the summer, however, before I made up my mind to speak to her on the subject; but one afternoon, in the month of August, I resolved to do so, and with that intent, walked leisurely over to Irville, and after calling on the Rev. Dr. Dinwiddie, the minister, I stepped in, as if by chance, to Mrs. Nugent's. I could see that she was a little surprised at my visit; however, she treated me with every possible civility, and her servant lass bringing in the tea things, in a most orderly manner, as punctually as the clock was striking, she invited me to sit still and drink my tea with her; which I did, being none displeased to get such encouragement. However, I said nothing that time, but returned to the manse, very well content with what I had observed, which made me fain to repeat my visit. So, in the course of the week, taking Janet, my daughter, with me, we walked over in the forenoon, and called at Mrs. Nugent's first, before going to any other house; and Janet saying, as we came out to go to the minister's, that she thought Mrs. Nugent an agreeable woman, I determined to knock the nail on the head without further delay.

Accordingly I invited the minister and his wife to dine with us on the Thursday following; and before leaving the town, I made Janet, while the minister and me were handling a subject, as a sort of thing of common civility, go to Mrs. Nugent, and invite her also. Dr. Dinwiddie was a gleg man, of a jocose nature; and he, guessing something of what I was ettling at, was very mirthful with me, but I kept my own counsel till a meet season.

On the Thursday, the company as invited came, and nothing extraordinary was seen, but in cutting up and helping a hen, Dr. Dinwiddie put one wing on Mrs. Nugent's plate, and the other wing on my plate, and said, there have been greater miracles than these two wings flying together, which was a sharp joke, that caused no little merriment, at the expense of Mrs. Nugent and me. I, however, to show that I

' A kindly nip on her sonsy arm.'

was none daunted, laid a leg also on her plate, and took another on my own, saying, in the words of the Reverend Doctor, there have been greater miracles than that these two legs should lie in the same nest, which was thought a very clever come off; and at the same time, I gave Mrs. Nugent a kindly nip on her sonsy arm, which was breaking the ice in as pleasant a way as could be. In short, before anything passed between ourselves on the subject, we were set down for a trysted pair; and this being the case, we were married as soon as a twelvemonth and a day had passed from the death of the second Mrs. Balwhidder; and neither of us have had occasion to rue the bargain. It is, however, but a piece of justice due to my second wife to say, that this was not a little owing to her good management; for she had left such a well-plenished house, that her successor said we had nothing to do but to contribute to one another's happiness.

In this year nothing more memorable happened in the parish, saving that the cotton-mill dam burst, about the time of the Lammas flood, and the waters went forth like a deluge of destruction, carrying off much victual, and causing a vast of damage to the mills that are lower down the stream. It was just a prodigy to see how calmly Mr. Cayenne acted on that occasion; for being at other times as crabbed as a wud terrier, folk were afraid to tell him till he came out himself in the morning and saw the devastation; at the sight of which he gave only a shrill whistle, and began to laugh at the idea of the men fearing to take him the news, as if he had not fortune and philosophy enough, as he called it, to withstand much greater misfortunes.

CHAPTER XXXVIII

YEAR 1797

Mr. Henry Melcomb comes to the parish to see his uncle, Mr. Cayenne— From some jocular behaviour on his part, Meg Gaffaw falls in love with him—The sad result of the adventure when he is married.

WHEN I have seen in my walks the irrational creatures of God, the birds and the beasts, governed by a kindly instinct in attendance on their young, often has it come into my head that love and charity, far more than reason or justice, formed the tie that holds the world, with all its jarring wants and woes, in social dependence and obligation together; and in this year a strong verification of the soundness of this notion was exemplified in the conduct of the poor haverel lassie, Meg Gaffaw, whose naturality on the occasion of her mother's death I have related at length in this chronicle.

In the course of the summer, Mr. Henry Melcomb, who was a nephew to Mr. Cayenne, came down from England to see his uncle. He had just completed his education at the College of Christ Church, in Oxford, and was the most perfect young gentleman that had ever been seen in this part of the country.

In his appearance he was a very paragon, with a fine manly countenance, frank-hearted, blithe, and, in many points of character, very like my old friend the Lord Eglesham who was shot. Indeed, in some respects, he was even above his lordship, for he had a great turn at ready wit, and could joke and banter in a most agreeable manner. He came very often to the manse to see me, and took great pleasure in my company, and really used a freedom that was so droll, I could scarcely keep my composity and decorum with him. Among others that shared in his attention was daft Meg Gaffaw, whom he had forgathered with one day in coming to see me, and after conversing with her for some time, he handed her, as she told me herself, over the kirk stile, like a lady of high degree, and came with her to the manse door linking by the arm.

From the ill-timed daffin of that hour, poor Meg fell deep in love with Mr. Melcomb, and it was just a play-acting to see the arts and antics she put in practice to win his attention. In her garb she had never any sense of a proper propriety, but went about the country asking for shapings of silks and satins, with which she patched her duds, calling them by the divers names of robes and *negligées*. All hitherto, however, had been moderation compared to the daffadile of vanity which she was now seen, when she had searched, as she said, to the bottom of her coffer. I cannot take it upon me to describe her, but she kithed in such a variety of cuffs and ruffles, feathers, old gum-flowers, painted paper knots, ribbons, and furs, and laces, and went about gecking and simpering with an old fan in her hand, that it was not in the power of nature to look at her with sobriety.

'*Handed her over the kirk stile.*'

Her first appearance in this masquerading was at the kirk on the Sunday following her adventure with Mr. Melcomb, and it was with a sore difficulty that I could keep my eyes off her, even in prayer; and when the kirk skailed, she walked before him, spreading all her grandeur to catch his eye in such a manner as had not been seen or heard of since the prank that Lady Macadam played Miss Betty Wudrife.

Any other but Mr. Melcomb would have been provoked by the fool's folly, but he humoured her wit, and, to the amazement of the whole people, presented her his hand, and allemanded her along in a manner that should not have been seen in any street out of a king's court, and far less on the Lord's day. But alas! this sport did not last long. Mr. Melcomb had come from England to be married to his cousin, Miss Virginia Cayenne, and poor daft Meg never heard of it till the banns for their purpose of marriage was read out by Mr. Lorimore on the Sabbath after. The words were scarcely out of his mouth, when the simple and innocent natural gave a loud shriek, that terrified the whole congregation, and ran out of the kirk demented. There was no more finery for poor Meg; but she went and sat opposite to the windows of Mr. Cayenne's house, where Mr. Melcomb was, with clasped hands and beseeching eyes, like a monumental statue in alabaster, and no entreaty could drive her away. Mr. Melcomb sent her money, and the bride many a fine thing, but Meg flung them from her, and clasped her hands again, and still sat. Mr. Cayenne would have let loose the house-dog on her, but was not permitted.

In the evening it began to rain, and they thought that and the coming darkness would drive her away, but when the servants looked out before barring the doors, there she was in the same posture. I was to perform the marriage ceremony at seven o'clock in the morning, for the young pair were to go that night to Edinburgh; and when I went, there was Meg sitting looking at the windows with her hands clasped. When she saw me she gave a shrill cry, and took me by the hand, and wised me to go back, crying out in a heart-breaking voice, 'Oh, sir! No yet—no yet! He'll maybe draw back and think of a far truer bride.' I was wae for her, and very angry with the servants for laughing at the fond folly of the ill-less thing.

When the marriage was over, and the carriage at the door,

the bridegroom handed in the bride. Poor Meg saw this, and jumping up from where she sat, was at his side like a spirit, as he was stepping in, and taking him by the hand, she looked in his face so piteously, that every heart was sorrowful, for she could say nothing. When he pulled away his hand, and the door was shut, she stood as if she had been charmed to the spot, and saw the chaise drive away. All that were about the door then spoke to her, but she heard us not. At last she gave a deep sigh, and the water coming into her eye, she said, 'The worm—the worm is my bonny bridegroom, and Jenny with the many-feet my bridal maid. The mill-dam water's the wine o' the wedding, and the clay and the clod shall be my bedding. A lang night is meet for a bridal, but none shall be langer than mine.' In saying which words, she fled from among us, with heels like the wind. The servants pursued, but long before they could stop her, she was past redemption in the deepest plumb of the cotton-mill dam.

Few deaths had for many a day happened in the parish to cause so much sorrow as that of this poor silly creature. She was a sort of household familiar among us, and there was much like the inner side of wisdom in the pattern of her sayings, many of which are still preserved as proverbs.

CHAPTER XXXIX

YEAR 1798

A dearth—Mr. Cayenne takes measures to mitigate the evil—He receives kindly some Irish refugees—His daughter's marriage.

THIS was one of the heaviest years in the whole course of my ministry. The spring was slow of coming, and cold and wet when it did come ; the dibs were full, the roads foul, and the ground that should have been dry at the seed-time was as claggy as clay and clung to the harrow. The labour of man and beast was thereby augmented, and all nature being in a state of sluggish indisposition, it was evident to every eye of experience that there would be a great disappointment to the hopes of the husbandman.

Foreseeing this I gathered the opinion of all the most sagacious of my parishioners, and consulted with them for a provision against the evil day, and we spoke to Mr. Cayenne on the subject, for he had a talent by common in matters of mercantile management. It was amazing, considering his hot temper, with what patience he heard the grounds of our apprehension, and how he questioned and sifted the experience of the old farmers, till he was thoroughly convinced that all similar seed-times were ever followed by a short crop. He then said, that he would prove himself a better friend to the parish than he was thought. Accordingly, as he afterwards told me himself, he wrote off that very night to his correspondents in America to buy for his account all the wheat and flour they could get, and ship it to arrive early in the fall ; and he bought up likewise in countries round the Baltic great store of victual, and he brought in two cargoes to Irville on purpose for the parish, against the time of need, making for the occasion a girnel of one of the warehouses of the cotton-mill.

The event came to pass as had been foretold ; the harvest fell short, and Mr. Cayenne's cargoes from America and the Baltic came home in due season, by which he made a terrible power of money, clearing thousands on thousands by post after post—making more profit, as he said himself, in the course of one month, he believed, than ever was made by any individual within the kingdom of Scotland in the course of a year. He said, however, that he might have made more if he had bought up the corn at home, but being convinced by us that there would be a scarcity, he thought it his duty as an honest man to draw from the stores and granaries of foreign countries, by which he was sure he would serve his country, and be abundantly rewarded. In short, we all reckoned him another Joseph when he opened his girnels at the cotton-mill, and after distributing a liberal portion to the poor and needy, selling the remainder at an easy rate to the generality of the people. Some of the neighbouring parishes, however, were angry that he would not serve them likewise, and called him a wicked and extortionate forestaller ; but he made it plain to the meanest capacity that if he did not circumscribe his dispensation to our own bounds it would be as nothing. So that, although he brought a wonderful prosperity in by the cotton-mill, and a plenteous supply of corn in a time of famine, doing more in these things for the people than all the other heritors had done from the beginning of time, he was much reviled ; even his bounty was little esteemed by my people, because he took a moderate profit on what he sold to them. Perhaps, however, these prejudices might be partly owing to their dislike of his hasty temper, at least I am willing to think so, for it would grieve me if they were really ungrateful for a benefit that made the pressure of the time lie but lightly on them.

The alarm of the Irish rebellion in this year was likewise another source of affliction to us, for many of the gentry coming over in great straits, especially ladies and their children, and some of them in the hurry of their flight having but little ready money, were very ill off. Some four or five families came to the Cross Keys in this situation, and the conduct of Mr. Cayenne to them was most exemplary. He remembered his own haste with his family from Virginia, when the Americans rebelled ; and immediately on hearing of these Irish refugees, he waited on them with his wife and daughter, supplied them with money, invited them to his house, made ploys to keep up their spirits, while the other gentry stood back till they knew something of the strangers.

Among these destitute ladies was a Mrs. Desmond and her two daughters, a woman of a most august presence, being indeed more like one ordained to reign over a kingdom, than for household purposes. The Miss Desmonds were only entering their teens, but they also had no ordinary stamp upon them. What made this party the more particular, was on account of Mr. Desmond, who was supposed to be a united man with the rebels, and it was known his son was deep in their plots ; yet although this was all told to Mr. Cayenne by some of the other Irish ladies who were of the loyal connection, it made no difference with him, but, on the contrary, he acted as if he thought the Desmonds the most of all the refugees entitled to his hospitable civilities. This was a wonderment to our strait-laced narrow lairds, as there was not a man of such strict government principles in the whole country-side as Mr. Cayenne : but he said he carried his political principles only to the camp and the council. ' To the hospital and the prison,' said he, ' I take those of a man '— which was almost a Christian doctrine, and from that declaration Mr. Cayenne and me began again to draw a little more cordially together; although he had still a very imperfect sense of religion, which I attributed to his being born in America, where even as yet, I am told, they have but a scanty sprinkling of grace.

But before concluding this year, I should tell the upshot of the visitation of the Irish, although it did not take place until some time after the peace with France.

In the putting down of the rebels Mr. Desmond and his son made their escape to Paris, where they staid till the Treaty was signed, by which, for several years after the return to Ireland of the grand lady and her daughters, as Mrs. Desmond was called by our commonality, we heard nothing of them. The other refugees repaid Mr. Cayenne his money with thankfulness, and on their restoration to their homes, could not sufficiently express their sense of his kindness. But the silence and seeming ingratitude of the Desmonds vexed him; and he could not abide to hear the Irish rebellion mentioned without flying into a passion against the rebels, which everybody knew was owing to the ill return he had received from that family. However, one afternoon, just about half an hour before his wonted dinner hour, a grand equipage, with four horses and outriders, stopped at his door, and who was in it but Mrs. Desmond and an elderly man, and a young gentleman with an aspect like a lord. It was her husband and son. They had come from Ireland in all their state on purpose to repay with interest the money Mr. Cayenne had counted so long lost, and to express in person the perpetual obligation which he had conferred upon the Desmond family, in all time coming. The lady then told him that she had been so straitened in helping the poor ladies that it was not in her power to make repayment till Desmond, as she called her husband, came home; and not choosing to assign the true reason, lest it might cause trouble, she rather submitted to be suspected of ingratitude than do an improper thing.

Mr. Cayenne was transported with this unexpected return, and a friendship grew up between the families which was afterwards cemented into relationship by the marriage of the young Desmond with Miss Caroline Cayenne. Some in the parish objected to this match, Mrs. Desmond being a papist; but as Miss Caroline had received an Episcopalian education,

I thought it of no consequence, and married them after their family chaplain from Ireland, as a young couple, both by beauty and fortune, well matched, and deserving of all conjugal felicity.

CHAPTER XL

YEAR 1799

My daughter's marriage—Her large portion—Mrs. Malcolm's death.

THERE are but two things to make me remember this year; the first was the marriage of my daughter Janet with the Reverend Dr. Kittleword of Swappington, a match in every way commendable, and on the advice of the third Mrs. Balwhidder, I settled a thousand pounds down, and promised five hundred more at my own death, if I died before my spouse, and a thousand at her death, if she survived me; which was the greatest portion ever minister's daughter had in our country-side. In this year, likewise, I advanced fifteen hundred pounds for my son in a concern in Glasgow,—all was the gathering of that indefatigable engine of industry the second Mrs. Balwhidder, whose talents her successor said were a wonder, when she considered the circumstances in which I had been left at her death, and made out of a narrow stipend.

The other memorable was the death of Mrs. Malcolm. If ever there was a saint on this earth she was surely one. She had been for some time bedfast, having all her days from the date of her widowhood been a tender woman; but no change made any alteration on the Christian contentment of her mind. She bore adversity with an honest pride, she toiled in the day of penury and affliction with thankfulness for her earnings, although ever so little. She bent her head to the Lord in resignation when her first-born fell in battle; nor was she puffed up with vanity when her daughters were married, as it was said, so far above their degree, though they showed it was but into their proper sphere by their demeanour after. She lived to see her second son, the captain, rise into affluence, married, and with a thriving young family; and she had the very great satisfaction, on the last day she was able to go to church, to see her youngest son the clergyman standing in my pulpit, a doctor of divinity, and the placed minister of a richer parish than mine. Well indeed might she have said on that day, ' Lord, let thy servant depart in peace, for mine eyes have seen thy salvation.'

For some time it had been manifest to all who saw her that her latter end was drawing nigh ; and therefore, as I had kept up a correspondence with her daughters, Mrs. Macadam and Mrs. Howard, I wrote them a particular account of her case, which brought them to the clachan. They both came in their own carriages, for Colonel Macadam was now a general, and had succeeded to a great property by an English uncle, his mother's brother ; and Captain Howard, by the death of his father, was also a man, as it was said, with a lord's living. Robert Malcolm, her son the captain, was in the West Indies at the time, but his wife came on the first summons, as did William the minister.

They all arrived about four o'clock in the afternoon, and at seven a message came for me and Mrs. Balwhidder to go over to them, which we did, and found the strangers seated by the heavenly patient's bedside. On my entering she turned her eyes towards me and said, ' Bear witness, sir, that I die thankful for an extraordinary portion of temporal mercies. The heart of my youth was withered like the leaf that is seared with the lightning, but in my children I have received a great indemnification for the sorrows of that trial.' She then requested me to pray, saying, ' No, let it be a thanksgiving. My term is out, and I have nothing more to hope or fear from the good or evil of this world. But I have had much to make me grateful ; therefore, sir, return thanks for the time I have been spared, for the goodness granted so long unto me, and the gentle hand with which the way from this world is smoothed for my passing.'

There was something so sweet and consolatory in the way she said this, that although it moved all present to tears, they were tears without the wonted bitterness of grief. Accordingly, I knelt down and did as she had required, and there was a great stillness while I prayed ; at the conclusion we looked to the bed, but the spirit had in the meantime departed, and there was nothing remaining but the clay tenement.

It was expected by the parish, considering the vast affluence of the daughters, that there would have been a grand funeral, and Mrs. Howard thought it was necessary; but her sister, who had from her youth upward a superior discernment of propriety, said, 'No, as my mother has lived so shall be her end.' Accordingly, everybody of any respect in the clachan was invited to the funeral; but none of the gentry, saving only such as had been numbered among the acquaintance of the deceased. But Mr. Cayenne came unbidden, saying to me, that although he did not know Mrs. Malcolm personally, he had often heard she was an amiable woman, and therefore he thought it a proper compliment to her family, who were out of the parish, to show in what respect she was held among us; for he was a man that would take his own way, and do what he thought was right, heedless alike of blame or approbation.

If, however, the funeral was plain, though respectable, the ladies distributed a liberal sum among the poor families; but before they went away, a silent token of their mother's virtue came to light, which was at once a source of sorrow and pleasure. Mrs. Malcolm was first well provided by the Macadams, afterwards the Howards settled on her an equal annuity, by which she spent her latter days in great comfort. Many a year before, she had repaid Provost Maitland the money he sent her in the day of her utmost distress, and at this period he was long dead, having died of a broken heart at the time of his failure. From that time his widow and her daughters had been in very straitened circumstances, but unknown to all but herself, and HIM from whom nothing is hid, Mrs. Malcolm from time to time had sent them, in a blank letter, an occasional note to the young ladies to buy a gown. After her death, a bank bill for a sum of money, her own savings, was found in her scrutoire, with a note of her own writing pinned to the same, stating, that the amount being more than she had needed for herself, belonged of right to those who had so generously provided for her, but as they were not in want of such a trifle, it would be a token of respect to her memory, if they would give the bill to Mrs. Maitland and her daughters, which was done with a most glad alacrity; and, in the doing of it, the private kindness was brought to light.

Thus ended the history of Mrs. Malcolm, as connected

with our Parish Annals. Her house was sold, and is the same now inhabited by the mill-wright, Mr. Periffery, and a neat house it still is, for the possessor is an Englishman, and the English have an uncommon taste for snod houses and trim gardens; but, at the time it was built, there was not a better in the town, though it's now but of the second class. Yearly we hear both from Mrs. Macadam and her sister, with a five-pound note from each to the poor of the parish, as a token of their remembrance; but they are far off, and were anything ailing me, I suppose the gift will not be continued. As for Captain Malcolm, he has proved, in many ways, a friend to such of our young men as have gone to sea. He has now left it off himself, and settled at London, where he latterly sailed from, and I understand is in a great way as a ship-owner. These things I have thought it fitting to record, and will now resume my historical narration.

CHAPTER XLI

YEAR 1800

Return of an inclination towards political tranquillity—Death of the schoolmistress.

THE same quietude and regularity that marked the progress of the last year continued throughout the whole of this. We sowed and reaped in tranquillity, though the sough of distant war came heavily from a distance. The cotton-mill did well for the company, and there was a sobriety in the minds of the spinners and weavers, which showed that the crisis of their political distemperature was over;—there was something more of the old prudence in men's reflections; and it was plain to me that the elements of reconciliation were coming together throughout the world. The conflagration of the French Revolution was indeed not extinguished, but it was evidently burning out, and their old reverence for the Grand Monarque was beginning to revive among them, though they only called him a Consul. Upon the king's fast I preached on this subject; and when the peace was concluded, I got great credit for my foresight, but there was no merit in't. I had only lived longer than the most of those around me, and had been all my days a close observer of the signs of the times; so that what was lightly called prophecy and prediction, were but a probability that experience had taught me to discern.

In the affairs of the parish, the most remarkable generality (for we had no particular catastrophe) was a great death of old people in the spring. Among others, Miss Sabrina, the schoolmistress, paid the debt of nature, but we could now better spare her than we did her predecessor; for at Cayenneville there was a broken manufacturer's wife, an excellent teacher, and a genteel and modernised woman, who took the better order of children; and Miss Sabrina having been long frail (for she was never stout), a decent and discreet carlin, Mrs. M'Caffie, the widow of a custom-house officer, that was a native of the parish, set up another for plainer work. Her opposition, Miss Sabrina did not mind, but she was sorely displeased at the interloping of Mrs. Pirn at Cayenneville, and some said it helped to kill her—of that, however, I am not so certain, for Dr. Tanzey had told me in the winter, that he thought the sharp winds in March would blow out her candle, as it was burnt to the snuff; accordingly she took her departure from this life, on the twenty-fifth day of that month, after there had, for some days prior, been a most cold and piercing east wind.

Miss Sabrina, who was always an oddity and aping grandeur, it was found, had made a will, leaving her gatherings to her favourites, with all regular formality. To one she bequeathed a gown, to another this, and a third that, and to me, a pair of black silk stockings. I was amazed when I heard this; but judge what I felt, when a pair of old marrowless stockings, darned in the heel, and not whole enough in the legs to make a pair of mittens to Mrs. Balwhidder, were delivered to me by her executor Mr. Caption, the lawyer. Saving, however, this kind of flummery, Miss Sabrina was a harmless creature, and could quote poetry in discourse more glibly than texts of Scripture—her father having spared no pains on her mind; as for her body, it could not be mended; but that was not her fault.

After her death, the Session held a consultation, and we agreed to give the same salary that Miss Sabrina enjoyed to

C.E.Brock
1894

'A pair of old marrowless stockings.'

Mrs. M'Caffie; which angered Mr. Cayenne, who thought it should have been given to the headmistress; and it made him give Mrs. Pirn, out of his own pocket, double the sum. But we considered that the parish funds were for the poor of the parish, and therefore it was our duty to provide for the instruction of the poor children. Saving, therefore, those few notations, I have nothing further to say concerning the topics and progress of this Ann. Dom.

CHAPTER XLII

YEAR 1801

An account of Colin Mavis, who becomes a poet.

IT is often to me very curious food for meditation, that as the parish increased in population, there should have been less cause for matter to record. Things that in former days would have occasioned great discourse and cogitation are forgotten, with the day in which they happen; and there is no longer that searching into personalities which was so much in vogue during the first epoch of my ministry, which I reckon the period before the American war; nor has there been any such germinal changes among us, as those which took place in the second epoch, counting backward from the building of the cotton-mill that gave rise to the town of Cayenneville. But still we were not, even at this era, of which this Ann. Dom. is the beginning, without occasional personality, or an event that deserved to be called a germinal.

Some years before, I had noted among the callans at Mr. Lorimore's school, a long soople laddie, who, like all bairns that grow fast and tall, had but little smeddum. He could not be called a dolt, for he was observant and thoughtful, and given to asking sagacious questions; but there was a sleepiness about him, especially in the kirk, and he gave, as the master said, but little application to his lessons, so that folk thought he would turn out a sort of gaunt-at-the-door, more mindful of meat than work. He was, however, a good-natured lad; and, when I was taking my solitary walks of meditation, I sometimes fell in with him, sitting alone on the brae by the water-side, and sometimes lying on the grass, with his hands under his head, on the sunny green knolls where Mr. Cylindar, the English engineer belonging to the cotton-work, has built the bonny house that he calls Diryhill Cottage. This was when Colin Mavis was a laddie at the school, and when I spoke to him, I was surprised at the discretion of his answers, so that gradually I began to think and say, that there was more about Colin than the neighbours knew. Nothing however, for many a day, came out to his advantage; so that his mother, who was by this time a widow woman, did not well know what to do with him, and folk pitied her heavy handful of such a droud.

By and by, however, it happened that one of the young clerks at the cotton-mill shattered his right-hand thumb by a gun bursting; and, being no longer able to write, was sent into the army to be an ensign, which caused a vacancy in the office; and, through the help of Mr. Cayenne, I got Colin Mavis into the place, where, to the surprise of everybody, he proved a wonderful eydent and active lad, and, from less to more, has come at the head of all the clerks, and deep in the confidentials of his employers. But although this was a great satisfaction to me, and to the widow woman his mother, it somehow was not so much so to the rest of the parish, who seemed, as it were, angry that poor Colin had not proved himself such a dolt as they had expected and foretold.

Among other ways that Colin had of spending his leisure, was that of playing music on an instrument, in which it was said he made a wonderful proficiency; but being long and thin, and of a delicate habit of body, he was obligated to refrain from this recreation; so he betook himself to books, and from reading, he began to try writing; but, as this was done in a corner, nobody jealoused what he was about, till one evening in this year, he came to the manse, and asked a word in private with me. I thought that perhaps he had fallen in with a lass and was come to consult me anent matrimony; but when we were by ourselves, in my study, he took out of his pocket a number of the *Scots Magazine*, and said, ' Sir, you have been long pleased to notice me more than any other body, and when I got this, I could not refrain from bringing it to let you see't. Ye maun ken, sir, that I have been long in secret given to trying my hand at rhyme, and, wishing to ascertain what others thought of my power in that way, I sent, by the post, twa three verses to the *Scots Magazine*, and they have not only inserted them, but placed them in the body of the book, in such a way, that I kenna what to think.' So I looked at the magazine, and read his verses, which were certainly very well made verses, for one who had no regular education. But I said to him, as the Greenock magistrates said to John Wilson, the author of *Clyde*, when they stipulated with him to give up the art, that poem-making was a profane and unprofitable trade, and he would do well to turn his talent to something of more solidity, which he promised to do; but he has since put out a book, whereby he has angered all those that had foretold he would be a do-nae-gude. Thus has our parish walked sidy for sidy with all the national improvements, having an author of its own, and getting a literary character in the ancient and famous republic of letters.

CHAPTER XLIII

YEAR 1802

The political condition of the world felt in the private concerns of individuals—Mr. Cayenne comes to ask my advice, and acts according to it.

'EXPERIENCE teaches fools,' was the first moral apothegm that I wrote in small text, when learning to write at the school, and I have ever since thought it was a very sensible reflection. For assuredly, as year after year has flown away on the swift wings of time, I have found my experience mellowing, and my discernment improving; by which I have, in the afternoon of life, been enabled to foresee what kings and nations would do, by the symptoms manifested within the bounds of the society around me. Therefore, at the beginning of the spring in this Ann. Dom., I had misgivings at the heart, a fluttering in my thoughts, and altogether a strange uneasiness as to the stability of the peace and harmony that was supposed to be founded upon a stedfast foundation between us and the French people. What my fears principally took their rise from was a sort of compliancy, on the part of those in power and authority, to cultivate the old relations and parts between them and the commonalty. It did not appear to me that this proceeded from any known or decided event, for I read the papers at this period daily, but from some general dread and fear, that was begotten, like a vapour, out of the fermentation of all sorts of opinions; most people of any sagacity, thinking that the state of things in France being so much of an antic, poetical, and play-actor-like guise, that it would never obtain that respect, far less that reverence from the world, which is necessary to the maintenance of all beneficial government. The consequence of this was a great distrust between man and man, and an aching restlessness among those who had their bread to bake in the world. Persons possessing the power to provide for their kindred, forcing them, as it were, down the throats of those who were dependent on them in business, a bitter morsel.

But the pith of these remarks chiefly applies to the manufacturing concerns of the new town of Cayenneville, for in the clachan we lived in the lea of the dike, and were more taken up with our own natural rural affairs, and the markets for victual, than the craft of merchandise. The only man interested in business, who walked in a steady manner at his old pace, though he sometimes was seen, being of a spunkie temper, grinding the teeth of vexation, was Mr. Cayenne himself.

One day, however, he came to me at the manse. 'Doctor,' says he, for so he always called me, 'I want your advice. I never choose to trouble others with my private affairs, but there are times when the word of an honest man may do good. I need not tell you, that when I declared myself a Royalist in America, it was at a considerable sacrifice. I have, however, nothing to complain of against government on that score, but I think it damn'd hard that those personal connections, whose interests I preserved, to the detriment of my own, should, in my old age, make such an ungrateful return. By the steps I took prior to quitting America, I saved the property of a great mercantile concern in London. In return for that, they took a share with me, and for me, in the cotton-mill; and being here on the spot as manager, I have both made and saved them money. I have, no doubt, bettered my own fortune in the meantime. Would you believe it, doctor, they have written a letter to me, saying, that they wish to provide for a relation, and requiring me to give up to him a portion of my share in the concern—a pretty sort of providing this, at another man's expense. But I'll be damn'd if I do any such thing. If they want to provide for their friend, let them do so from themselves, and not at my cost. What is your opinion?'

This appeared to me a very weighty concern, and not being versed in mercantile dealing, I did not well know what to say; but I reflected for some time, and then I replied, 'As far, Mr. Cayenne, as my observation has gone in this world, I think that the giffs and the gaffs nearly balance one another; and when they do not, there is a moral defect on the failing side. If a man long gives his labour to his employer, and is paid for that labour, it might be said that both are equal, but I say no. For it's in human nature to be prompt to change; and the employer, having always more in his power than his servant or agent, it seems to me a clear case, that in the course of a number of years, the master of the old servant is the obligated of the two; and, therefore, I say, in the first place, in your case there is no tie or claim, by which you may, in a moral sense, be called upon to submit to the dictates of your London correspondents; but there is a reason, in the nature of the thing and case, by which you may ask a favour from them. So, the advice I would give you would be this, write an answer to their letter, and tell them, that you have no objection to the taking in of a new partner, but you think it would be proper to revise all the copartnery, especially as you have, considering the manner in which you have advanced the business, been of opinion that your share should be considerably enlarged.'

I thought Mr. Cayenne would have louped out of his skin with mirth at this notion, and being a prompt man, he sat down at my scrutoire, and answered the letter which gave him so much uneasiness. No notice was taken of it for some time; but, in the course of a month, he was informed, that it was not considered expedient at that time to make any change in the Company. I thought the old man was gone by himself when he got this letter. He came over instantly in his chariot, from the cotton-mill office to the manse, and swore an oath, by some dreadful name, that I was a Solomon. However, I only mention this to show how experience had instructed me, and as a sample of that sinister provisioning of friends that was going on in the world at this time—all owing, as I do verily believe, to the uncertain state of governments and national affairs.

Besides these generalities, I observed another thing working to effect—mankind read more, and the spirit of reflection and reasoning was more awake than at any time within my remembrance. Not only was there a handsome bookseller's shop in Cayenneville, with a London newspaper daily, but magazines, and reviews, and other new publications.

Till this year, when a chaise was wanted, we had to send to Irville ; but Mr. Toddy of the Cross Keys being in at Glasgow, he bought an excellent one at the second hand, a portion of the effects of a broken merchant, by which, from that period, we had one of our own ; and it proved a great convenience, for I, who never but twice in my life before hired that kind of commodity, had it thrice during the summer, for a bit jaunt with Mrs. Balwhidder, to divers places and curiosities in the county, that I had not seen before, by which our ideas were greatly enlarged ; indeed, I have always had a partiality for travelling, as one of the best means of opening the faculty of the mind, and giving clear and correct notions of men and things.

CHAPTER XLIV

YEAR 1803

Fear of an invasion—Raising of volunteers in the parish—The young
ladies embroider a stand of colours for the regiment.

DURING the tempestuous times that ensued, from the death of the King of France, by the hands of the executioner, in 1793, there had been a political schism among my people that often made me very uneasy. The folk belonging to the cotton-mill, and the muslin-weavers in Cayenneville, were afflicted with the itch of Jacobinism, but those of the village were staunch and true to king and country ; and some of the heritors were desirous to make volunteers of the young men of them, in case of anything like the French anarchy and confusion rising on the side of the manufacturers. I, however, set myself, at that time, against this, for I foresaw that the French business was but a fever which would soon pass off, but no man could tell the consequence of putting arms in the hands of neighbour against neighbour, though it was but in the way of policy.

But when Bonaparte gathered his host fornent the English coast, and the government at London were in terror of their lives for an invasion, all in the country saw that there was danger, and I was not backward in sounding the trumpet to battle. For a time, however, there was a diffidence among us somewhere. The gentry had a distrust of the manufacturers, and the farming lads were wud with impatience, that those who should be their leaders would not come forth. I, knowing this, prepared a sermon suitable to the occasion, giving out from the pulpit myself, the Sabbath before preaching it, that it was my intent on the next Lord's day to deliver a religious and political exhortation on the present posture of public affairs. This drew a vast congregation of all ranks.

I trow that the stoor had no peace in the stuffing of the pulpit in that day, and the effect was very great and speedy, for next morning the weavers and cotton-mill folk held a meeting, and they, being skilled in the ways of committees and associating together, had certain resolutions prepared, by which a select few was appointed to take an enrolment of all willing in the parish to serve as volunteers in defence of their king and country, and to concert with certain gentlemen named therein, about the formation of a corps, of which, it was an understood thing, the said gentlemen were to be the officers. The whole of this business was managed with the height of discretion, and the weavers, and spinners, and farming lads vied with one another who should be first on the list. But that which the most surprised me, was the wonderful sagacity of the committee in naming the gentlemen that should be the officers. I could not have made a better choice myself, for they were the best built, the best bred, and the best natured in the parish. In short, when I saw the bravery that was in my people, and the spirit of wisdom by which it was directed, I said in my heart, The Lord of Hosts is with us, and the adversary shall not prevail.

The number of valiant men which at that time placed themselves around the banners of their country was so great, that the government would not accept of all who offered; so, like as in other parishes, we were obligated to make a selection, which was likewise done in a most judicious manner, all men above a certain age being reserved for the defence of the parish, in the day when the young might be called to England, to fight the enemy.

When the corps was formed, and the officers named, they made me their chaplain, and Dr. Marigold their doctor. He was a little man with a big belly, and was as crouse as a bantam cock; but it was not thought he could do so well in field exercises, on which account he was made the doctor, although he had no repute in that capacity, in comparison with Dr. Tanzey, who was not however liked, being a stiff-mannered man, with a sharp temper.

All things having come to a proper head, the young ladies of the parish resolved to present the corps with a stand of colours, which they embroidered themselves, and a day was fixed for the presentation of the same. Never was such a day seen in Dalmailing. The sun shone brightly on that scene of bravery and grandeur, and far and near the country folk came flocking in, and we had the regimental band of music hired from the soldiers that were in Ayr barracks. The very first sound o't made the hair on my old grey head to prickle up, and my blood to rise and glow, as if youth was coming again into my veins.

Sir Hugh Montgomery was the commandant, and he came in all the glory of war, on his best horse, and marched at the head of the men, to the green-head. The doctor and me were the rearguard: not being able, on account of my age, and his fatness, to walk so fast as the quick-step of the corps. On the field we took our place in front, near Sir Hugh and the ladies with the colours; and, after some salutations, according to the fashion of the army, Sir Hugh made a speech to the men, and then Miss Maria Montgomery came forward, with her sister Miss Eliza, and the other ladies, and the banners were unfurled, all glittering with gold, and the king's arms in needlework. Miss Maria then made a speech, which she had got by heart, but she was so agitated, that it was said she forgot the best part of it; however, it was very well considering. When this was done, I then stepped forward, and laying my hat on the ground, every man and boy taking off theirs, I said a prayer, which I had conned most carefully, and which I thought the most suitable I could devise, in unison with Christian principles, which are averse to the shedding of blood; and I particularly dwelt upon some of the specialities of our situation.

When I had concluded, the volunteers gave three great shouts, and the multitude answered them to the same tune, and all the instruments of music sounded, making such a bruit, as could not be surpassed for grandeur—a long and very circumstantial account of all which may be read in the newspapers of that time.

The volunteers, at the word of command, then showed us the way they were to fight with the French, in the doing of which a sad disaster happened; for when they were charging bayonets, they came towards us like a flood, and all the spectators ran, and I ran, and the doctor ran, but being laden with his belly, he could not run fast enough, so he lay down, and being just before me at the time, I tumbled over him, and such a shout of laughter shook the field as was never heard.

When the fatigues of the day were at an end, we marched to the cotton-mill, where, in one of the warehouses, a vast table was spread, and a dinner, prepared at Mr. Cayenne's own expense, sent in from the Cross Keys, and the whole corps, with many of the gentry of the neighbourhood, dined with great jollity, the band of music playing beautiful airs all the time. At night, there was a universal dance, gentle and semple mingled together. All which made it plain to me, that the Lord, by this unison of spirit, had decreed our national preservation; but I kept this in my own breast, lest it might have the effect to relax the vigilance of the kingdom. And I should note, that Colin Mavis, the poetical lad, of whom I have spoken in another part, made a song for this occasion, that was very mightily thought of, having in it a nerve of valiant genius, that kindled the very souls of those that heard it.

'So he lay down, and I tumbled over him.'

CHAPTER XLV

YEAR 1804

The Session agrees that church censures shall be commuted with fines—
Our parish has an opportunity of seeing a turtle, which is sent to Mr.
Cayenne—Some fears of popery—Also about a preacher of universal
redemption—Report of a French ship appearing in the west, which
sets the volunteers astir.

IN conformity with the altered fashions of the age, in this year
the Session came to an understanding with me, that we should
not inflict the common church censures for such as made
themselves liable thereto; but we did not formally promulge
our resolution as to this, wishing as long as possible to keep
the deterring rod over the heads of the young and thoughtless.
Our motive, on the one hand, was the disregard of the manufacturers in Cayenneville, who were, without the breach of
truth, an irreligious people, and, on the other, a desire to
preserve the ancient and wholesome admonitory and censorian
jurisdiction of the minister and elders. We therefore laid it
down as a rule to ourselves, that, in the case of transgressions
on the part of the inhabitants of the new district of Cayenneville, we should subject them rigorously to a fine; but that for
the farming lads, we would put it in their option to pay the
fine, or stand in the kirk.

We conformed also in another matter to the times, by consenting to baptize occasionally in private houses. Hitherto it
had been a strict rule with me only to baptize from the pulpit.
Other parishes, however, had long been in the practice of this
relaxation of ancient discipline.

But all this on my part was not done without compunction of
spirit; for I was of opinion, that the principle of Presbyterian
integrity should have been maintained to the uttermost.
Seeing, however, the elders set on an alteration, I distrusted my
own judgment, and yielded myself to the considerations that
weighed with them; for they were true men, and of a godly
honesty, and took the part of the poor in all contentions with the
heritors, often to the hazard and damage of their own temporal
welfare. .

I have now to note a curious thing, not on account of its importance, but to show to what lengths a correspondence had been opened in the parish with the farthest parts of the earth. Mr. Cayenne got a turtle-fish sent to him from a Glasgow merchant, and it was living when it came to the Wheatrig House, and was one of the most remarkable beasts that had ever been seen in our country-side. It weighed as much as a well-fed calf, and had three kinds of meat in its body, fish, flesh, and fowl, and it had four water-wings, for they could not be properly called fins; but what was little short of a miracle about the creature, happened after the head was cutted off, when, if a finger was offered to it, it would open its mouth and snap at it, and all this after the carcase was divided for dressing.

Mr. Cayenne made a feast on the occasion to many of the neighbouring gentry, to the which I was invited, and we drank lime-punch as we ate the turtle, which, as I understand, is the fashion in practice among the Glasgow West Indy merchants, who are famed as great hands with turtles and lime-punch. But it is a sort of food that I should not like to fare long upon. I was not right the next day; and I have heard it said, that, when eaten too often, it has a tendency to harden the heart and make it crave for greater luxuries.

But the story of the turtle is nothing to that of the Mass, which, with all its mummeries and abominations, was brought into Cayenneville by an Irish priest of the name of Father O'Grady, who was confessor to some of the poor deluded Irish labourers about the new houses and the cotton-mill. How he had the impudence to set up that memento of Satan, the crucifix, within my parish and jurisdiction, was what I never could get to the bottom of; but the soul was shaken within me, when, on the Monday after, one of the elders came to the manse, and told me, that the old dragon of Popery, with its seven heads and ten horns, had been triumphing in Cayenneville on the foregoing Lord's day! I lost no time in convening the Session to see what was to be done; much, however, to my surprise, the elders recommended no step to be taken, but only a zealous endeavour to greater Christian excellence on our part, by which we should put the beast and his worshippers to shame and flight. I am free to confess, that, at the time, I did not think this the wisest counsel which they might have given; for, in the heat of my alarm, I was for attacking the

'*Mr. Cayenne got a turtle-fish sent to him.*'

enemy in his camp. But they prudently observed, that the days of religious persecution were past, and it was a comfort to see mankind cherishing any sense of religion at all, after the vehement infidelity that had been sent abroad by the French Republicans; and to this opinion, now that I have had years to sift its wisdom, I own myself a convert and proselyte.

Fortunately, however, for my peace of mind, there proved to be but five Roman Catholics in Cayenneville; and Father O'Grady, not being able to make a living there, packed up his Virgin Marys, saints, and painted Agnuses in a portmanteau, and went off in the Ayr Fly one morning for Glasgow, where I hear he has since met with all the encouragement that might be expected from the ignorant and idolatrous inhabitants of that great city.

Scarcely were we well rid of Father O'Grady, when another interloper entered the parish. He was more dangerous, in the opinion of the Session, than even the Pope of Rome himself; for he came to teach the flagrant heresy of Universal Redemption, a most consolatory doctrine to the sinner that is loth to repent, and who loves to troll his iniquity like a sweet morsel under his tongue. Mr. Martin Siftwell, who was the last ta'en on elder, and who had received a liberal and judicious education, and was, moreover, naturally possessed of a quick penetration, observed, in speaking of this new doctrine, that the grossest papist sinner might have some qualms of fear after he had bought the Pope's pardon, and might thereby be led to a reformation of life; but that the doctrine of universal redemption was a bribe to commit sin, the wickedest mortal, according to it, being only liable to a few thousand years, more or less, of suffering, which, compared with eternity, was but a momentary pang, like having a tooth drawn for the toothache. Mr. Siftwell is a shrewd and clear-seeing man in points of theology, and I would trust a great deal to what he says, as I have not, at my advanced age, such a mind for the kittle crudities of polemical investigation that I had in my younger years, especially when I was a student in the Divinity Hall of Glasgow.

It will be seen from all I have herein recorded, that, in the course of this year, there was a general resuscitation of religious sentiments; for what happened in my parish was but a type and index to the rest of the world. We had, however, one memorable that must stand by itself; for although neither death nor bloodshed happened, yet was it cause of the fear of both.

A rumour reached us from the Clyde, that a French man-of-war had appeared in a Highland loch, and that all the Greenock volunteers had embarked in merchant-vessels to bring her in for a prize. Our volunteers were just jumping and yowling, like chained dogs, to be at her too; but the colonel, Sir Hugh, would do nothing without orders from his superiors. Mr. Cayenne, though an aged man, above seventy, was as bold as a lion, and came forth in the old garb of an American huntsman, like, as I was told, a Robin Hood in the play is; and it was just a sport to see him, feckless man, trying to march so crously with his lean, shaking hands. But the whole affair proved a false alarm, and our men, when they heard it, were as well pleased that they had been constrained to sleep in their warm beds at home, instead of lying on coils of cables, like the gallant Greenock sharp-shooters.

CHAPTER XLVI

YEAR 1805

Retrenchment of the extravagant expenses usual at burials—I use an expedient for putting even the second service out of fashion.

FOR some time I had meditated a reformation in the parish, and this year I carried the same into effect. I had often noticed with concern, that, out of a mistaken notion of paying respect to the dead, my people were wont to go to great lengths at their burials, and dealt round shortbread and sugar biscuit, with wine and other confections, as if there had been no ha'd in their hands; which straitened many a poor family, making the dispensation of the Lord a heavier temporal calamity than it should naturally have been. Accordingly, on consulting with Mrs. Balwhidder, who has a most judicious judgment, it was thought that my interference would go a great way to lighten the evil. I therefore advised with those whose friends were taken from them, not to make that amplitude of preparation which used to be the fashion, nor to continue handing about as long as the folk would take, but only at the very most to go no more than three times round with the service. Objections were made to this, as if it would be thought mean; but I put on a stern visage, and told them, that if they did more I would rise up and rebuke and forbid the extravagance. So three services became the uttermost modicum at all burials. This was doing much, but it was not all that I wished to do.

I considered that the best reformations are those which proceed step by step, and stop at that point where the consent to what has been established becomes general; and so I governed myself, and therefore interfered no farther; but I was determined to set an example. Accordingly, at the very next draigie, after I partook of one service, I made a bow to the servitors and they passed on, but all before me had partaken of the second service; some, however, of those after me did as I did, so I foresaw that in a quiet canny way I would bring in the fashion of being satisfied with one service. I therefore, from that time, always took my place as near as possible to the door, where the chief mourner sat, and made a point of nodding away the second service, which has now grown into a custom, to the great advantage of surviving relations.

But in this reforming business I was not altogether pleased with our poet; for he took a pawkie view of my endeavours, and indited a ballad on the subject, in the which he makes a clattering carlin describe what took place, so as to turn a very solemn matter into a kind of derision. When he brought his verse and read it to me, I told him that I thought it was overly natural; for I could not find another term to designate the cause of the dissatisfaction that I had with it; but Mrs. Balwhidder said that it might help my plan if it were made public, so upon her advice we got some of Mr. Lorimore's best writers to make copies of it for distribution, which was not without fruit and influence. But a sore thing happened at the very next burial. As soon as the nodding away of the second service began, I could see that the gravity of the whole meeting was discomposed, and some of the irreverent young chiels almost broke out into even-down laughter, which vexed me exceedingly. Mrs. Balwhidder, howsoever, comforted me by saying, that custom in time would make it familiar, and by and by the thing would pass as a matter of course, until one service would be all that folk would offer; and truly the thing is coming to that, for only two services are now handed round, and the second is regularly nodded by.

CHAPTER XLVII

YEAR 1806

The deathbed behaviour of Mr. Cayenne—A schism in the parish, and a subscription to build a meeting-house.

MR. CAYENNE of Wheatrig having for several years been in a declining way, partly brought on by the consuming fire of his furious passion, and partly by the decay of old age, sent for me on the evening of the first Sabbath of March in this year. I was surprised at the message, and went to the Wheatrig House directly, where, by the lights in the windows as I gaed up through the policy to the door, I saw something extraordinary was going on. Sambo, the blackamoor servant, opened the door, and without speaking shook his head; for he was an affectionate creature, and as fond of his master as if he had been his own father. By this sign I guessed that the old gentleman was thought to be drawing near his latter end, so I walked softly after Sambo up the stair, and was shown into the chamber where Mr. Cayenne, since he had been confined to the house, usually sat. His wife had been dead some years before.

Mr. Cayenne was sitting in his easy-chair, with a white cotton night-cap on his head, and a pillow at his shoulders to keep him straight. But his head had fallen down on his breast, and he breathed like a panting baby. His legs were swelled, and his feet rested on a footstool. His face, which was wont to be the colour of a peony rose, was of a yellow hue, with a patch of red on each cheek like a wafer, and his nose was shirpit and sharp, and of an unnatural purple. Death was evidently fighting with Nature for the possession of

173

the body. 'Heaven have mercy on his soul,' said I to myself, as I sat down beside him.

When I had been seated some time, the power was given him to raise his head as it were ajee, and he looked at me with the tail of his eye, which I saw was glittering and glassy. 'Doctor,' for he always called me doctor, though I am not of that degree, 'I am glad to see you,' were his words, uttered with some difficulty.

'How do you find yourself, sir?' I replied in a sympathising manner.

'Damned bad,' said he, as if I had been the cause of his suffering. I was daunted to the very heart to hear him in such an unregenerate state; but after a short pause I addressed myself to him again, saying, that 'I hoped he would soon be more at ease, and he should bear in mind that the Lord chasteneth whom He loveth.'

'The devil take such love,' was his awful answer, which was to me as a blow on the forehead with a mell. However, I was resolved to do my duty to the miserable sinner, let him say what he would. Accordingly, I stooped towards him with my hands on my knees, and said in a compassionate voice, 'It's very true, sir, that you are in great agony, but the goodness of God is without bound.'

'Curse me if I think so, doctor,' replied the dying uncircumcised Philistine. But he added at whiles, his breathlessness being grievous, and often broken by a sore hiccup, 'I am, however, no saint, as you know, doctor; so I wish you to put in a word for me, doctor; for you know that in these times, doctor, it is the duty of every good subject to die a Christian.'

This was a poor account of the state of his soul, but it was plain I could make no better o't by entering into any religious discourse or controversy with him, he being then in the last gasp; so I knelt down and prayed for him with great sincerity, imploring the Lord, as an awakening sense of grace to the dying man, that it would please Him to lift up, though it were but for the season of a minute, the chastening hand which was laid so heavily upon His aged servant; at which Mr. Cayenne, as if indeed the hand had been then lifted, cried out, 'None of that stuff, doctor; you know that I cannot call myself His servant.'

C.E. Brock

'*I knelt down and prayed for him with great sincerity.*'

Was ever a minister in his prayer so broken in upon by a perishing sinner! However, I had the weight of a duty upon me, and made no reply, but continued, 'Thou hearest, O Lord! how he confesses his unworthiness. Let not Thy compassion, therefore, be withheld, but verify to him the words that I have spoken in faith, of the boundlessness of Thy goodness, and the infinite multitude of Thy tender mercies.' I then calmly, but sadly, sat down, and presently, as if my prayer had been heard, relief was granted; for Mr. Cayenne raised his head, and, giving me a queer look, said, 'That last clause of your petition, doctor, was well put, and I think, too, it has been granted, for I am easier,'—adding, 'I have no doubt, doctor, given much offence in the world, and oftenest when I meant to do good; but I have wilfully injured no man, and as God is my judge, and His goodness, you say, is so great, He may, perhaps, take my soul into His holy keeping.' In saying which words, Mr. Cayenne dropped his head upon his breast, his breathing ceased, and he was wafted away out of this world with as little trouble as a blameless baby.

This event soon led to a change among us. In the settling of Mr. Cayenne's affairs in the Cotton-mill Company, it was found that he had left such a power of money, that it was needful to the concern, in order that they might settle with the doers under his testament, to take in other partners. By this Mr. Speckle came to be a resident in the parish, he having taken up a portion of Mr. Cayenne's share. He likewise took a tack of the house and policy of Wheatrig. But although Mr. Speckle was a far more conversible man than his predecessor, and had a wonderful plausibility in business, the affairs of the Company did not thrive in his hands. Some said this was owing to his having ower many irons in the fire; others, to the circumstances of the times; in my judgment, however, both helped; but the issue belongs to the events of another year. In the meanwhile, I should here note, that in the course of this current Ann. Dom. it pleased Heaven to visit me with a severe trial, the nature of which I will here record at length—the upshot I will make known hereafter.

From the planting of inhabitants in the cotton-mill town of Cayenneville, or, as the country folk, not used to such lang-nebbit words, now call it, Canaille, there had come in upon the parish various sectarians among the weavers, some of whom were not satisfied with the Gospel as I preached it, and endeavoured to practise it in my walk and conversation ; and they began to speak of building a kirk for themselves, and of getting a minister that would give them the Gospel more to their own ignorant fancies. I was exceedingly wroth and disturbed when the thing was first mentioned to me ; and I very earnestly, from the pulpit, next Lord's day, lectured on the growth of new-fangled doctrines ; which, however, instead of having the wonted effect of my discourses, set up the theological weavers in a bleeze, and the very Monday following they named a committee to raise money by subscription to build a meeting-house. This was the first overt act of insubordination collectively manifested in the parish ; and it was conducted with all that crafty dexterity, with which the infidel and Jacobin spirit of the French Revolution had corrupted the honest simplicity of our good old hameward fashions. In the course of a very short time, the Canaille folk had raised a large sum, and seduced not a few of my people into their schism, by which they were enabled to set about building their kirk ; the foundations thereof were not, however, laid till the following year, but their proceedings gave me a het heart, for they were like an open rebellion to my authority, and a contemptuous disregard of that religious allegiance which is due from the flock to the pastor.

On Christmas day the wind broke off the main arm of our Adam and Eve pear-tree, and I grieved for it more as a type and sign of the threatened partition, than on account of the damage, though the fruit was the juiciest in all the countryside.

CHAPTER XLVIII

YEAR 1807

Numerous marriages—Account of a pay-wedding, made to set up a shop.

THIS was a year to me of satisfaction, in many points, for a greater number of my younger flock married in it, than had done for any one of ten years prior. They were chiefly the

offspring of the marriages that took place at the close of the
American war; and I was pleased to see the duplification of
well-doing, as I think marrying is, having always considered
the command to increase and multiply, a holy ordinance,
which the circumstances of this world but too often interfere
to prevent.

It was also made manifest to me, that in this year there
was a very general renewal in the hearts of men, of a sense
of the utility, even in earthly affairs, of a religious life: in
some, I trust it was more than prudence, and really a birth
of grace. Whether this was owing to the upshot of the
French Revolution, all men being pretty well satisfied in their
minds that uproar and rebellion make but an ill way of
righting wrongs, or that the swarm of unruly youth, the offspring, as I have said, of the marriages after the American
war, had grown sobered from their follies, and saw things in
a better light, I cannot take upon me to say. But it was
very edifying to me, their minister, to see several lads, who
had been both wild and free in their principles, marrying with
sobriety, and taking their wives to the kirk, with the comely
decorum of heads of families.

But I was now growing old and could go seldomer out
among my people than in former days, so that I was less a
partaker of their ploys and banquets, either at birth, bridal,
or burial. I heard, however, all that went on at them, and
I made it a rule, after giving the blessing at the end of the
ceremony, to admonish the bride and bridegroom to ca' canny,
and join trembling with their mirth. It behoved me on one
occasion, however, to break through a rule, that age and
frailty had imposed upon me, and to go to the wedding of
Tibby Banes, the daughter of the betherel, because she had
once been a servant in the manse, besides the obligation upon
me from her father's part, both in the kirk and kirkyard.
Mrs. Balwhidder went with me, for she liked to countenance
the pleasantries of my people; and, over and above all, it
was a pay-wedding, in order to set up the bridegroom in a
shop.

There was, to be sure, a great multitude, gentle and semple,
of all denominations, with two fiddles and a bass, and the
volunteers' fife and drum, and the jollity that went on was a
perfect feast of itself, though the wedding-supper was a prodigy

of abundance. The auld carles kecklet with fainness, as they
saw the young dancers; and the carlins sat on forms, as
mim as May puddocks, with their shawls pinned apart, to
show their muslin napkins. But, after supper, when they had
got a glass of the punch, their heels showed their mettle,
and grannies danced with their oyes, holding out their hands
as if they had been spinning with two rocks. I told Colin
Mavis, the poet, that an *Infare* was a fine subject for his
muse, and soon after he indited an excellent ballad under
that title, which he projects to publish with other ditties by
subscription; and I have no doubt a liberal and discerning
public will give him all manner of encouragement, for that
is the food of talent of every kind, and without cheering, no
one can say what an author's faculty naturally is.

CHAPTER XLIX

YEAR 1808

Failure of Mr. Speckle, the proprietor of the cotton-mill—The melancholy
end of one of the overseers and his wife.

THROUGH all the wars that have raged from the time of the
king's accession to the throne, there has been a gradually
coming nearer and nearer to our gates, which is a very alarming thing to think of. In the first, at the time he came to
the crown, we suffered nothing. Not one belonging to the
parish was engaged in the battles thereof, and the news of
victories, before they reached us, which was generally by
word of mouth, were old tales. In the American war, as I
have related at length, we had an immediate participation,
but those that suffered were only a few individuals, and the
evil was done at a distance, and reached us not until the
worst of its effects were spent. And during the first term
of the present just and necessary contest for all that is dear
to us as a people, although, by the offswarming of some of
our restless youth, we had our part and portion in common
with the rest of the Christian world; yet still there was at
home a great augmentation of prosperity, and everything had

179

thriven in a surprising manner; somewhat, however, to the detriment of our country simplicity. By the building of the cotton-mill, and the rising up of the new town of Cayenneville, we had intromitted so much with concerns of trade, that we were become a part of the great web of commercial reciprocities, and felt in our corner and extremity every touch or stir that was made on any part of the texture. The consequence of this I have now to relate.

Various rumours had been floating about the business of the cotton manufacturers not being so lucrative as it had been; and Bonaparte, as it is well known, was a perfect limb of Satan against our prosperity, having recourse to the most wicked means and purposes to bring ruin upon us as a nation. His cantrips, in this year, began to have a dreadful effect.

For some time it had been observed in the parish, that Mr. Speckle, of the cotton-mill, went very often to Glasgow, and was sometimes off at a few minutes' warning to London, and the neighbours began to guess and wonder at what could be the cause of all this running here, and riding there, as if the littlegude was at his heels. Sober folk augured ill o't; and it was remarked, likewise, that there was a haste and confusion in his mind, which betokened a foretaste of some change of fortune. At last, in the fulness of time, the babe was born.

On a Saturday night, Mr. Speckle came out late from Glasgow; on the Sabbath he was with all his family at the kirk, looking as a man that had changed his way of life; and on the Monday, when the spinners went to the mill, they were told that the company had stopped payment. Never did a thunder-clap daunt the heart like this news, for the bread in a moment was snatched from more than a thousand mouths. It was a scene not to be described, to see the cotton-spinners and the weavers, with their wives and children, standing in bands along the road, all looking and speaking as if they had lost a dear friend or parent. For my part, I could not bear the sight, but hid myself in my closet, and prayed to the Lord to mitigate a calamity, which seemed to me past the capacity of man to remedy; for what could our parish fund do in the way of helping a whole town, thus suddenly thrown out of bread.

In the evening, however, I was strengthened, and convened the elders at the manse to consult with them on what was best to be done, for it was well known that the sufferers had made no provision for a sore foot. But all our gathered judgments could determine nothing ; and therefore we resolved to wait the issue, not doubting but that HE who sends the night, would bring the day in His good and gracious time, which so fell out. Some of them who had the largest experience of such vicissitudes, immediately began to pack up their ends and their awls, and to hie them into Glasgow and Paisley in quest of employ ; but those who trusted to the hopes that Mr. Speckle himself still cherished, lingered long, and were obligated to submit to sore distress. After a time, however, it was found that the company was ruined, and the mill being sold for the benefit of the creditors, it was bought by another Glasgow company, who, by getting it a good bargain, and managing well, have it still, and have made it again a blessing to the country. At the time of the stoppage, however, we saw that commercial prosperity, flush as it might be, was but a perishable commodity, and from thence, both by public discourse and private exhortation, I have recommended to the workmen to lay up something for a reverse ; and showed that, by doing with their bawbees and pennies, what the great do with their pounds, they might in time get a pose to help them in the day of need. This advice they have followed, and made up a Savings Bank, which is a pillow of comfort to many an industrious head of a family.

But I should not close this account of the disaster that befell Mr. Speckle, and the cotton-mill company, without relating a very melancholy case that was the consequence. Among the overseers there was a Mr. Dwining, an Englishman from Manchester, where he had seen better days, having had himself there of his own property, once as large a mill, according to report, as the Cayenneville mill. He was certainly a man above the common, and his wife was a lady in every point ; but they held themselves by themselves, and shunned all manner of civility, giving up their whole attention to their two little boys, who were really like creatures of a better race than the callans of our clachan.

On the failure of the company, Mr. Dwining was observed by those who were present to be particularly distressed : his salary being his all ; but he said little, and went thoughtfully home. Some days after he was seen walking by himself with a pale face, a heavy eye, and slow step—all tokens of a sorrowful heart. Soon after he was missed altogether ; nobody saw him. The door of his house was however open, and his two pretty boys were as lively as usual, on the green before the door. I happened to pass when they were there, and I asked them how their father and mother were. They said they were still in bed, and would no waken, and the innocent lambs took me by the hand, to make me waken their parents. I know not what was in it, but I trembled from head to foot, and I was led in by the babies, as if I had not the power to resist. Never shall I forget what I saw in that bed . . .

.　　　.　　　.　　　.　　　.

I found a letter on the table ; and I came away, locking the door behind me, and took the lovely prattling orphans home. I could but shake my head and weep, as I gave them to the care of Mrs. Balwhidder, and she was terrified but said nothing. I then read the letter. It was to send the bairns to a gentleman, their uncle, in London. Oh it is a terrible tale, but the winding-sheet and the earth is over it. I sent for two of my elders. I related what I had seen. Two coffins were got, and the bodies laid in them ; and the next day, with one of the fatherless bairns in each hand, I followed them to the grave, which was dug in that part of the kirkyard where unchristened babies are laid. We durst not take it upon us to do more, but few knew the reason, and some thought it was because the deceased were strangers, and had no regular lair.

I dressed the two bonny orphans in the best mourning at my own cost, and kept them in the manse till we could get an answer from their uncle, to whom I sent their father's letter. It stung him to the quick, and he came down all the way from London, and took the children away himself. Oh he was a vext man when the beautiful bairns, on being told he was their uncle, ran into his arms, and complained that their papa and mamma had slept so long, that they would never waken.

CHAPTER L

YEAR 1809

Opening of a meeting-house—The elders come to the manse,
and offer me a helper.

AS I come towards the events of these latter days, I am
surprised to find myself not at all so distinct in my recollection
of them, as in those of the first of my ministry; being apt to
confound the things of one occasion with those of another,
which Mrs. Balwhidder says is an admonishment to me to
leave off my writing. But, please God, I will endeavour to
fulfil this as I have through life tried, to the best of my
capacity, to do every other duty; and with the help of Mrs.
Balwhidder, who has·a very clear understanding, I think I
may get through my task in a creditable manner, which is all
I aspire after; not writing for a vain world, but only to testify
to posterity anent the great changes that have happened in
my day and generation—a period which all the best-informed
writers say, has not had its match in the history of the world
since the beginning of time.

By the failure of the cotton-mill company, whose affairs
were not settled till the spring of this year, there was great
suffering during the winter; but my people, those that still
adhered to the establishment, bore their share of the dispensation with meekness and patience, nor was there wanting
edifying monuments of resignation even among the stray-
vaggers.

On the day that the Canaille Meeting-house was opened,
which was in the summer, I was smitten to the heart to see
the empty seats that were in my kirk, for all the thoughtless,
and some that I had a better opinion of, went to hear the
opening discourse. Satan that day had power given to him to
buffet me as he did Job of old; and when I looked around
and saw the empty seats, my corruption rose, and I forgot
myself in the remembering prayer; for when I prayed for all
denominations of Christians, and worshippers, and infidels, I
could not speak of the schismatics with patience, but entreated

the Lord to do with the hobbleshow at Cayenneville as He saw meet in His displeasure, the which, when I came afterwards to think upon, I grieved at with a sore contrition.

In the course of the week following, the elders, in a body, came to me in the manse, and after much commendation of my godly ministry, they said, that seeing I was now growing old, they thought they could not testify their respect for me in a better manner, than by agreeing to get me a helper. But I would not at that time listen to such a proposal, for I felt no falling off in my powers of preaching ; on the contrary, I found myself growing better at it, as I was enabled to hold forth, in an easy manner, often a whole half-hour longer than I could do a dozen years before. Therefore nothing was done in this year anent my resignation ; but during the winter, Mrs. Balwhidder was often grieved, in the bad weather, that I should preach, and, in short, so worked upon my affections, that I began to think it was fitting for me to comply with the advice of my friends. Accordingly, in the course of the winter, the elders began to cast about for a helper, and during the bleak weather in the ensuing spring, several young men spared me from the necessity of preaching. But this relates to the concerns of the next and last year of my ministry. So I will now proceed to give an account of it, very thankful that I have been permitted, in unmolested tranquillity, to bring my history to such a point.

CHAPTER LI

YEAR 1810

Conclusion—I repair to the church for the last time—Afterwards receive a silver server from the parishioners—And still continue to marry and baptize.

My tasks are all near a close ; and in writing this final record of my ministry, the very sound of my pen admonishes me that my life is a burden on the back of flying Time, that he will soon be obliged to lay down in his great storehouse, the grave. Old age has, indeed, long warned me to prepare for rest, and the darkened windows of my sight show that the night is coming on, while deafness, like a door fast barred, has shut

'*The elders, in a body, came to me in the manse.*'
Copyright 1895 by Macmillan & Co.

out all the pleasant sounds of this world, and inclosed me, as it were, in a prison, even from the voices of my friends.

I have lived longer than the common lot of man, and I have seen, in my time, many mutations and turnings, and ups and downs, notwithstanding the great spread that has been in our national prosperity. I have beheld them that were flourishing like the green bay trees, made desolate, and their branches scattered. But, in my own estate, I have had a large and liberal experience of goodness.

At the beginning of my ministry I was reviled and rejected, but my honest endeavours to prove a faithful shepherd were blessed from on high, and rewarded with the affection of my flock. Perhaps, in the vanity of doting old age, I thought in this there was a merit due to myself, which made the Lord to send the chastisement of the Canaille schism among my people, for I was then wroth without judgment, and by my heat hastened into an open division the flaw that a more considerate manner might have healed. But I confess my fault, and submit my cheek to the smiter ; and now I see that the finger of Wisdom was in that probation, and it was far better that the weavers meddled with the things of God, which they could not change, than with those of the king, which they could only harm. In that matter, however, I was like our gracious monarch in the American war ; for though I thereby lost the pastoral allegiance of a portion of my people, in like manner as he did of his American subjects ; yet, after the separation, I was enabled so to deport myself, that they showed me many voluntary testimonies of affectionate respect, and which it would be a vainglory in me to rehearse here. One thing I must record, because it is as much to their honour as it is to mine.

When it was known that I was to preach my last sermon, every one of those who had been my hearers, and who had seceded to the Canaille meeting, made it a point that day to be in the parish kirk, and to stand in the crowd, that made a lane of reverence for me to pass from the kirk door to the back-yett of the manse. And shortly after a deputation of all their brethren, with their minister at their head, came to me one morning, and presented to me a server of silver, in token, as they were pleased to say, of their esteem for my blameless life, and the charity that I had practised towards the poor of all sects in the neighbourhood ; which is set forth in a well-penned inscription, written by a weaver lad that works for his daily bread. Such a thing would have been a prodigy at the beginning of my ministry, but the progress of book-learning and education has been wonderful since, and with it has come a spirit of greater liberality than the world knew before, bringing men of adverse principles and doctrines into a more humane communion with each other, showing, that it's by the mollifying influence of knowledge, the time will come to pass, when the tiger of papistry shall lie down with the lamb of reformation, and the vultures of prelacy be as harmless as the presbyterian doves; when the independent, the anabaptist, and every other order and denomination of Christians, not forgetting even those poor wee wrens of the Lord, the burghers and anti-burghers, who will pick from the hand of patronage, and dread no snare.

On the next Sunday, after my farewell discourse, I took the arm of Mrs. Balwhidder, and with my cane in my hand, walked to our own pew, where I sat some time, but owing to my deafness, not being able to hear, I have not since gone back to the church. But my people are fond of having their weans still christened by me, and the young folk, such as are of a serious turn, come to be married at my hands, believing, as they say, that there is something good in the blessing of an aged Gospel minister. But even this remnant of my gown I must lay aside, for Mrs. Balwhidder is now and then obliged to stop me in my prayers, as I sometimes wander—pronouncing the baptismal blessing upon a bride and bridegroom, talking as if they were already parents. I am thankful, however, that I have been spared with a sound mind to write this book to the end; but it is my last task, and, indeed, really I have no more to say, saving only to wish a blessing on all people from on High, where I soon hope to be, and to meet there all the old and long-departed sheep of my flock, especially the first and second Mrs. Balwhidders.

THE AYRSHIRE LEGATEES

'*Dr. Pringle received a letter.*'

THE AYRSHIRE LEGATEES:

OR

THE PRINGLE FAMILY

BY THE AUTHOR OF
ANNALS OF THE PARISH, THE ENTAIL, ETC.

INSCRIBED TO

KIRKMAN FINLAY, Esquire,

WITH THE BEST RESPECTS OF

THE AUTHOR

CONTENTS

THE AYRSHIRE LEGATEES

CHAPTER I

PAGE

THE DEPARTURE 1

CHAPTER II

THE VOYAGE 9

CHAPTER III

THE LEGACY 17

CHAPTER IV

THE TOWN 24

CHAPTER V

THE ROYAL FUNERAL 42

CHAPTER VI

PHILOSOPHY AND RELIGION 60

CHAPTER VII

DISCOVERIES AND REBELLIONS 79

CHAPTER VIII

THE QUEEN'S TRIAL 97

CHAPTER IX

PAGE

The Marriage 117

CHAPTER X

The Return 132

LIST OF ILLUSTRATIONS

'Dr. Pringle received a letter' . . . *Frontispiece*

'Trying to take the number of the coach' . . . 15

'My father turned his eyes upwards in thankfulness' . . 22

'Gathering wrath and holy indignation' . . . 33

'Miss Arabella took her harp' 54

'Mr. Snodgrass hastily removed the book' . . . 61

'What an inattentive congregation' 83

'To give us warning becas they were starvit' . . . 86

'Sir Marmaduke Towler' 95

'His fancy was exceedingly lively' 101

'A fine quiet canny sight of the queen' . . . 108

'Sabre has been brought to the point'. . . . 111

'Andrew became a man of fashion' 115

'Mr. Micklewham' 128

'The moment that the Doctor made his appearance' . . 141

CHAPTER I

THE DEPARTURE

ON New Year's day Dr. Pringle received a letter from India, informing him that his cousin, Colonel Armour, had died at Hydrabad, and left him his residuary legatee. The same post brought other letters on the same subject from the agent of the deceased in London, by which it was evident to the whole family that no time should be lost in looking after their interests in the hands of such brief and abrupt correspondents. 'To say the least of it,' as the Doctor himself sedately remarked, 'considering the greatness of the forthcoming property, Messieurs Richard Argent and Company, of New Broad Street, might have given a notion as to the particulars of the residue.' It was therefore determined that, as soon as the requisite arrangements could be made, the Doctor and Mrs. Pringle should set out for the metropolis, to obtain a speedy settlement with the agents, and, as Rachel had now, to use an expression of her mother's, 'a prospect before her,' that she also should accompany them: Andrew, who had just been called to the Bar, and who had come to the manse to spend a few days after attaining that distinction, modestly suggested, that, considering the various professional points which might be involved in the objects of his father's journey, and considering also the retired life which his father had led in the rural village of Garnock, it might be of importance to have the advantage of legal advice.

Mrs. Pringle interrupted this harangue, by saying, 'We see what you would be at, Andrew; ye're just wanting to come with us, and on this occasion I'm no for making step-bairns, so we'll a' gang thegither.'

1

The Doctor had been for many years the incumbent of
Garnock, which is pleasantly situated between Irvine and
Kilwinning, and, on account of the benevolence of his disposition, was much beloved by his parishioners. Some of the
pawkie among them used indeed to say, in answer to the
godly of Kilmarnock, and other admirers of the late great
John Russel, of that formerly orthodox town, by whom Dr.
Pringle's powers as a preacher were held in no particular
estimation,—'He kens our pu'pit's frail, and spar'st to save
outlay to the heritors.' As for Mrs. Pringle, there is not such
another minister's wife, both for economy and management,
within the jurisdiction of the Synod of Glasgow and Ayr, and
to this fact the following letter to Miss Mally Glencairn, a
maiden lady residing in the Kirkgate of Irvine, a street that
has been likened unto the Kingdom of Heaven, where there is
neither marriage nor giving in marriage, will abundantly testify.

LETTER I

Mrs. Pringle to Miss Mally Glencairn

GARNOCK MANSE.

DEAR MISS MALLY—The Doctor has had extraordinar news
from India and London, where we are all going, as soon as
me and Rachel can get ourselves in order, so I beg you will
go to Bailie Delap's shop, and get swatches of his best black
bombaseen, and crape, and muslin, and bring them over to
the manse the morn's morning. If you cannot come yourself,
and the day should be wat, send Nanny Eydent, the mantua-
maker, with them ; you'll be sure to send Nanny, onyhow, and
I requeesht that, on this okasion, ye'll get the very best the
Bailie has, and I'll tell you all about it when you come. You
will get, likewise, swatches of mourning print, with the lowest
prices. I'll no be so particular about them, as they are for
the servan lasses, and there's no need, for all the greatness of
God's gifts, that we should be wasterful. Let Mrs. Glibbans
know, that the Doctor's second cousin, the colonel, that
was in the East Indies, is no more ;—I am sure she will
sympatheese with our loss on this melancholy okasion. Tell
her, as I'll no be out till our mournings are made, I would
take it kind if she would come over and eate a bit of dinner

2

on Sunday. The Doctor will no preach himself, but there's to be an excellent young man, an acquaintance of Andrew's, that has the repute of being both sound and hellaquaint. But no more at present, and looking for you and Nanny Eydent, with the swatches,—I am, dear Miss Mally, your sinsare friend,

JANET PRINGLE.

The Doctor being of opinion that, until they had something in hand from the legacy, they should walk in the paths of moderation, it was resolved to proceed by the coach from Irvine to Greenock, there embark in a steam-boat for Glasgow, and, crossing the country to Edinburgh, take their passage at Leith in one of the smacks for London. But we must let the parties speak for themselves.

LETTER II

Miss Rachel Pringle to Miss Isabella Tod

GREENOCK.

MY DEAR ISABELLA—I know not why the dejection with which I parted from you still hangs upon my heart, and grows heavier as I am drawn farther and farther away. The uncertainty of the future—the dangers of the sea—all combine to sadden my too sensitive spirit. Still, however, I will exert myself, and try to give you some account of our momentous journey.

The morning on which we bade farewell for a time—alas ! it was to me as if for ever, to my native shades of Garnock— the weather was cold, bleak, and boisterous, and the waves came rolling in majestic fury towards the shore, when we arrived at the Tontine Inn of Ardrossan. What a monument has the late Earl of Eglinton left there of his public spirit ! It should embalm his memory in the hearts of future ages, as I doubt not but in time Ardrossan will become a grand emporium ; but the people of Saltcoats, a sordid race, complain that it will be their ruin ; and the Paisley subscribers to his lordship's canal grow pale when they think of profit.

The road, after leaving Ardrossan, lies along the shore. The blast came dark from the waters, and the clouds lay piled in every form of grandeur on the lofty peaks of Arran. The

3

view on the right hand is limited to the foot of a range of abrupt mean hills, and on the left it meets the sea—as we were obliged to keep the glasses up, our drive for several miles was objectless and dreary. When we had ascended a hill, leaving Kilbride on the left, we passed under the walls of an ancient tower. What delightful ideas are associated with the sight of such venerable remains of antiquity!

Leaving that lofty relic of our warlike ancestors, we descended again towards the shore. On the one side lay the Cumbra Islands, and Bute, dear to departed royalty. Afar beyond them, in the hoary magnificence of nature, rise the mountains of Argyllshire; the cairns, as my brother says, of a former world. On the other side of the road, we saw the cloistered ruins of the religious house of Southenan, a nunnery in those days of romantic adventure, when to live was to enjoy a poetical element. In such a sweet sequestered retreat, how much more pleasing to the soul it would have been, for you and I, like two captive birds in one cage, to have sung away our hours in innocence, than for me to be thus torn from you by fate, and all on account of that mercenary legacy, perchance the spoils of some unfortunate Hindoo Rajah!

At Largs we halted to change horses, and saw the barrows of those who fell in the great battle. We then continued our journey along the foot of stupendous precipices; and high, sublime, and darkened with the shadow of antiquity, we saw, upon its lofty station, the ancient Castle of Skelmorlie, where the Montgomeries of other days held their gorgeous banquets, and that brave knight who fell at Chevy-Chace came pricking forth on his milk-white steed, as Sir Walter Scott would have described him. But the age of chivalry is past, and the glory of Europe departed for ever!

When we crossed the stream that divides the counties of Ayr and Renfrew, we beheld, in all the apart and consequentiality of pride, the house of Kelly overlooking the social villas of Wemyss Bay. My brother compared it to a sugar hogshead, and them to cotton-bags; for the lofty thane of Kelly is but a West India planter, and the inhabitants of the villas on the shore are Glasgow manufacturers.

To this succeeded a dull drive of about two miles, and then at once we entered the pretty village of Inverkip. A slight snow-shower had given to the landscape a sort of copperplate

4

effect, but still the forms of things, though but sketched, as it were, with China ink, were calculated to produce interesting impressions. After ascending, by a gentle acclivity, into a picturesque and romantic pass, we entered a spacious valley, and, in the course of little more than half an hour, reached this town; the largest, the most populous, and the most superb that I have yet seen. But what are all its warehouses, ships, and smell of tar, and other odoriferous circumstances of fishery and the sea, compared with the green swelling hills, the fragrant bean-fields, and the peaceful groves of my native Garnock!

The people of this town are a very busy and clever race, but much given to litigation. My brother says, that they are the greatest benefactors to the Outer House, and that their law-suits are the most amusing and profitable before the courts, being less for the purpose of determining what is right than what is lawful. The chambermaid of the inn where we lodge pointed out to me, on the opposite side of the street, a magnificent edifice erected for balls; but the subscribers have resolved not to allow any dancing till it is determined by the Court of Session to whom the seats and chairs belong, as they were brought from another house where the assemblies were formerly held. I have heard a lawsuit compared to a country-dance, in which, after a great bustle and regular confusion, the parties stand still, all tired, just on the spot where they began; but this is the first time that the judges of the land have been called on to decide when a dance may begin.

We arrived too late for the steam-boat, and are obliged to wait till Monday morning; but to-morrow we shall go to church, where I expect to see what sort of creatures the beaux are. The Greenock ladies have a great name for beauty, but those that I have seen are perfect frights. Such of the gentlemen as I have observed passing the windows of the inn may do, but I declare the ladies have nothing of which any woman ought to be proud. Had we known that we ran a risk of not getting a steam-boat, my mother would have provided an introductory letter or two from some of her Irvine friends; but here we are almost entire strangers: my father, however, is acquainted with one of the magistrates, and has gone to see him. I hope he will be civil enough to ask us to his house, for an inn is a shocking place to live in, and my mother is terrified at the expense. My brother, however, has great confidence in our prospects, and orders and directs with a high hand. But my paper is full, and I am compelled to conclude with scarcely room to say how affectionately I am yours,

RACHEL PRINGLE.

LETTER III

The Rev. Dr. Pringle to Mr. Micklewham, Schoolmaster and Session-Clerk, Garnock

EDINBURGH.

DEAR SIR—We have got this length through many difficulties, both in the travel by land to, and by sea and land from Greenock, where we were obligated, by reason of no conveyance, to stop the Sabbath, but not without edification ; for we went to hear Dr. Drystour in the forenoon, who had a most weighty sermon on the tenth chapter of Nehemiah. He is surely a great orthodox divine, but rather costive in his delivery. In the afternoon we heard a correct moral lecture on good works, in another church, from Dr. Eastlight—a plain man, with a genteel congregation. The same night we took supper with a wealthy family, where we had much pleasant communion together, although the bringing in of the toddy-bowl after supper is a fashion that has a tendency to lengthen the sederunt to unseasonable hours.

On the following morning, by the break of day, we took shipping in the steam-boat for Glasgow. I had misgivings about the engine, which is really a thing of great docility ; but saving my concern for the boiler, we all found the place surprising comfortable. The day was bleak and cold ; but we had a good fire in a carron grate in the middle of the floor, and books to read, so that both body and mind are therein provided for.

Among the books, I fell in with a *History of the Rebellion*, anent the hand that an English gentleman of the name of Waverley had in it. I was grieved that I had not time to read it through, for it was wonderful interesting, and far more particular, in many points, than any other account of that affair I have yet met with ; but it's no so friendly to Protestant principles as I could have wished. However, if I get my

6

legacy well settled, I will buy the book, and lend it to you on my return, please God, to the manse.

We were put on shore at Glasgow by breakfast-time, and there we tarried all day, as I had a power of attorney to get from Miss Jenny Macbride, my cousin, to whom the colonel left the thousand pound legacy. Miss Jenny thought the legacy should have been more, and made some obstacle to signing the power; but both her lawyer and Andrew Pringle, my son, convinced her, that, as it was specified in the testament, she could not help it by standing out; so at long and last Miss Jenny was persuaded to put her name to the paper.

Next day we all four got into a fly coach, and, without damage or detriment, reached this city in good time for dinner in Macgregor's hotel, a remarkable decent inn, next door to one Mr. Blackwood, a civil and discreet man in the bookselling line.

Really the changes in Edinburgh since I was here, thirty years ago, are not to be told. I am confounded; for although I have both heard and read of the New Town in the *Edinburgh Advertiser*, and the *Scots Magazine*, I had no notion of what has come to pass. It's surprising to think wherein the decay of the nation is; for at Greenock I saw nothing but shipping and building; at Glasgow, streets spreading as if they were one of the branches of cotton-spinning; and here, the houses grown up as if they were sown in the seed-time with the corn, by a drill-machine, or dibbled in rigs and furrows like beans and potatoes.

To-morrow, God willing, we embark in a smack at Leith, so that you will not hear from me again till it please HIM to take us in the hollow of His hand to London. In the meantime, I have only to add, that, when the Session meets, I wish you would speak to the elders, particularly to Mr. Craig, no to be overly hard on that poor donsie thing, Meg Milliken, about her bairn; and tell Tam Glen, the father o't, from me, that it would have been a sore heart to that pious woman, his mother, had she been living, to have witnessed such a thing; and therefore I hope and trust, he will yet confess a fault, and own Meg for his wife, though she is but something of a tawpie. However, you need not diminish her to Tam. I hope Mr. Snodgrass will give as much satisfaction to the parish as can reasonably be expected in my absence; and I remain, dear sir, your friend and pastor,   ZACHARIAH PRINGLE.

Mr. Micklewham received the Doctor's letter about an hour before the Session met on the case of Tam Glen and Meg Milliken, and took it with him to the session-house, to read it to the elders before going into the investigation.   Such a long and particular letter from the Doctor was, as they all justly remarked, kind and dutiful to his people, and a great pleasure to them.

Mr. Daff observed, 'Truly the Doctor's a vera funny man, and wonderfu' jocose about the toddy-bowl.'   But Mr. Craig said, that 'sic a thing on the Lord's night gi'es me no pleasure; and I am for setting my face against Waverley's *History of the Rebellion*, whilk I hae heard spoken of among the ungodly, both at Kilwinning and Dalry; and if it has no respect to Protestant principles, I doubt it's but another dose o' the radical poison in a new guise.'   Mr. Icenor, however, thought that 'the observe on the great Doctor Drystour was very edifying; and that they should see about getting him to help at the summer Occasion.'[1]

While they were thus reviewing, in their way, the first epistle of the Doctor, the betherel came in to say that Meg and Tam were at the door.   'Oh, man,' said Mr. Daff, slyly, 'ye shouldna hae left them at the door by themselves.'   Mr. Craig looked at him austerely, and muttered something about the growing immorality of this backsliding age; but before the smoke of his indignation had kindled into eloquence, the delinquents were admitted.   However, as we have nothing to do with the business, we shall leave them to their own deliberations.

[1] The administration of the Sacrament.

8

CHAPTER II

THE VOYAGE

ON the fourteenth day after the departure of the family from the manse, the Rev. Mr. Charles Snodgrass, who was appointed to officiate during the absence of the Doctor, received the following letter from his old chum, Mr. Andrew Pringle. It would appear that the young advocate is not so solid in the head as some of his elder brethren at the Bar; and therefore many of his flights and observations must be taken with an allowance on the score of his youth.

LETTER IV

Andrew Pringle, Esq., Advocate, to the Rev. Charles Snodgrass

LONDON.

MY DEAR FRIEND—We have at last reached London, after a stormy passage of seven days. The accommodation in the smacks looks extremely inviting in port, and in fine weather, I doubt not, is confortable, even at sea; but in February, and in such visitations of the powers of the air as we have endured, a balloon must be a far better vehicle than all the vessels that have been constructed for passengers since the time of Noah. In the first place, the waves of the atmosphere cannot be so dangerous as those of the ocean, being but 'thin air'; and I am sure they are not so disagreeable; then the speed of the balloon is so much greater,—and it would puzzle Professor Leslie to demonstrate that its motions are more unsteady; besides, who ever heard of sea-sickness in a balloon? the consideration of which alone would, to any reason-

9

able person actually suffering under the pains of that calamity, be deemed more than an equivalent for all the little fractional difference of danger between the two modes of travelling. I shall henceforth regard it as a fine characteristic trait of our national prudence, that, in their journies to France and Flanders, the Scottish witches always went by air on broomsticks and benweeds, instead of venturing by water in sieves, like those of England. But the English are under the influence of a maritime genius.

When we had got as far up the Thames as Gravesend, the wind and tide came against us, so that the vessel was obliged to anchor, and I availed myself of the circumstance, to induce the family to disembark and go to London by LAND; and I esteem it a fortunate circumstance that we did so, the day, for the season, being uncommonly fine. After we had taken some refreshment, I procured places in a stage-coach for my mother and sister, and, with the Doctor, mounted myself on the outside. My father's old - fashioned notions boggled a little at first to this arrangement, which he thought somewhat derogatory to his ministerial dignity; but his scruples were in the end overruled.

The country in this season is, of course, seen to disadvantage, but still it exhibits beauty enough to convince us what England must be when in leaf. The old gentleman's admiration of the increasing signs of what he called civilisation, as we approached London, became quite eloquent; but the first view of the city from Blackheath (which, by the bye, is a fine common, surrounded with villas and handsome houses) overpowered his faculties, and I shall never forget the impression it made on myself. The sun was declined towards the horizon; vast masses of dark low-hung clouds were mingled with the smoky canopy, and the dome of St. Paul's, like the enormous idol of some terrible deity, throned amidst the smoke of sacrifices and magnificence, darkness, and mystery, presented altogether an object of vast sublimity. I felt touched with reverence, as if I was indeed approaching the city of THE HUMAN POWERS.

The distant view of Edinburgh is picturesque and romantic, but it affects a lower class of our associations. It is, compared to that of London, what the poem of the *Seasons* is with respect to *Paradise Lost*—the castellated descriptions of Walter

10

Scott to the *Darkness* of Byron—the *Sabbath* of Grahame to the *Robbers* of Schiller. In the approach to Edinburgh, leisure and cheerfulness are on the road; large spaces of rural and pastoral nature are spread openly around, and mountains, and seas, and headlands, and vessels passing beyond them, going like those that die, we know not whither, while the sun is bright on their sails, and hope with them; but, in coming to this Babylon, there is an eager haste and a hurrying on from all quarters, towards that stupendous pile of gloom, through which no eye can penetrate; an unceasing sound, like the enginery of an earthquake at work, rolls from the heart of that profound and indefinable obscurity—sometimes a faint and yellow beam of the sun strikes here and there on the vast expanse of edifices; and churches, and holy asylums, are dimly seen lifting up their countless steeples and spires, like so many lightning rods to avert the wrath of Heaven.

The entrance to Edinburgh also awakens feelings of a more pleasing character. The rugged veteran aspect of the Old Town is agreeably contrasted with the bright smooth forehead of the New, and there is not such an overwhelming torrent of animal life, as to make you pause before venturing to stem it; the noises are not so deafening, and the occasional sound of a ballad-singer, or a Highland piper, varies and enriches the discords; but here, a multitudinous assemblage of harsh alarms, of selfish contentions, and of furious carriages, driven by a fierce and insolent race, shatter the very hearing, till you partake of the activity with which all seem as much possessed as if a general apprehension prevailed, that the great clock of Time would strike the doom-hour before their tasks were done. But I must stop, for the postman with his bell, like the betherel of some ancient 'borough's town' summoning to a burial, is in the street, and warns me to conclude.
—Yours, ANDREW PRINGLE.

LETTER V

The Rev. Dr. Pringle to Mr. Micklewham, Schoolmaster and Session-Clerk, Garnock

LONDON, 49 NORFOLK STREET, STRAND.

DEAR SIR—On the first Sunday forthcoming after the receiving hereof, you will not fail to recollect in the remembering prayer, that we return thanks for our safe arrival in London, after a dangerous voyage. Well, indeed, is it ordained that we should pray for those who go down to the sea in ships, and do business on the great deep; for what me and mine have come through is unspeakable, and the hand of Providence was visibly manifested.

On the day of our embarkation at Leith, a fair wind took us onward at a blithe rate for some time; but in the course of that night the bridle of the tempest was slackened, and the curb of the billows loosened, and the ship reeled to and fro like a drunken man, and no one could stand therein. My wife and daughter lay at the point of death; Andrew Pringle, my son, also was prostrated with the grievous affliction; and the very soul within me was as if it would have been cast out of the body.

On the following day the storm abated, and the wind blew favourable; but towards the heel of the evening it again became vehement, and there was no help unto our distress. About midnight, however, it pleased HIM, whose breath is the tempest, to be more sparing with the whip of His displeasure on our poor bark, as she hirpled on in her toilsome journey through the waters; and I was enabled, through His strength, to lift my head from the pillow of sickness, and ascend the deck, where I thought of Noah looking out of the window in the ark, upon the face of the desolate flood, and of Peter walking on the sea; and I said to myself, it matters not where we are, for we can be in no place where Jehovah is not there likewise, whether it be on the waves of the ocean, or the mountain tops, or in the valley and shadow of death.

The third day the wind came contrary, and in the fourth, and the fifth, and the sixth, we were also sorely buffeted; but on the night of the sixth we entered the mouth of the river

12

Thames, and on the morning of the seventh day of our departure, we cast anchor near a town called Gravesend, where, to our exceeding great joy, it pleased HIM, in whom alone there is salvation, to allow us once more to put our foot on the dry land.

When we had partaken of a repast, the first blessed with the blessing of an appetite, from the day of our leaving our native land, we got two vacancies in a stage-coach for my wife and daughter; but with Andrew Pringle, my son, I was obligated to mount aloft on the outside. I had some scruple of conscience about this, for I was afraid of my decorum. I met, however, with nothing but the height of discretion from the other outside passengers, although I jealoused that one of them was a light woman. Really I had no notion that the English were so civilised; they were so well bred, and the very duddiest of them spoke such a fine style of language, that when I looked around on the country, I thought myself in the land of Canaan. But it's extraordinary what a power of drink the coachmen drink, stopping and going into every change-house, and yet behaving themselves with the greatest sobriety. And then they are all so well dressed, which is no doubt owing to the poor rates. I am thinking, however, that for all they cry against them, the poor rates are but a small evil, since they keep the poor folk in such food and raiment, and out of the temptations to thievery; indeed, such a thing as a common beggar is not to be seen in this land, excepting here and there a sorner or a ne'er-do-weel.

When we had got to the outskirts of London, I began to be ashamed of the sin of high places, and would gladly have got into the inside of the coach, for fear of anybody knowing me; but although the multitude of by-goers was like the kirk scailing at the Sacrament, I saw not a kent face, nor one that took the least notice of my situation. At last we got to an inn, called *The White Horse*, Fetter-Lane, where we hired a hackney to take us to the lodgings provided for us here in Norfolk Street, by Mr. Pawkie, the Scotch solicitor, a friend of Andrew Pringle, my son. Now it was that we began to experience the sharpers of London; for it seems that there are divers Norfolk Streets. Ours was in the Strand (mind that when you direct), not very far from Fetter-Lane; but the hackney driver took us away to one afar off, and when we

13

knocked at the number we thought was ours, we found ourselves at a house that should not be told. I was so mortified,
that I did not know what to say; and when Andrew Pringle,
my son, rebuked the man for the mistake, he only gave a
cunning laugh, and said we should have told him whatna
Norfolk Street we wanted. Andrew stormed at this—but I
discerned it was all owing to our own inexperience, and put an
end to the contention, by telling the man to take us to Norfolk
Street in the Strand, which was the direction we had got.
But when we got to the door, the coachman was so extortionate, that another hobbleshaw arose. Mrs. Pringle had been
told that, in such disputes, the best way of getting redress
was to take the number of the coach; but, in trying to do so,
we found it fastened on, and I thought the hackneyman would
have gone by himself with laughter. Andrew, who had not
observed what we were doing, when he saw us trying to take
off the number, went like one demented, and paid the man, I
cannot tell what, to get us out, and into the house, for fear we
should have been mobbit.

I have not yet seen the colonel's agents, so can say nothing
as to the business of our coming; for, landing at Gravesend,
we did not bring our trunks with us, and Andrew has gone to
the wharf this morning to get them, and, until we get them,
we can go nowhere, which is the occasion of my writing so
soon, knowing also how you and the whole parish would be
anxious to hear what had become of us; and I remain, dear
sir, your friend and pastor,   ZACHARIAH PRINGLE.

On Saturday evening, Saunders Dickie, the Irvine postman,
suspecting that this letter was from the Doctor, went with it
himself, on his own feet, to Mr. Micklewham, although the
distance is more than two miles; but Saunders, in addition to
the customary *twal pennies* on the postage, had a dram for his
pains. The next morning being wet, Mr. Micklewham had
not an opportunity of telling any of the parishioners in the
churchyard of the Doctor's safe arrival, so that when he read
out the request to return thanks (for he was not only schoolmaster and session-clerk, but also precentor), there was a
murmur of pleasure diffused throughout the congregation, and
the greatest curiosity was excited to know what the dangers
were, from which their worthy pastor and his whole family

14

Trying to take the number of the coach.

Copyright 1895 by Macmillan & Co.

had so thankfully escaped in their voyage to London ; so that, when the service was over, the elders adjourned to the session-house to hear the letter read ; and many of the heads of families, and other respectable parishioners, were admitted to the honours of the sitting, who all sympathised, with the greatest sincerity, in the sufferings which their minister and his family had endured. Mr. Daff, however, was justly chided by Mr. Craig, for rubbing his hands, and giving a sort of sniggering laugh, at the Doctor's sitting on high with a light woman. But even Mr. Snodgrass was seen to smile at the incident of taking the number off the coach, the meaning of which none but himself seemed to understand.

When the epistle had been thus duly read, Mr. Micklewham promised, for the satisfaction of some of the congregation, that he would get two or three copies made by the best writers in his school, to be handed about the parish, and Mr. Icenor remarked, that truly it was a thing to be held in remembrance, for he had not heard of greater tribulation by the waters since the shipwreck of the Apostle Paul.

CHAPTER III

THE LEGACY

SOON after the receipt of the letters which we had the pleasure of communicating in the foregoing chapter, the following was received from Mrs. Pringle, and the intelligence it contains is so interesting and important, that we hasten to lay it before our readers :—

LETTER VI

Mrs. Pringle to Miss Mally Glencairn

LONDON.

MY DEAR MISS MALLY—You must not expect no particulars from me of our journey ; but as Rachel is writing all the calamities that befell us to Bell Tod, you will, no doubt, hear of them. But all is nothing to my losses. I bought from the first hand, Mr. Treddles the manufacturer, two pieces of muslin, at Glasgow, such a thing not being to be had on any reasonable terms here, where they get all their fine muslins from Glasgow and Paisley ; and in the same bocks with them I packit a small crock of our ain excellent poudered butter, with a delap cheese, for I was told that such commodities are not to be had genuine in London. I likewise had in it a pot of marmlet, which Miss Jenny Macbride gave me at Glasgow, assuring me that it was not only dentice, but a curiosity among the English, and my best new bumbeseen goun in peper. Howsomever, in the nailing of the bocks, which I did carefully with my oun hands, one of the nails gaed in ajee, and broke the pot of marmlet, which, by the jolting of the ship, ruined the muslin, rottened the peper round the goun, which the shivers cut into more than twenty great holes. Over and

17

above all, the crock with the butter was, no one can tell how, crackit, and the pickle lecking out, and mixing with the seerip of the marmlet, spoilt the cheese.   In short, at the object I beheld, when the bocks was opened, I could have ta'en to the greeting ; but I behaved with more composity on the occasion, than the Doctor thought it was in the power of nature to do. Howsomever, till I get a new goun and other things, I am obliged to be a prisoner ; and as the Doctor does not like to go to the counting-house of the agents without me, I know not what is yet to be the consequence of our journey.   But it would need to be something ; for we pay four guineas and a half a week for our dry lodgings, which is at a degree more than the Doctor's whole stipend.   As yet, for the cause of these misfortunes, I can give you no account of London ; but there is, as everybody kens, little thrift in their housekeeping.   We just buy our tea by the quarter a pound, and our loaf sugar, broken in a peper bag, by the pound, which would be a disgrace to a decent family in Scotland ; and when we order dinner, we get no more than just serves, so that we have no cold meat if a stranger were coming by chance, which makes an unco bare house.   The servan lasses I cannot abide ; they dress better at their wark than ever I did on an ordinaire week-day at the manse ; and this very morning I saw madam, the kitchen lass, mounted on a pair of pattens, washing the plain stenes before the door ; na, for that matter, a bare foot is not to be seen within the four walls of London, at the least I have na seen no such thing.

In the way of marketing, things are very good here, and considering, not dear ; but all is sold by the licht weight, only the fish are awful ; half a guinea for a cod's head, and no bigger than the drouds the cadgers bring from Ayr, at a shilling and eighteenpence apiece.

Tell Miss Nanny Eydent that I have seen none of the fashions as yet ; but we are going to the burial of the auld king next week, and I'll write her a particular account how the leddies are dressed ; but everybody is in deep mourning. Howsomever I have seen but little, and that only in a manner from the window ; but I could not miss the opportunity of a frank that Andrew has got, and as he's waiting for the pen, you must excuse haste.   From your sincere friend,

JANET PRINGLE.

LETTER VII

Andrew Pringle, Esq., to the Rev. Charles Snodgrass

LONDON.

MY DEAR FRIEND—It will give you pleasure to hear that my father is likely to get his business speedily settled without any equivocation ; and that all those prudential considerations which brought us to London were but the phantasms of our own inexperience. I use the plural, for I really share in the shame of having called in question the high character of the agents : it ought to have been warrantry enough that everything would be fairly adjusted. But I must give you some account of what has taken place, to illustrate our provincialism, and to give you some idea of the way of doing business in London.

After having recovered from the effects, and repaired some of the accidents of our voyage, we yesterday morning sallied forth, the Doctor, my mother, and your humble servant, in a hackney coach, to Broad Street, where the agents have their counting-house, and were ushered into a room among other legatees or clients, waiting for an audience of Mr. Argent, the principal of the house.

I know not how it is, that the little personal peculiarities, so amusing to strangers, should be painful when we see them in those whom we love and esteem ; but I own to you, that there was a something in the demeanour of the old folks on this occasion, that would have been exceedingly diverting to me, had my filial reverence been less sincere for them.

The establishment of Messrs. Argent and Company is of vast extent, and has in it something even of a public magnitude ; the number of the clerks, the assiduity of all, and the order that obviously prevails throughout, give at the first sight, an impression that bespeaks respect for the stability and integrity of the concern. When we had been seated about ten minutes, and my father's name taken to Mr. Argent, an answer was brought, that he would see us as soon as possible ; but we were obliged to wait at least half an hour more. Upon our being at last admitted, Mr. Argent received us standing, and in an easy gentlemanly manner said to my father, 'You are the residuary

19

legatee of the late Colonel Armour. I am sorry that you did not apprise me of this visit, that I might have been prepared to give the information you naturally desire ; but if you will call here to-morrow at 12 o'clock, I shall then be able to satisfy you on the subject. Your lady, I presume ?' he added, turning to my mother ; ' Mrs. Argent will have the honour of waiting on you ; may I therefore beg the favour of your address ?' Fortunately I was provided with cards, and having given him one, we found ourselves constrained, as it were, to take our leave. The whole interview did not last two minutes, and I never was less satisfied with myself. The Doctor and my mother were in the greatest anguish ; and when we were again seated in the coach, loudly expressed their apprehensions. They were convinced that some stratagem was meditated ; they feared that their journey to London would prove as little satisfactory as that of the Wrongheads, and that they had been throwing away good money in building castles in the air.

It had been previously arranged, that we were to return for my sister, and afterwards visit some of the sights ; but the clouded visages of her father and mother darkened the very spirit of Rachel, and she largely shared in their fears. This, however, was not the gravest part of the business ; for, instead of going to St. Paul's and the Tower, as we had intended, my mother declared, that not one farthing would they spend more till they were satisfied that the expenses already incurred were likely to be reimbursed ; and a Chancery suit, with all the horrors of wig and gown, floated in spectral haziness before their imagination.

We sat down to a frugal meal, and although the remainder of a bottle of wine, saved from the preceding day, hardly afforded a glass apiece, the Doctor absolutely prohibited me from opening another.

This morning, faithful to the hour, we were again in Broad Street, with hearts knit up into the most peremptory courage ; and, on being announced, were immediately admitted to Mr. Argent. He received us with the same ease as in the first interview, and, after requesting us to be seated (which, by the way, he did not do yesterday, a circumstance that was ominously remarked), he began to talk on indifferent matters. I could see that a question, big with law and fortune, was gathering in the breasts both of the Doctor and my mother, and that they were in a state far from that of the blessed. But one of the clerks, before they had time to express their indignant suspicions, entered with a paper, and Mr. Argent, having glanced it over, said to the Doctor—' I congratulate you, sir, on the amount of the colonel's fortune. I was not indeed aware before that he had died so rich. He has left about £120,000 ; seventy-five thousand of which is in the five per cents ; the remainder in India bonds and other securities. The legacies appear to be inconsiderable, so that the residue to you, after paying them and the expenses of Doctors' Commons, will exceed a hundred thousand pounds.'

My father turned his eyes upwards in thankfulness. ' But,' continued Mr. Argent, ' before the property can be transferred, it will be necessary for you to provide about four thousand pounds to pay the duty and other requisite expenses.' This was a thunderclap. ' Where can I get such a sum ? ' exclaimed my father, in a tone of pathetic simplicity. Mr. Argent smiled and said, ' We shall manage that for you ' ; and having in the same moment pulled a bell, a fine young man entered, whom he introduced to us as his son, and desired him to explain what steps it was necessary for the Doctor to take. We accordingly followed Mr. Charles Argent to his own room.

Thus, in less time than I have been in writing it, were we put in possession of all the information we required, and found those whom we feared might be interested to withhold the settlement, alert and prompt to assist us.

Mr. Charles Argent is naturally more familiar than his father. He has a little dash of pleasantry in his manner, with a shrewd good-humoured fashionable air, that renders him soon an agreeable acquaintance. He entered with singular felicity at once into the character of the Doctor and my mother, and waggishly drolled, as if he did not understand them, in order, I could perceive, to draw out the simplicity of their apprehensions. He quite won the old lady's economical heart, by offering to frank her letters, for he is in Parliament. ' You have probably,' said he slyly, ' friends in the country, to whom you may be desirous of communicating the result of your journey to London ; send your letters to me, and I will forward them, and any that you expect may also come under cover to my address, for postage is very expensive.'

As we were taking our leave, after being fully instructed in all the preliminary steps to be taken before the transfers of the funded property can be made, he asked me, in a friendly

'*My father turned his eyes upwards in thankfulness.*'
Copyright 1895 by Macmillan & Co.

manner, to dine with him this evening, and I never accepted an invitation with more pleasure. I consider his acquaintance a most agreeable acquisition, and not one of the least of those advantages which this new opulence has put it in my power to attain. The incidents, indeed, of this day, have been all highly gratifying, and the new and brighter phase in which I have seen the mercantile character, as it is connected with the greatness and glory of my country—is in itself equivalent to an accession of useful knowledge. I can no longer wonder at the vast power which the British Government wielded during the late war, when I reflect that the method and promptitude of the house of Messrs. Argent and Company is common to all the great commercial concerns from which the statesmen derived, as from so many reservoirs, those immense pecuniary supplies, which enabled them to beggar all the resources of a political despotism, the most unbounded, both in power and principle, of any tyranny that ever existed so long.—Yours, etc.,   ANDREW PRINGLE.

CHAPTER IV

THE TOWN

THERE was a great tea-drinking held in the Kirkgate of Irvine, at the house of Miss Mally Glencairn ; and at that assemblage of rank, beauty, and fashion, among other delicacies of the season, several new-come-home Clyde skippers, roaring from Greenock and Port-Glasgow, were served up—but nothing contributed more to the entertainment of the evening than a proposal, on the part of Miss Mally, that those present who had received letters from the Pringles should read them for the benefit of the company. This was, no doubt, a preconcerted scheme between her and Miss Isabella Tod, to hear what Mr. Andrew Pringle had said to his friend Mr. Snodgrass, and likewise what the Doctor himself had indited to Mr. Micklewham ; some rumour having spread of the wonderful escapes and adventures of the family in their journey and voyage to London. Had there not been some prethought of this kind, it was not indeed probable, that both the helper and session-clerk of Garnock could have been there together, in a party, where it was an understood thing, that not only Whist and Catch Honours were to be played, but even obstreperous Birky itself, for the diversion of such of the company as were not used to gambling games. It was in consequence of what took place at this Irvine route, that we were originally led to think of collecting the letters.

LETTER VIII

Miss Rachel Pringle to Miss Isabella Tod

LONDON.

MY DEAR BELL—It was my heartfelt intention to keep a regular journal of all our proceedings, from the sad day on which I bade a long adieu to my native shades—and I persevered with a constancy becoming our dear and youthful friendship, in writing down everything that I saw, either rare or beautiful, till the hour of our departure from Leith. In that faithful register of my feelings and reflections as a traveller, I described our embarkation at Greenock, on board the steam-boat,—our sailing past Port-Glasgow, an insignificant town, with a steeple;—the stupendous rock of Dumbarton Castle, that Gibraltar of antiquity;—our landing at Glasgow;—my astonishment at the magnificence of that opulent metropolis of the muslin manufacturers; my brother's remark, that the punch-bowls on the roofs of the Infirmary, the Museum, and the Trades Hall, were emblematic of the universal estimation in which that celebrated mixture is held by all ranks and degrees—learned, commercial, and even medical, of the inhabitants;—our arrival at Edinburgh—my emotion on beholding the Castle, and the visionary lake which may be nightly seen from the windows of Princes Street, between the Old and New Town, reflecting the lights of the lofty city beyond—with a thousand other delightful and romantic circumstances, which render it no longer surprising that the Edinburgh folk should be, as they think themselves, the most accomplished people in the world. But, alas! from the moment I placed my foot on board that cruel vessel, of which the very idea is anguish, all thoughts were swallowed up in suffering—swallowed, did I say? Ah, my dear Bell, it was the odious reverse—but imagination alone can do justice to the subject. Not, however, to dwell on what is past, during the whole time of our passage from Leith, I was unable to think, far less to write; and, although there was a handsome young Hussar officer also a passenger, I could not even listen to the elegant compliments which he seemed disposed to offer by way of consolation, when he had got the better of his own sickness. Neither love nor

25

valour can withstand the influence of that sea-demon. The interruption thus occasioned to my observations made me destroy my journal, and I have now to write to you only about London—only about London! What an expression for this human universe, as my brother calls it, as if my weak feminine pen were equal to the stupendous theme!

But, before entering on the subject, let me first satisfy the anxiety of your faithful bosom with respect to my father's legacy. All the accounts, I am happy to tell you, are likely to be amicably settled; but the exact amount is not known as yet, only I can see, by my brother's manner, that it is not less than we expected, and my mother speaks about sending me to a boarding-school to learn accomplishments. Nothing, however, is to be done until something is actually in hand. But what does it all avail to me? Here am I, a solitary being in the midst of this wilderness of mankind, far from your sympathising affection, with the dismal prospect before me of going a second time to school, and without the prospect of enjoying, with my own sweet companions, that light and bounding gaiety we were wont to share, in skipping from tomb to tomb in the breezy churchyard of Irvine, like butterflies in spring flying from flower to flower, as a Wordsworth or a Wilson would express it.

We have got elegant lodgings at present in Norfolk Street, but my brother is trying, with all his address, to get us removed to a more fashionable part of the town, which, if the accounts were once settled, I think will take place; and he proposes to hire a carriage for a whole month. Indeed, he has given hints about the saving that might be made by buying one of our own; but my mother shakes her head, and says, 'Andrew, dinna be carri't.' From all which it is very plain, though they don't allow me to know their secrets, that the legacy is worth the coming for. But to return to the lodgings; —we have what is called a first and second floor, a drawing-room, and three handsome bedchambers. The drawing-room is very elegant; and the carpet is the exact same pattern of the one in the dress-drawing-room of Eglintoun Castle. Our landlady is indeed a lady, and I am surprised how she should think of letting lodgings, for she dresses better, and wears finer lace, than ever I saw in Irvine. But I am interrupted.—

I now resume my pen. We have just had a call from Mrs.

and Miss Argent, the wife and daughter of the colonel's man of business. They seem great people, and came in their own chariot, with two grand footmen behind; but they are pleasant and easy, and the object of their visit was to invite us to a family dinner to-morrow, Sunday. I hope we may become better acquainted; but the two livery servants make such a difference in our degrees, that I fear this is a vain expectation. Miss Argent was, however, very frank, and told me that she was herself only just come to London for the first time since she was a child, having been for the last seven years at a school in the country. I shall, however, be better able to say more about her in my next letter. Do not, however, be afraid that she shall ever supplant you in my heart. No, my dear friend, companion of my days of innocence,—that can never be. But this call from such persons of fashion looks as if the legacy had given us some consideration; so that I think my father and mother may as well let me know at once what my prospects are, that I might show you how disinterestedly and truly I am, my dear Bell, yours, RACHEL PRINGLE.

When Miss Isabella Tod had read the letter, there was a solemn pause for some time—all present knew something, more or less, of the fair writer; but a carriage, a carpet like the best at Eglintoun, a Hussar officer, and two footmen in livery, were phantoms of such high import, that no one could distinctly express the feelings with which the intelligence affected them. It was, however, unanimously agreed, that the Doctor's legacy had every symptom of being equal to what it was at first expected to be, namely, twenty thousand pounds; —a sum which, by some occult or recondite moral influence of the Lottery, is the common maximum, in popular estimation, of any extraordinary and indefinite windfall of fortune. Miss Becky Glibbans, from the purest motives of charity, devoutly wished that poor Rachel might be able to carry her full cup with a steady hand; and the Rev. Mr. Snodgrass, that so commendable an expression might not lose its edifying effect by any lighter talk, requested Mr. Micklewham to read his letter from the Doctor.

LETTER IX

The Rev. Z. Pringle, D.D., to Mr. Micklewham, Schoolmaster and Session-Clerk of Garnock

LONDON.

DEAR SIR—I have written by the post that will take this to hand, a letter to Banker M——y, at Irvine, concerning some small matters of money that I may stand in need of his opinion anent ; and as there is a prospect now of a settlement of the legacy business, I wish you to take a step over to the banker, and he will give you ten pounds, which you will administer to the poor, by putting a twenty-shilling note in the plate on Sunday, as a public testimony from me of thankfulness for the hope that is before us ; the other nine pounds you will quietly, and in your own canny way, divide after the following manner, letting none of the partakers thereof know from what other hand than the Lord's the help comes, for, indeed, from whom but HIS does any good befall us !

You will give to auld Mizy Eccles ten shillings. She's a careful creature, and it will go as far with her thrift as twenty will do with Effy Hopkirk ; so you will give Effy twenty. Mrs. Binnacle, who lost her husband, the sailor, last winter, is, I am sure, with her two sickly bairns, very ill off; I would therefore like if you will lend her a note, and ye may put half-a-crown in the hand of each of the poor weans for a playock, for she's a proud spirit, and will bear much before she complain. Thomas Dowy has been long unable to do a turn of work, so you may give him a note too. I promised that donsie body, Willy Shachle, the betherel, that when I got my legacy, he should get a guinea, which would be more to him than if the colonel had died at home, and he had had the howking of his grave ; you may therefore, in the meantime, give Willy a crown, and be sure to warn him well no to get fou with it, for I'll be very angry if he does. But what in this matter will need all your skill, is the giving of the remaining five pounds to auld Miss Betty Peerie ; being a gentlewoman both by blood and education, she's a very slimmer affair to handle in a doing of this kind. But I am persuaded she's in as great necessity as many that seem far poorer, especially since the muslin

28

flowering has gone so down. Her bits of brats are sairly worn, though she keeps out an apparition of gentility. Now, for all this trouble, I will give you an account of what we have been doing since my last.

When we had gotten ourselves made up in order, we went, with Andrew Pringle, my son, to the counting-house, and had a satisfactory vista of the residue; but it will be some time before things can be settled—indeed, I fear, not for months to come—so that I have been thinking, if the parish was pleased with Mr. Snodgrass, it might be my duty to my people to give up to him my stipend, and let him be appointed not only helper, but successor likewise. It would not be right of me to give the manse, both because he's a young and inexperienced man, and cannot, in the course of nature, have got into the way of visiting the sick-beds of the frail, which is the main part of a pastor's duty, and likewise, because I wish to die, as I have lived, among my people. But, when all's settled, I will know better what to do.

When we had got an inkling from Mr. Argent of what the colonel has left,—and I do assure you, that money is not to be got, even in the way of legacy, without anxiety,—Mrs. Pringle and I consulted together, and resolved, that it was our first duty, as a token of our gratitude to the Giver of all Good, to make our first outlay to the poor. So, without saying a word either to Rachel, or to Andrew Pringle, my son, knowing that there was a daily worship in the Church of England, we slipped out of the house by ourselves, and, hiring a hackney conveyance, told the driver thereof to drive us to the high church of St. Paul's. This was out of no respect to the pomp and pride of prelacy, but to Him before whom both pope and presbyter are equal, as they are seen through the merits of Christ Jesus. We had taken a gold guinea in our hand, but there was no broad at the door; and, instead of a venerable elder, lending sanctity to his office by reason of his age, such as we see in the effectual institutions of our own national church—the door was kept by a young man, much more like a writer's whipper-snapper-clerk, than one qualified to fill that station, which good King David would have preferred to dwelling in tents of sin. However, we were not come to spy the nakedness of the land, so we went up the outside stairs, and I asked at him for the plate; 'Plate!' says he; 'why, it's on the altar!' I should have known this—the custom of old being to lay the offerings on the altar, but I had forgot; such is the force, you see, of habit, that the Church of England is not so well reformed and purged as ours is from the abominations of the leaven of idolatry. We were then stepping forward, when he said to me, as sharply as if I was going to take an advantage, 'You must pay here.' 'Very well, wherever it is customary,' said I, in a meek manner, and gave him the guinea. Mrs. Pringle did the same. 'I cannot give you change,' cried he, with as little decorum as if we had been paying at a playhouse. 'It makes no odds,' said I; 'keep it all.' Whereupon he was so converted by the mammon of iniquity, that he could not be civil enough, he thought—but conducted us in, and showed us the marble monuments, and the French colours that were taken in the war, till the time of worship—nothing could surpass his discretion.

At last the organ began to sound, and we went into the place of worship; but oh, Mr. Micklewham, yon is a thin kirk. There was not a hearer forby Mrs. Pringle and me, saving and excepting the relics of popery that assisted at the service. What was said, I must, however, in verity confess, was not far from the point. But it's still a comfort to see that prelatical usurpations are on the downfall; no wonder that there is no broad at the door to receive the collection for the poor, when no congregation entereth in. You may, therefore, tell Mr. Craig, and it will gladden his heart to hear the tidings, that the great Babylonian madam is now, indeed, but a very little cutty.

On our return home to our lodgings, we found Andrew Pringle, my son, and Rachel, in great consternation about our absence. When we told them that we had been at worship, I saw they were both deeply affected; and I was pleased with my children, the more so, as you know I have had my doubts that Andrew Pringle's principles have not been strengthened by the reading of the *Edinburgh Review*. Nothing more passed at that time, for we were disturbed by a Captain Sabre that came up with us in the smack, calling to see how we were after our journey; and as he was a civil well-bred young man, which I marvel at, considering he's a Hussar dragoon, we took a coach, and went to see the lions, as he said; but, instead of taking us to the Tower of London, as I expected, he ordered the man to drive us round the town. In our way through the city he showed us the Temple Bar, where Lord Kilmarnock's head was placed after the Rebellion, and pointed out the Bank of England and Royal Exchange. He said the steeple of the Exchange was taken down shortly ago—and that the late improvements at the Bank were very grand. I remembered having read in the *Edinburgh Advertiser*, some years past, that there was a great deal said in Parliament about the state of the Exchange, and the condition of the Bank, which I could never thoroughly understand. And, no doubt, the taking down of an old building, and the building up of a new one so near together, must, in such a crowded city as this, be not only a great detriment to business, but dangerous to the community at large.

After we had driven about for more than two hours, and neither seen lions nor any other curiosity, but only the outside of houses, we returned home, where we found a copperplate card left by Mr. Argent, the colonel's agent, with the name of his private dwelling-house. Both me and Mrs. Pringle were confounded at the sight of this thing, and could not but think that it prognosticated no good; for we had seen the gentleman himself in the forenoon. Andrew Pringle, my son, could give no satisfactory reason for such an extraordinary manifestation of anxiety to see us; so that, after sitting on thorns at our dinner, I thought that we should see to the bottom of the business. Accordingly, a hackney was summoned to the door, and me and Andrew Pringle, my son, got into it, and told the man to drive to second in the street where Mr. Argent lived, and which was the number of his house. The man got up, and away we went; but, after he had driven an awful time, and stopping and inquiring at different places, he said there was no such house as Second's in the street; whereupon Andrew Pringle, my son, asked him what he meant, and the man said that he supposed it was one Second's Hotel, or Coffee-house, that we wanted. Now, only think of the craftiness of the ne'er-da-weel; it was with some difficulty that I could get him to understand, that second was just as good as number two; for Andrew Pringle, my son, would not interfere, but lay back in the coach, and was like to split his sides at my confabulating with the hackney man. At long and length we got to the house, and were admitted to

31

Mr. Argent, who was sitting by himself in his library reading, with a plate of oranges, and two decanters with wine before him. I explained to him, as well as I could, my surprise and anxiety at seeing his card, at which he smiled, and said, it was merely a sort of practice that had come into fashion of late years, and that, although we had been at his counting-house in the morning, he considered it requisite that he should call on his return from the city. I made the best excuse I could for the mistake ; and the servant having placed glasses on the table, we were invited to take wine. But I was grieved to think that so respectable a man should have had the bottles before him by himself, the more especially as he said his wife and daughters had gone to a party, and that he did not much like such sort of things. But for all that, we found him a wonderful conversible man ; and Andrew Pringle, my son, having read all the new books put out at Edinburgh, could speak with him on any subject. In the course of conversation they touched upon politick economy, and Andrew Pringle, my son, in speaking about cash in the Bank of England, told him what I had said concerning the alterations of the Royal Exchange steeple, with which Mr. Argent seemed greatly pleased, and jocosely proposed as a toast,—'May the country never suffer more from the alterations in the Exchange, than the taking down of the steeple.' But as Mrs. Pringle is wanting to send a bit line under the same frank to her cousin, Miss Mally Glencairn, I must draw to a conclusion, assuring you, that I am, dear sir, your sincere friend and pastor,

ZACHARIAH PRINGLE.

The impression which this letter made on the auditors of Mr. Micklewham was highly favourable to the Doctor—all bore testimony to his benevolence and piety ; and Mrs. Glibbans expressed, in very loquacious terms, her satisfaction at the neglect to which prelacy was consigned. The only person who seemed to be affected by other than the most sedate feelings on the occasion was the Rev. Mr. Snodgrass, who was observed to smile in a very unbecoming manner at some parts of the Doctor's account of his reception at St. Paul's. Indeed, it was apparently with the utmost difficulty that the young clergyman could restrain himself from giving liberty to his risible faculties. It is really surprising how differently

32

the same thing affects different people. 'The Doctor and Mrs. Pringle giving a guinea at the door of St. Paul's for the

'Gathering wrath and holy indignation.'

poor need not make folk laugh,' said Mrs. Glibbans; 'for is it not written, that whosoever giveth to the poor lendeth to the

Lord?' 'True, my dear madam,' replied Mr. Snodgrass, 'but the Lord to whom our friends in this case gave their money is the Lord Bishop of London; all the collection made at the doors of St. Paul's Cathedral is, I understand, a perquisite of the Bishop's.' In this the reverend gentleman was not very correctly informed, for, in the first place, it is not a collection, but an exaction; and, in the second place, it is only sanctioned by the Bishop, who allows the inferior clergy to share the gains among themselves. Mrs. Glibbans, however, on hearing his explanation, exclaimed, 'Gude be about us!' and pushing back her chair with a bounce, streaking down her gown at the same time with both her hands, added, 'No wonder that a judgment is upon the land, when we hear of money-changers in the temple.' Miss Mally Glencairn, to appease her gathering wrath and holy indignation, said facetiously, 'Na, na, Mrs. Glibbans, ye forget, there was nae changing of money there. The man took the whole guineas. But not to make a controversy on the subject, Mr. Snodgrass will now let us hear what Andrew Pringle, "my son," has said to him':—And the reverend gentleman read the following letter with due circumspection, and in his best manner:—

LETTER X

Andrew Pringle, Esq., to the Reverend Charles Snodgrass

MY DEAR FRIEND—I have heard it alleged, as the observation of a great traveller, that the manners of the higher classes of society throughout Christendom are so much alike, that national peculiarities among them are scarcely perceptible. This is not correct; the differences between those of London and Edinburgh are to me very striking. It is not that they talk and perform the little etiquettes of social intercourse differently; for, in these respects, they are apparently as similar as it is possible for imitation to make them; but the difference to which I refer is an indescribable something, which can only be compared to peculiarities of accent. They both speak the same language; perhaps in classical purity of phraseology the fashionable Scotchman is even superior to the Englishman; but there is a flatness of tone in his accent—a lack of what the musicians call expression, which gives a local and provincial effect to his conversation, however, in other respects, learned and intelligent. It is so with his manners; he conducts himself with equal ease, self-possession, and discernment, but the flavour of the metropolitan style is wanting.

I have been led to make these remarks by what I noticed in the guests whom I met on Friday at young Argent's. It was a small party, only five strangers; but they seemed to be all particular friends of our host, and yet none of them appeared to be on any terms of intimacy with each other. In Edinburgh, such a party would have been at first a little cold; each of the guests would there have paused to estimate the characters of the several strangers before committing himself with any topic of conversation. But here, the circumstance of being brought together by a mutual friend, produced at once the purest gentlemanly confidence; each, as it were, took it for granted, that the persons whom he had come among were men of education and good-breeding, and, without deeming it at all necessary that he should know something of their respective political and philosophical principles, before venturing to speak on such subjects, discussed frankly, and as things unconnected with party feelings, incidental occurrences which, in Edinburgh, would have been avoided as calculated to awaken animosities.

But the most remarkable feature of the company, small as it was, consisted of the difference in the condition and character of the guests. In Edinburgh the landlord, with the scrupulous care of a herald or genealogist, would, for a party, previously unacquainted with each other, have chosen his guests as nearly as possible from the same rank of life; the London host had paid no respect to any such consideration—all the strangers were as dissimilar in fortune, profession, connections, and politics, as any four men in the class of gentlemen could well be. I never spent a more delightful evening.

The ablest, the most eloquent, and the most elegant man present, without question, was the son of a saddler. No expense had been spared on his education. His father, proud of his talents, had intended him for a seat in Parliament; but Mr. T—— himself prefers the easy enjoyments of private life, and has kept himself aloof from politics and parties. Were I

35

to form an estimate of his qualifications to excel in public speaking, by the clearness and beautiful propriety of his colloquial language, I should conclude that he was still destined to perform a distinguished part. But he is content with the liberty of a private station, as a spectator only, and, perhaps, in that he shows his wisdom ; for undoubtedly such men are not cordially received among hereditary statesmen, unless they evince a certain suppleness of principle, such as we have seen in the conduct of more than one political adventurer.

The next in point of effect was young C—— G——. He evidently languished under the influence of indisposition, which, while it added to the natural gentleness of his manners, diminished the impression his accomplishments would otherwise have made. I was greatly struck with the modesty with which he offered his opinions, and could scarcely credit that he was the same individual whose eloquence in Parliament is by many compared even to Mr. Canning's, and whose firmness of principle is so universally acknowledged, that no one ever suspects him of being liable to change. You may have heard of his poem ' On the Restoration of Learning in the East,' the most magnificent prize essay that the English Universities have produced for many years. The passage in which he describes the talents, the researches, and learning of Sir William Jones, is worthy of the imagination of Burke ; and yet, with all this oriental splendour of fancy, he has the reputation of being a patient and methodical man of business. He looks, however, much more like a poet or a student, than an orator and a statesman ; and were statesmen the sort of personages which the spirit of the age attempts to represent them, I, for one, should lament that a young man, possessed of so many amiable qualities, all so tinted with the bright lights of a fine enthusiasm, should ever have been removed from the moon-lighted groves and peaceful cloisters of Magdalen College, to the lamp-smelling passages and factious debates of St. Stephen's Chapel. Mr. G—— certainly belongs to that high class of gifted men who, to the honour of the age, have redeemed the literary character from the charge of unfitness for the concerns of public business ; and he has shown that talents for affairs of state, connected with literary predilections, are not limited to mere reviewers, as some of your old classfellows would have the world to believe. When I contrast the quiet unobtrusive development of Mr. G——'s character with that bustling and obstreperous elbowing into notice of some of those to whom the *Edinburgh Review* owes half its fame, and compare the pure and steady lustre of his elevation, to the rocket-like aberrations and perturbed blaze of their still uncertain course, I cannot but think that we have overrated, if not their ability, at least their wisdom in the management of public affairs.

The third of the party was a little Yorkshire baronet. He was formerly in Parliament, but left it, as he says, on account of its irregularities, and the bad hours it kept. He is a Whig, I understand, in politics, and indeed one might guess as much by looking at him; for I have always remarked, that your Whigs have something odd and particular about them. On making the same sort of remark to Argent, who, by the way, is a high ministerial man, he observed, the thing was not to be wondered at, considering that the Whigs are exceptions to the generality of mankind, which naturally accounts for their being always in the minority. Mr. T——, the saddler's son, who overheard us, said slyly, 'That it might be so; but if it be true that the wise are few compared to the multitude of the foolish, things would be better managed by the minority than as they are at present.'

The fourth guest was a stock-broker, a shrewd compound, with all charity be it spoken, of knavery and humour. He is by profession an epicure, but I suspect his accomplishments in that capacity are not very well founded; I would almost say, judging by the evident traces of craft and dissimulation in his physiognomy, that they have been assumed as part of the means of getting into good company, to drive the more earnest trade of money-making. Argent evidently understood his true character, though he treated him with jocular familiarity. I thought it a fine example of the intellectual tact and superiority of T——, that he seemed to view him with dislike and contempt. But I must not give you my reasons for so thinking, as you set no value on my own particular philosophy; besides, my paper tells me, that I have only room left to say, that it would be difficult in Edinburgh to bring such a party together; and yet they affect there to have a metropolitan character. In saying this, I mean only with reference to manners; the methods of behaviour in each of the company were precisely similar—there was no eccentricity, but only that distinct and decided individuality which nature gives, and which no acquired habits can change. Each, however, was the representative of a class; and Edinburgh has no classes exactly of the same kind as those to which they belonged.—Yours truly,

ANDREW PRINGLE.

Just as Mr. Snodgrass concluded the last sentence, one of the Clyde skippers, who had fallen asleep, gave such an extravagant snore, followed by a groan, that it set the whole company a-laughing, and interrupted the critical strictures which would otherwise have been made on Mr. Andrew Pringle's epistle. 'Damn it,' said he, 'I thought myself in a fog, and could not tell whether the land ahead was Plada or the Lady Isle.' Some of the company thought the observation not inapplicable to what they had been hearing.

Miss Isabella Tod then begged that Miss Mally, their hostess, would favour the company with Mrs. Pringle's communication. To this request that considerate maiden ornament of the Kirkgate deemed it necessary, by way of preface to the letter, to say, 'Ye a' ken that Mrs. Pringle's a managing woman, and ye maunna expect any metaphysical philosophy from her.' In the meantime, having taken the letter from her pocket, and placed her spectacles on that functionary of the face which was destined to wear spectacles, she began as follows :—

LETTER XI

Mrs. Pringle to Miss Mally Glencairn

MY DEAR MISS MALLY—We have been at the counting-house, and gotten a sort of a satisfaction; what the upshot may be, I canna take it upon myself to prognosticate; but when the waur comes to the worst, I think that baith Rachel and Andrew will have a nest egg, and the Doctor and me may sleep sound on their account, if the nation doesna break, as the argle-barglers in the House of Parliament have been threatening: for all the cornal's fortune is sunk at present in the pesents. Howsomever, it's our notion, when the legacies

38

are paid off, to lift the money out of the funds, and place it at good interest on hairetable securitie. But ye will hear aften from us, before things come to that, for the delays, and the goings, and the comings in this town of London are past all expreshon.

As yet, we have been to see no fairlies, except going in a coach from one part of the toun to another; but the Doctor and me was at the he-kirk of Saint Paul's for a purpose that I need not tell you, as it was adoing with the right hand what the left should not know. I couldna say that I had there great pleasure, for the preacher was very cauldrife, and read every word, and then there was such a beggary of popish prelacy, that it was compassionate to a Christian to see.

We are to dine at Mr. Argent's, the cornal's hadgint, on Sunday, and me and Rachel have been getting something for the okasion. Our landlady, Mrs. Sharkly, has recommended us to ane of the most fashionable millinders in London, who keeps a grand shop in Cranburn Alla, and she has brought us arteecles to look at; but I was surprised they were not finer, for I thought them of a very inferior quality, which she said was because they were not made for no costomer, but for the public.

The Argents seem as if they would be discreet people, which, to us who are here in the jaws of jeopardy, would be a great confort—for I am no overly satisfeet with many things. What would ye think of buying coals by the stimpert, for anything that I know, and then setting up the poker afore the ribs, instead of blowing with the bellies to make the fire burn? I was of a pinion that the Englishers were naturally wasterful; but I can ashure you this is no the case at all—and I am beginning to think that the way of leeving from hand to mouth is great frugality, when ye consider that all is left in the logive hands of uncercumseezed servans.

But what gives me the most concern at this time is one Captain Sabre of the Dragoon Hozars, who come up in the smak with us from Leith, and is looking more after our Rachel than I could wish, now that she might set her cap to another sort of object. But he's of a respectit family, and the young lad himself is no to be despisid; howsomever, I never likit officir-men of any description, and yet the thing that makes me look down on the captain is all owing to the cornal, who was an officer of the native poors of India, where the pay must indeed have been extraordinar, for who ever heard either of a cornal, or any officer whomsoever, making a hundred thousand pounds in our regiments ? no that I say the cornal has left so meikle to us.

Tell Mrs. Glibbans that I have not heard of no sound preacher as yet in London—the want of which is no doubt the great cause of the crying sins of the place. What would she think to hear of newspapers selling by tout of horn on the Lord's day? and on the Sabbath night, the change-houses are more throng than on the Saturday! I am told, but as yet I cannot say that I have seen the evil myself with my own eyes, that in the summer time there are tea-gardens, where the tradesmen go to smoke their pipes of tobacco, and to entertain their wives and children, which can be nothing less than a bringing of them to an untimely end. But you will be surprised to hear, that no such thing as whusky is to be had in the public-houses, where they drink only a dead sort of beer ; and that a bottle of true jennyinn London porter is rarely to be seen in the whole town—all kinds of piple getting their porter in pewter cans, and a laddie calls for in the morning to take away what has been yoused over night. But what I most miss is the want of creem. The milk here is just skimm, and I doot not, likewise well watered—as for the water, a drink of clear wholesome good water is not within the bounds of London ; and truly, now may I say, that I have learnt what the blessing of a cup of cold water is.

Tell Miss Nanny Eydent, that the day of the burial is now settled, when we are going to Windsor Castle to see the precesson—and that, by the end of the wick, she may expect the fashions from me, with all the particulars. Till then, I am, my dear Miss Mally, your friend and well-wisher,

JANET PRINGLE.

Noto Beny.—Give my kind compliments to Mrs. Glibbans, and let her know, that I will, after Sunday, give her an account of the state of the Gospel in London.

Miss Mally paused when she had read the letter, and it was unanimously agreed, that Mrs. Pringle gave a more full account of London than either father, son, or daughter.

By this time the night was far advanced, and Mrs. Glibbans was rising to go away, apprehensive, as she observed, that they were going to bring 'the carts' into the room. Upon Miss Mally, however, assuring her that no such transgression was meditated, but that she intended to treat them with a bit nice Highland mutton ham, and eggs, of her own laying, that worthy pillar of the Relief Kirk consented to remain.

It was past eleven o'clock when the party broke up; Mr. Snodgrass and Mr. Micklewham walked home together, and as they were crossing the Red Burn Bridge, at the entrance of Eglintoun Wood,—a place well noted from ancient times for preternatural appearances, Mr. Micklewham declared that he thought he heard something purring among the bushes; upon which Mr. Snodgrass made a jocose observation, stating, that it could be nothing but the effect of Lord North's strong ale in his head; and we should add, by way of explanation, that the Lord North here spoken of was Willy Grieve, celebrated in Irvine for the strength and flavour of his brewing, and that, in addition to a plentiful supply of his best, Miss Mally had entertained them with tamarind punch, constituting a natural cause adequate to produce all the preternatural purring that terrified the dominie.

CHAPTER V

THE ROYAL FUNERAL

TAM GLEN having, in consequence of the exhortations of Mr. Micklewham, and the earnest entreaties of Mr. Daff, backed by the pious animadversions of the rigidly righteous Mr. Craig, confessed a fault, and acknowledged an irregular marriage with Meg Milliken, their child was admitted to church privileges. But before the day of baptism, Mr. Daff, who thought Tam had given but sullen symptoms of penitence, said, to put him in better humour with his fate,—'Noo, Tam, since ye hae beguiled us of the infare, we maun mak up for't at the christening; so I'll speak to Mr. Snodgrass to bid the Doctor's friens and acquaintance to the ploy, that we may get as meikle amang us as will pay for the bairn's baptismal frock.'

Mr. Craig, who was present, and who never lost an opportunity of testifying, as he said, his 'discountenance of the crying iniquity,' remonstrated with Mr. Daff on the unchristian nature of the proposal, stigmatising it with good emphasis 'as a sinful nourishing of carnality in his day and generation.' Mr. Micklewham, however, interfered, and said, 'It was a matter of weight and concernment, and therefore it behoves you to consult Mr. Snodgrass on the fitness of the thing. For if the thing itself is not fit and proper, it cannot expect his countenance; and, on that account, before we reckon on his compliance with what Mr. Daff has propounded, we should first learn whether he approves of it at all.' Whereupon the two elders and the session-clerk adjourned to the manse, in which Mr. Snodgrass, during the absence of the incumbent, had taken up his abode.

The heads of the previous conversation were recapitulated by Mr. Micklewham, with as much brevity as was consistent with perspicuity ; and the matter being duly digested by Mr. Snodgrass, that orthodox young man—as Mrs. Glibbans denominated him, on hearing him for the first time—declared that the notion of a pay-christening was a benevolent and kind thought : ' For, is not the order to increase and multiply one of the first commands in the Scriptures of truth ? ' said Mr. Snodgrass, addressing himself to Mr. Craig. ' Surely, then, when children are brought into the world, a great law of our nature has been fulfilled, and there is cause for rejoicing and gladness ! And is it not an obligation imposed upon all Christians, to welcome the stranger, and to feed the hungry, and to clothe the naked ; and what greater stranger can there be than a helpless babe ? Who more in need of sustenance than the infant, that knows not the way even to its mother's bosom ? And whom shall we clothe, if we do not the wailing innocent, that the hand of Providence places in poverty and nakedness before us, to try, as it were, the depth of our Christian principles, and to awaken the sympathy of our humane feelings ? '

Mr. Craig replied, ' It's a' very true and sound what Mr. Snodgrass has observed ; but Tam Glen's wean is neither a stranger, nor hungry, nor naked, but a sturdy brat, that has been rinning its lane for mair than sax weeks.' ' Ah ! ' said Mr. Snodgrass familiarly, ' I fear, Mr. Craig, ye're a Malthusian in your heart.' The sanctimonious elder was thunderstruck at the word. Of many a various shade and modification of sectarianism he had heard, but the Malthusian heresy was new to his ears, and awful to his conscience, and he begged Mr. Snodgrass to tell him in what it chiefly consisted, pro-testing his innocence of that, and of every erroneous doctrine.

Mr. Snodgrass happened to regard the opinions of Malthus on Population as equally contrary to religion and nature, and not at all founded in truth. ' It is evident, that the reproductive principle in the earth and vegetables, and all things and animals which constitute the means of subsistence, is much more vigorous than in man. It may be therefore affirmed, that the multiplication of the means of subsistence is an effect of the multiplication of population, for the one is augmented in quantity, by the skill and care of the other,'

43

said Mr. Snodgrass, seizing with avidity this opportunity of stating what he thought on the subject, although his auditors were but the session-clerk, and two elders of a country parish. We cannot pursue the train of his argument, but we should do injustice to the philosophy of Malthus, if we suppressed the observation which Mr. Daff made at the conclusion. 'Gude sate's!' said the good-natured elder, 'if it's true that we breed faster than the Lord provides for us, we maun drown the poor folks' weans like kittlings.' 'Na, na!' exclaimed Mr. Craig, 'ye're a' out, neighbour; I see now the utility of church-censures.' 'True!' said Mr. Micklewham; 'and the ordination of the stool of repentance, the horrors of which, in the opinion of the fifteen Lords at Edinburgh, palliated child-murder, is doubtless a Malthusian institution.' But Mr. Snodgrass put an end to the controversy, by fixing a day for the christening, and telling he would do his best to procure a good collection, according to the benevolent suggestion of Mr. Daff. To this cause we are indebted for the next series of the Pringle correspondence; for, on the day appointed, Miss Mally Glencairn, Miss Isabella Tod, Mrs. Glibbans and her daughter Becky, with Miss Nanny Eydent, together with other friends of the minister's family, dined at the manse, and the conversation being chiefly about the concerns of the family, the letters were produced and read.

LETTER XII

Andrew Pringle, Esq., to the Rev. Charles Snodgrass

WINDSOR, CASTLE-INN.

MY DEAR FRIEND—I have all my life been strangely susceptible of pleasing impressions from public spectacles where great crowds are assembled. This, perhaps, you will say, is but another way of confessing, that, like the common vulgar, I am fond of sights and shows. It may be so, but it is not from the pageants that I derive my enjoyment. A multitude, in fact, is to me as it were a strain of music, which, with an irresistible and magical influence, calls up from the unknown abyss of the feelings new combinations of fancy, which, though vague and obscure, as those nebulæ of light that astronomers have supposed to be the rudiments of

44

unformed stars, afterwards become distinct and brilliant acquisitions. In a crowd, I am like the somnambulist in the highest degree of the luminous crisis, when it is said a new world is unfolded to his contemplation, wherein all things have an intimate affinity with the state of man, and yet bear no resemblance to the objects that address themselves to his corporeal faculties. This delightful experience, as it may be called, I have enjoyed this evening, to an exquisite degree, at the funeral of the king ; but, although the whole succession of incidents is indelibly imprinted on my recollection, I am still so much affected by the emotion excited, as to be incapable of conveying to you any intelligible description of what I saw. It was indeed a scene witnessed through the medium of the feelings, and the effect partakes of the nature of a dream.

I was within the walls of an ancient castle,

> ' So old as if they had for ever stood,
> So strong as if they would for ever stand,'

and it was almost midnight. The towers, like the vast spectres of departed ages, raised their embattled heads to the skies, monumental witnesses of the strength and antiquity of a great monarchy. A prodigious multitude filled the courts of that venerable edifice, surrounding on all sides a dark embossed structure, the sarcophagus, as it seemed to me at the moment, of the heroism of chivalry.

'A change came o'er the spirit of my dream,' and I beheld the scene suddenly illuminated, and the blaze of torches, the glimmering of arms, and warriors and horses, while a mosaic of human faces covered like a pavement the courts. A deep low under sound pealed from a distance ; in the same moment, a trumpet answered with a single mournful note from the stateliest and darkest portion of the fabric, and it was whispered in every ear, ' It is coming.' Then an awful cadence of solemn music, that affected the heart like silence, was heard at intervals, and a numerous retinue of grave and venerable men,

> ' The fathers of their time,
> Those mighty master spirits, that withstood
> The fall of monarchies, and high upheld
> Their country's standard, glorious in the storm,'

passed slowly before me, bearing the emblems and trophies of a king. They were as a series of great historical events, and I beheld behind them, following and followed, an awful and indistinct image, like the vision of Job. It moved on, and I could not discern the form thereof, but there were honours and heraldries, and sorrow, and silence, and I heard the stir of a profound homage performing within the breasts of all the witnesses. But I must not indulge myself farther on this subject. I cannot hope to excite in you the emotions with which I was so profoundly affected. In the visible objects of the funeral of George the Third there was but little magnificence ; all its sublimity was derived from the trains of thought and currents of feeling, which the sight of so many illustrious characters, surrounded by circumstances associated with the greatness and antiquity of the kingdom, was necessarily calculated to call forth. In this respect, however, it was perhaps the sublimest spectacle ever witnessed in this island ; and I am sure, that I cannot live so long as ever again to behold another, that will equally interest me to the same depth and extent.—Yours,   ANDREW PRINGLE.

We should ill perform the part of faithful historians, did we omit to record the sentiments expressed by the company on this occasion. Mrs. Glibbans, whose knowledge of the points of orthodoxy had not their equal in the three adjacent parishes, roundly declared, that Mr. Andrew Pringle's letter was nothing but a peesemeal of clishmaclavers ; that there was no sense in it ; and that it was just like the writer, a canary idiot, a touch here and a touch there, without anything in the shape of cordiality or satisfaction.

Miss Isabella Tod answered this objection with that sweetness of manner and virgin diffidence, which so well becomes a youthful member of the establishment, controverting the dogmas of a stoop of the Relief persuasion, by saying, that she thought Mr. Andrew had shown a fine sensibility. ' What is sensibility without judgment,' cried her adversary, ' but a thrashing in the water, and a raising of bells ? Couldna the fallow, without a' his parleyvoos, have said, that such and such was the case, and that the Lord giveth and the Lord taketh away ?—but his clouds, and his spectres, and his visions of Job !—Oh, an he could but think like Job !—Oh, an he would but think like the patient man !—and was obliged to claut

46

his flesh with a bit of a broken crock, we might have some hope of repentance unto life. But Andrew Pringle, he's a gone dick; I never had comfort or expectation of the free-thinker, since I heard that he was infected with the blue and yellow calamity of the *Edinburgh Review;* in which, I am credibly told, it is set forth, that women have nae souls, but only a gut, and a gaw, and a gizzard, like a pigeon-dove, or a raven-crow, or any other outcast and abominated quadruped.'

Here Miss Mally Glencairn interposed her effectual media-tion, and said, 'It is very true that Andrew deals in the diplomatics of obscurity; but it's well known that he has a nerve for genius, and that, in his own way, he kens the loan from the crown of the causeway, as well as the duck does the midden from the adle dib.' To this proverb, which we never heard before, a learned friend, whom we consulted on the subject, has enabled us to state, that middens were formerly of great magnitude, and often of no less antiquity in the west of Scotland; in so much, that the Trongate of Glasgow owes all its spacious grandeur to them. It being within the recollec-tion of persons yet living, that the said magnificent street was at one time an open road, or highway, leading to the Trone, or market-cross, with thatched houses on each side, such as may still be seen in the pure and immaculate royal borough of Rutherglen; and that before each house stood a luxuriant midden, by the removal of which, in the progress of modern degeneracy, the stately architecture of Argyle Street was formed. But not to insist at too great a length on such topics of antiquarian lore, we shall now insert Dr. Pringle's account of the funeral, and which, patly enough, follows our digression concerning the middens and magnificence of Glasgow, as it contains an authentic anecdote of a manufacturer from that city, drinking champaign at the king's dirgie.

LETTER XIII

The Rev. Z. Pringle, D.D., to Mr. Micklewham, Schoolmaster and Session-Clerk of Garnock

LONDON.

DEAR SIR—I have received your letter, and it is a great pleasure to me to hear that my people were all so much concerned at our distress in the Leith smack; but what gave me the most contentment was the repentance of Tam Glen. I hope, poor fellow, he will prove a good husband; but I have my doubts; for the wife has really but a small share of common sense, and no married man can do well unless his wife will let him. I am, however, not overly pleased with Mr. Craig on the occasion, for he should have considered frail human nature, and accepted of poor Tam's confession of a fault, and allowed the bairn to be baptized without any more ado. I think honest Mr. Daff has acted like himself, and I trust and hope there will be a great gathering at the christening, and, that my mite may not be wanting, you will slip in a guinea note when the dish goes round, but in such a manner, that it may not be jealoused from whose hand it comes.

Since my last letter, we have been very thrang in the way of seeing the curiosities of London; but I must go on regular, and tell you all, which, I think, it is my duty to do, that you may let my people know. First, then, we have been at Windsor Castle, to see the king lying in state, and, afterwards, his interment; and sorry am I to say, it was not a sight that could satisfy any godly mind on such an occasion. We went in a coach of our own, by ourselves, and found the town of Windsor like a cried fair. We were then directed to the Castle gate, where a terrible crowd was gathered together; and we had not been long in that crowd, till a pocket-picker, as I thought, cutted off the tail of my coat, with my pocket-book in my pocket, which I never missed at the time. But it seems the coat tail was found, and a policeman got it, and held it up on the end of his stick, and cried, whose pocket is this? showing the book that was therein in his hand. I was confounded to see my pocket-book there, and could scarcely believe my own eyes; but Mrs. Pringle knew it at the first glance, and said, 'It's my gudeman's'; at the which, there was a great shout of derision among the multitude, and we would baith have then been glad to disown the pocket-book, but it was returned to us, I may almost say, against our will; but the scorners, when they saw our confusion, behaved with great civility towards us, so that we got into the Castle-yard with no other damage than the loss of the flap of my coat tail.

Being in the Castle-yard, we followed the crowd into another gate, and up a stair, and saw the king lying in state, which was a very dismal sight — and I thought of Solomon in all his glory, when I saw the coffin, and the mutes, and the mourners ; and reflecting on the long infirmity of mind of the good old king, I said to myself, in the words of the book of Job, ' Doth not their excellency which is in them go away ? they die even without wisdom ! '

When we had seen the sight, we came out of the Castle, and went to an inn to get a chack of dinner ; but there was such a crowd, that no resting-place could for a time be found for us. Gentle and semple were there, all mingled, and no respect of persons ; only there was, at a table nigh unto ours, a fat Glasgow manufacturer, who ordered a bottle of champaign wine, and did all he could in the drinking of it by himself, to show that he was a man in well-doing circumstances. While he was talking over his wine, a great peer of the realm, with a star on his breast, came into the room, and ordered a glass of brandy and water ; and I could see, when he saw the Glasgow manufacturer drinking champaign wine on that occasion, that he greatly marvelled thereat.

When we had taken our dinner, we went out to walk and see the town of Windsor ; but there was such a mob of coaches going and coming, and men and horses, that we left the streets, and went to inspect the king's policy, which is of great compass, but in a careless order, though it costs a world of money to keep it up. Afterwards, we went back to the inns, to get tea for Mrs. Pringle and her daughter, while Andrew Pringle, my son, was seeing if he could get tickets to buy, to let us into the inside of the Castle, to see the burial—but he came back without luck, and I went out myself, being more experienced in the world, and I saw a gentleman's servant with a ticket in his hand, and I asked him to sell it to me, which the man did with thankfulness, for five shillings, although the price was said to be golden guineas. But as this ticket admitted only one person, it was hard to say what should be done with it when I got back to my family. However, as by this time we were all very much fatigued, I gave it to Andrew Pringle, my son, and Mrs. Pringle, and her daughter Rachel, agreed to bide with me in the inns.

Andrew Pringle, my son, having got the ticket, left us sitting, when shortly after in came a nobleman, high in the cabinet, as I think he must have been, and he having politely asked leave to take his tea at our table, because of the great throng in the house, we fell into a conversation together, and he, understanding thereby that I was a minister of the Church of Scotland, said he thought he could help us into a place to see the funeral; so, after he had drank his tea, he took us with him, and got us into the Castle-yard, where we had an excellent place, near to the Glasgow manufacturer that drank the champaign. The drink by this time, however, had got into that poor man's head, and he talked so loud, and so little to the purpose, that the soldiers who were guarding were obliged to make him hold his peace, at which he was not a little nettled, and told the soldiers that he had himself been a soldier, and served the king without pay, having been a volunteer officer. But this had no more effect than to make the soldiers laugh at him, which was not a decent thing at the interment of their master, our most gracious Sovereign that was.

However, in this situation we saw all; and I can assure you it was a very edifying sight; and the people demeaned themselves with so much propriety, that there was no need for any guards at all; indeed, for that matter, of the two, the guards, who had eaten the king's bread, were the only ones there, saving and excepting the Glasgow manufacturer, that manifested an irreverent spirit towards the royal obsequies. But they are men familiar with the king of terrors on the field of battle, and it was not to be expected that their hearts would be daunted like those of others by a doing of a civil character.

When all was over, we returned to the inns, to get our chaise, to go back to London that night, for beds were not to be had for love or money at Windsor, and we reached our temporary home in Norfolk Street about four o'clock in the morning, well satisfied with what we had seen,—but all the meantime I had forgotten the loss of the flap of my coat, which caused no little sport when I came to recollect what a pookit like body I must have been, walking about in the king's policy like a peacock without my tail. But I must conclude, for Mrs. Pringle has a letter to put in the frank for Miss Nanny Eydent, which you will send to her by one of your scholars, as it contains information that may be serviceable to Miss Nanny in her business, both as a mantua-maker and a superintendent of the genteeler sort of burials at Irvine and our vicinity. So that this is all from your friend and pastor,

ZACHARIAH PRINGLE.

'I think,' said Miss Isabella Tod, as Mr. Micklewham finished the reading of the Doctor's epistle, 'that my friend Rachel might have given me some account of the ceremony ; but Captain Sabre seems to have been a much more interesting object to her than the pride and pomp to her brother, or even the Glasgow manufacturer to her father.' In saying these words, the young lady took the following letter from her pocket, and was on the point of beginning to read it, when Miss Becky Glibbans exclaimed, 'I had aye my fears that Rachel was but light-headed, and I'll no be surprised to hear more about her and the dragoon or a's done.' Mr. Snodgrass looked at Becky, as if he had been afflicted at the moment with unpleasant ideas ; and perhaps he would have rebuked the spitefulness of her insinuations, had not her mother sharply snubbed the uncongenial maiden, in terms at least as pungent as any which the reverend gentleman would have employed. 'I'm sure,' replied Miss Becky, pertly, 'I meant no ill ; but if Rachel Pringle can write about nothing but this Captain Sabre, she might as well let it alone, and her letter canna be worth the hearing.' 'Upon that,' said the clergyman, 'we can form a judgment when we have heard it, and I beg that Miss Isabella may proceed,'—which she did accordingly.

LETTER XIV

Miss Rachel Pringle to Miss Isabella Tod

LONDON.

MY DEAR BELL—I take up my pen with a feeling of disappointment such as I never felt before. Yesterday was the day appointed for the funeral of the good old king, and it was agreed that we should go to Windsor, to pour the tribute of our tears upon the royal hearse. Captain Sabre promised to go with us, as he is well acquainted with the town, and the interesting objects around the Castle, so dear to chivalry, and embalmed by the genius of Shakespeare and many a minor bard, and I promised myself a day of unclouded felicity—but the captain was ordered to be on duty,—and the crowd was so rude and riotous, that I had no enjoyment whatever; but, pining with chagrin at the little respect paid by the rabble to the virtues of the departed monarch, I would fainly have retired into some solemn and sequestered grove, and breathed my sorrows to the listening waste. Nor was the loss of the captain, to explain and illuminate the different baronial circumstances around the Castle, the only thing I had to regret in this ever-memorable excursion—my tender and affectionate mother was so desirous to see everything in the most particular manner, in order that she might give an account of the funeral to Nanny Eydent, that she had no mercy either upon me or my father, but obliged us to go with her to the most difficult and inaccessible places. How vain was all this meritorious assiduity! for of what avail can the ceremonies of a royal funeral be to Miss Nanny, at Irvine, where kings never die, and where, if they did, it is not at all probable that Miss Nanny would be employed to direct their solemn obsequies? As for my brother, he was so entranced with his own enthusiasm, that he paid but little attention to us, which made me the more sensible of the want we suffered from the absence of Captain Sabre. In a word, my dear Bell, never did I pass a more unsatisfactory day, and I wish it blotted for ever from my remembrance. Let it therefore be consigned to the abysses of oblivion, while I recall the more pleasing incidents that have happened since I wrote you last.

On Sunday, according to invitation, as I told you, we dined with the Argents—and were entertained by them in a style at once most splendid, and on the most easy footing. I shall not attempt to describe the consumable materials of the table, but call your attention, my dear friend, to the intellectual portion of the entertainment, a subject much more congenial to your delicate and refined character.

Mrs. Argent is a lady of considerable personal magnitude, of an open and affable disposition. In this respect, indeed, she bears a striking resemblance to her nephew, Captain Sabre, with whose relationship to her we were unacquainted before that day. She received us as friends in whom she felt a peculiar interest; for when she heard that my mother had got her dress and mine from Cranbury Alley, she expressed the greatest astonishment, and told us, that it was not at all a place where persons of fashion could expect to be properly served. Nor can I disguise the fact, that the flounced and gorgeous garniture of our dresses was in shocking contrast to the amiable simplicity of hers and the fair Arabella, her daughter, a charming girl, who, notwithstanding the fashionable splendour in which she has been educated, displays a delightful sprightliness of manner, that, I have some notion, has not been altogether lost on the heart of my brother.

When we returned upstairs to the drawing-room, after dinner, Miss Arabella took her harp, and was on the point of favouring us with a Mozart; but her mother, recollecting that we were Presbyterians, thought it might not be agreeable, and she desisted, which I was sinful enough to regret; but my mother was so evidently alarmed at the idea of playing on the harp on a Sunday night, that I suppressed my own wishes, in filial veneration for those of that respected parent. Indeed, fortunate it was that the music was not performed; for, when we returned home, my father remarked with great solemnity, that such a way of passing the Lord's night as we had passed it, would have been a great sin in Scotland.

Captain Sabre, who called on us next morning, was so delighted when he understood that we were acquainted with his aunt, that he lamented he had not happened to know it before, as he would, in that case, have met us there. He is indeed very attentive, but I assure you that I feel no particular interest about him; for although he is certainly a very handsome young man, he is not such a genius as my brother, and has no literary partialities. But literary accomplishments are, you know, foreign to the military profession, and if the captain has not distinguished himself by cutting up authors in the reviews, he has acquired an honourable medal, by overcoming the enemies of the civilised world at Waterloo.

To-night the playhouses open again, and we are going to the Oratorio, and the captain goes with us, a circumstance which I am the more pleased at, as we are strangers, and he will tell us the names of the performers. My father made some scruple of consenting to be of the party; but when he heard that an Oratorio was a concert of sacred music, he thought it would be only a sinless deviation if he did, so he goes likewise.

53

'Miss Arabella took her harp.'

The captain, therefore, takes an early dinner with us at five o'clock. Alas! to what changes am I doomed,—that was the tea hour at the manse of Garnock. Oh, when shall I revisit the primitive simplicities of my native scenes again! But neither time nor distance, my dear Bell, can change the affection with which I subscribe myself, ever affectionately, yours,

RACHEL PRINGLE.

At the conclusion of this letter, the countenance of Mrs. Glibbans was evidently so darkened, that it daunted the company, like an eclipse of the sun, when all nature is saddened. 'What think you, Mr. Snodgrass,' said that spirit-stricken lady, —'what think you of this dining on the Lord's day,—this playing on the harp; the carnal Mozarting of that ungodly family, with whom the corrupt human nature of our friends has been chambering?' Mr. Snodgrass was at some loss for an answer, and hesitated, but Miss Mally Glencairn relieved him from his embarrassment, by remarking, that 'the harp was a holy instrument,' which somewhat troubled the settled orthodoxy of Mrs. Glibbans's visage. 'Had it been an organ,' said Mr. Snodgrass, dryly, 'there might have been, perhaps, more reason to doubt; but, as Miss Mally justly remarks, the harp has been used from the days of King David in the performances of sacred music, together with the psalter, the timbrel, the sackbut, and the cymbal.' The wrath of the polemical Deborah of the Relief-Kirk was somewhat appeased by this explanation, and she inquired in a more diffident tone, whether a Mozart was not a metrical paraphrase of the song of Moses after the overthrow of the Egyptians in the Red Sea; 'in which case, I must own,' she observed, 'that the sin and guilt of the thing is less grievous in the sight of HIM before whom all the actions of men are abominations.' Miss Isabella Tod, availing herself of this break in the conversation, turned round to Miss Nanny Eydent, and begged that she would read her letter from Mrs. Pringle. We should do injustice, however, to honest worth and patient industry, were we, in thus introducing Miss Nanny to our readers, not to give them some account of her lowly and virtuous character.

Miss Nanny was the eldest of three sisters, the daughters of a shipmaster, who was lost at sea when they were very young; and his all having perished with him, they were indeed, as their mother said, the children of Poverty and Sorrow. By the help of a little credit, the widow contrived, in a small shop, to eke out her days till Nanny was able to assist her. It was the intention of the poor woman to take up a girl's school for reading and knitting, and Nanny was destined to instruct the pupils in that higher branch of accomplishment—the different stitches of the sampler. But about the time that Nanny was advancing to the requisite degree of perfection in chain-steek and pie-holes—indeed had made some progress in the Lord's prayer between two yew trees— tambouring was introduced at Irvine, and Nanny was sent to acquire a competent knowledge of that classic art, honoured by the fair hands of the beautiful Helen and the chaste and domestic Andromache. In this she instructed her sisters ; and such was the fruit of their application and constant industry, that her mother abandoned the design of keeping school, and continued to ply her little huxtry in more easy circumstances. The fluctuations of trade in time taught them that it would not be wise to trust to the loom, and accordingly Nanny was at some pains to learn mantua-making ; and it was fortunate that she did so—for the tambouring gradually went out of fashion, and the flowering which followed suited less the infirm constitution of poor Nanny. The making of gowns for ordinary occasions led to the making of mournings, and the making of mournings naturally often caused Nanny to be called in at deaths, which, in process of time, promoted her to have the management of burials ; and in this line of business she has now a large proportion of the genteelest in Irvine and its vicinity ; and in all her various engagements her behaviour has been as blameless and obliging as her assiduity has been uniform ; insomuch, that the numerous ladies to whom she is known take a particular pleasure in supplying her with the newest patterns, and earliest information, respecting the varieties and changes of fashions ; and to the influence of the same good feelings in the breast of Mrs. Pringle, Nanny was indebted for the following letter. How far the information which it contains may be deemed exactly suitable to the circumstances in which Miss Nanny's lot is cast, our readers may judge for themselves ; but we are happy to state, that it has proved of no small advantage to her : for since it has been known that she had received a full, true, and particular account, of all manner of London fashions, from so managing and notable a woman as the minister's wife of Garnock, her consideration has been so augmented in the opinion of the neighbouring gentlewomen, that she is not only consulted as to funerals, but is often called in to assist in the decoration and arrangement of wedding-dinners, and other occasions of sumptuous banqueting; by which she is enabled, during the suspension of the flowering trade, to earn a lowly but a respected livelihood.

LETTER XV

*Mrs. Pringle to Miss Nanny Eydent, Mantua-maker,
Seagate Head, Irvine*

LONDON.

DEAR MISS NANNY—Miss Mally Glencairn would tell you all how it happent that I was disabled, by our misfortunes in the ship, from riting to you konserning the London fashons as I promist; for I wantit to be partikylor, and to say nothing but what I saw with my own eyes, that it might be servisable to you in your bizness—so now I will begin with the old king's burial, as you have sometimes okashon to lend a helping hand in that way at Irvine, and nothing could be more genteeler of the kind than a royal obsakew for a patron; but no living sole can give a distink account of this matter, for you know the old king was the father of his piple, and the croud was so great. Howsomever we got into our oun hired shaze at daylight; and when we were let out at the castel yett of Windsor, we went into the mob, and by and by we got within the castel walls, when great was the lamentation for the purdition of shawls and shoos, and the Doctor's coat pouch was clippit off by a pocket-picker. We then ran to a wicket-gate, and up an old timber-stair with a rope ravel, and then we got to a great pentit chamber called King George's Hall: After that we were allowt to go into another room full of guns and guards, that told us all to be silent: so then we all went like sawlies, holding our tongues in an awful manner, into a dysmal room hung with black cloth, and lighted with dum wax-candles in silver skonses, and men in a row all in mulancholic posters. At length and at last we came to the coffin; but although I was as partikylar as possoble, I could see nothing that I would recommend. As for the interment, there was nothing but even-down wastrie—wax-candles blowing away in the wind, and flunkies as fou as pipers, and an unreverent mob that scarsely could demean themselves with decency as the body was going by; only the Duke of York, who carrit the head, had on no hat, which I think was the newest identical thing in the affair: but really there was nothing that could be recommended. Howsomever I understood that there was no draigie, which was a saving; for the bread and wine for such a multitude would have been a destruction to a lord's living: and this is the only point that the fashon set in the king's feunoral may be follot in Irvine.

Since the burial, we have been to see the play, where the leddies were all in deep murning; but excepting that some had black gum-floors on their heads, I saw leetil for admiration —only that bugles, I can ashure you, are not worn at all this season; and surely this murning must be a vast detrimint to bizness—for where there is no verietie, there can be but leetil to do in your line. But one thing I should not forget, and that is, that in the vera best houses, after tea and coffee after dinner, a cordial dram is handed about; but likewise I could observe, that the fruit is not set on with the cheese, as in our part of the country, but comes, after the cloth is drawn, with the wine; and no such a thing as a punch-bowl is to be heard of within the four walls of London. Howsomever, what I principally notised was, that the tea and coffee is not made by the lady of the house, but out of the room, and brought in without sugar or milk, on servors, every one helping himself, and only plain flimsy loaf and butter is served—no such thing as shortbread, seed-cake, bun, marmlet, or jeelly to be seen, which is an okonomical plan, and well worthy of adaptation in ginteel families with narrow incomes, in Irvine or elsewhere.

But when I tell you what I am now going to say, you will not be surprizt at the great wealth in London. I paid for a bumbeseen gown, not a bit better than the one that was made by you that the sore calamity befell, and no so fine neither, more than three times the price; so you see, Miss Nanny, if you were going to pouse your fortune, you could not do better than pack up your ends and your awls and come to London. But ye're far better at home—for this is not a town for any creditable young woman like you, to live in by herself, and I am wearying to be back, though it's hard to say when the Doctor will get his counts settlet. I wish you, howsomever, to mind the patches for the bed-cover that I was going to patch, for a licht afternoon seam, as the murning for the king will no be so general with you, and the spring fashons will be coming on to help my gathering—so no more at present from your friend and well-wisher, JANET PRINGLE.

CHAPTER VI

PHILOSOPHY AND RELIGION

On Sunday morning, before going to church, Mr. Micklewham called at the manse, and said that he wished particularly to speak to Mr. Snodgrass. Upon being admitted, he found the young helper engaged at breakfast, with a book lying on his table, very like a volume of a new novel called *Ivanhoe*, in its appearance, but of course it must have been sermons done up in that manner to attract fashionable readers. As soon, however, as Mr. Snodgrass saw his visitor, he hastily removed the book, and put it into the table-drawer.

The precentor having taken a seat at the opposite side of the fire, began somewhat diffidently to mention, that he had received a letter from the Doctor, that made him at a loss whether or not he ought to read it to the elders, as usual, after worship, and therefore was desirous of consulting Mr. Snodgrass on the subject, for it recorded, among other things, that the Doctor had been at the playhouse, and Mr. Micklewham was quite sure that Mr. Craig would be neither to bind nor to hold when he heard that, although the transgression was certainly mollified by the nature of the performance. As the clergyman, however, could offer no opinion until he saw the letter, the precentor took it out of his pocket, and Mr. Snodgrass found the contents as follows :—

60

'*Mr. Snodgrass hastily removed the book.*'

LETTER XVI

The Rev. Z. Pringle, D.D., to Mr. Micklewham, Schoolmaster and Session-Clerk, Garnock

LONDON.

DEAR SIR—You will recollect that, about twenty years ago, there was a great sound throughout all the West that a playhouse in Glasgow had been converted into a tabernacle of religion. I remember it was glad tidings to our ears in the parish of Garnock; and that Mr. Craig, who had just been ta'en on for an elder that fall, was for having a thanksgiving-day on the account thereof, holding it to be a signal manifestation of a new birth in the of-old-godly town of Glasgow, which had become slack in the way of well-doing, and the church therein lukewarm, like that of Laodicea. It was then said, as I well remember, that when the Tabernacle was opened, there had not been seen, since the Kaimslang wark, such a congregation as was there assembled, which was a great proof that it's the matter handled, and not the place, that maketh pure; so that when you and the elders hear that I have been at the theatre of Drury Lane, in London, you must not think that I was there to see a carnal stage play, whether tragical or comical, or that I would so far demean myself and my cloth, as to be a witness to the chambering and wantonness of ne'er-du-weel play-actors. No, Mr. Micklewham, what I went to see was an Oratorio, a most edifying exercise of psalmody and prayer, under the management of a pious gentleman, of the name of Sir George Smart, who is, as I am informed, at the greatest pains to instruct the exhibitioners, they being, for the most part, before they get into his hands, poor uncultivated creatures, from Italy, France, and Germany, and other atheistical and popish countries.

They first sung a hymn together very decently, and really with as much civilised harmony as could be expected from novices; indeed so well, that I thought them almost as melodious as your own singing class of the trades lads from Kilwinning. Then there was one Mr. Braham, a Jewish proselyte, that was set forth to show us a specimen of his proficiency. In the praying part, what he said was no

62

objectionable as to the matter ; but he drawled in his manner
to such a pitch, that I thought he would have broken out into
an even-down song, as I sometimes think of yourself when you
spin out the last word in reading out the line in a warm
summer afternoon. In the hymn by himself, he did better ;
he was, however, sometimes like to lose the tune, but the
people gave him great encouragement when he got back again.
Upon the whole, I had no notion that there was any such
Christianity in practice among the Londoners, and I am
happy to tell you, that the house was very well filled, and the
congregation wonderful attentive. No doubt that excellent
man, Mr. W——, has a hand in these public strainings
after grace, but he was not there that night ; for I have seen
him ; and surely at the sight I could not but say to myself,
that it's beyond the compass of the understanding of man to
see what great things Providence worketh with small means,
for Mr. W—— is a small creature. When I beheld his
diminutive stature, and thought of what he had achieved for
the poor negroes and others in the house of bondage, I said
to myself, that here the hand of Wisdom is visible, for the
load of perishable mortality is laid lightly on his spirit, by
which it is enabled to clap its wings and crow so crously on
the dunghill top of this world ; yea even in the House of
Parliament.

I was taken last Thursday morning to breakfast with him
in his house at Kensington, by an East India man, who is
likewise surely a great saint. It was a heart-healing meeting
of many of the godly, which he holds weekly in the season ;
and we had such a warsle of the spirit among us that
the like cannot be told. I was called upon to pray, and a
worthy gentleman said, when I was done, that he never had
met with more apostolic simplicity—indeed, I could see with
the tail of my eye, while I was praying, that the chief saint
himself was listening with a curious pleasant satisfaction.

As for our doings here anent the legacy, things are going
forward in the regular manner ; but the expense is terrible,
and I have been obliged to take up money on account ; but,
as it was freely given by the agents, I am in hopes all will
end well ; for, considering that we are but strangers to them,
they would not have assisted us in this matter had they not
been sure of the means of payment in their own hands.

The people of London are surprising kind to us; we need not, if we thought proper ourselves, eat a dinner in our own lodgings; but it would ill become me, at my time of life, and with the character for sobriety that I have maintained, to show an example in my latter days of riotous living; therefore, Mrs. Pringle, and her daughter, and me, have made a point of going nowhere three times in the week; but as for Andrew Pringle, my son, he has forgathered with some acquaintance, and I fancy we will be obliged to let him take the length of his tether for a while. But not altogether without a curb neither, for the agent's son, young Mr. Argent, had almost persuaded him to become a member of Parliament, which he said he could get him made, for more than a thousand pounds less than the common price—the state of the new king's health having lowered the commodity of seats. But this I would by no means hear of; he is not yet come to years of discretion enough to sit in council; and, moreover, he has not been tried; and no man, till he has out of doors shown something of what he is, should be entitled to power and honour within. Mrs. Pringle, however, thought he might do as well as young Dunure; but Andrew Pringle, my son, has not the solidity of head that Mr. K——dy has, and is over free and outspoken, and cannot take such pains to make his little go a great way, like that well-behaved young gentleman. But you will be grieved to hear that Mr. K——dy is in opposition to the government; and truly I am at a loss to understand how a man of Whig principles can be an adversary to the House of Hanover. But I never meddled much in politick affairs, except at this time, when I prohibited Andrew Pringle, my son, from offering to be a member of Parliament, notwithstanding the great bargain that he would have had of the place.

And since we are on public concerns, I should tell you, that I was minded to send you a newspaper at the second-hand, every day when we were done with it. But when we came to inquire, we found that we could get the newspaper for a shilling a week every morning but Sunday, to our breakfast, which was so much cheaper than buying a whole paper, that Mrs. Pringle thought it would be a great extravagance; and, indeed, when I came to think of the loss of time a newspaper every day would occasion to my people, I considered it would be very wrong of me to send you any at all. For I do think that honest folks in a far-off country parish should not make or meddle with the things that pertain to government,—the more especially, as it is well known, that there is as much falsehood as truth in newspapers, and they have not the means of testing their statements. Not, however, that I am an advocate for passive obedience ; God forbid. On the contrary, if ever the time should come, in my day, of a saint-slaying tyrant attempting to bind the burden of prelatic abominations on our backs, such a blast of the gospel trumpet would be heard in Garnock, as it does not become me to say, but I leave it to you and others, who have experienced my capacity as a soldier of the word so long, to think what it would then be. Meanwhile, I remain, my dear sir, your friend and pastor,   Z. PRINGLE.

When Mr. Snodgrass had perused this epistle, he paused some time, seemingly in doubt, and then he said to Mr. Micklewham, that, considering the view which the Doctor had taken of the matter, and that he had not gone to the play-house for the motives which usually take bad people to such places, he thought there could be no possible harm in reading the letter to the elders, and that Mr. Craig, so far from being displeased, would doubtless be exceedingly rejoiced to learn that the playhouses of London were occasionally so well employed as on the night when the Doctor was there.

Mr. Micklewham then inquired if Mr. Snodgrass had heard from Mr. Andrew, and was answered in the affirmative ; but the letter was not read. Why it was withheld our readers must guess for themselves ; but we have been fortunate enough to obtain the following copy.

LETTER XVII

Andrew Pringle, Esq., to the Rev. Mr. Charles Snodgrass

LONDON.

MY DEAR FRIEND—As the season advances, London gradu-ally unfolds, like Nature, all the variety of her powers and pleasures. By the Argents we have been introduced effectu-ally into society, and have now only to choose our acquaintance among those whom we like best. I should employ another word than choose, for I am convinced that there is no choice in the matter. In his friendships and affections, man is subject to some inscrutable moral law, similar in its effects to what the chemists call affinity. While under the blind influence of this sympathy, we, forsooth, suppose ourselves free agents ! But a truce with philosophy.

The amount of the legacy is now ascertained. The stock, however, in which a great part of the money is vested being shut, the transfer to my father cannot be made for some time ; and till this is done, my mother cannot be persuaded that we have yet got anything to trust to—an unfortunate notion which renders her very unhappy. The old gentleman himself takes no interest now in the business. He has got his mind at ease by the payment of all the legacies ; and having fallen in with some of the members of that political junto, the Saints, who are worldly enough to link, as often as they can, into their association, the powerful by wealth or talent, his whole time is occupied in assisting to promote their humbug ; and he has absolutely taken it into his head, that the attention he receives from them for his subscriptions is on account of his eloquence as a preacher, and that hitherto he has been altogether in an error with respect to his own abilities. The effect of this is abundantly amusing ; but the source of it is very evident. Like most people who pass a sequestered life, he had formed an exaggerated opinion of public characters ; and on seeing them in reality so little superior to the generality of mankind, he imagines that he was all the time nearer to their level than he had ventured to suppose ; and the discovery has placed him on the happiest terms with himself. It is impossible that I can respect his manifold excellent qualities and goodness of heart more than I do ; but there is an innocency in this simplicity, which, while it often compels me to smile, makes me feel towards him a degree of tenderness, somewhat too familiar for that filial reverence that is due from a son.

Perhaps, however, you will think me scarcely less under the influence of a similar delusion when I tell you, that I have been somehow or other drawn also into an association, not indeed so public or potent as that of the Saints, but equally persevering in the objects for which it has been formed. The drift of the Saints, as far as I can comprehend the matter, is to procure the advancement to political power of men distinguished for the purity of their lives, and the integrity of their conduct; and in that way, I presume, they expect to effect the accomplishment of that blessed epoch, the Millennium, when the Saints are to rule the whole earth. I do not mean to say that this is their decided and determined object; I only infer, that it is the necessary tendency of their proceedings; and I say it with all possible respect and sincerity, that, as a public party, the Saints are not only perhaps the most powerful, but the party which, at present, best deserves power.

The association, however, with which I have happened to become connected, is of a very different description. Their object is, to pass through life with as much pleasure as they can obtain, without doing anything unbecoming the rank of gentlemen, and the character of men of honour. We do not assemble such numerous meetings as the Saints, the Whigs, or the Radicals, nor are our speeches delivered with so much vehemence. We even, I think, tacitly exclude oratory. In a word, our meetings seldom exceed the perfect number of the muses; and our object on these occasions is not so much to deliberate on plans of prospective benefits to mankind, as to enjoy the present time for ourselves, under the temperate inspiration of a well-cooked dinner, flavoured with elegant wine, and just so much of mind as suits the fleeting topics of the day. T——, whom I formerly mentioned, introduced me to this delightful society. The members consist of about fifty gentlemen, who dine occasionally at each other's houses; the company being chiefly selected from the brotherhood, if that term can be applied to a circle of acquaintance, who, without any formal institution of rules, have gradually acquired a consistency that approximates to organisation. But the universe of this vast city contains a plurality of systems; and the one into which I have been attracted may be described as that of the idle intellects. In general society, the members of our party are looked up to as men of taste and refinement, and are received with a degree of deference that bears some resemblance to the respect paid to the hereditary endowment of rank. They consist either of young men who have acquired distinction at college, or gentlemen of fortune who have a relish for intellectual pleasures, free from the acerbities of politics, or the dull formalities which so many of the pious think essential to their religious pretensions. The wealthy furnish the entertainments, which are always in a superior style, and the ingredient of birth is not requisite in the qualifications of a member, although some jealousy is entertained of professional men, and not a little of merchants. T——, to whom I am also indebted for this view of that circle of which he is the brightest ornament, gives a felicitous explanation of the reason. He says, professional men, who are worth anything at all, are always ambitious, and endeavour to make their acquaintance subservient to their own advancement; while merchants are liable to such casualties, that their friends are constantly exposed to the risk of being obliged to sink them below their wonted equality, by granting them favours in times of difficulty, or, what is worse, by refusing to grant them.

I am much indebted to you for the introduction to your friend G——. He is one of us; or rather, he moves in an eccentric sphere of his own, which crosses, I believe, almost all the orbits of all the classed and classifiable systems of London. I found him exactly what you described; and we were on the frankest footing of old friends in the course of the first quarter of an hour. He did me the honour to fancy that I belonged, as a matter of course, to some one of the literary fraternities of Edinburgh, and that I would be curious to see the associations of the learned here. What he said respecting them was highly characteristic of the man. 'They are,' said he, 'the dullest things possible. On my return from abroad, I visited them all, expecting to find something of that easy disengaged mind which constitutes the charm of those of France and Italy. But in London, among those who have a character to keep up, there is such a vigilant circumspection, that I should as soon expect to find nature in the ballets of the Opera-house, as genius at the established haunts of authors, artists, and men of science. Bankes gives, I suppose officially, a public breakfast weekly, and opens his house for conversations on the Sundays. I found at his breakfasts, tea and coffee, with hot rolls, and men of celebrity afraid to speak. At the conversations, there was something even worse. A few plausible talking fellows created a buzz in the room, and the merits of some paltry nick-nack of mechanism or science was discussed. The party consisted undoubtedly of the most eminent men of their respective lines in the world; but they were each and all so apprehensive of having their ideas purloined, that they took the most guarded care never to speak of anything that they deemed of the slightest consequence, or to hazard an opinion that might be called in question. The man who either wishes to augment his knowledge, or to pass his time agreeably, will never expose himself to a repetition of the fastidious exhibitions of engineers and artists who have their talents at market. But such things are among the curiosities of London; and if you have any inclination to undergo the initiating mortification of being treated as a young man who may be likely to interfere with their professional interests, I can easily get you introduced.'

I do not know whether to ascribe these strictures of your friend to humour or misanthropy; but they were said without bitterness; indeed so much as matters of course, that, at the moment, I could not but feel persuaded they were just. I spoke of them to T——, who says, that undoubtedly G——'s account of the exhibitions is true in substance, but that it is his own sharp-sightedness which causes him to see them so offensively; for that ninety-nine out of the hundred in the world would deem an evening spent at the conversations of Sir Joseph Bankes a very high intellectual treat.

G—— has invited me to dinner, and I expect some amusement; for T——, who is acquainted with him, says, that it is his fault to employ his mind too much on all occasions; and that, in all probability, there will be something, either in the fare or the company, that I shall remember as long as I live. However, you shall hear all about it in my next.—Yours,

ANDREW PRINGLE.

On the same Sunday on which Mr. Micklewham consulted Mr. Snodgrass as to the propriety of reading the Doctor's letter to the elders, the following epistle reached the post-office of Irvine, and was delivered by Saunders Dickie himself, at the door of Mrs. Glibbans to her servan lassie, who, as her mistress had gone to the Relief Church, told him, that he would have to come for the postage the morn's morning. 'Oh,' said Saunders, 'there's naething to pay but my ain trouble, for it's frankit; but aiblins the mistress will gie me a bit drappie, and so I'll come betimes i' the morning.'

LETTER XVIII

Mrs. Pringle to Mrs. Glibbans

LONDON.

MY DEAR MRS. GLIBBANS—The breking up of the old Parlament has been the cause why I did not right you before, it having taken it out of my poor to get a frank for my letter till yesterday; and I do ashure you, that I was most extraordinar uneasy at the great delay, wishing much to let you know the decayt state of the Gospel in thir perts, which is the pleasure of your life to study by day, and meditate on in the watches of the night.

There is no want of going to church, and, if that was a sign of grease and peese in the kingdom of Christ, the toun of London might hold a high head in the tabernacles of the faithful and true witnesses. But saving Dr. Nichol of Swallo-Street, and Dr. Manuel of London-Wall, there is nothing sound in the way of preeching here; and when I tell you that Mr. John Gant, your friend, and some other flea-lugged fallows, have set up a Heelon congregation, and got a young man to preach Erse to the English, ye maun think in what a state sinful souls are left in London. But what I have been the most consarned about is the state of the dead. I am no meaning those who are dead in trespasses and sins, but the true dead. Ye will hardly think, that they are buried in a popish-like manner, with prayers, and white gowns, and ministers, and spadefuls of yerd cast upon them, and laid in vauts, like kists of orangers in a grocery seller—and I am told that, after a time, they are taken out when the vaut is shurfeeted, and their bones brunt, if they are no made into lampblack by a secret wark—which is a clean proof to me that a right doctrine cannot be established in this land—there being so little respec shone to the dead.

The worst point, howsomever, of all is, what is done with the prayers—and I have heard you say, that although there was nothing more to objec to the wonderful Doctor Chammers of Glasgou, that his reading of his sermons was testimony against him in the great controversy of sound doctrine; but what will you say to reading of prayers, and no only reading of prayers, but printed prayers, as if the contreet heart of the sinner had no more to say to the Lord in the hour of fasting and humiliation, than what a bishop can indite, and a bookseller make profit o'. 'Verily,' as I may say, in a word of scripter, I doobt if the glad tidings of salvation have yet been preeched in this land of London; but the ministers have good stipends, and where the ground is well manured, it may in time bring forth fruit meet for repentance.

There is another thing that behoves me to mention, and that is, that an elder is not to be seen in the churches of London, which is a sore signal that the piple are left to themselves; and in what state the morality can be, you may guess with an eye of pity. But on the Sabbath nights, there is such a going and coming, that it's more like a cried fair than the Lord's night—all sorts of poor people, instead of meditating on their bygane toil and misery of the week, making the Sunday their own day, as if they had not a greater Master to serve on that day, than the earthly man whom they served in the week-days. It is, howsomever, past the poor of nature to tell you of the sinfulness of London; and you may well think what is to be the end of all things, when I ashure you, that there is a newspaper sold every Sabbath morning, and read by those that never look at their Bibles. Our landlady asked us if we would take one; but I thought the Doctor would have fired the house, and you know it is not a small thing that kindles his passion. In short, London is not a place to come to hear the tidings of salvation preeched,—no that I mean to deny that there is not herine more than five righteous persons in it, and I trust the cornal's hagent is one; for if he is not, we are undone, having been obligated to take on already more than a hundred pounds of debt, to the account of our living, and the legacy yet in the dead thraws. But as I mean this for a spiritual letter, I will say no more about the root of all evil, as it is called in the words of truth and holiness; so referring you to what I have told Miss Mally Glencairn about the legacy and other things nearest my heart, I remain, my dear Mrs. Glibbans, your fellou Christian and sinner,   JANET PRINGLE.

Mrs. Glibbans received this letter between the preachings, and it was observed by all her acquaintance during the after-

noon service, that she was a laden woman. Instead of standing up at the prayers, as her wont was, she kept her seat,
sitting with downcast eyes, and ever and anon her left hand,
which was laid over her book on the reading-board of the
pew, was raised and allowed to drop with a particular moral
emphasis, bespeaking the mournful cogitations of her spirit.
On leaving the church, somebody whispered to the minister,
that surely Mrs. Glibbans had heard some sore news; upon
which that meek, mild, and modest good soul hastened
towards her, and inquired, with more than his usual kindness,
How she was? Her answer was brief and mysterious; and
she shook her head in such a manner that showed him all
was not right. 'Have you heard lately of your friends the
Pringles?' said he, in his sedate manner—'when do they
think of leaving London?'

'I wish they may ever get out o't,' was the agitated reply
of the afflicted lady.

'I am very sorry to hear you say so,' responded the minister.
'I thought all was in a fair way to an issue of the settlement.
I'm very sorry to hear this.'

'Oh, sir,' said the mourner, 'don't think that I am grieved
for them and their legacy—filthy lucre—no, sir; but I have
had a letter that has made my hair stand on end. Be none
surprised if you hear of the earth opening, and London swallowed
up, and a voice crying in the wilderness, "Woe, woe."'

The gentle priest was much surprised by this information;
it was evident that Mrs. Glibbans had received a terrible
account of the wickedness of London; and that the weight
upon her pious spirit was owing to that cause. He, therefore,
accompanied her home, and administered all the consolation
he was able to give; assuring her, that it was in the power
of Omnipotence to convert the stony heart into one of flesh
and tenderness, and to raise the British metropolis out of the
miry clay, and place it on a hill, as a city that could not be
hid; which Mrs. Glibbans was so thankful to hear, that, as
soon as he had left her, she took her tea in a satisfactory
frame of mind, and went the same night to Miss Mally Glencairn to hear what Mrs. Pringle had said to her. No visit
ever happened more opportunely; for just as Mrs. Glibbans
knocked at the door, Miss Isabella Tod made her appearance.
She had also received a letter from Rachel, in which it will

be seen that reference was made likewise to Mrs. Pringle's epistle to Miss Mally.

LETTER XIX

Miss Rachel Pringle to Miss Isabella Tod

LONDON.

MY DEAR BELL—How delusive are the flatteries of fortune ! The wealth that has been showered upon us, beyond all our hopes, has brought no pleasure to my heart, and I pour my unavailing sighs for your absence, when I would communicate the cause of my unhappiness. Captain Sabre has been most assiduous in his attentions, and I must confess to your sympathising bosom, that I do begin to find that he has an interest in mine. But my mother will not listen to his proposals, nor allow me to give him any encouragement, till the fatal legacy is settled. What can be her motive for this, I am unable to divine ; for the captain's fortune is far beyond what I could ever have expected without the legacy, and equal to all I could hope for with it. If, therefore, there is any doubt of the legacy being paid, she should allow me to accept him ; and if there is none, what can I do better ? In the meantime, we are going about seeing the sights ; but the general mourning is a great drawback on the splendour of gaiety. It ends, however, next Sunday ; and then the ladies, like the spring flowers, will be all in full blossom. I was with the Argents at the opera on Saturday last, and it far surpassed my ideas of grandeur. But the singing was not good—I never could make out the end or the beginning of a song, and it was drowned with the violins ; the scenery, however, was lovely ; but I must not say a word about the dancers, only that the females behaved in a manner so shocking, that I could scarcely believe it was possible for the delicacy of our sex to do. They are, however, all foreigners, who are, you know, naturally of a licentious character, especially the French women.

We have taken an elegant house in Baker Street, where we go on Monday next, and our own new carriage is to be home in the course of the week. All this, which has been done by the advice of Mrs. Argent, gives my mother great uneasiness, in case anything should yet happen to the legacy. My brother, however, who knows the law better than her, only laughs at her fears, and my father has found such a wonderful deal to do in religion here, that he is quite delighted, and is busy from morning to night in writing letters, and giving charitable donations. I am soon to be no less busy, but in another manner. Mrs. Argent has advised us to get in accomplished masters for me, so that, as soon as we are removed into our own local habitation, I am to begin with drawing and music, and the foreign languages. I am not, however, to learn much of the piano; Mrs. A. thinks it would take up more time than I can now afford; but I am to be cultivated in my singing, and she is to try if the master that taught Miss Stephens has an hour to spare—and to use her influence to persuade him to give it to me, although he only receives pupils for perfectioning, except they belong to families of distinction.

My brother had a hankering to be made a member of Parliament, and got Mr. Charles Argent to speak to my father about it, but neither he nor my mother would hear of such a thing, which I was very sorry for, as it would have been so convenient to me for getting franks; and I wonder my mother did not think of that, as she grudges nothing so much as the price of postage. But nothing do I grudge so little, especially when it is a letter from you. Why do you not write me oftener, and tell me what is saying about us, particularly by that spiteful toad, Becky Glibbans, who never could hear of any good happening to her acquaintance, without being as angry as if it was obtained at her own expense?

I do not like Miss Argent so well on acquaintance as I did at first; not that she is not a very fine lassie, but she gives herself such airs at the harp and piano—because she can play every sort of music at the first sight, and sing, by looking at the notes, any song, although she never heard it, which may be very well in a play-actor, or a governess, that has to win her bread by music; but I think the education of a modest young lady might have been better conducted.

Through the civility of the Argents, we have been introduced to a great number of families, and been much invited; but all the parties are so ceremonious, that I am never at my ease, which my brother says is owing to my rustic education, which I cannot understand; for, although the people are finer dressed, and the dinners and rooms grander than what I have seen, either at Irvine or Kilmarnock, the company are no wiser; and I have not met with a single literary character among them. And what are ladies and gentlemen without mind, but a well-dressed mob! It is to mind alone that I am at all disposed to pay the homage of diffidence.

The acquaintance of the Argents are all of the first circle, and we have got an invitation to a route from the Countess of J——y, in consequence of meeting her with them. She is a charming woman, and I anticipate great pleasure. Miss Argent says, however, she is ignorant and presuming; but how is it possible that she can be so, as she was an earl's daughter, and bred up for distinction? Miss Argent may be presuming, but a countess is necessarily above that, at least it would only become a duchess or marchioness to say so. This, however, is not the only occasion in which I have seen the detractive disposition of that young lady, who, with all her simplicity of manners and great accomplishments, is, you will perceive, just like ourselves, rustic as she doubtless thinks our breeding has been.

I have observed that nobody in London inquires about who another is; and that in company every one is treated on an equality, unless when there is some remarkable personal peculiarity, so that one really knows nothing of those whom one meets. But my paper is full, and I must not take another sheet, as my mother has a letter to send in the same frank to Miss Mally Glencairn. Believe me, ever affectionately yours,

RACHEL PRINGLE.

The three ladies knew not very well what to make of this letter. They thought there was a change in Rachel's ideas, and that it was not for the better; and Miss Isabella expressed, with a sentiment of sincere sorrow, that the acquisition of fortune seemed to have brought out some unamiable traits in her character, which, perhaps, had she not been exposed to the companions and temptations of the great world, would have slumbered, unfelt by herself, and unknown to her friends.

Mrs. Glibbans declared, that it was a waking of original sin, which the iniquity of London was bringing forth, as the heat of summer causes the rosin and sap to issue from the bark of the tree. In the meantime, Miss Mally had opened her letter, of which we subjoin a copy.

LETTER XX

Mrs. Pringle to Miss Mally Glencairn

LONDON.

DEAR MISS MALLY—I greatly stand in need of your advise and counsel at this time. The Doctor's affair comes on at a fearful slow rate, and the money goes like snow off a dyke. It is not to be told what has been paid for legacy-duty, and no legacy yet in hand; and we have been obligated to lift a whole hundred pounds out of the residue, and what that is to be the Lord only knows. But Miss Jenny Macbride, she has got her thousand pound, all in one bank bill, sent to her; Thomas Bowie, the doctor in Ayr, he has got his five hundred pounds; and auld Nanse Sorrel, that was nurse to the cornal, she has got the first year of her twenty pounds a year; but we have gotten nothing, and I jealouse, that if things go on at this rate, there will be nothing to get; and what will become of us then, after all the trubble and outlay that we have been pot too by this coming to London?

Howsomever, this is the black side of the story; for Mr. Charles Argent, in a jocose way, proposed to get Andrew made a Parliament member for three thousand pounds, which he said was cheap; and surely he would not have thought of such a thing, had he not known that Andrew would have the money to pay for't; and, over and above this, Mrs. Argent has been recommending Captain Sabre to me for Rachel, and she says he is a stated gentleman, with two thousand pounds rental, and her nephew; and surely she would not think Rachel a match for him, unless she had an inkling from her gudeman of what Rachel's to get. But I have told her that we would think of nothing of the sort till the counts war settled, which she may tell to her gudeman, and if he approves the match, it will make him hasten on the settlement, for really I am growing tired of this London, whar I am just like a fish out of the water. The Englishers are sae obstinate in their own way, that I can get them to do nothing like Christians; and, what is most provoking of all, their ways are very good when you know them; but they have no instink to teach a body how to learn them. Just this very morning, I told the

76

lass to get a jiggot of mutton for the morn's dinner, and she said there was not such a thing to be had in London, and threeppit it till I couldna stand her ; and, had it not been that Mr. Argent's French servan' man happened to come with a cart, inviting us to a ball, and who understood what a jiggot was, I might have reasoned till the day of doom without redress. As for the Doctor, I declare he's like an enchantit person, for he has falling in with a party of the elect here, as he says, and they have a kilfud yoking every Thursday at the house of Mr. W——, where the Doctor has been, and was asked to pray, and did it with great effec, which has made him so up in the buckle, that he does nothing but go to Bible soceeyetis, and mishonary meetings, and cherity sarmons, which cost a poor of money.

But what consarns me more than all is, that the temptations of this vanity fair have turnt the head of Andrew, and he has bought two horses, with an English man-servan', which you know is an eating moth. But how he payt for them, and whar he is to keep them, is past the compass of my understanding. In short, if the legacy does not cast up soon, I see nothing left for us but to leave the world as a legacy to you all, for my heart will be broken—and I often wish that the cornel hadna made us his residees, but only given us a clean soom, like Miss Jenny Macbride, although it had been no more ; for, my dear Miss Mally, it does not doo for a woman of my time of life to be taken out of her element, and, instead of looking after her family with a thrifty eye, to be sitting dressed all day seeing the money fleeing like sclate stanes. But what I have to tell is worse than all this ; we have been persuaded to take a furnisht house, where we go on Monday ; and we are to pay for it, for three months, no less than a hundred and fifty pounds, which is more than the half of the Doctor's whole stipend is, when the meal is twenty-pence the peck ; and we are to have three servan' lassies, besides Andrew's man, and the coachman that we have hired altogether for ourselves, having been persuaded to trist a new carriage of our own by the Argents, which I trust the Argents will find money to pay for ; and masters are to come in to teach Rachel the fasionable accomplishments, Mrs. Argent thinking she was rather old now to be sent to a boarding-school. But what I am to get to do for so many vorashous servants, is dreadful to think, there being no such thing as a wheel within the four walls of London ; and, if there was, the Englishers no nothing about spinning. In short, Miss Mally, I am driven dimentit, and I wish I could get the Doctor to come home with me to our manse, and leave all to Andrew and Rachel, with kurators ; but, as I said, he's as mickle bye himself as onybody, and says that his candle has been hidden under a bushel at Garnock more than thirty years, which looks as if the poor man was fey ; howsomever, he's happy in his delooshon, for if he was afflictit with that forethought and wisdom that I have, I know not what would be the upshot of all this calamity. But we maun hope for the best ; and, happen what will, I am, dear Miss Mally, your sincere friend, JANET PRINGLE.

Miss Mally sighed as she concluded, and said, ' Riches do not always bring happiness, and poor Mrs. Pringle would have been far better looking after her cows and her butter, and keeping her lassies at their wark, than with all this galravitching and grandeur.' ' Ah ! ' added Mrs. Glibbans, ' she's now a testifyer to the truth—she's now a testifyer ; happy it will be for her if she's enabled to make a sanctified use of the dispensation.'

CHAPTER VII

DISCOVERIES AND REBELLIONS

ONE evening as Mr. Snodgrass was taking a solitary walk towards Irvine, for the purpose of calling on Miss Mally Glencairn, to inquire what had been her latest accounts from their mutual friends in London, and to read to her a letter, which he had received two days before, from Mr. Andrew Pringle, he met, near Eglintoun Gates, that pious woman, Mrs. Glibbans, coming to Garnock, brimful of some most extraordinary intelligence. The air was raw and humid, and the ways were deep and foul; she was, however, protected without, and tempered within, against the dangers of both. Over her venerable satin mantle, lined with cat-skin, she wore a scarlet duffle Bath cloak, with which she was wont to attend the tent sermons of the Kilwinning and Dreghorn preachings in cold and inclement weather. Her black silk petticoat was pinned up, that it might not receive injury from the nimble paddling of her short steps in the mire; and she carried her best shoes and stockings in a handkerchief to be changed at the manse, and had fortified her feet for the road in coarse worsted hose, and thick plain-soled leather shoes.

Mr. Snodgrass proposed to turn back with her, but she would not permit him. 'No, sir,' said she, 'what I am about you cannot meddle in. You are here but a stranger—come to-day, and gane to-morrow;—and it does not pertain to you to sift into the doings that have been done before your time. Oh dear; but this is a sad thing—nothing like it since the silencing of M'Auly of Greenock. What will the worthy Doctor say when he hears tell o't? Had it fa'n out with that neighering body, James Daff, I wouldna hae car't a snuff of

79

tobacco, but wi' Mr. Craig, a man so gifted wi' the power of the Spirit, as I hae often had a delightful experience! Ay, ay, Mr. Snodgrass, take heed lest ye fall; we maun all lay it to heart; but I hope the trooper is still within the jurisdiction of church censures. She shouldna be spairt. Nae doubt, the fault lies with her, and it is that I am going to search; yea, as with a lighted candle.'

Mr. Snodgrass expressed his inability to understand to what Mrs. Glibbans alluded, and a very long and interesting disclosure took place, the substance of which may be gathered from the following letter; the immediate and instigating cause of the lady's journey to Garnock being the alarming intelligence which she had that day received of Mr. Craig's servant-damsel Betty having, by the style and title of Mrs. Craig, sent for Nanse Swaddle, the midwife, to come to her in her own case, which seemed to Mrs. Glibbans nothing short of a miracle, Betty having, the very Sunday before, helped the kettle when she drank tea with Mr. Craig, and sat at the room door, on a buffet-stool brought from the kitchen, while he performed family worship, to the great solace and edification of his visitor.

LETTER XXI

The Rev. Z. Pringle, D.D., to Mr. Micklewham, Schoolmaster and Session-Clerk, Garnock

DEAR SIR—I have received your letter of the 24th, which has given me a great surprise to hear, that Mr. Craig was married as far back as Christmas, to his own servant lass Betty, and me to know nothing of it, nor you neither, until it was time to be speaking to the midwife. To be sure, Mr. Craig, who is an elder, and a very rigid man, in his animadversions on the immoralities that come before the session, must have had his own good reasons for keeping his marriage so long a secret. Tell him, however, from me, that I wish both him and Mrs. Craig much joy and felicity; but he should be milder for the future on the thoughtlessness of youth and headstrong passions. Not that I insinuate that there has been any occasion in the conduct of such a godly man to cause a suspicion; but it's wonderful how he was married in December, and I cannot say that I am altogether so proud to hear it as I am at all times of the well-doing of my people. Really the way that Mr. Daff has comported himself in this matter is greatly to his credit ; and I doubt if the thing had happened with him, that Mr. Craig would have sifted with a sharp eye how he came to be married in December, and without bridal and banquet. For my part, I could not have thought it of Mr. Craig, but it's done now, and the less we say about it the better ; so I think with Mr. Daff, that it must be looked over ; but when I return, I will speak both to the husband and wife, and not without letting them have an inkling of what I think about their being married in December, which was a great shame, even if there was no sin in it. But I will say no more ; for truly, Mr. Micklewham, the longer we live in this world, and the farther we go, and the better we know ourselves, the less reason have we to think slightingly of our neighbours ; but the more to convince our hearts and understandings, that we are all prone to evil, and desperately wicked. For where does hypocrisy not abound ? and I have had my own experience here, that what a man is to the world, and to his own heart, is a very different thing.

In my last letter, I gave you a pleasing notification of the growth, as I thought, of spirituality in this Babylon of deceitfulness, thinking that you and my people would be gladdened with the tidings of the repute and estimation in which your minister was held, and I have dealt largely in the way of public charity. But I doubt that I have been governed by a spirit of ostentation, and not with that lowly-mindedness, without which all almsgiving is but a serving of the altars of Belzebub ; for the chastening hand has been laid upon me, but with the kindness and pity which a tender father hath for his dear children.

I was requested by those who come so cordially to me with their subscription papers, for schools and suffering worth, to preach a sermon to get a collection. I have no occasion to tell you, that when I exert myself, what effect I can produce ; and I never made so great an exertion before, which in itself was a proof that it was with the two bladders, pomp and vanity, that I had committed myself to swim on the uncertain waters of London ; for surely my best exertions were due to my people. But when the Sabbath came upon which I was to hold forth, how were my hopes withered, and my expectations frustrated. Oh, Mr. Micklewham, what an inattentive congregation was yonder! many slumbered and slept, and I sowed the words of truth and holiness in vain upon their barren and stoney hearts. There is no true grace among some that I shall not name, for I saw them whispering and smiling like the scorners, and altogether heedless unto the precious things of my discourse, which could not have been the case had they been sincere in their professions, for I never preached more to my own satisfaction on any occasion whatsoever—and, when I return to my own parish, you shall hear what I said, as I will preach the same sermon over again, for I am not going now to print it, as I did once think of doing, and to have dedicated it to Mr. W——.

We are going about in an easy way, seeing what is to be seen in the shape of curiosities; but the whole town is in a state of ferment with the election of members to Parliament. I have been to see't, both in the Guildhall and at Covent Garden, and it's a frightful thing to see how the Radicals roar like bulls of Bashan, and put down the speakers in behalf of the government. I hope no harm will come of yon, but I must say, that I prefer our own quiet canny Scotch way at Irvine. Well do I remember, for it happened in the year I was licensed, that the town council, the Lord Eglinton that was shot being then provost, took in the late Thomas Bowet to be a counsellor; and Thomas, not being versed in election matters, yet minding to please his lordship (for, like the rest of the council, he had always a proper veneration for those in power), he, as I was saying, consulted Joseph Boyd the weaver, who was then Dean of Guild, as to the way of voting; whereupon Joseph, who was a discreet man, said to him, 'Ye'll just say as I say, and I'll say what Bailie Shaw says, for he will do what my lord bids him'; which was as peaceful a way of sending up a member to Parliament as could well be devised.

But you know that politics are far from my hand—they belong to the temporalities of the community; and the ministers of peace and goodwill to man should neither make nor meddle with them. I wish, however, that these tumultuous elections were well over, for they have had an effect on the per cents, where our bit legacy is funded; and it would terrify you to hear what we have thereby already lost. We have not, how-

'What an inattentive congregation.'

Copyright 1895 by Macmillan & Co.

ever, lost so much but that I can spare a little to the poor
among my people; so you will, in the dry weather, after the
seed-time, hire two-three thackers to mend the thack on the
roofs of such of the cottars' houses as stand in need of mending,
and banker M——y will pay the expense; and I beg you to
go to him on receipt hereof, for he has a line for yourself,
which you will be sure to accept as a testimony from me for
the great trouble that my absence from the parish has given
to you among my people, and I am, dear sir, your friend and
pastor,   Z. PRINGLE.

As Mrs. Glibbans would not permit Mr. Snodgrass to return
with her to the manse, he pursued his journey alone to the
Kirkgate of Irvine, where he found Miss Mally Glencairn on
the eve of sitting down to her solitary tea. On seeing her
visitor enter, after the first compliments on the state of health
and weather were over, she expressed her hopes that he had
not drank tea; and, on receiving a negative, which she did
not quite expect, as she thought he had been perhaps invited
by some of her neighbours, she put in an additional spoonful
on his account; and brought from her corner cupboard with
the glass door, an ancient French pickle-bottle, in which she
had preserved, since the great tea-drinking formerly mentioned,
the remainder of the two ounces of carvey, the best, Mrs.
Nanse bought for that memorable occasion. A short conversation then took place relative to the Pringles; and, while
the tea was masking, for Miss Mally said it took a long time
to draw, she read to him the following letter:—

LETTER XXII

Mrs. Pringle to Miss Mally Glencairn

MY DEAR MISS MALLY—Trully, it may be said, that the
croun of England is upon the downfal, and surely we are all
seething in the pot of revolution, for the scum is mounting
uppermost. Last week, no farther gone than on Mononday,
we came to our new house heer in Baker Street, but it's nather
to be bakit nor brewt what I hav sin syne suffert. You no
my way, and that I like a been house, but no wastrie, and so
I needna tell yoo, that we hav had good diners; to be sure,

there was not a meerakle left to fill five baskets every day, but an abundance, with a proper kitchen of breed, to fill the bellies of four dumasticks. Howsomever, lo and behold, what was clecking downstairs. On Saturday morning, as we were sitting at our breakfast, the Doctor reading the newspapers, who shoud com intil the room but Andrew's grum, follo't by the rest, to give us warning that they were all going to quat our sairvice, becas they were starvit. I thocht that I would hav fentit cauld deed, but the Doctor, who is a consiederat man, inquairt what made them starve, and then there was such an approbrious cry about cold meet and bare bones, and no beer. It was an evendoun resurection—a rebellion waur than the forty-five. In short, Miss Mally, to make a leettle of a lang tail, they would have a hot joint day and day about, and a tree of yill to stand on the gauntress for their draw and drink, with a cock and a pail; and we were obligated to evacuate to their terms, and to let them go to their wark with flying colors; so you see how dangerous it is to live among this piple, and their noshans of liberty.

You will see by the newspapers that ther's a lection going on for parliament. It maks my corruption to rise to hear of such doings, and if I was a government as I'm but a woman, I woud put them doon with the strong hand, just to be revenged on the proud stomaks of these het and fou English.

We have gotten our money in the pesents put into our name; but I have had no peese since, for they have fallen in price three eight parts, which is very near a half, and if they go at this rate, where will all our legacy soon be? I have no goo of the pesents; so we are on the look-out for a landed estate, being a shure thing.

Captain Saber is still sneking after Rachel, and if she were awee perfited in her accomplugments, it's no saying what might happen, for he's a fine lad, but she's o'er young to be the heed of a family. Howsomever, the Lord's will maun be done, and if there is to be a match, she'll no have to fight for gentility with a straitent circumstance.

As for Andrew, I wish he was weel settlt, and we have our hopes that he's beginning to draw up with Miss Argent, who will have, no doobt, a great fortune, and is a treasure of a creeture in herself, being just as simple as a lamb; but, to be

' To give us warning becas they were starvit.'

Copyright 1895 by Macmillan & Co.

sure, she has had every advantage of edication, being brought up in a most fashonible boarding-school.

I hope you have got the box I sent by the smak, and that you like the patron of the goon. So no more at present, but remains, dear Miss Mally, your sinsaire friend,

JANET PRINGLE.

'The box,' said Miss Mally, 'that Mrs. Pringle speaks about came last night. It contains a very handsome present to me and to Miss Bell Tod. The gift to me is from Mrs. P. herself, and Miss Bell's from Rachel; but that ettercap, Becky Glibbans, is flying through the town like a spunky, mislikening the one and misca'ing the other: everybody, however, kens that it's only spite that gars her speak. It's a great pity that she cou'dna be brought to a sense of religion like her mother, who, in her younger days, they say, wasna to seek at a clashing.'

Mr. Snodgrass expressed his surprise at this account of the faults of that exemplary lady's youth; but he thought of her holy anxiety to sift into the circumstances of Betty, the elder's servant, becoming in one day Mrs. Craig, and the same afternoon sending for the midwife, and he prudently made no other comment; for the characters of all preachers were in her hands, and he had the good fortune to stand high in her favour, as a young man of great promise. In order, therefore, to avoid any discussion respecting moral merits, he read the following letter from Andrew Pringle:—

LETTER XXIII

Andrew Pringle, Esq., to the Reverend Charles Snodgrass

MY DEAR FRIEND—London undoubtedly affords the best and the worst specimens of the British character; but there is a certain townish something about the inhabitants in general, of which I find it extremely difficult to convey any idea. Compared with the English of the country, there is apparently very little difference between them; but still there is a difference, and of no small importance in a moral point of view. The country peculiarity is like the bloom of the plumb, or the down of the peach, which the fingers of infancy cannot touch without injuring ; but this felt but not describable quality of the town character, is as the varnish which brings out more vividly the colours of a picture, and which may be freely and even rudely handled. The women, for example, although as chaste in principle as those of any other community, possess none of that innocent untempted simplicity, which is more than half the grace of virtue ; many of them, and even young ones too, ' in the first freshness of their virgin beauty,' speak of the conduct and vocation of 'the erring sisters of the sex,' in a manner that often amazes me, and has, in more than one instance, excited unpleasant feelings towards the fair satirists. This moral taint, for I can consider it as nothing less, I have heard defended, but only by men who are supposed to have had a large experience of the world, and who, perhaps, on that account, are not the best judges of female delicacy. 'Every woman,' as Pope says, 'may be at heart a rake'; but it is for the interests of the domestic affections, which are the very elements of virtue, to cherish the notion, that women, as they are physically more delicate than men, are also so morally.

But the absence of delicacy, the bloom of virtue, is not peculiar to the females, it is characteristic of all the varieties of the metropolitan mind. The artifices of the medical quacks are things of universal ridicule ; but the sin, though in a less gross form, pervades the whole of that sinister system by which much of the superiority of this vast metropolis is supported. The state of the periodical press, that great organ of political instruction—the unruly tongue of liberty, strikingly confirms the justice of this misanthropic remark.

G—— had the kindness, by way of a treat to me, to collect, the other day, at dinner, some of the most eminent editors of the London journals. I found them men of talent, certainly, and much more men of the world, than 'the cloistered student from his paling lamp'; but I was astonished to find it considered, tacitly, as a sort of maxim among them, that an intermediate party was not bound by any obligation of honour to withhold, farther than his own discretion suggested, any information of which he was the accidental depositary, whatever the consequences might be to his informant, or to those affected by the communication. In a word, they seemed all to care less about what might be true than what would produce effect, and that effect for their own particular advantage. It is impossible to deny, that if interest is made the criterion by which the confidences of 'social intercourse are to be respected, the persons who admit this doctrine will have but little respect for the use of names, or deem it any reprehensible delinquency to suppress truth, or to blazon falsehood. In a word, man in London is not quite so good a creature as he is out of it. The rivalry of interests is here too intense; it impairs the affections, and occasions speculations both in morals and politics, which, I much suspect, it would puzzle a casuist to prove blameless. Can anything, for example, be more offensive to the calm spectator, than the elections which are now going on? Is it possible that this country, so much smaller in geographical extent than France, and so inferior in natural resources, restricted too by those ties and obligations which were thrown off as fetters by that country during the late war, could have attained, in despite of her, such a lofty pre-eminence—become the foremost of all the world—had it not been governed in a manner congenial to the spirit of the people, and with great practical wisdom? It is absurd to assert, that there are no corruptions in the various modifications by which the affairs of the British empire are administered; but it would be difficult to show, that, in the present state of morals and interests among mankind, corruption is not a necessary evil. I do not mean necessary, as evolved from those morals and interests, but necessary to the management of political trusts. I am afraid, however, to insist on this, as the natural integrity of your own heart, and the dignity of your vocation, will alike induce you to condemn it as Machiavellian. It is, however, an observation forced on me by what I have seen here.

It would be invidious, perhaps, to criticise the different candidates for the representation of London and Westminster very severely. I think it must be granted, that they are as sincere in their professions as their opponents, which at least bleaches away much of that turpitude of which their political conduct is accused by those who are of a different way of thinking. But it is quite evident, at least to me, that no government could exist a week, managed with that subjection to public opinion to which Sir Francis Burdett and Mr. Hobhouse apparently submit; and it is no less certain, that no government ought to exist a single day that would act in complete defiance of public opinion.

I was surprised to find Sir Francis Burdett an uncommonly mild and gentlemanly-looking man. I had pictured somehow to my imagination a dark and morose character ; but, on the contrary, in his appearance, deportment, and manner of speaking, he is eminently qualified to attract popular applause. His style of speaking is not particularly oratorical, but he has the art of saying bitter things in a sweet way. In his language, however, although pungent, and sometimes even eloquent, he is singularly incorrect. He cannot utter a sequence of three sentences without violating common grammar in the most atrocious way ; and his tropes and figures are so distorted, hashed, and broken—such a patchwork of different patterns, that you are bewildered if you attempt to make them out ; but the earnestness of his manner, and a certain fitness of character, in his observations a kind of Shaksperian pithiness, redeem all this. Besides, his manifold blunders of syntax do not offend the taste of those audiences where he is heard with the most approbation.

Hobhouse speaks more correctly, but he lacks in the conciliatory advantages of personal appearance ; and his physiognomy, though indicating considerable strength of mind, is not so prepossessing. He is evidently a man of more education than his friend, that is, of more reading, perhaps also of more various observation, but he has less genius. His tact is coarser, and though he speaks with more vehemence, he seldomer touches the sensibilities of his auditors. He may have observed mankind in general more extensively than Sir Francis, but he is far less acquainted with the feelings and associations of the English mind. There is also a wariness about him, which I do not like so well as the imprudent ingenuousness of the baronet. He seems to me to have a cause in hand—Hobhouse *versus* Existing Circumstances— and that he considers the multitude as the jurors, on whose decision his advancement in life depends. But in this I may be uncharitable. I should, however, think more highly of his sincerity as a patriot, if his stake in the country were greater ; and yet I doubt, if his stake were greater, if he is that sort of man who would have cultivated popularity in Westminster. He seems to me to have qualified himself for Parliament as others do for the bar, and that he will probably be considered in the House for some time merely as a political adventurer. But if he has the talent and prudence requisite to ensure distinction in the line of his profession, the mediocrity of his original condition will reflect honour on his success, should he hereafter acquire influence and consideration as a statesman. Of his literary talents I know you do not think very highly, nor am I inclined to rank the powers of his mind much beyond those of any common well-educated English gentleman. But it will soon be ascertained whether his pretensions to represent Westminster be justified by a sense of conscious superiority, or only prompted by that ambition which overleaps itself.

Of Wood, who was twice Lord Mayor, I know not what to say. There is a queer and wily cast in his pale countenance, that puzzles me exceedingly. In common parlance I would call him an empty vain creature ; but when I look at that indescribable spirit, which indicates a strange and out-of-the-way manner of thinking, I humbly confess that he is no common man. He is evidently a person of no intellectual accomplishments ; he has neither the language nor the deportment of a gentleman, in the usual understanding of the term ; and yet there is something that I would almost call genius about him. It is not cunning, it is not wisdom, it is far from being prudence, and yet it is something as wary as prudence, as effectual as wisdom, and not less sinister than cunning. I would call it intuitive skill, a sort of instinct, by which he is enabled to attain his ends in defiance of a capacity naturally narrow, a judgment that topples with vanity, and an address at once mean and repulsive. To call him a great man, in any possible approximation of the word, would be ridiculous ; that he is a good one, will be denied by those who envy his success, or hate his politics ; but nothing, save the blindness of fanaticism, can call in question his possession of a rare and singular species of ability, let it be exerted in what cause it may. But my paper is full, and I have only room to subscribe myself, faithfully, yours, A. PRINGLE.

'It appears to us,' said Mr. Snodgrass, as he folded up the letter to return it to his pocket, 'that the Londoners, with all their advantages of information, are neither purer nor better than their fellow-subjects in the country.' 'As to their betterness,' replied Miss Mally, ' I have a notion that they are far waur ; and I hope you do not think that earthly knowledge of any sort has a tendency to make mankind, or womankind either, any better ; for was not Solomon, who had more of it than any other man, a type and testification, that knowledge without grace is but vanity ? ' The young clergyman was somewhat startled at this application of a remark on which he laid no particular stress, and was thankful in his heart that Mrs. Glibbans was not present. He was not aware that Miss Mally had an orthodox corn, or bunyan, that could as little bear a touch from the royne-slippers of philosophy, as the inflamed gout of polemical controversy, which had gumfiated every mental joint and member of that zealous prop of the Relief Kirk. This was indeed the tender point of Miss Mally's character ; for she was left unplucked on the stalk of single blessedness, owing entirely to a conversation on this very subject with the only lover she ever had, Mr. Dalgliesh, formerly helper in the neighbouring parish of Dintonknow. He happened incidentally to observe, that education was requisite to promote the interests of religion. But Miss Mally, on that occasion, jocularly maintained, that education had only a tendency to promote the sale of books. This, Mr. Dalgliesh thought, was a sneer at himself, he having some time before unfortunately published a short tract, entitled, ' The moral union of our temporal and eternal interests considered, with respect to the establishment of parochial seminaries,' and which fell still-born from the press. He therefore retorted with some acrimony, until, from less to more, Miss Mally ordered him to keep his distance ; upon which he bounced out of the room, and they were never afterwards on speaking terms. Saving, however, and excepting this particular dogma, Miss Mally was on all other topics as liberal and beneficent as could be expected from a maiden lady, who was obliged to eke out her stinted income with a nimble needle and a close-clipping economy. The conversation with Mr. Snodgrass was not, however, lengthened into acrimony ; for immediately after the remark which we have noticed, she proposed that they should call on Miss Isabella Tod to see Rachel's letter ; indeed, this was rendered necessary by the state of the fire, for after boiling the kettle she had allowed it to fall low. It was her nightly practice after tea to take her evening seam, in a friendly way, to some of her neighbours' houses, by which she saved both coal and candle, while she acquired the news of the day, and was occasionally invited to stay supper.

On their arrival at Mrs. Tod's, Miss Isabella understood the purport of their visit, and immediately produced her letter, receiving, at the same time, a perusal of Mr. Andrew Pringle's. Mrs. Pringle's to Miss Mally she had previously seen.

LETTER XXIV

Miss Rachel Pringle to Miss Isabella Tod

My dear Bell—Since my last, we have undergone great changes and vicissitudes. Last week we removed to our present house, which is exceedingly handsome and elegantly furnished; and on Saturday there was an insurrection of the servants, on account of my mother not allowing them to have their dinners served up at the usual hour for servants at other genteel houses. We have also had the legacy in the funds transferred to my father, and only now wait the settling of the final accounts, which will yet take some time. On the day that the transfer took place, my mother made me a present of a twenty pound note, to lay out in any way I thought fit, and in so doing, I could not but think of you; I have, therefore, in a box which she is sending to Miss Mally Glencairn, sent you an evening dress from Mrs. Bean's, one of the most fashionable and tasteful dressmakers in town, which I hope you will wear with pleasure for my sake. I have got one exactly like it, so that when you see yourself in the glass, you will behold in what state I appeared at Lady ——'s route.

Ah! my dear Bell, how much are our expectations disappointed! How often have we, with admiration and longing wonder, read the descriptions in the newspapers of the fashionable parties in this great metropolis, and thought of the Grecian lamps, the ottomans, the promenades, the ornamented floors, the cut glass, the *coup d'œil*, and the *tout ensemble*. 'Alas!' as Young the poet says, 'the things unseen do not deceive us.' I have seen more beauty at an Irvine ball, than all the fashionable world could bring to market at my Lady ——'s emporium for the disposal of young ladies, for indeed I can consider it as nothing else.

I went with the Argents. The hall door was open, and filled with the servants in their state liveries; but although the door was open, the porter, as each carriage came up, rung a peal upon the knocker, to announce to all the square the successive arrival of the guests. We were shown upstairs to the drawing-rooms. They were very well, but neither so grand nor so great as I expected. As for the company, it was a suffocating crowd of fat elderly gentlewomen, and misses that stood in need of all the charms of their fortunes. One thing I could notice—for the press was so great, little could be seen—it was, that the old ladies wore rouge. The white satin sleeve of my dress was entirely ruined by coming in contact with a little round, dumpling duchess's cheek—as vulgar a body as could well be. She seemed to me to have spent all her days behind a counter, smirking thankfulness to bawbee customers.

When we had been shown in the drawing-rooms to the men for some time, we then adjourned to the lower apartments, where the refreshments were set out. This, I suppose, is arranged to afford an opportunity to the beaux to be civil to the belles, and thereby to scrape acquaintance with those whom they approve, by assisting them to the delicacies. Altogether, it was a very dull well-dressed affair, and yet I ought to have been in good spirits, for Sir Marmaduke Towler, a great Yorkshire baronet, was most particular in his attentions to me; indeed so much so, that I saw it made poor Sabre very uneasy. I do not know why it should, for I have given him no positive encouragement to hope for anything; not that I have the least idea that the baronet's attentions were more than commonplace politeness, but he has since called. I cannot, however, say that my vanity is at all flattered by this circumstance. At the same time, there surely could be no harm in Sir Marmaduke making me an offer, for you know I am not bound to accept it. Besides, my father does not like him, and my mother thinks he's a fortune-hunter; but I cannot conceive how that may be, for, on the contrary, he is said to be rather extravagant.

Before we return to Scotland, it is intended that we shall

'Sir Marmaduke Towler.'

Copyright 1895 by Macmillan & Co.

visit some of the watering-places ; and, perhaps, if Andrew can manage it with my father, we may even take a trip to Paris. The Doctor himself is not averse to it, but my mother is afraid that a new war may break out, and that we may be detained prisoners. This fantastical fear we shall, however, try to overcome. But I am interrupted. Sir Marmaduke is in the drawing-room, and I am summoned.—Yours truly,

RACHEL PRINGLE.

When Mr. Snodgrass had read this letter, he paused for a moment, and then said dryly, in handing it to Miss Isabella, ' Miss Pringle is improving in the ways of the world.'

The evening by this time was far advanced, and the young clergyman was not desirous to renew the conversation ; he therefore almost immediately took his leave, and walked sedately towards Garnock, debating with himself as he went along, whether Dr. Pringle's family were likely to be benefited by their legacy. But he had scarcely passed the minister's carse, when he met with Mrs. Glibbans returning. ' Mr. Snodgrass ! Mr. Snodgrass ! ' cried that ardent matron from her side of the road to the other where he was walking, and he obeyed her call ; ' yon's no sic a black story as I thought. Mrs. Craig is to be sure far gane, but they were married in December ; and it was only because she was his servan' lass that the worthy man didna like to own her at first for his wife. It would have been dreadful had the matter been jealoused at the first. She gaed to Glasgow to see an auntie that she has there, and he gaed in to fetch her out, and it was then the marriage was made up, which I was glad to hear ; for, oh, Mr. Snodgrass, it would have been an awfu' judgment had a man like Mr. Craig turn't out no better than a Tam Pain or a Major Weir. But a's for the best ; and Him that has the power of salvation can blot out all our iniquities. So good-night—ye'll have a lang walk.'

CHAPTER VIII

THE QUEEN'S TRIAL

As the spring advanced, the beauty of the country around
Garnock was gradually unfolded; the blossom was unclosed,
while the church was embraced within the foliage of more
umbrageous boughs. The schoolboys from the adjacent
villages were, on the Saturday afternoons, frequently seen
angling along the banks of the Lugton, which ran clearer
beneath the churchyard wall, and the hedge of the minister's
glebe; and the evenings were so much lengthened, that the
occasional visitors at the manse could prolong their walk after
tea. These, however, were less numerous than when the
family were at home; but still Mr. Snodgrass, when the
weather was fine, had no reason to deplore the loneliness of
his bachelor's court.

It happened that, one fair and sunny afternoon, Miss Mally
Glencairn and Miss Isabella Tod came to the manse. Mrs.
Glibbans and her daughter Becky were the same day paying
their first ceremonious visit, as the matron called it, to Mr. and
Mrs. Craig, with whom the whole party were invited to take
tea; and, for lack of more amusing chit-chat, the Reverend
young gentleman read to them the last letter which he had
received from Mr. Andrew Pringle. It was conjured naturally
enough out of his pocket, by an observation of Miss Mally's
'Nothing surprises me,' said that amiable maiden lady, 'so
much as the health and good-humour of the commonality. It
is a joyous refutation of the opinion, that the comfort and
happiness of this life depends on the wealth of worldly
possessions.'

'It is so,' replied Mr. Snodgrass, 'and I do often wonder,

97

when I see the blithe and hearty children of the cottars, frolicking in the abundance of health and hilarity, where the means come from to enable their poor industrious parents to supply their wants.'

'How can you wonder at ony sic things, Mr. Snodgrass? Do they not come from on high,' said Mrs. Glibbans, 'whence cometh every good and perfect gift? Is there not the flowers of the field, which neither card nor spin, and yet Solomon, in all his glory, was not arrayed like one of these?'

'I was not speaking in a spiritual sense,' interrupted the other, 'but merely made the remark, as introductory to a letter which I have received from Mr. Andrew Pringle, respecting some of the ways of living in London.'

Mrs. Craig, who had been so recently translated from the kitchen to the parlour, pricked up her ears at this, not doubting that the letter would contain something very grand and wonderful, and exclaimed, 'Gude safe's, let's hear't—I'm unco fond to ken about London, and the king and the queen; but I believe they are baith dead noo.'

Miss Becky Glibbans gave a satirical keckle at this, and showed her superior learning, by explaining to Mrs. Craig the unbroken nature of the kingly office. Mr. Snodgrass then read as follows:—

LETTER XXV

Andrew Pringle, Esq., to the Rev. Charles Snodgrass

MY DEAR FRIEND—You are not aware of the task you impose, when you request me to send you some account of the general way of living in London. Unless you come here, and actually experience yourself what I would call the London ache, it is impossible to supply you with any adequate idea of the necessity that exists in this wilderness of mankind, to seek refuge in society, without being over fastidious with respect to the intellectual qualifications of your occasional associates. In a remote desart, the solitary traveller is subject to apprehensions of danger; but still he is the most important thing 'within the circle of that lonely waste'; and the sense of his own dignity enables him to sustain the shock of considerable hazard with spirit and fortitude. But, in London, the feeling

98

of self-importance is totally lost and suppressed in the bosom of a stranger. A painful conviction of insignificance—of nothingness, I may say—is sunk upon his heart, and murmured in his ear by the million, who divide with him that consequence which he unconsciously before supposed he possessed in a general estimate of the world. While elbowing my way through the unknown multitude that flows between Charing Cross and the Royal Exchange, this mortifying sense of my own insignificance has often come upon me with the energy of a pang ; and I have thought, that, after all we can say of any man, the effect of the greatest influence of an individual on society at large, is but as that of a pebble thrown into the sea. Mathematically speaking, the undulations which the pebble causes, continue until the whole mass of the ocean has been disturbed to the bottom of its most secret depths and farthest shores ; and, perhaps, with equal truth it may be affirmed, that the sentiments of the man of genius are also infinitely propagated ; but how soon is the physical impression of the one lost to every sensible perception, and the moral impulse of the other swallowed up from all practical effect.

But though London, in the general, may be justly compared to the vast and restless ocean, or to any other thing that is either sublime, incomprehensible, or affecting, it loses all its influence over the solemn associations of the mind when it is examined in its details. For example, living on the town, as it is slangishly called, the most friendless and isolated condition possible, is yet fraught with an amazing diversity of enjoyment. Thousands of gentlemen, who have survived the relish of active fashionable pursuits, pass their life in that state without tasting the delight of one new sensation. They rise in the morning merely because Nature will not allow them to remain longer in bed. They begin the day without motive or purpose, and close it after having performed the same unvaried round as the most thoroughbred domestic animal that ever dwelt in manse or manor-house. If you ask them at three o'clock where they are to dine, they cannot tell you ; but about the wonted dinner-hour, batches of these forlorn bachelors find themselves diurnally congregated, as if by instinct, around a cozy table in some snug coffee-house, where, after inspecting the contents of the bill of fare, they discuss the news of the day, reserving the scandal, by way of dessert, for their wine.

Day after day their respective political opinions give rise to keen encounters, but without producing the slightest shade of change in any of their old ingrained and particular sentiments.

Some of their haunts, I mean those frequented by the elderly race, are shabby enough in their appearance and circumstances, except perhaps in the quality of the wine. Everything in them is regulated by an ancient and precise economy, and you perceive, at the first glance, that all is calculated on the principle of the house giving as much for the money as it can possibly afford, without infringing those little etiquettes which persons of gentlemanly habits regard as essentials. At half price the junior members of these unorganised or natural clubs retire to the theatres, while the elder brethren mend their potations till it is time to go home. This seems a very comfortless way of life, but I have no doubt it is the preferred result of a long experience of the world, and that the parties, upon the whole, find it superior, according to their early formed habits of dissipation and gaiety, to the sedate but not more regular course of a domestic circle.

The chief pleasure, however, of living on the town, consists in accidentally falling in with persons whom it might be otherwise difficult to meet in private life. I have several times enjoyed this. The other day I fell in with an old gentleman, evidently a man of some consequence, for he came to the coffee-house in his own carriage. It happened that we were the only guests, and he proposed that we should therefore dine together. In the course of conversation it came out, that he had been familiarly acquainted with Garrick, and had frequented the Literary Club in the days of Johnson and Goldsmith. In his youth, I conceive, he must have been an amusing companion; for his fancy was exceedingly lively, and his manners altogether afforded a very favourable specimen of the old, the gentlemanly school. At an appointed hour his carriage came for him, and we parted, perhaps never to meet again.

Such agreeable incidents, however, are not common, as the frequenters of the coffee-houses are, I think, usually taciturn characters, and averse to conversation. I may, however, be myself in fault. Our countrymen in general, whatever may be their address in improving acquaintance to the promotion of their own interests, have not the best way, in the first

'*His fancy was exceedingly lively.*'

Copyright 1895 by Macmillan & Co.

instance, of introducing themselves. A raw Scotchman, contrasted with a sharp Londoner, is very inadroit and awkward, be his talents what they may; and I suspect, that even the most brilliant of your old class-fellows have, in their professional visits to this metropolis, had some experience of what I mean.

ANDREW PRINGLE.

When Mr. Snodgrass paused, and was folding up the letter, Mrs. Craig, bending with her hands on her knees, said, emphatically, 'Noo, sir, what think you of that?' He was not, however, quite prepared to give an answer to a question so abruptly propounded, nor indeed did he exactly understand to what particular the lady referred. 'For my part,' she resumed, recovering her previous posture—'for my part, it's a very caldrife way of life to dine every day on coffee; broth and beef would put mair smeddum in the men; they're just a whin auld fogies that Mr. Andrew describes, an' no wurth a single woman's pains.' 'Wheesht, wheesht, mistress,' cried Mr. Craig; 'ye mauna let your tongue rin awa with your sense in that gait.' 'It has but a light load,' said Miss Becky, whispering Isabella Tod. In this juncture, Mr. Micklewham happened to come in, and Mrs. Craig, on seeing him, cried out, 'I hope, Mr. Micklewham, ye have brought the Doctor's letter. He's such a funny man! and touches off the Londoners to the nines.'

'He's a good man,' said Mrs. Glibbans, in a tone calculated to repress the forwardness of Mrs. Craig; but Miss Mally Glencairn having, in the meanwhile, taken from her pocket an epistle which she had received the preceding day from Mrs. Pringle, Mr. Snodgrass silenced all controversy on that score by requesting her to proceed with the reading. 'She's a clever woman, Mrs. Pringle,' said Mrs. Craig, who was resolved to cut a figure in the conversation in her own house. 'She's a discreet woman, and may be as godly, too, as some that make mair wark about the elect.' Whether Mrs. Glibbans thought this had any allusion to herself is not susceptible of legal proof; but she turned round and looked at their 'most kind hostess' with a sneer that might almost merit the appellation of a snort. Mrs. Craig, however, pacified her, by proposing, 'that, before hearing the letter, they should take a dram of wine, or pree her cherry bounce'—adding, 'our maister likes a been house, and ye a' ken that we are providing for a handling.' The wine was accordingly served, and, in due time, Miss Mally Glencairn edified and instructed the party with the contents of Mrs. Pringle's letter.

LETTER XXVI

Mrs. Pringle to Miss Mally Glencairn

DEAR MISS MALLY—You will have heard, by the peppers, of the gret hobbleshow heer aboot the queen's coming over contrary to the will of the nation; and, that the king and parlement are so angry with her, that they are going to put her away by giving to her a bill of divorce. The Doctor, who has been searchin the Scriptures on the okashon, says this is not in their poor, although she was found guilty of the fact; but I tell him, that as the king and parlement of old took upon them to change our religion, I do not see how they will be hampered now by the word of God.

You may well wonder that I have no ritten to you about the king, and what he is like, but we have never got a sight of him at all, whilk is a gret shame, paying so dear as we do for a king, who shurely should be a publik man. But, we have seen her majesty, who stays not far from our house heer in Baker Street, in dry lodgings, which, I am creditably informed, she is obligated to pay for by the week, for nobody will trust her; so you see what it is, Miss Mally, to have a light character. Poor woman, they say she might have been going from door to door, with a staff and a meal pock, but for ane Mr. Wood, who is a baillie of London, that has ta'en her by the hand. She's a woman advanced in life, with a short neck, and a pentit face; housomever, that, I suppose, she canno help, being a queen, and obligated to set the fashons to the court, where it is necessar to hide their faces with pent, our Andrew says, that their looks may not betray them—there being no shurer thing than a false-hearted courtier.

But what concerns me the most, in all this, is, that there will be no coronashon till the queen is put out of the way— and nobody can take upon them to say when that will be, as the law is so dootful and endless—which I am verra sorry for, as it was my intent to rite Miss Nanny Eydent a true account of the coronashon, in case there had been any partiklars that might be servisable to her in her bisness.

The Doctor and me, by ourselves, since we have been settlt, go about at our convenience, and have seen far mae farlies than baith Andrew and Rachel, with all the acquaintance they have forgathert with—but you no old heeds canno be expectit on young shouthers, and they have not had the experience of the world that we have had.

The lamps in the streets here are lighted with gauze, and not with crusies, like those that have lately been put up in your toun; and it is brought in pips aneath the ground from the manufactors, which the Doctor and me have been to see—an awful place—and they say as fey to a spark as poother, which made us glad to get out o't when we heard so;—and we have been to see a brew-house, where they mak the London porter, but it is a sight not to be told. In it we saw a barrel, whilk the Doctor said was by gauging bigger than the Irvine muckle kirk, and a masking fat, like a barn for mugnited. But all thae were as nothing to a curiosity of a steam-ingine, that minches minch collops as natural as life—and stuffs the sosogees itself, in a manner past the poor of nature to consiv. They have, to be shure, in London, many things to help work —for in our kitchen there is a smoking-jack to roast the meat, that gangs of its oun free will, and the brisker the fire, the faster it runs; but a potatoe-beetle is not to be had within the four walls of London, which is a great want in a house; Mrs. Argent never hard of sic a thing.

Me and the Doctor have likewise been in the Houses of Parliament, and the Doctor since has been again to heer the argol-bargoling aboot the queen. But, cepting the king's throne, which is all gold and velvet, with a croun on the top, and stars all round, there was nothing worth the looking at in them baith. Howsomever, I sat in the king's seat, and in the preses chair of the House of Commons, which, you no, is something for me to say; and we have been to see the printing of books, where the very smallest dividual syllib is taken up by itself and made into words by the hand, so as to be quite confounding how it could ever read sense. But there is ane piece of industry and froughgalaty I should not forget, whilk is wives going about with whirl-barrows, selling horses' flesh to the cats and dogs by weight, and the cats and dogs know them very well by their voices. In short, Miss Mally, there is nothing heer that the hand is not turnt to ; and there is, I can see, a better order and method really among the Londoners than among our Scotch folks, notwithstanding their advantages of edicashion, but my pepper will hold no more at present, from your true friend,

JANET PRINGLE.

There was a considerable diversity of opinion among the commentators on this epistle. Mrs. Craig was the first who broke silence, and displayed a great deal of erudition on the minch-collop-engine, and the potatoe-beetle, in which she was interrupted by the indignant Mrs. Glibbans, who exclaimed, ' I am surprised to hear you, Mrs. Craig, speak of sic baubles, when the word of God's in danger of being controverted by an Act of Parliament. But, Mr. Snodgrass, dinna ye think that this painting of the queen's face is a Jezebitical testification against her ? ' Mr. Snodgrass replied, with an unwonted sobriety of manner, and with an emphasis that showed he intended to make some impression on his auditors—' It is impossible to judge correctly of strangers by measuring them according to our own notions of propriety. It has certainly long been a practice in courts to disfigure the beauty of the human countenance with paint ; but what, in itself, may have been originally assumed for a mask or disguise, may, by usage, have grown into a very harmless custom. I am not, therefore, disposed to attach any criminal importance to the circumstance of her majesty wearing paint. Her late majesty did so herself.' ' I do not say it was criminal,' said Mrs. Glibbans ; ' I only meant it was sinful, and I think it is.' The accent of authority in which this was said, prevented Mr. Snodgrass from offering any reply ; and, a brief pause ensuing, Miss Molly Glencairn observed, that it was a surprising thing how the Doctor and Mrs. Pringle managed their matters so well. ' Ay,' said Mrs. Craig, ' but we a' ken what a manager the mistress is—she's the bee that mak's the hiney—she does not gang bizzing aboot, like a thriftless wasp, through her neighbours' houses.' ' I tell you, Betty, my dear,' cried Mr. Craig, ' that you shouldna make comparisons—what's past is gane— and Mrs. Glibbans and you maun now be friends.' ' They're a' friends to me that's no faes, and am very glad to see Mrs. Glibbans sociable in my house ; but she needna hae made sae light of me when she was here before.' And, in saying this, the amiable hostess burst into a loud sob of sorrow, which induced Mr. Snodgrass to beg Mr. Micklewham to read the Doctor's letter, by which a happy stop was put to the further manifestation of the grudge which Mrs. Craig harboured against Mrs. Glibbans for the lecture she had received, on what the latter called ' the incarnated effect of a more than Potipharian claught o' the godly Mr. Craig.'

LETTER XXVII

The Rev. Z. Pringle, D.D., to Mr. Micklewham, Schoolmaster and Session-Clerk of Garnock

DEAR SIR—I had a great satisfaction in hearing that Mr. Snodgrass, in my place, prays for the queen on the Lord's Day, which liberty, to do in our national church, is a thing to be upholden with a fearless spirit, even with the spirit of martyrdom, that we may not bow down in Scotland to the prelatic Baal of an order in Council, whereof the Archbishop of Canterbury, that is cousin-german to the Pope of Rome, is art and part. Verily, the sending forth of that order to the General Assembly was treachery to the solemn oath of the new king, whereby he took the vows upon him, conform to the Articles of the Union, to maintain the Church of Scotland as by law established, so that for the Archbishop of Canterbury to meddle therein was a shooting out of the horns of aggressive domination.

I think it is right of me to testify thus much, through you, to the Session, that the elders may stand on their posts to bar all such breaking in of the Episcopalian boar into our corner of the vineyard.

Anent the queen's case and condition, I say nothing ; for be she guilty, or be she innocent, we all know that she was born in sin, and brought forth in iniquity—prone to evil, as the sparks fly upwards—and desperately wicked, like you and me, or any other poor Christian sinner, which is reason enough to make us think of her in the remembering prayer.

Since she came over, there has been a wonderful work

doing here ; and it is thought that the crown will be taken off her head by a strong handling of the Parliament ; and really, when I think of the bishops sitting high in the peerage, like owls and rooks in the bartisans of an old tower, I have my fears that they can bode her no good. I have seen them in the House of Lords, clothed in their idolatrous robes ; and when I looked at them so proudly placed at the right hand of the king's throne, and on the side of the powerful, egging on, as I saw one of them doing in a whisper, the Lord Liverpool, before he rose to speak against the queen, the blood ran cold in my veins, and I thought of their woeful persecutions of our national church, and prayed inwardly that I might be keepit in the humility of a zealous presbyter, and that the corruption of the frail human nature within me might never be tempted by the pampered whoredoms of prelacy.

Saving the Lord Chancellor, all the other temporal peers were just as they had come in from the crown of the causeway —none of them having a judicial garment, which was a shame ; and as for the Chancellor's long robe, it was not so good as my own gown ; but he is said to be a very narrow man. What he spoke, however, was no doubt sound law ; yet I could observe he has a bad custom of taking the name of God in vain, which I wonder at, considering he has such a kittle conscience, which, on less occasions, causes him often to shed tears.

Mrs. Pringle and me, by ourselves, had a fine quiet canny sight of the queen, out of the window of a pastry baxter's shop, opposite to where her majesty stays. She seems to be a plump and jocose little woman ; gleg, blithe, and throwgaun for her years, and on an easy footing with the lower orders— coming to the window when they call for her, and becking to them, which is very civil of her, and gets them to take her part against the government.

The baxter in whose shop we saw this told us that her majesty said, on being invited to take her dinner at an inn on the road from Dover, that she would be content with a mutton-chop at the King's Arms in London,[1] which shows that she is a lady of a very hamely disposition. Mrs. Pringle thought her not big enough for a queen ; but we cannot expect every

[1] The honest Doctor's version of this *bon mot* of her majesty is not quite correct ; her expression was, 'I mean to take a chop at the King's Head when I get to London.'

C E Brock

'*A fine quiet canny sight of the queen.*'
Copyright 1895 by Macmillan & Co.

one to be like that bright occidental star, Queen Elizabeth, whose effigy we have seen preserved in armour in the Tower of London, and in wax in Westminster Abbey, where they have a living-like likeness of Lord Nelson, in the very identical regimentals that he was killed in. They are both wonderful places, but it costs a power of money to get through them, and all the folk about them think of nothing but money; for when I inquired, with a reverent spirit, seeing around me the tombs of great and famous men, the mighty and wise of their day, what department it was of the Abbey—'It's the eighteenpence department,' said an uncircumcised Philistine, with as little respect as if we had been treading the courts of the darling Dagon.

Our concerns here are now drawing to a close; but before we return, we are going for a short time to a town on the seaside, which they call Brighton. We had a notion of taking a trip to Paris, but that we must leave to Andrew Pringle, my son, and his sister Rachel, if the bit lassie could get a decent gudeman, which maybe will cast up for her before we leave London. Nothing, however, is settled as yet upon that head, so I can say no more at present anent the same.

Since the affair of the sermon, I have withdrawn myself from trafficking so much as I did in the missionary and charitable ploys that are so in vogue with the pious here, which will be all the better for my own people, as I will keep for them what I was giving to the unknown; and it is my design to write a book on almsgiving, to show in what manner that Christian duty may be best fulfilled, which I doubt not will have the effect of opening the eyes of many in London to the true nature of the thing by which I was myself beguiled in this Vanity Fair, like a bird ensnared by the fowler.

I was concerned to hear of poor Mr. Witherspoon's accident, in falling from his horse in coming from the Dalmailing occasion. How thankful he must be, that the Lord made his head of a durability to withstand the shock, which might otherwise have fractured his skull. What you say about the promise of the braird gives me pleasure on account of the poor; but what will be done with the farmers and their high rents, if the harvest turn out so abundant? Great reason have I to be thankful that the legacy has put me out of the reverence of my stipend; for when the meal was cheap, I own to you that I felt my carnality grudging the horn of abundance that

109

the Lord was then pouring into the lap of the earth. In short, Mr. Micklewham, I doubt it is o'er true with us all, that the less we are tempted, the better we are ; so with my sincere prayers that you may be delivered from all evil, and led out of the paths of temptation, whether it is on the highway, or on the footpaths, or beneath the hedges, I remain, dear sir, your friend and pastor,   ZACHARIAH PRINGLE.

'The Doctor,' said Mrs. Glibbans, as the schoolmaster concluded, ' is there like himself—a true orthodox Christian, standing up for the word, and overflowing with charity even for the sinner. But, Mr. Snodgrass, I did not ken before that the bishops had a hand in the making of the Acts of the Parliament ; I think, Mr. Snodgrass, if that be the case, there should be some doubt in Scotland about obeying them. However that may be, sure am I that the queen, though she was a perfect Deliah, has nothing to fear from them ; for have we not read in the Book of Martyrs, and other church histories, of their concubines and indulgences, in the papist times, to all manner of carnal iniquity? But if she be that noghty woman that they say '——' Gude safe's,' cried Mrs. Craig, ' if she be a noghty woman, awa' wi' her, awa' wi' her —wha kens the cantrips she may play us ? '
Here Miss Mally Glencairn interposed, and informed Mrs. Craig, that a noghty woman was not, as she seemed to think, a witch wife. ' I am sure,' said Miss Becky Glibbans, ' that Mrs. Craig might have known that.' ' Oh, ye're a spiteful deevil,' whispered Miss Mally, with a smile to her ; and turning in the same moment to Miss Isabella Tod, begged her to read Miss Pringle's letter—a motion which Mr. Snodgrass seconded chiefly to abridge the conversation, during which, though he wore a serene countenance, he often suffered much.

LETTER XXVIII

Miss Rachel Pringle to Miss Isabella Tod

MY DEAR BELL—I am much obliged by your kind expressions for my little present. I hope soon to send you something better, and gloves at the same time ; for Sabre has been brought to the point by an alarm for the Yorkshire baronet

110

'*Sabre has been brought to the point.*'

Copyright 1895 by Macmillan & Co.

that I mentioned, as showing symptoms of the tender passion for my fortune. The friends on both sides being satisfied with the match, it will take place as soon as some preliminary arrangements are made. When we are settled, I hope your mother will allow you to come and spend some time with us at our country-seat in Berkshire; and I shall be happy to repay all the expenses of your journey, as a jaunt to England is what your mother would, I know, never consent to pay for.

It is proposed that, immediately after the ceremony, we shall set out for France, accompanied by my brother, where we are to be soon after joined at Paris by some of the Argents, who, I can see, think Andrew worth the catching for Miss. My father and mother will then return to Scotland; but whether the Doctor will continue to keep his parish, or give it up to Mr. Snodgrass, will depend greatly on the circumstances in which he finds his parishioners. This is all the domestic intelligence I have got to give, but its importance will make up for other deficiencies.

As to the continuance of our discoveries in London, I know not well what to say. Every day brings something new, but we lose the sense of novelty. Were a fire in the same street where we live, it would no longer alarm me. A few nights ago, as we were sitting in the parlour after supper, the noise of an engine passing startled us all; we ran to the windows—there was haste and torches, and the sound of other engines, and all the horrors of a conflagration reddening the skies. My father sent out the footboy to inquire where it was; and when the boy came back, he made us laugh, by snapping his fingers, and saying the fire was not worth so much—although, upon further inquiry, we learnt that the house in which it originated was burnt to the ground. You see, therefore, how the bustle of this great world hardens the sensibilities, but I trust its influence will never extend to my heart.

The principal topic of conversation at present is about the queen. The Argents, who are our main instructors in the proprieties of London life, say that it would be very vulgar in me to go to look at her, which I am sorry for, as I wish above all things to see a personage so illustrious by birth, and renowned by misfortune. The Doctor and my mother, who are less scrupulous, and who, in consequence, somehow, by themselves, contrive to see, and get into places that are inaccessible to all gentility, have had a full view of her majesty. My father has since become her declared partisan, and my mother too has acquired a leaning likewise towards her side of the question; but neither of them will permit the subject to be spoken of before me, as they consider it detrimental to good morals. I, however, read the newspapers.

What my brother thinks of her majesty's case is not easy to divine; but Sabre is convinced of the queen's guilt, upon some private and authentic information which a friend of his, who has returned from Italy, heard when travelling in that country. This information he has not, however, repeated to me, so that it must be very bad. We shall know all when the trial comes on. In the meantime, his majesty, who has lived in dignified retirement since he came to the throne, has taken up his abode, with rural felicity, in a cottage in Windsor Forest; where he now, contemning all the pomp and follies of his youth, and this metropolis, passes his days amidst his cabbages, like Dioclesian, with innocence and tranquillity, far from the intrigues of courtiers, and insensible to the murmuring waves of the fluctuating populace, that set in with so strong a current towards 'the mob-led queen,' as the divine Shakespeare has so beautifully expressed it.

You ask me about Vauxhall Gardens;—I have not seen them—they are no longer in fashion—the theatres are quite vulgar—even the opera-house has sunk into a second-rate place of resort. Almack's balls, the Argyle-rooms, and the Philharmonic concerts, are the only public entertainments frequented by people of fashion; and this high superiority they owe entirely to the difficulty of gaining admission. London, as my brother says, is too rich, and grown too luxurious, to have any exclusive place of fashionable resort, where price alone is the obstacle. Hence, the institution of these select aristocratic assemblies. The Philharmonic concerts, however, are rather professional than fashionable entertainments; but everybody is fond of music, and, therefore, everybody, that can be called anybody, is anxious to get tickets to them; and this anxiety has given them a degree of *éclat*, which I am persuaded the performance would never have excited had the tickets been purchasable at any price.

The great thing here is, either to be somebody, or to be patronised by a person that is a somebody; without this, though you were as rich as Crœsus, your golden chariots, like the comets of a season, blazing and amazing, would speedily roll away into the obscurity from which they came, and be remembered no more.

At first when we came here, and when the amount of our legacy was first promulgated, we were in a terrible flutter. Andrew became a man of fashion, with all the haste that tailors, and horses, and dinners, could make him. My father, honest man, was equally inspired with lofty ideas, and began a career that promised a liberal benefaction of good things to the poor—and my mother was almost distracted with calculations about laying out the money to the best advantage, and the sum she would allow to be spent. I alone preserved my natural equanimity; and foreseeing the necessity of new accomplishments to suit my altered circumstances, applied myself to the instructions of my masters, with an assiduity that won their applause. The advantages of this I now experience —my brother is sobered from his champaign fumes—my father has found out that charity begins at home—and my mother, though her establishment is enlarged, finds her happiness, notwithstanding the legacy, still lies within the little circle of her household cares. Thus, my dear Bell, have I proved the sweets of a true philosophy; and, unseduced by the blandishments of rank, rejected Sir Marmaduke Towler, and accepted the humbler but more disinterested swain, Captain Sabre, who requests me to send you his compliments, not altogether content that you should occupy so much of the bosom of your affectionate   RACHEL PRINGLE.

'Rachel had ay a gude roose of hersel',' said Becky Glibbans, as Miss Isabella concluded. In the same moment, Mr. Snodgrass took his leave, saying to Mr. Micklewham, that he had something particular to mention to him. 'What can it be about?' inquired Mrs. Glibbans at Mr. Craig, as soon as the helper and schoolmaster had left the room : 'Do you think it can be concerning the Doctor's resignation of the parish in his favour?' 'I'm sure,' interposed Mrs. Craig, before her husband could reply, 'it winna be wi' my gudewill that he shall come in upon us—a pridefu' wight, whose saft

'*Andrew became a man of fashion.*'

Copyright 1895 by Macmillan & Co.

words, and a' his politeness, are but lip-deep ; na, na, Mrs. Glibbans, we maun hae another on the leet forbye him.'

'And wha would ye put on the leet noo, Mrs. Craig, you that's sic a judge ? ' said Mrs. Glibbans, with the most ineffable consequentiality.

' I'll be for young Mr. Dirlton, who is baith a sappy preacher of the word, and a substantial hand at every kind of civility.'

'Young Dirlton !—young Deevilton ! ' cried the orthodox Deborah of Irvine ; 'a fallow that knows no more of a gospel dispensation than I do of the Arian heresy, which I hold in utter abomination. No, Mrs. Craig, you have a godly man for your husband—a sound and true follower ; tread ye in his footsteps, and no try to set up yoursel' on points of doctrine. But it's time, Miss Mally, that we were taking the road ; Becky and Miss Isabella, make yourselves ready. Noo, Mrs. Craig, ye'll no be a stranger ; you see I have no been lang of coming to give you my countenance ; but, my leddy, ca' canny, it's no easy to carry a fu' cup ; ye hae gotten a great gift in your gudeman. Mr. Craig, I wish you a good-night ; I would fain have stopped for your evening exercise, but Miss Mally was beginning, I saw, to weary—so good-night ; and, Mrs. Craig, ye'll take tent of what I have said—it's for your gude.' So exeunt Mrs. Glibbans, Miss Mally, and the two young ladies. ' Her bark's waur than her bite,' said Mrs. Craig, as she returned to her husband, who felt already some of the ourie symptoms of a henpecked destiny.

CHAPTER IX

THE MARRIAGE

MR. SNODGRASS was obliged to walk into Irvine one evening, to get rid of a raging tooth, which had tormented him for more than a week. The operation was so delicately and cleverly performed by the surgeon to whom he applied—one of those young medical gentlemen, who, after having been educated for the army or navy, are obliged, in this weak piping time of peace, to glean what practice they can amid their native shades —that the amiable divine found himself in a condition to call on Miss Isabella Tod.

During this visit, Saunders Dickie, the postman, brought a London letter to the door, for Miss Isabella ; and Mr. Snodgrass having desired the servant to inquire if there were any for him, had the good fortune to get the following from Mr. Andrew Pringle :—

LETTER XXIX

Andrew Pringle, Esq., to the Rev. Mr. Charles Snodgrass

MY DEAR FRIEND—I never receive a letter from you without experiencing a strong emotion of regret, that talents like yours should be wilfully consigned to the sequestered vegetation of a country pastor's life. But we have so often discussed this point, that I shall only offend your delicacy if I now revert to it more particularly. I cannot, however, but remark, that although a private station may be the happiest, a public is the proper sphere of virtue and talent, so clear, superior, and decided as yours. I say this with the more confidence, as I

117

have really, from your letter, obtained a better conception of the queen's case, than from all that I have been able to read and hear upon the subject in London. The rule you lay down is excellent. Public safety is certainly the only principle which can justify mankind in agreeing to observe and enforce penal statutes ; and, therefore, I think with you, that unless it could be proved in a very simple manner, that it was requisite for the public safety to institute proceedings against the queen— her sins or indiscretions should have been allowed to remain in the obscurity of her private circle.

I have attended the trial several times. For a judicial proceeding, it seems to me too long—and for a legislative, too technical. Brougham, it is allowed, has displayed even greater talent than was expected ; but he is too sharp ; he seems to me more anxious to gain a triumph, than to establish truth. I do not like the tone of his proceedings, while I cannot sufficiently admire his dexterity. The style of Denman is more lofty, and impressed with stronger lineaments of sincerity. As for their opponents, I really cannot endure the Attorney-General as an orator ; his whole mind consists, as it were, of a number of little hands and claws—each of which holds some scrap or portion of his subject ; but you might as well expect to get an idea of the form and character of a tree, by looking at the fallen leaves, the fruit, the seeds, and the blossoms, as anything like a comprehensive view of a subject, from an intellect so constituted as that of Sir Robert Gifford. He is a man of application, but of meagre abilities, and seems never to have read a book of travels in his life. The Solicitor-General is somewhat better ; but he is one of those who think a certain artificial gravity requisite to professional consequence ; and which renders him somewhat obtuse in the tact of propriety.

Within the bar, the talent is superior to what it is without ; and I have been often delighted with the amazing fineness, if I may use the expression, with which the Chancellor discriminates the shades of difference in the various points on which he is called to deliver his opinion. I consider his mind as a curiosity of no ordinary kind. It deceives itself by its own acuteness. The edge is too sharp ; and, instead of cutting straight through, it often diverges—alarming his conscience with the dread of doing wrong. This singular subtlety has the effect of impairing the reverence which the endowments

118

and high professional accomplishments of this great man are otherwise calculated to inspire. His eloquence is not effective —it touches no feeling nor affects any passion; but still it affords wonderful displays of a lucid intellect. I can compare it to nothing but a pencil of sunshine; in which, although one sees countless motes flickering and fluctuating, it yet illuminates, and steadily brings into the most satisfactory distinctness, every object on which it directly falls.

Lord Erskine is a character of another class, and whatever difference of opinion may exist with respect to their professional abilities and attainments, it will be allowed by those who contend that Eldon is the better lawyer—that Erskine is the greater genius. Nature herself, with a constellation in her hand, playfully illuminates his path to the temple of reasonable Justice; while Precedence with her guide-book, and Study with a lantern, cautiously show the road in which the Chancellor warily plods his weary way to that of legal Equity. The sedateness of Eldon is so remarkable, that it is difficult to conceive that he was ever young; but Erskine cannot grow old; his spirit is still glowing and flushed with the enthusiasm of youth. When impassioned, his voice acquires a singularly elevated and pathetic accent; and I can easily conceive the irresistible effect he must have had on the minds of a jury, when he was in the vigour of his physical powers, and the case required appeals of tenderness or generosity. As a parliamentary orator, Earl Grey is undoubtedly his superior; but there is something much less popular and conciliating in his manner. His eloquence is heard to most advantage when he is contemptuous; and he is then certainly dignified, ardent, and emphatic; but it is apt, I should think, to impress those who hear him, for the first time, with an idea that he is a very supercilious personage, and this unfavourable impression is liable to be strengthened by the elegant aristocratic languor of his appearance.

I think that you once told me you had some knowledge of the Marquis of Lansdowne, when he was Lord Henry Petty. I can hardly hope that, after an interval of so many years, you will recognise him in the following sketch :—His appearance is much more that of a Whig than Lord Grey—stout and sturdy—but still withal gentlemanly; and there is a pleasing simplicity, with somewhat of good-nature, in the expression of his countenance, that renders him, in a quiescent state, the more agreeable character of the two. He speaks exceedingly well—clear, methodical, and argumentative; but his eloquence, like himself, is not so graceful as it is upon the whole manly; and there is a little tendency to verbosity in his language, as there is to corpulency in his figure; but nothing turgid, while it is entirely free from affectation. The character of respectable is very legibly impressed, in everything about the mind and manner of his lordship. I should, now that I have seen and heard him, be astonished to hear such a man represented as capable of being factious.

I should say something about Lord Liverpool, not only on account of his rank as a minister, but also on account of the talents which have qualified him for that high situation. The greatest objection that I have to him as a speaker, is owing to the loudness of his voice—in other respects, what he does say is well digested. But I do not think that he embraces his subject with so much power and comprehension as some of his opponents; and he has evidently less actual experience of the world. This may doubtless be attributed to his having been almost constantly in office since he came into public life; than which nothing is more detrimental to the unfolding of natural ability, while it induces a sort of artificial talent, connected with forms and technicalities, which, though useful in business, is but of minor consequence in a comparative estimate of moral and intellectual qualities. I am told that in his manner he resembles Mr. Pitt; be this, however, as it may, he is evidently a speaker, formed more by habit and imitation, than one whom nature prompts to be eloquent. He lacks that occasional accent of passion, the melody of oratory; and I doubt if, on any occasion, he could at all approximate to that magnificent intrepidity which was admired as one of the noblest characteristics of his master's style.

But all the display of learning and eloquence, and intellectual power and majesty of the House of Lords, shrinks into insignificance when compared with the moral attitude which the people have taken on this occasion. You know how much I have ever admired the attributes of the English national character—that boundless generosity, which can only be compared to the impartial benevolence of the sunshine—that heroic magnanimity, which makes the hand ever ready to succour a fallen foe; and that sublime courage, which rises with the energy of a conflagration roused by a tempest, at every insult or menace of an enemy. The compassionate interest taken by the populace in the future condition of the queen is worthy of this extraordinary people. There may be many among them actuated by what is called the radical spirit; but malignity alone would dare to ascribe the bravery of their compassion to a less noble feeling than that which has placed the kingdom so proudly in the van of all modern nations. There may be an amiable delusion, as my Lord Castlereagh has said, in the popular sentiments with respect to the queen. Upon that, as upon her case, I offer no opinion. It is enough for me to have seen, with the admiration of a worshipper, the manner in which the multitude have espoused her cause.

But my paper is filled, and I must conclude. I should, however, mention that my sister's marriage is appointed to take place to-morrow, and that I accompany the happy pair to France.—Yours truly, ANDREW PRINGLE.

'This is a dry letter,' said Mr. Snodgrass, and he handed it to Miss Isabella, who, in exchange, presented the one which she had herself at the same time received; but just as Mr. Snodgrass was on the point of reading it, Miss Becky Glibbans was announced. 'How lucky this is,' exclaimed Miss Becky, 'to find you both thegither! Now you maun tell me all the particulars; for Miss Mally Glencairn is no in, and her letter lies unopened. I am just gasping to hear how Rachel conducted herself at being married in the kirk before all the folk —married to the hussar captain, too, after all! who would have thought it?'

'How, have you heard of the marriage already?' said Miss Isabella. 'Oh, it's in the newspapers,' replied the amiable inquisitant,—'Like ony tailor or weaver's—a' weddings maun nowadays gang into the papers. The whole toun, by this time, has got it; and I wouldna wonder if Rachel Pringle's marriage ding the queen's divorce out of folk's heads for the next nine days to come. But only to think of her being married in a public kirk. Surely her father would never submit to hae't done by a bishop? And then to put it in the London paper, as if Rachel Pringle had been somebody of distinction. Perhaps it might have been more to the purpose, considering

121

what dragoon officers are, if she had got the doited Doctor, her father, to publish the intended marriage in the papers beforehand.'

'Haud that condumacious tongue of yours,' cried a voice, panting with haste as the door opened, and Mrs. Glibbans entered. 'Becky, will you never devawl wi' your backbiting. I wonder frae whom the misleart lassie takes a' this passion of clashing.'

The authority of her parent's tongue silenced Miss Becky, and Mrs. Glibbans having seated herself, continued,—'Is it your opinion, Mr. Snodgrass, that this marriage can hold good, contracted, as I am told it is mentioned in the papers to hae been, at the horns of the altar of Episcopalian apostacy?'

'I can set you right as to that,' said Miss Isabella. 'Rachel mentions, that, after returning from the church, the Doctor himself performed the ceremony anew, according to the Presbyterian usage.' 'I am glad to hear't, very glad indeed,' said Mrs. Glibbans. 'It would have been a judgment-like thing, had a bairn of Dr. Pringle's—than whom, although there may be abler, there is not a sounder man in a' the West of Scotland—been sacrificed to Moloch, like the victims of prelatic idolatry.'

At this juncture, Miss Mally Glencairn was announced: she entered, holding a letter from Mrs. Pringle in her hand, with the seal unbroken. Having heard of the marriage from an acquaintance in the street, she had hurried home, in the well-founded expectation of hearing from her friend and well-wisher, and taking up the letter, which she found on her table, came with all speed to Miss Isabella Tod to commune with her on the tidings.

Never was any confluence of visitors more remarkable than on this occasion. Before Miss Mally had well explained the cause of her abrupt intrusion, Mr. Micklewham made his appearance. He had come to Irvine to be measured for a new coat, and meeting by accident with Saunders Dickie, got the Doctor's letter from him, which, after reading, he thought he could do no less than call at Mrs. Tod's, to let Miss Isabella know the change which had taken place in the condition of her friend.

Thus were all the correspondents of the Pringles assembled, by the merest chance, like the *dramatis personæ* at the end of a play. After a little harmless bantering, it was agreed that Miss Mally should read her communication first—as all the others were previously acquainted with the contents of their respective letters, and Miss Mally read as follows :—

LETTER XXX

Mrs. Pringle to Miss Mally Glencairn

DEAR MISS MALLY—I hav a cro to pik with you conserning yoor comishon aboot the partickels for your friends. You can hav no noshon what the Doctor and me suffert on the head of the flooring shrubs. We took your Nota Beny as it was spilt, and went from shop to shop enquirin in a most partiklar manner for 'a Gardner's Bell, or the least of all flowering plants'; but sorrow a gardner in the whole tot here in London ever had heard of sic a thing ; so we gave the porshoot up in despare. Howsomever, one of Andrew's acquaintance—a decent lad, who is only son to a saddler in a been way, that keeps his own carriage, and his son a coryikel, happent to call, and the Doctor told him what ill socsess we had in our serch for the gardner's bell ; upon which he sought a sight of your yepissle, and read it as a thing that was just wonderful for its whorsogroffie ; and then he sayid, that looking at the prinsipol of your spilling, he thought we should reed, 'a gardner's bill, or a list of all flooring plants'; whilk being no doot your intent, I have proqurt the same, and it is included heerin. But, Miss Mally, I would advize you to be more exac in your inditing, that no sic torbolashon may hippen on a future okashon.

What I hav to say for the present is, that you will, by a smak, get a bocks of kumoddities, whilk you will destraboot as derekit on every on of them, and you will before have resievit by the post-offis, an account of what has been don. I need say no forther at this time, knowin your discreshon and prooduns, septs that our Rachel and Captain Sabor will, if it pleese the Lord, be off to Parish, by way of Bryton, as man and wife, the morn's morning. What her father the Doctor gives for tocher, what is settlt on her for jontor, I will tell you all aboot when we meet ; for it's our dishire noo to lose no tim in retorning to the manse, this being the last of our diploma-

ticals in London, where we have found the Argents a most
discrit family, payin to the last farding the Cornal's legacy,
and most seevil, and well bred to us.

As I am naterally gretly okypt with this matteromoneal
afair, you cannot expect ony news ; but the queen is going on
with a dreadful rat, by which the pesents hav falen more than
a whole entirr pesent.   I wish our fonds were well oot of them,
and in yird and stane, which is a constansie.   But what is to
become of the poor donsie woman, no one can expound.
Some think she will be pot in the Toor of London, and her
head chappit off; others think she will raise sic a stramash,
that she will send the whole government into the air, like
peelings of ingons, by a gunpoother plot.   But it's my opinion,
and I have weighed the matter well in my understanding, that
she will hav to fight with sword in hand, be she ill, or be she
good.   How els can she hop to get the better of more than
two hundred lords, as the Doctor, who has seen them, tells me,
with princes of the blood-royal, and the prelatic bishops, whom,
I need not tell you, are the worst of all.

But the thing I grudge most, is to be so long in Lundon,
and no to see the king.   Is it not a hard thing to come to
London, and no to see the king ?   I am not pleesed with him,
I assure you, becose he does not set himself out to public view,
like ony other curiosity, but stays in his palis, they say, like
one of the anshent wooden images of idolatry, the which is a
great peety, he beeing, as I am told, a beautiful man, and
more the gentleman than all the coortiers of his court.

The Doctor has been minting to me that there is an address
from Irvine to the queen ; and he, being so near a neighbour
to your toun, has been thinking to pay his respecs with it, to
see her near at hand.   But I will say nothing ; he may take
his own way in matters of gospel and spiritualety ; yet I have
my scroopols of conshence, how this may not turn out a
rebellyon against the king ; and I would hav him to sift and
see who are at the address, before he pits his han to it.   For,
if it's a radikol job, as I jealoos it is, what will the Doctor then
say ? who is an orthodox man, as the world nose.

In the maitre of our dumesticks, no new axsident has cast
up ; but I have seen such a wonder as could not have been
forethocht.   Having a washin, I went down to see how the
lassies were doing ; but judge of my feelings, when I saw them

triomphing on the top of pattons, standing upright before the
boyns on chairs, rubbin the clothes to juggins between their
hands, above the sapples, with their gouns and stays on, and
round-eared mutches.   What would you think of such a
miracle at the washing-house in the Goffields, or the Gallows-
knows of Irvine?   The cook, howsomever, has shown me a
way to make rice-puddings without eggs, by putting in a bit of
shoohet, which is as good—and this you will tell Miss Nanny
Eydent; likewise, that the most fashionable way of boiling
green pis, is to pit a blade of speermint in the pot, which gives
a fine flavour.   But this is a long letter, and my pepper is
done; so no more, but remains your friend and well-wisher,

JANET PRINGLE.

'A great legacy, and her dochtir married, in ae journey to
London, is doing business,' said Mrs. Glibbans, with a sigh, as
she looked to her only get, Miss Becky; 'but the Lord's will
is to be done in a' thing;—sooner or later something of the
same kind will come, I trust, to all our families.' 'Ay,'
replied Miss Mally Glencairn, 'marriage is like death—it's
what we are a' to come to.'

'I have my doubts of that,' said Miss Becky with a sneer.
'Ye have been lang spair't from it, Miss Mally.'

'Ye're a spiteful puddock; and if the men hae the e'en
and lugs they used to hae, gude pity him whose lot is cast
with thine, Becky Glibbans,' replied the elderly maiden ornament of the Kirkgate, somewhat tartly.

Here Mr. Snodgrass interposed, and said, he would read to
them the letter which Miss Isabella had received from the
bride; and without waiting for their concurrence, opened and
read as follows :—

LETTER XXXI

Mrs. Sabre to Miss Isabella Tod

MY DEAREST BELL—Rachel Pringle is no more! My
heart flutters as I write the fatal words.   This morning, at
nine o'clock precisely, she was conducted in bridal array to the
new church of Mary-le-bone; and there, with ring and book,
sacrificed to the Minotaur, Matrimony, who devours so many
of our bravest youths and fairest maidens.

My mind is too agitated to allow me to describe the scene. The office of handmaid to the victim, which, in our young simplicity, we had fondly thought one of us would perform for the other, was gracefully sustained by Miss Argent.

On returning from church to my father's residence in Baker Street, where we breakfasted, he declared himself not satisfied with the formalities of the English ritual, and obliged us to undergo a second ceremony from himself, according to the wonted forms of the Scottish Church. All the advantages and pleasures of which, my dear Bell, I hope you will soon enjoy.

But I have no time to enter into particulars. The captain and his lady, by themselves, in their own carriage, set off for Brighton in the course of less than an hour. On Friday they are to be followed by a large party of their friends and relations ; and, after spending a few days in that emporium of salt-water pleasures, they embark, accompanied with their beloved brother, Mr. Andrew Pringle, for Paris ; where they are afterwards to be joined by the Argents. It is our intention to remain about a month in the French capital ; whether we shall extend our tour, will depend on subsequent circumstances : in the meantime, however, you will hear frequently from me.

My mother, who has a thousand times during these important transactions wished for the assistance of Nanny Eydent, transmits to Miss Mally Glencairn a box containing all the requisite bridal recognisances for our Irvine friends. I need not say that the best is for the faithful companion of my happiest years. As I had made a vow in my heart that Becky Glibbans should never wear gloves for my marriage, I was averse to sending her any at all, but my mother insisted that no exceptions should be made. I secretly took care, however, to mark a pair for her, so much too large, that I am sure she will never put them on. The asp will be not a little vexed at the disappointment. Adieu for a time, and believe that, although your affectionate Rachel Pringle be gone that way in which she hopes you will soon follow, one not less sincerely attached to you, though it be the first time she has so subscribed herself, remains in   RACHEL SABRE.

Before the ladies had time to say a word on the subject,

the prudent young clergyman called immediately on Mr. Micklewham to read the letter which he had received from the Doctor ; and which the worthy dominie did without delay, in that rich and full voice with which he is accustomed to teach his scholars elocution by example.

LETTER XXXII

The Rev. Z. Pringle, D.D., to Mr. Micklewham, Schoolmaster and Session-Clerk, Garnock

LONDON.

DEAR SIR—I have been much longer of replying to your letter of the 3rd of last month, than I ought in civility to have been, but really time, in this town of London, runs at a fast rate, and the day passes before the dark's done. What with Mrs. Pringle and her daughter's concernments, anent the marriage to Captain Sabre, and the trouble I felt myself obliged to take in the queen's affair, I assure you, Mr. Micklewham, that it's no to be expressed how I have been occupied for the last four weeks. But all things must come to a conclusion in this world. Rachel Pringle is married, and the queen's weary trial is brought to an end—upon the subject and motion of the same, I offer no opinion, for I made it a point never to read the evidence, being resolved to stand by THE WORD from the first, which is clearly and plainly written in the queen's favour, and it does not do in a case of conscience to stand on trifles ; putting, therefore, out of consideration the fact libelled, and looking both at the head and the tail of the proceeding, I was of a firm persuasion, that all the sculduddery of the business might have been well spared from the eye of the public, which is of itself sufficiently prone to keek and kook, in every possible way, for a glimpse of a black story ; and, therefore, I thought it my duty to stand up in all places against the trafficking that was attempted with a divine institution. And I think, when my people read how their prelatic enemies, the bishops (the heavens defend the poor Church of Scotland from being subjected to the weight of their paws), have been visited with a constipation of the understanding on that point, it must to them be a great satisfaction to know how clear and collected their minister was on this

127

'Mr. Micklewham.'

Copyright 1895 by Macmillan & Co.

fundamental of society. For it has turned out, as I said to Mrs. Pringle, as well as others, it would do, that a sense of grace and religion would be manifested in some quarter before all was done, by which the devices for an unsanctified repudiation or divorce would be set at nought.

As often as I could, deeming it my duty as a minister of the word and gospel, I got into the House of Lords, and heard the trial; and I cannot think how ever it was expected that justice could be done yonder; for although no man could be more attentive than I was, every time I came away I was more confounded than when I went; and when the trial was done, it seemed to me just to be clearing up for a proper beginning —all which is a proof that there was a foul conspiracy. Indeed, when I saw Duke Hamilton's daughter coming out of the coach with the queen, I never could think after, that a lady of her degree would have countenanced the queen had the matter laid to her charge been as it was said. Not but in any circumstance it behoved a lady of that ancient and royal blood, to be seen beside the queen in such a great historical case as a trial.

I hope, in the part I have taken, my people will be satisfied; but whether they are satisfied or not, my own conscience is content with me. I was in the House of Lords when her majesty came down for the last time, and saw her handed up the stairs by the usher of the black-rod, a little stumpy man, wonderful particular about the rules of the House, insomuch that he was almost angry with me for stopping at the stair-head. The afflicted woman was then in great spirits, and I saw no symptoms of the swelled legs that Lord Lauderdale, that jooking man, spoke about, for she skippit up the steps like a lassie. But my heart was wae for her when all was over, for she came out like an astonished creature, with a wild steadfast look, and a sort of something in the face that was as if the rational spirit had fled away; and she went down to her coach as if she had submitted to be led to a doleful destiny. Then the shouting of the people began, and I saw and shouted too in spite of my decorum, which I marvel at sometimes, thinking it could be nothing less than an involuntary testification of the spirit within me.

Anent the marriage of Rachel Pringle, it may be needful in me to state, for the satisfaction of my people, that although by stress of law we were obligated to conform to the practice of the Episcopalians, by taking out a bishop's license, and going to their church, and vowing, in a pagan fashion, before their altars, which are an abomination to the Lord ; yet, when the young folk came home, I made them stand up, and be married again before me, according to all regular marriages in our national Church. For this I had two reasons : first, to satisfy myself that there had been a true and real marriage ; and, secondly, to remove the doubt of the former ceremony being sufficient ; for marriage being of divine appointment, and the English form and ritual being a thing established by Act of Parliament, which is of human ordination, I was not sure that marriage performed according to a human enactment could be a fulfilment of a divine ordinance. I therefore hope that my people will approve what I have done ; and in order that there may be a sympathising with me, you will go over to Banker M——y, and get what he will give you, as ordered by me, and distribute it among the poorest of the parish, according to the best of your discretion, my long absence having taken from me the power of judgment in a matter of this sort. I wish indeed for the glad sympathy of my people, for I think that our Saviour turning water into wine at the wedding, was an example set that we should rejoice and be merry at the fulfilment of one of the great obligations imposed on us as social creatures ; and I have ever regarded the unhonoured treatment of a marriage occasion as a thing of evil bodement, betokening heavy hearts and light purses to the lot of the bride and bridegroom. You will hear more from me by and by ; in the meantime, all I can say is, that when we have taken our leave of the young folks, who are going to France, it is Mrs. Pringle's intent, as well as mine, to turn our horses' heads northward, and make our way with what speed we can, for our own quiet home, among you. So no more at present from your friend and pastor,

Z. PRINGLE.

Mrs. Tod, the mother of Miss Isabella, a respectable widow lady, who had quiescently joined the company, proposed that they should now drink health, happiness, and all manner of prosperity, to the young couple ; and that nothing might be wanting to secure the favourable auspices of good omens to the toast, she desired Miss Isabella to draw fresh bottles of white and red. When all manner of felicity was duly wished in wine to the captain and his lady, the party rose to seek their respective homes. But a bustle at the street-door occasioned a pause. Mrs. Tod inquired the matter; and three or four voices at once replied, that an express had come from Garnock for Nanse Swaddle the midwife, Mrs. Craig being taken with her pains. 'Mr. Snodgrass,' said Mrs. Glibbans, instantly and emphatically, 'ye maun let me go with you, and we can spiritualise on the road; for I hae promis't Mrs. Craig to be wi' her at the crying, to see the upshot—so I hope you will come awa.'

It would be impossible in us to suppose, that Mr. Snodgrass had any objections to spiritualise with Mrs. Glibbans on the road between Irvine and Garnock; but, notwithstanding her urgency, he excused himself from going with her; however, he recommended her to the special care and protection of Mr. Micklewham, who was at that time on his legs to return home. 'Oh! Mr. Snodgrass,' said the lady, looking slyly, as she adjusted her cloak, at him and Miss Isabella, 'there will be marrying and giving in marriage till the day of judgment.' And with these oracular words she took her departure.

CHAPTER X

THE RETURN

ON Friday, Miss Mally Glencairn received a brief note from Mrs. Pringle, informing her, that she and the Doctor would reach the manse, 'God willing,' in time for tea on Saturday; and begging her, therefore, to go over from Irvine, and see that the house was in order for their reception. This note was written from Glasgow, where they had arrived, in their own carriage, from Carlisle on the preceding day, after encountering, as Mrs. Pringle said, 'more hardships and extorshoning than all the dangers of the sea which they met with in the smack of Leith that took them to London.'

As soon as Miss Mally received this intelligence, she went to Miss Isabella Tod, and requested her company for the next day to Garnock, where they arrived betimes to dine with Mr. Snodgrass. Mrs. Glibbans and her daughter Becky were then on a consolatory visit to Mr. Craig. We mentioned in the last chapter, that the crying of Mrs. Craig had come on; and that Mrs. Glibbans, according to promise, and with the most anxious solicitude, had gone to wait the upshot. The upshot was most melancholy,—Mrs. Craig was soon no more; —she was taken, as Mrs. Glibbans observed on the occasion, from the earthly arms of her husband, to the spiritual bosom of Abraham, Isaac, and Jacob, which was far better. But the baby survived; so that, what with getting a nurse, and the burial, and all the work and handling that a birth and death in one house at the same time causes, Mr. Craig declared, that he could not do without Mrs. Glibbans; and she, with all that Christianity by which she was so zealously distinguished, sent for Miss Becky, and took up her abode with him, till it would please Him, without whom there is no comfort, to wipe the eyes of the pious elder. In a word, she staid so long, that a rumour began to spread that Mr. Craig would need a wife to look after his bairn ; and that Mrs. Glibbans was destined to supply the desideratum.

Mr. Snodgrass, after enjoying his dinner society with Miss Mally and Miss Isabella, thought it necessary to dispatch a courier, in the shape of a barefooted servant lass, to Mr. Micklewham, to inform the elders that the Doctor was expected home in time for tea, leaving it to their discretion either to greet his safe return at the manse, or in any other form or manner that would be most agreeable to themselves. These important news were soon diffused through the clachan. Mr. Micklewham dismissed his school an hour before the wonted time, and there was a universal interest and curiosity excited, to see the Doctor coming home in his own coach. All the boys of Garnock assembled at the braehead which commands an extensive view of the Kilmarnock road, the only one from Glasgow that runs through the parish ; the wives with their sucklings were seated on the large stones at their respective door-cheeks ; while their cats were calmly reclining on the window soles. The lassie weans, like clustering bees, were mounted on the carts that stood before Thomas Birlpenny the vintner's door, churming with anticipated delight ; the old men took their stations on the dike that incloses the side of the vintner's kail-yard, and 'a batch of wabster lads,' with green aprons and thin yellow faces, planted themselves at the gable of the malt kiln, where they were wont, when trade was better, to play at the hand-ball ; but, poor fellows, since the trade fell off, they have had no heart for the game, and the vintner's half-mutchkin stoups glitter in empty splendour unrequired on the shelf below the brazen sconce above the bracepiece, amidst the idle pewter pepper-boxes, the bright copper tea-kettle, the coffee-pot that has never been in use, and lids of saucepans that have survived their principals,—the wonted ornaments of every trig change-house kitchen.

The season was far advanced ; but the sun shone at his setting with a glorious composure, and the birds in the hedges and on the boughs were again gladdened into song. The leaves had fallen thickly, and the stubble-fields were bare, but Autumn, in a many-coloured tartan plaid, was seen still walking with matronly composure in the woodlands, along the brow of the neighbouring hills.

133

About half-past four o'clock, a movement was seen among the callans at the braehead, and a shout announced that a carriage was in sight. It was answered by a murmuring response of satisfaction from the whole village. In the course of a few minutes the carriage reached the turnpike—it was of the darkest green and the gravest fashion,—a large trunk, covered with Russian matting, and fastened on with cords, prevented from chafing it by knots of straw rope, occupied the front,—behind, other two were fixed in the same manner, the lesser of course uppermost; and deep beyond a pile of light bundles and bandboxes, that occupied a large portion of the interior, the blithe faces of the Doctor and Mrs. Pringle were discovered. The boys huzzaed, the Doctor flung them penny-pieces, and the mistress baubees.

As the carriage drove along, the old men on the dike stood up and reverently took off their hats and bonnets. The weaver lads gazed with a melancholy smile; the lassies on the carts clapped their hands with joy; the women on both sides of the street acknowledged the recognising nods; while all the village dogs, surprised by the sound of chariot wheels, came baying and barking forth, and sent off the cats that were so doucely sitting on the window soles, clambering and scampering over the roofs in terror of their lives.

When the carriage reached the manse door, Mr. Snodgrass, the two ladies, with Mr. Micklewham, and all the elders except Mr. Craig, were there ready to receive the travellers. But over this joy of welcoming we must draw a veil; for the first thing that the Doctor did, on entering the parlour and before sitting down, was to return thanks for his safe restoration to his home and people.

The carriage was then unloaded, and as package, bale, box, and bundle were successively brought in, Miss Mally Glencairn expressed her admiration at the great capacity of the chaise. 'Ay,' said Mrs. Pringle, 'but you know not what we have suffert for't in coming through among the English taverns on the road; some of them would not take us forward when there was a hill to pass, unless we would take four horses, and every one after another reviled us for having no mercy in loading the carriage like a waggon,—and then the drivers were so gleg and impudent, that it was worse than martyrdom to come with them. Had the Doctor taken my advice, he would

have brought our own civil London coachman, whom we hired
with his own horses by the job; but he said it behoved us to
gi'e our ain fish guts to our ain sea-maws, and that he designed
to fee Thomas Birlpenny's hostler for our coachman, being a
lad of the parish. This obliged us to post it from London;
but, oh! Miss Mally, what an outlay it has been!'

The Doctor, in the meantime, had entered into conversation
with the gentlemen, and was inquiring, in the most particular
manner, respecting all his parishioners, and expressing his
surprise that Mr. Craig had not been at the manse with the
rest of the elders. 'It does not look well,' said the Doctor.
Mr. Daff, however, offered the best apology for his absence
that could be made. 'He has had a gentle dispensation, sir—
Mrs. Craig has won awa' out of this sinful world, poor woman,
she had a large experience o't; but the bairn's to the fore, and
Mrs. Glibbans, that has such a cast of grace, has ta'en charge
of the house since before the interment. It's thought, considering what's by gane, Mr. Craig may do waur than make
her mistress, and I hope, sir, your exhortation will no be wanting to egg the honest man to think o't seriously.'

Mr. Snodgrass, before delivering the household keys,
ordered two bottles of wine, with glasses and biscuit, to be set
upon the table, while Mrs. Pringle produced from a paper
package, that had helped to stuff one of the pockets of the
carriage, a piece of rich plum-cake, brought all the way from
a confectioner's in Cockspur Street, London, not only for the
purpose of being eaten, but, as she said, to let Miss Nanny
Eydent pree, in order to direct the Irvine bakers how to bake
others like it.

Tea was then brought in; and, as it was making, the
Doctor talked aside to the elders, while Mrs. Pringle recounted
to Miss Mally and Miss Isabella the different incidents of her
adventures subsequent to the marriage of Miss Rachel.

'The young folk,' said she, 'having gone to Brighton, we
followed them in a few days, for we were told it was a curiosity,
and that the king has a palace there, just a warld's wonder!
and, truly, Miss Mally, it is certainly not like a house for a
creature of this world, but for some Grand Turk or Chinaman.
The Doctor said, it put him in mind of Miss Jenny Macbride's
sideboard in the Stockwell of Glasgow; where all the pepper-
boxes, poories, and teapots, punch-bowls, and china-candlesticks

of her progenitors are set out for a show, that tells her visitors, they are but seldom put to use. As for the town of Brighton, it's what I would call a gawky piece of London. I could see nothing in it but a wheen idlers, hearing twa lads, at night, crying, " Five, six, seven for a shilling," in the booksellers' shops, with a play-actor lady singing in a corner, because her voice would not do for the players' stage. Therefore, having seen the Captain and Mrs. Sabre off to France, we came home to London ; but it's not to be told what we had to pay at the hotel where we staid in Brighton. Howsomever, having come back to London, we settled our counts, and, buying a few necessars, we prepared for Scotland,—and here we are. But travelling has surely a fine effect in enlarging the understanding ; for both the Doctor and me thought, as we came along, that everything had a smaller and poorer look than when we went away ; and I dinna think this room is just what it used to be. What think ye o't, Miss Isabella ? How would ye like to spend your days in't ? '

Miss Isabella reddened at this question ; but Mrs. Pringle, who was as prudent as she was observant, affecting not to notice this, turned round to Miss Mally Glencairn, and said softly in her ear,—' Rachel was Bell's confidante, and has told us all about what's going on between her and Mr. Snodgrass. We have agreed no to stand in their way, as soon as the Doctor can get a mailing or two to secure his money upon.'

Meantime, the Doctor received from the elders a very satisfactory account of all that had happened among his people, both in and out of the Session, during his absence ; and he was vastly pleased to find there had been no inordinate increase of wickedness ; at the same time, he was grieved for the condition in which the poor weavers still continued, saying, that among other things of which he had been of late meditating, was the setting up of a lending bank in the parish for the labouring classes, where, when they were out of work, ' bits of loans for a house-rent, or a brat of claes, or sic like, might be granted, to be repaid when trade grew better, and thereby take away the objection that an honest pride had to receiving help from the Session.'

Then some lighter general conversation ensued, in which the Doctor gave his worthy counsellors a very jocose description of many of the lesser sort of adventures which he had met with; and the ladies having retired to inspect the great bargains that Mrs. Pringle had got, and the splendid additions she had made to her wardrobe, out of what she denominated the dividends of the present portion of the legacy, the Doctor ordered in the second biggest toddy-bowl, the guardevine with the old rum, and told the lassie to see if the tea-kettle was still boiling. 'Ye maun drink our welcome hame,' said he to the elders; 'it would nae otherwise be canny. But I'm sorry Mr. Craig has nae come.' At these words the door opened, and the absent elder entered, with a long face and a deep sigh. 'Ha!' cried Mr. Daff, 'this is very droll. Speak of the Evil One, and he'll appear';—which words dinted on the heart of Mr. Craig, who thought his marriage in December had been the subject of their discourse. The Doctor, however, went up and shook him cordially by the hand, and said, 'Now I take this very kind, Mr. Craig; for I could not have expected you, considering ye have got, as I am told, your jo in the house'; at which words the Doctor winked paukily to Mr. Daff, who rubbed his hands with fainness, and gave a good-humoured sort of keckling laugh. This facetious stroke of policy was a great relief to the afflicted elder, for he saw by it that the Doctor did not mean to trouble him with any inquiries respecting his deceased wife; and, in consequence, he put on a blither face, and really affected to have forgotten her already more than he had done in sincerity.

Thus the night passed in decent temperance and a happy decorum; insomuch, that the elders when they went away, either by the influence of the toddy-bowl, or the Doctor's funny stories about the Englishers, declared that he was an excellent man, and, being none lifted up, was worthy of his rich legacy.

At supper, the party, besides the minister and Mrs. Pringle, consisted of the two Irvine ladies, and Mr. Snodgrass. Miss Becky Glibbans came in when it was about half over, to express her mother's sorrow at not being able to call that night, 'Mr. Craig's bairn having taken an ill turn.' The truth, however, was, that the worthy elder had been rendered somewhat tozy by the minister's toddy, and wanted an opportunity to inform the old lady of the joke that had been played upon him by the Doctor calling her his jo, and to see how she would relish it. So by a little address Miss Becky was sent out of the way, with the excuse we have noticed; at the same time, as the night was rather sharp, it is not to be supposed that she would have been the bearer of any such message, had her own curiosity not enticed her.

During supper the conversation was very lively. Many 'pickant jokes,' as Miss Becky described them, were cracked by the Doctor; but, soon after the table was cleared, he touched Mr. Snodgrass on the arm, and, taking up one of the candles, went with him to his study, where he then told him, that Rachel Pringle, now Mrs. Sabre, had informed him of a way in which he could do him a service. 'I understand, sir,' said the Doctor, 'that you have a notion of Miss Bell Tod, but that until ye get a kirk there can be no marriage. But the auld horse may die waiting for the new grass; and, therefore, as the Lord has put it in my power to do a good action both to you and my people,—whom I am glad to hear you have pleased so well,—if it can be brought about that you could be made helper and successor, I'll no object to give up to you the whole stipend, and, by and by, maybe the manse to the bargain. But that is if you marry Miss Bell; for it was a promise that Rachel gar't me make to her on her wedding morning. Ye know she was a forcasting lassie, and, I have reason to believe, has said nothing anent this to Miss Bell herself; so that if you have no partiality for Miss Bell, things will just rest on their own footing; but if you have a notion, it must be a satisfaction to you to know this, as it will be a pleasure to me to carry it as soon as possible into effect.'

Mr. Snodgrass was a good deal agitated; he was taken by surprise, and without words the Doctor might have guessed his sentiments; he, however, frankly confessed that he did entertain a very high opinion of Miss Bell, but that he was not sure if a country parish would exactly suit him. 'Never mind that,' said the Doctor; 'if it does not fit at first, you will get used to it; and if a better casts up, it will be no obstacle.'

The two gentlemen then rejoined the ladies, and, after a short conversation, Miss Becky Glibbans was admonished to depart, by the servants bringing in the Bibles for the worship of the evening. This was usually performed before supper, but, owing to the bowl being on the table, and the company jocose, it had been postponed till all the guests who were not to sleep in the house had departed.

The Sunday morning was fine and bright for the season;

the hoar-frost, till about an hour after sunrise, lay white on the grass and tombstones in the churchyard; but before the bell rung for the congregation to assemble, it was exhaled away, and a freshness, that was only known to be autumnal by the fallen and yellow leaves that strewed the church-way path from the ash and plane trees in the avenue, encouraged the spirits to sympathise with the universal cheerfulness of all nature.

The return of the Doctor had been bruited through the parish with so much expedition, that, when the bell rung for public worship, none of those who were in the practice of stopping in the churchyard to talk about the weather were so ignorant as not to have heard of this important fact. In consequence, before the time at which the Doctor was wont to come from the back-gate which opened from the manse-garden into the churchyard, a great majority of his people were assembled to receive him.

At the last jingle of the bell, the back-gate was usually opened, and the Doctor was wont to come forth as punctually as a cuckoo of a clock at the striking of the hour; but a deviation was observed on this occasion. Formerly, Mrs. Pringle and the rest of the family came first, and a few minutes were allowed to elapse before the Doctor, laden with grace, made his appearance. But at this time, either because it had been settled that Mr. Snodgrass was to officiate, or for some other reason, there was a breach in the observance of this time-honoured custom.

As the ringing of the bell ceased, the gate unclosed, and the Doctor came forth. He was of that easy sort of feather-bed corpulency of form that betokens good-nature, and had none of that smooth, red, well-filled protuberancy, which indicates a choleric humour and a testy temper. He was in fact what Mrs. Glibbans denominated 'a man of a gausy external.' And some little change had taken place during his absence in his visible equipage. His stockings, which were wont to be of worsted, had undergone a translation into silk; his waistcoat, instead of the venerable Presbyterian flap-covers to the pockets, which were of Johnsonian magnitude, was become plain—his coat in all times single-breasted, with no collar, still, however, maintained its ancient characteristics; instead, however, of the former bright black cast horn, the buttons

139

were covered with cloth. But the chief alteration was discernible in the furniture of the head. He had exchanged the simplicity of his own respectable grey hairs for the cauliflower hoariness of a PARRISH[1] wig, on which he wore a broad-brimmed hat, turned up a little at each side behind, in a portentous manner, indicatory of Episcopalian predilections. This, however, was not justified by any alteration in his principles, being merely an innocent variation of fashion, the natural result of a Doctor of Divinity buying a hat and wig in London.

The moment that the Doctor made his appearance, his greeting and salutation was quite delightful; it was that of a father returned to his children, and a king to his people.

Almost immediately after the Doctor, Mrs. Pringle, followed by Miss Mally Glencairn and Miss Isabella Tod, also debouched from the gate, and the assembled females remarked, with no less instinct, the transmutation which she had undergone. She was dressed in a dark blue cloth pelisse, trimmed with a dyed fur, which, as she told Miss Mally, 'looked quite as well as sable, without costing a third of the money.' A most matronly muff, that, without being of sable, was of an excellent quality, contained her hands; and a very large Leghorn straw bonnet, decorated richly, but far from excess, with a most substantial band and bow of a broad crimson satin ribbon around her head.

If the Doctor was gratified to see his people so gladly thronging around him, Mrs. Pringle had no less pleasure also in her thrice-welcome reception. It was an understood thing, that she had been mainly instrumental in enabling the minister to get his great Indian legacy; and in whatever estimation she may have been previously held for her economy and management, she was now looked up to as a personage skilled in the law, and particularly versed in testamentary erudition. Accordingly, in the customary testimonials of homage with which she was saluted in her passage to the church door, there was evidently a sentiment of veneration mingled, such as had never been evinced before, and which was neither unobserved nor unappreciated by that acute and perspicacious lady.

[1] See the *Edinburgh Review*, for an account of our old friend, Dr. Parr's wig, and Spital Sermon.

'*The moment that the Doctor made his appearance.*'

Copyright 1895 by Macmillan & Co

The Doctor himself did not preach, but sat in the minister's pew till Mr. Snodgrass had concluded an eloquent and truly an affecting sermon ; at the end of which, the Doctor rose and went up into the pulpit, where he publicly returned thanks for the favours and blessings he had obtained during his absence, and for the safety in which he had been restored, after many dangers and tribulations, to the affections of his parishioners.

Such were the principal circumstances that marked the return of the family. In the course of the week after, the estate of Moneypennies being for sale, it was bought for the Doctor as a great bargain. It was not, however, on account of the advantageous nature of the purchase that our friend valued this acquisition, but entirely because it was situated in his own parish, and part of the lands marching with the Glebe.

The previous owner of Moneypennies had built an elegant house on the estate, to which Mrs. Pringle is at present actively preparing to remove from the manse ; and it is understood, that, as Mr. Snodgrass was last week declared helper, and successor to the Doctor, his marriage with Miss Isabella Tod will take place with all convenient expedition. There is also reason to believe, that, as soon as decorum will permit, any scruple which Mrs. Glibbans had to a second marriage is now removed, and that she will soon again grace the happy circle of wives by the name of Mrs. Craig. Indeed, we are assured that Miss Nanny Eydent is actually at this time employed in making up her wedding garments ; for, last week, that worthy and respectable young person was known to have visited Bailie Delap's shop, at a very early hour in the morning, and to have priced many things of a bridal character, besides getting swatches ; after which she was seen to go to Mrs. Glibbans's house, where she remained a very considerable time, and to return straight therefrom to the shop, and purchase divers of the articles which she had priced and inspected ; all of which constitute sufficient grounds for the general opinion in Irvine, that the union of Mr. Craig with Mrs. Glibbans is a happy event drawing near to consummation.